About the Authors

Maureen Child is the author of more than 130 romance novels and novellas that routinely appear on bestseller lists and have won numerous awards, including the National Reader's Choice Award. A seven-time nominee for the prestigious *RITA*® award from Romance Writers of America, one of her books was made into a CBS-TV movie called *The Soul Collector.* Maureen recently moved from California to the mountains of Utah and is trying to get used to snow.

New York Times and *USA Today* bestselling, award-winning author **Lisa Childs** has written more than eighty-five novels. Published in twenty countries, she's also appeared on the *Publisher's Weekly*, Barnes & Nobles and Nielsen Top 100 bestseller lists. Lisa writes contemporary romance, romantic suspense, paranormal and women's fiction. She's a wife, mum, bonus mum, an avid reader and a less avid runner. Readers can reach her through Facebook or her website: lisachilds.com

Award-winning author **Jennifer Hayward** emerged on the publishing scene as the winner of the So You Think You Can Write global writing competition and recipient of a *RT* Reviewer's Choice Award. Jennifer's careers in journalism and PR, including years of working alongside powerful, charismatic CEOs and travelling the world, have provided perfect fodder for the fast-paced, sexy stories she likes to write.

The Crown

April 2023
Duty to the Crown

May 2023
Promised to the Crown

June 2023
Reunited with the Crown

July 2023
Protecting the Crown

August 2023
Trading the Crown

September 2023
Falling for the Crown

Protecting the Crown

MAUREEN CHILD

LISA CHILDS

JENNIFER HAYWARD

MILLS & BOON

First Published in Great Britain 2023
by Mills & Boon, an imprint of HarperCollins*Publishers* Ltd,
1 London Bridge Street, London, SE1 9GF

www.harpercollins.co.uk

HarperCollins*Publishers*
Macken House, 39/40 Mayor Street Upper,
Dublin 1, D01 C9W8, Ireland

ISBN: 978-0-263-31946-0

This book is produced from independently certified FSC™ paper to ensure responsible forest management.

For more information visit: www.harpercollins.co.uk/green

Printed and Bound in the UK using 100% Renewable Electricity at CPI Group (UK) Ltd, Croydon, CR0 4YY

TO KISS A KING

MAUREEN CHILD

To Susan Mallery, a great writer and an
even better friend. For all of the shared dreams,
all of the good laughs and all those yet to come.
Thanks, Susan.

One

Garrett King was in Hell.

Dozens of screaming, laughing children raced past him and he winced as their voices hit decibels only dogs should have been able to hear. Happiest Place on Earth? He didn't think so.

How he had let himself be talked into this, he had no idea.

"Getting soft," he muttered darkly and leaned one hand on the hot metal balustrade in front of him only to wrench his hand back instantly. He glanced at his palm, sighed and reached for a napkin out of his cousin's bag to wipe the sticky cotton candy off his skin.

"You could be at the office," he told himself sternly, wadding up the napkin and tossing it into a trash can. "You could be checking invoices, keeping tabs on the new client. But no, you had to say yes to your cousin instead."

Jackson King had pulled out all the stops getting Garrett to go along with this little family adventure. Jackson's wife, Casey, was apparently "worried" because Garrett was alone too much. Nice woman Casey, he told himself. But did no one ever consider that maybe a man was alone because he *wanted* to be?

But he still could have begged off if it had been just Casey and Jackson doing the asking. But Garrett's cousin had cheated.

He had had his daughters ask "Uncle" Garrett to go with them and frankly, when faced with three of the cutest kids in the world, it would have been impossible to say no. And Jackson knew it, the clever bastard.

"Hey, cuz!" Jackson's shout sounded out and Garrett turned to give him a hard look.

Jackson only laughed. "Casey, honey," he said, turning to his stunning wife, "did you see that? I don't think Garrett's having any fun."

"About that," Garrett cut in, lifting his voice to be heard over the raucous noise rising from the crowd, "I was thinking I'd just head out now. Leave you guys to some family fun."

"You *are* family, Garrett," Casey pointed out.

Before he could speak, Garrett felt a tug at his pants leg. He looked down into Mia's upturned face. "Uncle Garrett, we're going on the fast mountain ride. You wanna come?"

At five, Mia King was already a heartbreaker. From her King blue eyes to the missing front tooth to the dimple in her cheek, she was absolutely adorable. And not being a dummy, she knew how to work it already, too.

"Uh…" Garrett glanced behind Mia to her younger sisters Molly and Mara. Molly was three and Mara was just beginning to toddle. The three of them were unstoppable, Garrett told himself wryly.

There was just no way he was getting out of this day

early. One girl pouting was hard to resist. Three were too much for any man to stand against.

"How about I stand here and watch your stuff while you guys go on the ride?"

Jackson snorted a laugh that Garrett ignored. For God's sake, he owned the most respected security company in the country and here he was haggling with a five-year-old.

Garrett and Jackson had been good friends for years. Most of the King cousins were close, but he and Jackson had worked closely together over the years. Garrett's security company and Jackson's company, King Jets, fed off each other. With Garrett's high-priced clients renting Jackson's luxury jets, both companies were thriving for the loosely defined partnership.

Jackson's wife, Casey, on the other hand, was one of those happily married women who saw every determined bachelor as a personal challenge.

"You going on the Matterhorn with us?" Jackson asked, plucking Mara from his wife's arms. The chubby toddler slapped at his cheeks gleefully and Garrett watched with some amusement as Jackson practically melted. The man was a sap when it came to his family. Funny, because in business, Jackson King was a cutthroat kind of guy that nobody wanted to cross.

"Nope," Garrett told him and lifted the baby out of his cousin's arms. With the crazed population explosion in the King family, Garrett was getting used to dealing with kids. Comfortably settling the tiny girl on his hip, he said, "I'll wait here with Mara and the rest of your—" he paused to glance down at the stroller and the bags already piled high on it "—stuff."

"You could ride with me," Mia insisted, turning those big blue eyes on him.

"Oh, she's good," Jackson whispered on a laugh.

Garrett went down on one knee and looked her in the eye. "How about I stay here with your sister and you tell me all about the ride when you get off?"

She scowled a little, clearly unused to losing, then grinned. "Okay."

Casey took both of the girls' hands, smiled at Garrett and headed for the line.

"I didn't ask you to come along so you could just stand around, you know," Jackson said.

"Yeah. Why did you ask me along? Better yet, why'd I say yes?"

Jackson laughed, looked over his shoulder at his wife and then said, "One word. Casey. She thinks you're lonely. And if you think I'm going to listen to her worry about you all by myself, you're nuts."

Mara slapped Garrett's face. He swiveled his head to smile at the baby. "Your daddy's scared of your mommy."

"Damn straight," Jackson admitted with a laugh. He headed off after the rest of his family and called back, "If she gets cranky, there's a bottle in the diaper bag."

"I think I can handle a baby," he shouted back, but Jackson was already swallowed by the crowd.

"It's just you and me, kid," Garrett told the girl who laughed delightedly and squirmed as if she wanted to be turned loose to run. "Oh, no, you don't. I put you down, you disappear and your mommy kills me."

"Down." Mara looked mutinous.

"No."

She scowled again then tried a coy smile.

"Man," Garrett said with a smile. "Are women *born* knowing how to do that?"

Bright, cheerful calliope music erupted from somewhere nearby and the smell of popcorn floated on the breeze. A dog wearing a top hat was waltzing with Cinderella to the cheers of the crowd. And Garrett was holding a baby and feeling as out of place as—hell, he couldn't even think of anything as out of place as he felt at the moment.

This was not his world, he thought, jiggling Mara when she started fussing. Give Garrett King a dangerous situation, a shooter going after a high-profile target, a kidnapping, even a jewelry heist, and he was in his element.

This happy, shiny stuff? Not so much.

Owning and operating the biggest, most successful security company in the country was bound to color your outlook on the world. Their clients ranged from royalty to wealthy industrialists, computer billionaires and politicians. Because of their own immense wealth, the King brothers knew how to blend in when arranging security. Because of their expertise, their reputation kept growing. Their firm was the most sought-after of its kind on the planet. The King twins flew all over the world to meet the demands of their clients. And he and his twin, Griffin, were good with that. Not everyone could be relaxed and optimistic. There had to be people like he and Griff around to take care of the dirty jobs.

That was his comfort zone, he told himself as he watched Jackson and his family near the front of the line. Casey was holding Molly and Jackson had Mia up on his shoulders. They looked…perfect. And Garrett was glad for his cousin, really. In fact, he was happy for all of the Kings who had recently jumped off a cliff into the uncharted waters of marriage and family. But he wouldn't be joining them.

Guys like him didn't do happy endings.

"That's okay, though," he whispered, planting a kiss on Mara's forehead. "I'll settle for spending time with you guys. How's that?"

She burbled something he took as agreement then fixed her gaze on a bright pink balloon. "Boon!"

Garrett was just going to buy it for her when he noticed the woman.

Alexis Morgan Wells was having a *wonderful* day. Disneyland was everything she had hoped it would be. She loved everything about it. The music, the laughter. The cartoon characters wandering around interacting with the crowd. She loved the gardens, the topiary statues; she even loved the smell of the place. It was like childhood and dreams and magic all at once.

The music from the last ride she'd been on was still dancing through her mind—she had a feeling it would be for hours—when she noticed the man coming up to her. Her good mood quickly drained away as the same man who had followed her on to It's a Small World hurried to catch up. He'd had the seat behind her in the boat and had come close to ruining the whole experience for her as he insisted on trying to talk to her.

Just as he was now.

"Come on, babe. I'm not a crazy person or anything. I just want to buy you lunch. Is that so bad?"

She half turned and gave him a patient, if tight, smile. "I've already told you I'm not interested, so please go away."

Instead of being rebuffed, his eyes lit up. "You're British, aren't you? The accent's cool."

"Oh, for heaven's sake."

She was really going to have to work on that, she told herself sternly. If she wasn't paying close attention, her clipped accent immediately branded her as "different." Though it would take a much better ear than that of the man currently bothering her, to recognize that her accent wasn't British, but Cadrian.

But if she worked at it, she could manage an American accent—since her mother had been born in California. Thinking about her mom brought a quick zip of guilt shooting through her, but Alex tamped it down. She'd deal with it later. She was absolutely sure her mother would understand why Alex had had to leave—she was just in no hurry to hear how much worry she'd caused by taking off.

After all, Alex was a bright, capable adult and if she wanted a vacation, why should she have to jump through hoops to take one? There, she was feeling better already. Until she picked up on the fact that her would-be admirer was still talking. Honestly, she was trying to stay under the radar and this man was drawing way too much attention to her.

Trying to ignore him, Alex quickened her steps, moving in and out of the ever-shifting crowd with the grace earned from years of dance lessons. She wore a long, tunic-style white blouse, blue jeans and blue platform heels, and, at the moment, she was wishing she'd worn sneakers. Then she could have sprinted for some distance.

The minute that thought entered her mind, she dismissed it, though. Running through a crowd like a lunatic would only draw the notice she was trying to avoid.

"C'mon, babe, it's *lunch.* What could it hurt?"

"I don't eat," she told him, "I'm an oxygenarian."

He blinked at her. "What?"

"Nothing," she muttered, hurrying again. Stop talking to him, she told herself. Ignore him and he'll go away.

She headed for the landmark right ahead of her. The snow-topped mountain in the middle of Anaheim, California. This particular mountain was probably one of the best known peaks in the world. Alex smiled just looking at it. She lifted her gaze and watched as toboggans filled with screaming, laughing people jolted around curves and splashed through lagoons, sending waves of water into the air. The line for the mountain was a long one and as her gaze moved over the people there, she saw *him*. He was watching her. A big man with black hair, a stern jaw and a plump baby on his hip.

In one quick instant, she felt a jolt of something like "recognition." As if something inside her, *knew* him. Had been searching for him. Unfortunately, judging by the black-haired little girl he was holding, some other woman had found him first.

"Quit walking so fast, will ya?" the annoying guy behind her whined.

Alex fixed her gaze on the sharp-eyed man and felt his stare hit her as powerfully as a touch. Then his eyes shifted from her to the man behind her and back again. He seemed to understand the situation instantly.

"There you are, honey!" he called out, smiling directly at Alex. "What took you so long?"

Smiling broadly, she accepted the help he was offering and ran to him. He greeted her with a grin then dropped one arm around her shoulders, pulling her in close to his side. Only then did he shift his gaze to the disappointed man.

"There a problem here?" Her Knight in Shining Denim demanded.

"No," the guy muttered, shaking his head. "No problem. Later."

And he was gone.

Alex watched him go with a sigh of relief. Not that he had ever scared her or anything, but she hadn't wanted to waste her first day in Disneyland being irritated. The big man beside her still had his arm around her and Alex liked it. He was big and strong and it was hard not to appreciate a guy who had seen you needed help and offered it without a qualm.

"Boon!"

The little girl's voice shattered the moment and with that reminder that her hero was probably someone else's husband, Alex slipped out from under his arm. Glancing up at the little girl, she smiled. "You're a beauty, aren't you? Your daddy must be very proud."

"Oh, he is," the man beside her said, his voice so deep it seemed to sink right inside her. "And he's got two more just like her."

"Really." She wasn't sure why the news that he was the father of three was so disappointing, but there it was.

"Yeah. My cousin and his wife have the other two on the ride right now. I'm just watching this one for them."

"Oh." She smiled, pleasure rushing through her. "Then you're not her father?"

He smiled, too, as if he knew exactly what she was thinking. "Not a chance. I wouldn't do that to some poor, unsuspecting kid."

Alex looked into his eyes and enjoyed the sparkle she found there. He was relishing this little flirtation as much as she was. "Oh, I don't know. A hero might make a very good father."

"Hero? I'm hardly that."

"You were for me a minute ago," she said. "I couldn't seem to convince that man to leave me alone, so I really appreciate your help."

"You're welcome. But you could have gone to a security guard and had the guy thrown out. Probably should have."

No, going to a security guard would have involved making statements, filling out paperwork and then her identity would be revealed and the lovely day she'd planned would have been ruined.

She shook her head, pushed her long blond hair back from her face and turned to sweep her gaze across the manicured flower gardens, the happy kids and the brilliant blue sky overhead. "No, he wasn't dangerous. Just irritating."

He laughed and she liked the sound of it.

"Boon, Gar," the little girl said in a voice filled with the kind of determination only a single-minded toddler could manage.

"Right. Balloon." He lifted one hand to the balloon seller, and the guy stepped right up, gently tying the string of a bright pink balloon to the baby's wrist. While Garrett paid the man, the baby waved her arm, squealing with delight as the balloon danced and jumped to her whim.

"So, I think introductions are in order," he said. "This demanding female is Mara and I'm Garrett."

"Alexis, but call me Alex," she said, holding her right hand out to him.

He took her hand in his and the instant her skin brushed along his, Alex felt ripples of something really intriguing washing throughout her body. Then he let her go and the delightful heat dissipated.

"So, Alex, how's your day going?"

She laughed a little. "Until that one little moment, it was going great. I love it here. It's my first time, and I've heard so much about this place..."

"Ah," he said nodding, "that explains it."

She tensed. "Explains what?"

"If it's your first time here, you're having so much fun that all of these crowds don't bother you."

"Oh, no. I think it's wonderful. Everyone seems so nice, well, except for—"

"That one little moment?" he asked, repeating her words to her.

"Yes, exactly." Alex smiled again and reluctantly took a step back. As lovely as this was, talking to a handsome man who had no idea who she was, it would be better for her if she ended it now and went on her way. "Thank you again for the rescue, but I should really be going…"

He tipped his head to one side and looked at her. "Meeting someone?"

"No, but—"

"Then what's your hurry?"

Her heartbeat sped up at the invitation in his eyes. He didn't want her to leave. And how nice that was. He actually liked her.

The darling little girl was still playing with her balloon, paying no attention at all to the two adults with her.

Alex looked up into Garrett's pale blue eyes and did some fast thinking. She had to keep a low profile, true. But that didn't mean she had to be a hermit during her… vacation, did it? And what kind of holiday would it be if there were no "romance" included?

"What do you say," he added, "hang with us today. Rescue me from a day filled with too many kids?"

"*You* need rescuing?"

She saw the teasing glint in his eyes and responded to it with a smile.

"Trust me. My cousin's girls all have my number. If you're not there to protect me, who knows what might happen?"

Tempting, she thought. So very tempting. She'd only been in America for three days and already she was feeling a little isolated. Being on her own was liberating, but, as it turned out, *lonely*. And it wasn't as if she could call the few friends she had in the States—the moment she did, word would get back to her family and, just like that, her bid for freedom would end.

What could it hurt to spend the day with a man who made her toes curl and the family he clearly loved? She took a breath and made the leap. "All right, thank you. I would love to rescue you."

"Excellent. My cousin and his family should be back any minute now. So while we wait, why don't you tell me where you're from. I can't quite place your accent. It's British, but…not."

She jolted a little and fought to keep him from seeing it. "You've a good ear."

"So I've been told. But that's not really an answer, is it?"

No, it wasn't, and how astute of him to notice. She'd been trained in how to answer questions without really answering them from the time she was a child. Her father would have been proud. *Never answer a question directly, Alexis. Always be vague. Watch what you say, Alexis. You've a responsibility to your family. Your heritage. Your people…*

"Hey. Alex."

At the sound of his concerned voice, she shook her head, coming out of her thoughts with relief. That was the second time Garrett had rescued her today. She didn't want to think about her duties. Her role in history. She didn't want to be anything but Alex.

So instead of being evasive again, she said, "Why don't you try to figure out where I'm from and I'll let you know when you've got it right?"

One dark eyebrow lifted. "Oh, you're challenging the wrong guy. But you're on. Five bucks says I've got it by the end of the day."

Oh, she hoped not. If he did, that would ruin everything. But she braved it out and asked, "Five dollars? Not much of a wager."

He gave her a slow grin that sent new flashes of heat dancing through her system. "I'm open to negotiation."

She actually *felt* her blood sizzle and hum.

"No, no. That's all right." She backed up quickly. Maybe she wasn't as prepared for that zing of romance as she had thought. Or maybe Garrett the Gorgeous was just too much for her to handle. Either way, she was nervous enough to try to cool things down between them just a little. "Five dollars will do. It's a bargain."

"Agreed," he said, one corner of his mouth lifting tantalizingly. "But just so you know, you should never bet with me, Alex. I always win."

"Confident, aren't you?"

"You have no idea."

A thrill of something hot and delicious swept through her veins. Nerves or not, she really enjoyed what he was doing to her. What was it about him that affected her so?

"That was fun, Uncle Garrett!"

A tiny whirlwind rushed up to them and threw both arms around Garrett's knees. The girl gave him a wide smile then shifted suspicious eyes to Alex. "Who are you?"

"This is Alex," Garrett told her. "Alex, meet Mia."

She smiled at the child and couldn't help noticing that the little girl held on to Garrett's legs just a little more tightly.

"Mia, don't run from me in these crowds," a deep male voice shouted.

Alex turned to watch an impossibly attractive couple approach, the man holding on to a smaller version of the still-wary Mia.

"Alex," Garrett said briskly, "this is my cousin Jackson and his wife, Casey, and that pretty girl with them is Molly."

"It's lovely to meet you all."

Jackson gave her a quick up and down, then winked at his wife. "Wow, leave Garrett alone for a few minutes and he finds the most beautiful woman in the whole place—"

His wife nudged him with an elbow.

"—not counting you of course, sweetie. You're the most beautiful woman in the *world*."

"Nice recovery," Casey told him with a laugh and a smile for Alex.

"Always were a smooth one, Jackson," Garrett mused.

"It's why she loves me," his cousin answered, dropping a kiss on his wife's head.

Alex smiled at all of them. It was lovely to see the open affection in this family, though she felt a sharp pang of envy slice at her, as well. To get some time for herself she'd had to run from her own family. She missed them, even her dictatorial father, and being around these people only brought up their loss more sharply.

"It's nice to meet you, Alex," Casey said, extending her right hand in welcome.

"Thank you. I must admit I'm a little overwhelmed by everything. This is my first trip to Disneyland and—"

"Your *first* time?" Mia interrupted. "But you're *old*."

"Mia!" Casey was horrified.

Garrett and Jackson laughed and Alex joined them. Bending down slightly, she met Mia's gaze and said, "It's horrible I know. But I live very far away from here, so this is the first chance I've ever had to visit."

"Oh." Nodding her head, Mia thought about it for a minute then looked at her mother. "I think we should take Alex to the ghost ride."

"Mia, that's *your* favorite ride," her father said.

"But she would like it, wouldn't you, Alex?" She turned her eyes up and gave her a pleading look.

"You know," Alex said, "I was just wishing I knew how to find the ghost ride."

"I'll show you!" Mia took her hand and started walking, fully expecting her family to follow.

"Guess you'll be spending the day with us for sure, now," Garrett teased.

"Looks that way." She grinned, delighted with this turn of events. She was in a place she'd heard about her whole life and she wasn't alone. There were children to enjoy and people to talk to and it was very near to perfect.

Then she looked up at Garrett's blue eyes and told herself maybe it was closer to perfect than she knew.

"And after the ghost ride, we can ride the jungle boats and then the pirate one." Mia was talking a mile a minute.

"Molly, honey, don't pick up the bug," Jackson said patiently.

"Bug?" Casey repeated, horrified.

Still holding Mara, Garrett came up beside Alex and said softly, "I promise, after the ghost ride, I'll ride herd on my family and you can do what you want to do."

The funny thing was, he didn't know it, but she was already doing what she had always wanted to do.

She *wanted* to be accepted. To spend a day with nothing more to worry about than enjoying herself. And mostly, she wanted to meet people and have them like her because she was Alex Wells.

Not because she was Her Royal Highness Princess Alexis Morgan Wells of Cadria.

Two

She was driving Garrett just a little crazy.

And not only because she was beautiful and funny and smart. But because he'd never seen a woman let go and really enjoy herself so much. Most of the women who came and went from his life were more interested in how their hair looked. Or in being sophisticated enough that a ride on spinning teacups would never have entered their heads.

But Alex was different. She had the girls eating out of her hand, and, without even trying, she was reaching Garrett in ways that he never would have expected. He couldn't take his eyes off her.

That wide smile was inviting, sexy—and familiar, somehow.

He knew he'd seen her before somewhere, but damned if he could remember where. And that bothered him, too. Because a woman like Alex wasn't easily forgotten.

At lunch, she had bitten into a burger with a sigh of pleasure so rich that all he could think of was cool sheets and hot sex. She sat astride a carousel horse and he imagined her straddling him. She licked at an ice cream cone and he—

Garrett shook his head and mentally pulled back fast from that particular image. As it was, he was having a hard time walking. A few more thoughts like that one and he'd be paralyzed.

Alex loved everything about Disneyland. He saw it in her eyes because she didn't hide a thing. Another way she was different from the women he knew. They were all about artful lies, strategic moves and studied flirtation.

Alex was just…herself.

"You'll like this, Alex," said Mia, who had appointed herself Alex's personal tour guide. "The pirate ships shoot cannons and there's a fire and singing, too. And it's dark inside."

"Okay, kiddo," Jackson told his daughter, interrupting her flood of information, "how about we give Alex a little rest?" He grinned at her and Garrett as he steered his family into the front row of the boat.

Garrett took the hint gratefully and pulled Alexis into the last row. A bit of separation for the duration of the ride would give them a little time to themselves.

"She's wonderful," Alex murmured. "So bright. So talkative."

"Oh, she is that," Garrett said with a laugh. "Mia has an opinion on everything and doesn't hesitate to share it. Her kindergarten teacher calls her 'precocious.' I call her a busybody."

She laughed again and Garrett found himself smiling in response. There was no cautious titter. No careful chuckle. When Alex laughed, she threw her soul into it and everything about her lit up. Oh, he was getting in way too deep. This was ridiculous. Not only did he not even know her last name, but he hadn't been able to pin down what country she was from, either.

Not for lack of trying, though.

The sense of familiarity he had for her was irritating as hell. There was something there. Something just out of reach, that would tell him how he knew her. Who she was. And yet, he couldn't quite grab hold of it.

The ride jolted into motion and Alex leaned forward, eager to see everything. He liked that about her, too. Her curiosity. Her appreciation for whatever was happening. It wasn't something enough people did, living in the moment. For most, it was all about "tomorrow." What they would do when they had the time or the money or the energy.

He'd seen it all too often. People who had everything in the world and didn't seem to notice because they were always looking forward to the next thing.

"Wonderful," she whispered. Their boat rocked lazily on its tracks, water slapping at its hull. She looked behind them at the people awaiting the next boat then shifted her gaze to his.

Overhead, a night sky was filled with stars and animatronic fireflies blinked on and off. A sultry, hot breeze wafted past them. Even in the darkness, he saw delight shining in her eyes and the curve of her mouth was something he just didn't want to resist any longer.

Leaning forward, he caught her by the back of the neck and pulled her toward him. Then he slanted his mouth over hers for a taste of the mouth that had been driving him nuts for hours.

She was worth the wait.

After a second's surprise, she recovered and kissed him

back. Her mouth moved against his with a soft, languid touch that stirred fires back into life and made him wish they were all alone in the dark—rather than surrounded by singing pirates and chattering tourists.

She sighed and leaned into him and that fired him up so fast, it took his breath away. But who needed breathing anyway? She lifted one hand to his cheek and when she pulled back, breaking the kiss, her fingertips stroked his jaw. She drew a breath and let it go again with a smile. Leaning into him, she whispered, "That was lovely."

He took her hand in his and kissed the center of her palm. "It was way better than lovely."

A kid squealed, a pirate's gun erupted too close to the boat and Alex jolted in surprise. Then she laughed with delight and eased back against him, pillowing her head on his shoulder. He pulled her in more closely to him and, instead of watching the ride, indulged himself by watching her reactions to their surroundings instead.

Her eyes never stopped shifting. Her smile never faltered. She took it all in, as if she were soaking up experiences like a sponge. And in that moment, Garrett was pitifully glad Jackson had talked him into going to Disneyland.

"I'm having such a nice day," she whispered in a voice pitched low enough that Garrett almost missed it.

"*Nice?* That's it?"

She tipped her head back and smiled up at him. "*Very* nice."

"Oh, well then, that's better." He snorted and shook his head. Nothing a man liked better than hearing the woman he was fantasizing about telling him she was having a "nice" time.

"Oh, look! The dog has the jail cell keys!" She was off again, losing herself in the moment and Garrett was charmed. The pirates were singing, water lapped at the sides of their boat and up ahead of them he could hear Mia singing along. He smiled to himself and realized that astonishing as it was, he, too, was having a *very* nice day.

After the ride, they walked into twilight. Sunset stained the sky with the last shreds of color before night crept in. The girls were worn-out. Molly was dragging, Mara was asleep on Casey's shoulder and Mia was so far beyond tired, her smile was fixed more in a grimace. But before they could go home, they had to make their traditional last stop.

"You'll like the castle, Alex," Mia said through a yawn. "Me and Molly are gonna be princesses someday and we're gonna have a castle like this one and we'll have puppies, too..."

"Again with the dog," Jackson said with a sigh at what was apparently a very familiar topic.

Alex chuckled and slipped her hand into Garrett's. His fingers closed over hers as he cut a glance her way. In the soft light, her eyes shone with the same excitement he'd seen earlier. She wasn't tired out by all the kids and the crowds. She was thriving on this.

Her mouth curved slightly and another ping of recognition hit him. Frowning to himself, Garrett tried to pin down where he'd seen her before. He knew he'd never actually *met* her before today. He wouldn't have forgotten that. But she was so damned familiar...

The castle shone with a pink tinge and as they approached, lights carefully hidden behind rocks and in the shrubbery blinked on to make it seem even more of a fairy-tale palace.

Garrett shook his head and smiled as Mia cooed in delight. Swans were floating gracefully in the lake. A cool wind rustled the trees and lifted the scent of the neatly trimmed rosebushes into the air.

"Can I have a princess hat?" Mia asked.

"Sure you can, sweetie," Jackson said, scooping his oldest into his arms for a fast hug.

Garrett watched the byplay and, for the first time, felt a twinge of regret. Not that it would last long, but for the moment, he could admit that the thought of having kids like Mia and her sisters wasn't an entirely hideous idea. For other people, of course. Not for him.

"Alex, look!" Mia grabbed Alex's hand and half dragged her up to the stone balustrade overlooking the lake. The two of them stood together, watching the swans, the pink castle in the background and Garrett stopped dead. And stared.

In one blinding instant, he knew why she looked so familiar.

Several years ago, he'd done some work for her father.

Her father, the King of Cadria.

Which meant that Alex the delicious, Alex the sexiest woman he'd ever known, was actually the Crown Princess Alexis.

And he'd kissed her.

Damn.

He scrubbed one hand across the back of his neck, took a deep breath and held it. This changed things. Radically.

"Do you want to live in a castle, Alex?" Mia asked.

Garrett listened for her answer.

Alex ran one hand over Mia's long black hair and said, "I think a castle might get lonely. They're awfully big, you know. And drafty, as well."

Garrett watched her face as she described what he knew was her home. Funny, he'd never imagined that a princess might not like her life. After all, in the grand scheme, being royalty had to be better than a lot of other alternatives.

"But I could have lots of puppies," Mia said thoughtfully.

"Yes, but you'd never see them because princesses can't play with puppies. They have more important things to do. They have to say all the right things, do all the right things. There's not a lot of time for playing."

Mia frowned at that.

So did Garrett. Was that how she really felt about her life? Was that why she was here, trying to be incognito? To escape her world? And what would she do if she knew he had figured out her real identity? Would she bolt?

Alex smiled and said, "I think you might not like a real castle as much as you do this one."

Nodding, the little girl murmured, "Maybe I'll just be a pretend princess."

"Excellent idea," Alex told her with another smile. Then she turned her head to look at Garrett and their gazes collided.

He felt the slam of attraction hit him like a fist to the chest. He was in deep trouble here. A princess, for God's sake? He'd kissed a *princess?* He took a good long look at her, from her platform heels to the blue jeans and the pair of sunglasses perched on top of her head.

She had worked very hard to disguise herself, he thought, and wondered why. As a princess, she could have had a guided tour through the park, swept through all of the lines and been treated like—well, royalty. Instead, she had spent her day wandering through Disneyland just like any other tourist.

Alone.

That word shouted through his mind and instantly, his professional side sat up and took notice. Letting go, for the moment, of the fact that she'd lied about who she was—where was her security detail? Where were her bodyguards? The entourage? Didn't she know how dangerous it was for someone like her to be unprotected? The world was a dangerous place and helping out the wackos by giving them a clear shot at you didn't seem like a good plan to him.

So just what was she up to?

As if reading his troubled thoughts from the emotions in his eyes, Alex's smile faded slightly. Garrett noticed and immediately put his game face on. She was keeping her identity a secret for a reason. Until he found out what that was, he'd play along.

And until he knew everything that was happening, he'd make damn sure she was safe.

In the huge parking lot, they all said goodbye and Jackson and Casey herded their girls off toward their car. The parking lot lights above them flickered weirdly as tourists streamed past like zombies in search of the best way home.

Garrett turned to look at Alex again. "Where's your car?"

"Oh, I don't have one," she said quickly. "I never learned to drive, so I took a cab here from the hotel."

A cab, he thought grimly. On her own. She was asking for disaster. It was a freaking miracle she'd made it here without somebody recognizing her and tipping off the press. "Where are you staying?"

"In Huntington Beach."

Not too far, he thought, but far enough that he didn't want her repeating the "grab a cab" thing. His gaze scanning the crowded lot and the people passing by them, he said, "I'll give you a ride back to your hotel."

"Oh, you don't have to do that," she argued automatically.

He wondered if it was sheer politeness or a reaction to his change in attitude. The closeness, the heat that had been between them earlier and definitely cooled. But how could it not? She was a runaway princess, and he was the guy who knew better than to give in to his urges, now that he knew the truth.

She was a *princess* for God's sake. Didn't matter that his bank account was probably close to hers. There was wealth and then there was *royalty.* The two didn't necessarily mix.

"Yeah," he told her, "I really do."

"I can take care of myself," she said.

"I'm sure you can. But why wait for a cab when I'm here and ready?"

No way was he going to let her out of his sight until he knew she was safe. She was too high-profile. Princess Alexis's pretty face had adorned more magazine covers than he could count. Reporters and photographers usually followed after her like rats after the Pied Piper. Her luck was bound to run out soon and once it did, she'd have people crowding all around her. And not all of them would be trustworthy.

Nope. He'd be with her until he got her back to her hotel, at least. Then he'd figure out what to do next.

"Well, all right then," she said with a smile. "Thank you."

The traffic gods were smiling on them and it didn't take more than twenty minutes before he was steering his BMW up to the waterfront hotel. He left his keys with the valet, took Alex's arm and escorted her into the hotel. His gaze never quit moving, checking out the area, the people, the situation. The hotel lobby was elegant and mostly empty. Live trees stood in huge, terra cotta pots on the inside of the double doors. A marble floor gleamed under pearly lights and tasteful paintings hung on cream-colored walls.

A couple of desk clerks were busily inputting things into computers. A guest stood at the concierge, asking questions, and an elevator hushed open to allow an elderly couple to exit. It all looked fine to his studied eyes, but as he knew all too well, things could change in an instant. An ordinary moment could become the stuff of nightmares in a heartbeat.

Alex was blissfully unaware of his tension, though, and kept up a steady stream of comments as they walked toward the bank of elevators. “It’s this one,” she said and used her key card to activate it.

While they waited, he took another quick look around and noted that no one had paid the slightest attention to them. Good. Seemed that her identity was still a secret. Somehow that made him feel a bit better about his own failure to recognize her.

But in his own defense, you didn’t normally see a princess in blue jeans taking a cab to Disneyland.

She was staying in the penthouse suite, of course, and he was glad to see that there was a special elevator for that floor that required a key card. At least she had semiprotection. Not from the hotel staff of course, and he knew how easily bribed a staff member could be. For the right price, some people would sell off their souls.

When the elevator opened, they stepped into a marble-floored entryway with a locked door opposite them. He waited for her to open the door then before she could say anything, he stepped inside, to assure himself that all was as it should be. His practiced gaze swept over the interior of the plushly decorated suite. Midnight-blue couches and chairs made up conversation areas. An unlit fireplace took up most of one wall and the sliding glass doors along a wall of windows afforded an amazing view of the ocean. Starlight filled the dark sky and the moon shone down on the water with a sparkling silver light.

He stalked across the suite to the bedroom, gave it and the master bath a quick, thorough look then moved back into the living room. He checked the balcony then swept his gaze around the room. No sign of anything and just the stillness in the room told him that there hadn't been any intruders.

"What're you doing?" she asked, tossing the key card onto the nearest table.

"Just making sure you're okay." He brushed it off as if it were nothing more than any other guy would have done. But she was no dummy and her blue eyes narrowed slightly in suspicion.

Her nose was sunburned, her hair was a wild tangle and she looked, he thought, absolutely edible. His body stirred in reaction and he told himself to get a grip. There wouldn't be any more kisses. No more fantasies. Not now that he knew who she was.

Alex was strictly off-limits. Oh, he wanted her. Bad. But damned if he was going to start an international incident or something. He'd met her father. He knew the king was not the kind of man to take it lightly if some commoner was sniffing around the royal princess. And Garrett didn't need the extra hassle anyway. Yeah, she was gorgeous. And hot. And funny and smart. But that crown of hers was just getting in the way. And beside all that was the fact that she was here. Alone. Unprotected. Garrett was hardwired to think more of her safety than of his own wants. And mixing the two never worked well.

"Well, I appreciate it," she said softly, "but I'm really

fine. The hotel is a good one and they have excellent security."

Uh-huh. He wasn't so sure of that, but he'd be doing some checking into the situation, that was for damn sure. True, it was a five-star hotel and that usually meant guests were safe. But as he had found out the hard way, mistakes happened.

"Thank you again."

Alex walked toward him and everything in him wanted to reach out, grab her and pull her in close. He could still taste her, damn it, and he knew he wouldn't be forgetting anytime soon just how good she felt, pressed up against him. His body was hard and aching like a bad tooth, which didn't do much for his attitude.

"I had a wonderful day." Her smile widened and she threw her arms out. "Actually, it was perfect. Just as I'd always imagined my first day at Disneyland would be."

That statement caught him off guard and he laughed. "You imagined a five-year-old talking your ears off?"

"I imagined a day spent with friends and finding someone who—" She broke off there, letting the rest of what she might have said die unuttered.

Just as well, Garrett told himself. He might be a professional security expert, but he was also a guy. And knowing that she felt the same pulse of desire he did was almost more than he could take.

Hell, if he didn't get out of there soon, he might forget all about his principles and better judgment.

"Guess I'd better go," he said, stepping past her for the open doorway while he could still manage it.

"Oh. Are you sure?" She waved one hand at the wet bar across the room. "Maybe one drink first? Or I could call room service…"

She wasn't making this easy, he told himself. Need

grabbed him at the base of the throat and squeezed. It would be so easy to stay here. To kiss her again and take his time about it. To feel her body respond to his and to forget all about who she was. Who he was. And why this was a really bad idea.

"I don't think so," he said, "but thanks. Another time."

"Of course." Disappointment clouded her features briefly. And after a day of watching her smile and enjoy herself, damned if he could stand her feeling badly.

"How about breakfast?" He heard himself say it and couldn't call the words back.

That smile of hers appeared again and his heart thudded painfully in his chest. Garrett King, master of bad mistakes.

"I'd like that."

"I'll see you then," he said and stepped out of the penthouse, closing the door quietly behind him.

In the elevator, he stood perfectly still and let the annoying Muzak fill his mind and, temporarily at least, drive out his churning thoughts. But it couldn't last. He had to think about this. Figure out how to handle this situation.

Yes, he wanted Alex.

But his own code of behavior demanded that he protect—not bed—the princess.

He watched the numbers over the elevator doors flash and as they hit the first floor and those doors sighed open, he told himself that maybe he could do both.

The question was, should he?

Three

"Did you and Mickey have a good time?"

"Funny." Garrett dropped into his favorite, bloodred leather chair and propped his feet up on the matching hassock. Clutching his cell phone in one hand and a cold bottle of beer in the other, he listened to his twin's laughter.

"Sorry, man," Griff finally said, "but made me laugh all day thinking about you hauling your ass around the happiest place on Earth. All day. Still can't believe you let Jackson con you into going."

"Wasn't Jackson," Garrett told him. "It was Casey."

"Ah. Well then, that's different." Griffin sighed. "What is it about women? How do they get us to do things we would never ordinarily do?"

"Beats the hell outta me," Garrett said. In his mind, he was seeing Alex again as he said goodbye. Her eyes shining, her delectable mouth curved…

"So was it hideous?"

"What?"

"I swear, when I went to Knott's Berry Farm with them last summer, Mia about wore me into the ground. That kid is like the Tiny Terminator."

"Good description," Garrett agreed with a laugh. "And she was pumped today. Only time she sat down was when we were on a ride."

Sympathy in his tone, Griffin said, "Man, that sounds miserable."

"Would have been."

"Yeah…?"

Garrett took a breath, considered what he was about to do, then went with his gut. He was willing to keep Alex's secret, for the time being anyway, but not from Griffin. Not only were they twins, but they were partners in the security firm they had built together.

"So, talk. Explain what saved you from misery."

"Right to the point, as always," Garrett murmured. His gaze swept the room. His condo wasn't big, but it suited him. He'd tried living in hotels for a while like his cousin Rafe had done for years until meeting his wife, Katie. But hotels got damned impersonal and on the rare occasions when Garrett *wasn't* traveling all over the damn globe, he had wanted a place that was *his.* Something familiar to come home to.

He wasn't around enough to justify a house, and he didn't like the idea of leaving it empty for weeks at a stretch, either. But this condo had been just right. A home that he could walk away from knowing the home owner's association was looking after the property.

It was decorated for comfort, and the minute he walked in, he always felt whatever problems he was thinking about slide away. Maybe it was the view of the ocean.

Maybe it was the knowledge that this was his space, one that no one could take from him. Either way, over the past couple of years, it really had become *home*.

The study where he sat now was a man's room, from the dark paneling to the leather furniture to the stone hearth on the far wall. There were miles of bookshelves stuffed with novels, the classics and several gifts presented to him by grateful clients.

And beyond the glass doors, there was a small balcony where he could stand and watch the water. Just like the view from Alex's hotel room. Amazing how quickly his mind could turn and focus back on her.

"Hello? Garrett? You still there?"

"Yes, I'm here."

"Then talk. No more stalling. What's going on?"

"I met a woman today."

"Well, shout hallelujah and alert the media!" Griffin hooted a laugh that had Garrett wrenching the phone away from his ear. "'Bout time you got lucky. I've been telling you for months you needed to loosen up some. What's she like?"

"Believe me when I say she defies description."

"Right. You met a goddess at Disneyland."

"Not exactly."

"What's that mean?"

"She's a princess."

"Oh, no," Griffin groaned dramatically. "You didn't hook up with some snotty society type, did you? Because that's just wrong."

Frowning, Garrett said, "No, she's a *princess*."

"Now I'm confused. Are we talking a real princess? Crown? Throne?"

"Yep."

"What the—"

"Remember that job we did for the King of Cadria a few years ago?"

Silence, while his brother thought about it, then, "Yeah. I remember. They were doing some big show of the crown jewels and we set up the security for the event. Good job."

"Yeah. Remember the daughter?"

"Hah. Of course I remember her. Never met her face-to-face, but I saw her around the palace from a distance once or twice. Man she was—" Another long pause. "Are you kidding me?"

Garrett had gotten a few of those long-distance glances, too. He remembered not paying much attention to her, either. When he was on a job, his concentration was laser-like. Nothing but security concerns had registered for him and once that had been accomplished, he and his brother had left Cadria.

Since the small island nation was just off the coast of England, he and Griffin had flown to Ireland to visit their cousin Jefferson and his family. And never once had Garrett given the crown princess another thought.

Until today.

"Nope. Not kidding. Princess Alexis was at Disneyland today."

"I didn't see anything about it on the news."

"You won't, either." Garrett took a swig of his beer and hoped the icy brew would cool him off. His body was still thrumming, his groin hot and hard, and he had a feeling it was only going to get worse for him, the longer he spent in her company. "She's hiding out or some damn thing. Told us her name was Alex, that's all."

"What about her security?"

"Doesn't have any that I could see."

Griffin inhaled sharply. "That's not good, bro."

"No kidding?" Garrett shook his head as Griffin's concern flashed his own worries into higher gear. Alex was all alone in a hotel room and *Garrett* was the only one who knew where she was. He couldn't imagine her family allowing her to be unprotected, so that told him she had slipped away from her guards. Which left her vulnerable. Hell, anything could happen to her.

"What're you gonna do about it?"

He checked the time on the grandfather clock on the far wall. "I'm going to wait another hour or so, then I'm calling her father."

Griffin laughed. "Yeah, cuz it's that easy to just pick up a phone and call the palace. Hello, King? This is King."

Garrett rolled his eyes at his brother's lame joke. They'd heard plenty just like that one while they were doing the job for Alex's father. Kings working for kings and all that.

"Why am I talking to you again?"

"Because I'm your twin. The one that got all the brains."

"Must explain why I got all the looks," Garrett muttered with a smile.

"In your dreams."

It was an old game. Since they were identical, neither of them had anything to lose by the insults. Griffin was the one person in his life Garrett could always count on. There were four other King brothers in their branch of the family, and they were all close. But being twins had set Garrett and Griffin apart from the rest of their brothers. Growing up, they'd been a team, standing against their older brothers' teasing. They'd played ball together, learned how to drive together and dated cheerleaders together. They were still looking out for each other.

To Kings, nothing was more important than family. Family came first. Always.

Griffin finally stopped laughing and asked, "Seriously, what are you going to do?"

"Just what I said. I'm going to call her father. He gave us a private number, remember?"

"Oh, right."

Nodding, Garrett said, "First, I want to find out if the king knows where she is."

"You think she ran away?"

"I think she's going to a lot of trouble to avoid having people recognize her, so yeah." He remembered the blue jeans, the simple white shirt, the platform heels and her wild tangle of hair. Nope. Not how anyone would expect a princess to look. "Wouldn't be surprised to find out no one but us knows where she is. Anyway, I'll let the king know she's okay and find out how he wants me to handle this."

"And how do *you* want to handle it?" Griffin asked.

Garrett didn't say a word, which pretty much answered Griffin's question more eloquently than words could have. What could he possibly have said anyway? That he didn't want to handle the situation—he wanted to handle *Alex?* Yeah, that'd be good.

"She must be something else."

"Y'know? She really is," he said tightly. "And she's going to stay safe."

Memories flew around him like a cloud of mosquitoes. Nagging. Irritating. He couldn't stop them. Never had been able to make them fade. And that was as it should be, he told himself. He'd made a mistake and someone had died. He should never be allowed to forget.

"Garrett," Griffin said quietly, "you've got to let the past go."

He winced and took another drink of his beer. As twins, they had always been finely attuned to each other. Not exactly reading each other's minds or anything—thank God for small favors. But there was usually an undercurrent that each of them could pick up on. Clearly, Griffin's twin radar was on alert.

"Who's talking about the past?" Bristling, Garrett pushed haunting memories aside and told himself that Alex's situation had nothing to do with what had happened so long ago. And he would do whatever he could to see that it stayed that way.

"Fine. Be stubborn. Keep torturing yourself for something that you did. Not. Do."

"I'm done talking about it," Garrett told his brother.

"Whatever. Always were a hard head."

"Hello, pot? This is kettle. You're black."

"Hey," Griffin complained, "I'm the funny one, remember?"

"What was I thinking?" Garrett smiled to himself and sipped at his beer.

"Look, just keep me posted on this. Let me know what her father has to say and if you need backup, *call*."

"I will," he promised, even though he knew he wouldn't be calling. He didn't want backup with Alex. He wanted to watch over her himself. He trusted his brother with his life. But he would trust *no one* with Alex's. The only way to make sure she stayed safe was to take care of her himself.

Alex couldn't sleep.

Every time she closed her eyes, her mind dredged up images snatched from her memories of the day. Mostly, of course, images of Garrett—laughing, teasing his nieces, carrying a sleeping baby…and images of him as he leaned in to kiss her.

Oh, that kiss had been…well, way too short, but aside

from that, wonderful. She could still hear the water sloshing against the boat, the singing from the pirates and feel the hot wind buffeting their faces. Still feel his mouth moving over hers.

It had been, she told herself with a small smile, *magic.*

She picked up her hot tea off the room service cart and stepped onto the balcony of her suite. A summer wind welcomed her with the cool kiss of the sea. She stared up at the night sky then shifted her gaze to the ocean where the moon's light danced across the surface of the water, leaving a silvery trail, as if marking a path to be followed. In the middle of the night, everything was quiet, as if the whole world was dreaming.

And if she could sleep, Alex knew her dreams would be filled with Garrett.

She took a sip of the tea and sighed in satisfaction.

Alexis knew she should feel guilty for having left Cadria the way she had, but she just couldn't manage it. Maybe it was because of the years she had spent doing all the "right" things. She had been a dutiful daughter, a helpful sister, a perfect princess. She was always in the right place at the right time saying the right things.

She loved her father, but the man was practically medieval. If it weren't for her mother's restraining influence, King Gregory of Cadria would probably have had his only daughter fitted for a chastity belt and tucked away in a tower. Until he picked out the right husband for her, of course.

Alex had had to fight for every scrap of independence she had found over the past few years. She hadn't wanted to be seen only at state occasions. Or to christen a new ship or open a new park. She wanted more. She wanted her life to mean something.

And if that meant a twenty-eight-year-old woman had to run away from home—then so be it.

She only hoped her father would eventually forgive her. Maybe he would understand one day just how important her independence was to her.

Nothing had ever been *hers.* The palace deemed what she should do and when she should do it.

Even her work with single mothers in need, in the capital city of Cadria, had been co-opted by the palace press. They made her out to be a saint. To be the gently bred woman reaching out to the less fortunate. Which just infuriated her and embarrassed the women she was trying to help.

Her entire life had been built around a sense of duty and privilege, and it was choking her.

Shaking her head, she tried to push that thought aside because she knew very well how pitiful that sounded. Poor little rich girl, such a trying life. But being a princess was every bit as suffocating as she had tried to tell little Mia earlier.

Mia.

Alexis smiled to herself in spite of her rushing thoughts. That little girl and her family had given Alex one of the best days of her life. Back at the palace, she had felt as though her life was slipping away from her, disappearing into the day-to-day repetitiveness of the familiar. The safe.

There were no surprises in her world. No days of pure enjoyment. No rush of attraction or sizzle of sexual heat. Though she had longed for all of those for most of her life.

She had grown up on tales of magic. Romance. Her mom had always insisted that there was something special about Disneyland. That the joy that infused the place somehow made it more enchanted than anywhere else.

Alex's mother had been nineteen and working in one

of the gift shops on Main Street when she met the future King of Cadria. Of course, Mom hadn't known then that the handsome young man flirting with her was a prince. She had simply fallen for his kind eyes and quiet smile. He kept his title a secret until Alex's mother was in love—and that, Alexis had always believed, was the secret. Find a man who didn't know who she was. Someone who would want her for herself, not for who her father was.

Today, she thought, she might have found him. And in the same spot where her own mother had found the magic that changed her life.

"I can't feel guilty because it was worth it," she murmured a moment later, not caring that she was talking to herself. One of the downsides of being by yourself was that you had no one to talk things over with. But the upside was, if she talked to herself instead, there was no one to notice or care.

Her mind drifted back to thoughts of her family and she winced a little as she realized that they were probably worried about her. No doubt her father was half crazed, her mother was working to calm him down and her older brothers were torn between exasperation and pride at what she'd managed to do.

She would call them in a day or two and let them know she was safe. But until then, she was simply going to *be*. For the first time in her life, she was just like any other woman. There was no one to dress her, advise her, hand her the day's agenda. Her time was her own and she had no one to answer to.

Freedom was a heady sensation.

Still, she couldn't believe she had actually gotten away with it. Ditching her personal guards—who she really hoped didn't get into too much trouble with her father—disguising herself, buying an airplane ticket and slipping out of Cadria unnoticed. Her father was no doubt furious, but truth to tell, all of this was really his fault. If he hadn't started making noises about Alex "settling down," finding an "appropriate" husband and taking up her royal duties, then maybe she wouldn't have run.

Not that her father was an ogre, she assured herself. He was really a nice man, but, in spite of the fact that he had married an American woman who had a mind of her own and a spine of steel, he couldn't see that his daughter needed to find her own way.

Which meant that today, she was going to make the most of what she might have found with Garrett—she frowned. God, she didn't even know his last name.

She laughed and shook her head. Names didn't matter. All that mattered was that the stories her mother had told her were true.

"Mom, you were *right,*" she said, cradling her cup between her palms, allowing the heat to seep into her. "Disneyland is a special place filled with magic. And I think I found some for myself."

He had already been cleared for the penthouse elevator, so when Garrett arrived early in the morning, he went right up. The hum of the machinery was a white noise that almost drowned out the quiet strains of the Muzak pumping down on him from overhead speakers.

His eyes felt gritty from lack of sleep, but his body was wired. He was alert. Tense. And, he silently admitted, eager to see Alex again.

Stupid, he knew, but there it was. He had no business allowing desire to blind him. She was a princess, for God's sake and he was now, officially, her bodyguard.

Garrett caught his own reflection in the mirrored wall opposite him and scowled. He should have seen it coming, what had happened when he finally got through to the King of Cadria. The fact that he had been surprised only underlined exactly how off course his brain was.

In the seconds it took for the elevator to make its climb, he relived that conversation.

"She's in California?"

The king's thundering shout probably could have been heard even without the telephone.

Well, Garrett told himself, that answered his first question. He had been right. The king had had no idea where Alex was.

"Is she safe?"

"Yes," Garrett said quickly as his measure of the king went up a notch or two. Sure he was pissed, but he was also more concerned about his daughter's safety than anything else. "She's safe, but she's on her own. I'm not comfortable with that."

"Nor am I, Mr. King."

"Garrett, please."

"Garrett, then." He muttered to someone in the room with him, "Yes, yes, I will ask, give me a moment, Teresa," he paused, then said, "Pardon me. My wife is very concerned for Alexis, as are we all."

"I understand." In fact Garrett was willing to bet that "very concerned" was a major understatement.

"So, Garrett. My wife wished to know how you found Alexis."

"Interestingly enough, I was with my family at Disneyland," he said, still amused by it all. Imagine stumbling across a runaway princess in the heart of an amusement park. "We met outside one of the rides."

No point telling the king that Garrett had come to Alex's rescue, not knowing who she was. No point in mention-

ing the kiss he had stolen in the darkness of a pirate ride, either.

"I knew it!" The king shouted then spoke to his wife in the room with him. "Teresa, this is your fault, filling our daughter's head with romantic nonsense until she—"

Listening in on a royal argument just underscored what Garrett had learned long ago. People were people. Didn't matter if they wore a king's crown or a baseball cap. They laughed, they fought, they cried—all of them. And it sounded to Garrett that the King of Cadria, like any other man, didn't have a clue how to deal with women.

The king's voice broke off and a moment later a soft, feminine voice spoke up. The queen, Garrett guessed, and smiled as he realized that she clearly didn't let her husband's blustering bother her.

"Hello, Garrett?"

"Yes, ma'am."

"Is Alexis well?"

"Yes, ma'am, as I told your husband, she was fine when I took her back to her hotel last night."

"Oh, that's such good news, thank you. You say you met her at Disneyland?"

"Yes, ma'am."

More to herself than to him, the queen murmured, "She always dreamed of visiting the park. I should have guessed she would go there, but—"

A princess dreaming about Disneyland. Well, other young girls dreamed of being a princess, so he supposed it made sense. Garrett heard the worry in the queen's voice and he wondered if Alex was even the slightest bit concerned about what her family was going through.

"Thank you again for looking out for my daughter," the queen said, "and now, my husband wants to speak to you again."

Garrett smiled to himself imagining the phone shuffle going on in a palace a few thousand miles away. When the king came back on the line, his tone was quieter.

"Yes, my dear, you're right. Of course. Garrett?"

"I'm here, sir."

"I would like to hire you to protect our daughter."

Instantly, Garrett did a quick mental step backward. This wasn't what he'd had in mind. He didn't want to guard her body. He just wanted her. Not the best basis for a protection detail.

"I don't think that's a good idea—"

"We will pay whatever you ask, but frankly my wife feels that Alexis needs this time to herself so I can't very well drag her back home, much as I would prefer it. At the same time, I'm unwilling to risk her safety."

Good point, Garrett couldn't help but admit. Whether she thought so or not, there was potential danger all around Alexis. Which is why he had placed this call in the first place. He thought she should be protected—just not by him. "I agree that the princess needs a bodyguard, but..."

"Excellent." The king interrupted him neatly. "You will keep us informed of what she's doing, where she's going?"

Instantly, Garrett bristled. That wasn't protection; that was being an informant. Not once in all the years he and his twin had run their agency had they resorted to snapping pictures of cheating spouses and damned if he was going to start down that road now.

"I'm not interested in being a spy, your majesty."

A dismissive chuckle sounded. "A spy. This isn't the situation at all. I'm asking that you protect my daughter—for a handsome fee—and along the way that you merely observe and report. What, Teresa?" Garrett heard furious whispers during the long pause and finally the king came back on the line. "Fine, it is spying. Very well. Observe and not report?"

He still didn't like it. Then the king spoke again.

"Garrett, my daughter wants her holiday, but she's managed to lose every guard I've ever assigned her. We would appreciate it very much if you would watch over Alexis."

Which was why he had finally agreed to this.

Garrett came back out of his memories with a thoughtful frown at his image. He had the distinct feeling that this was not going to end well.

But what the hell else was he supposed to do? Tell a man, a king, that he *wouldn't* protect his daughter? And still, he would have refused outright if the king had insisted on the spying.

But damned if he could think of a way to get out of guarding her. The king didn't want Alex's presence announced to the world, for obvious reasons, and since Garrett had already met her, and was a trained security specialist besides, how could he *not* take the assignment?

If he had said no and something happened to Alexis, he'd never be able to live with himself. His frown deepened as he silently admitted that the truth was, he already had one dead girl haunting him—he wouldn't survive another.

Four

At the knock on her door, Alex opened it and smiled up at Garrett.

The slam of what she had felt around him the day before came back harder and faster than ever. He was so tall. Broad shoulders, narrow hips. He wore black jeans, a dark green pullover shirt—open at the collar, with short sleeves that displayed tanned, muscular forearms. His boots were scuffed and well worn, just adding to the whole "danger" mystique. His features were stark, but somehow beautiful. His eyes shone like a summer sky and the mouth she had thought about way too often was quirked in a half smile.

"I'm impressed."

"You are?" she asked. "With what?"

"You're ready to go," he said, sweeping his gaze up and down her before meeting her gaze again. "Not going to have me sit in the living room while you finish your hair or put on makeup or decide what to wear?"

Her eyebrows lifted. He had no way of knowing of course, but she had been raised to be punctual. The King of Cadria never kept people waiting and he expected the same of his family.

"Well," she said, "that was completely sexist. Good morning to you, too."

He grinned, obviously unapologetic. "Wasn't meant to be sexist, merely grateful," he said, stepping past her into the living room of her suite. "I hate waiting around while a woman drags her feet just so she can make an entrance." He gave her a long, slow look, then said, "Although, you would have been worth the wait."

She flushed with pleasure. A simple compliment simply given, and it meant so much more than the flowery stuff she was used to hearing. As for "entrances," she got way too many of those when she was at home. People standing when she entered a room, crowds thronging for a chance at a handshake or a photo. A band striking up when she was escorted into a formal affair.

And none of those experiences gave her the same sort of pleasure she found in seeing Garrett's reaction to her. Alex threw her hair back over her shoulder and tugged at the hem of her short-sleeved, off-the-shoulder, dark red shirt. She had paired the top with white slacks and red, sky-high heels that gave her an extra three inches in height. Yet still she wasn't at eye level with Garrett.

And the gleam in his eyes sent pinpricks of expectation dancing along her skin. Funny, she'd been awake half the night, but Alex had never felt more alert. More…alive. She should have done this years ago, she thought. Striking out on her own. Going incognito, meeting people who had no idea who she was. But then, even as those thoughts raced through her mind, she had to admit, if only to herself, that the real reason she was feeling so wired wasn't her little holiday. It was Garrett.

She'd never known a man like him. Gorgeous, yes. But there was more to him than the kind of face that should be on the pages of a magazine. There was his laughter, his kindness to his little cousins—and the fact that he'd ridden to her rescue.

And the fact that the black jeans he wore looked amazing on him didn't hurt anything, either.

Alex watched him now as he scanned the perimeter of the room as if looking for people hiding behind the couches and chairs. Frowning slightly, she realized that she'd seen a similar concentrated, laserlike focus before. From the palace guards and her own personal protection detail. He had the air of a man on a mission. As if it were his *job* to keep her safe. Doubt wormed its way through her mind.

Was it possible this had all been a setup? Had her father somehow discovered her whereabouts and sent Garrett to watch over her?

Then she silently laughed and shook her head at the thought. Garrett had been at Disneyland with his family. Their meeting was accidental. Serendipity. She was reading too much into this, letting her imagination spiral out of control. Alex was projecting her concerns onto Garrett's presence with absolutely no reason at all to do so. The man was simply looking around the penthouse suite.

She was so used to staying in hotels like this one she tended to forget that not everyone in the world was blasé about a penthouse. Inwardly smiling at the wild turns paranoia could take, she ordered herself to calm down and patiently waited for Garrett's curiosity to be satiated.

Finally, he turned to look at her, his features unreadable. "So. Breakfast?"

"Yes, thanks. I'm starving."

He gave her that grin that seemed designed to melt her knees and leave her sprawling on the rug. Really, the man had a presence that was nearly overpowering.

"Another thing I like about you, Alex. You admit when you're hungry."

She shook off the sexual hunger clawing at her and smiled back at him. "Let me guess, most women you know don't eat?"

He shrugged as if the women in his life meant nothing and she really hoped that was the case.

"Let's just say the ones I've known consider splitting an M&M a hearty dessert."

She laughed at the image. "I know some women like that, too," she said, snatching up her red leather bag off the closest chair. "I've never understood it. Me, I love to eat."

"Good to know," he said, one corner of his mouth lifting.

And there went the swirl of something hot and delicious in the pit of her stomach. How was she supposed to keep a lid on her imagination if every look and smile he gave her set off incendiary devices inside her?

This holiday was becoming more interesting every minute. When he took her hand and drew her from the penthouse, Alex savored the heat of his skin against hers and told herself to stop overthinking everything and just enjoy every moment she was with him.

They had breakfast down the coast in Laguna Beach, at a small café on Pacific Coast Highway. On one side of the patio dining area, the busy street was clogged with cars and the sidewalks bustled with pedestrian traffic. On the other side, the Pacific Ocean stretched out to the horizon.

Seagulls wheeled and dipped in the air currents, surfers

rode waves in to shore and pleasure boats bobbed lazily on the water. And Alex was only vaguely aware of any of it. How could she be distracted by her surroundings when she could hardly take her eyes off Garrett? His thick, black hair lifted in a capricious breeze and she nearly sighed when he reached up to push his hair off his forehead. The man was completely edible, she thought, and wondered vaguely what he might look like in a suit. Probably just as gorgeous, she decided silently, but she preferred him like this. There were too many suits in her world.

This man was nothing like the other men in her life. Which was only one of the reasons he so intrigued her.

But Garrett seemed…different this morning. Less relaxed, somehow, although that was probably perfectly natural. People were bound to be more casual and laid-back at an amusement park than they were in everyday situations. The interesting part was she liked him even more now.

There was something about his air of casual danger that appealed to her. Not that she was afraid of him in any way, but the sense of tightly reined authority bristling off him said clearly that he was in charge and no one with him had to worry about a thing.

She laughed to herself. Funny, but the very thing she found so intriguing about him was what drove her the craziest about her father.

"Want to share the joke?" he asked, that deep voice of his rumbling along every single one of her nerve endings.

"No," she said abruptly. "Not really."

"Okay, but when a woman is chuckling to herself, a man always assumes she's laughing at *him*."

"Oh, I doubt that." Alex reached for her coffee cup and took a sip. When she set it down again, she added, "I can't imagine too many women laugh at you."

Amusement sparkled in his eyes. "Never more than once."

Now she did laugh and he gave her a reluctant smile.

"Not intimidated by me at all, are you?" he asked.

"Should I be?"

"Most people are."

"I'm not most people."

"Yeah," he said wryly, "I'm getting that." He leaned back in his chair and asked, "So what next, Alex? Anything else on your 'must see' list besides Disneyland?"

She grinned. It was wonderful. Being here. Alone. With him. No palace guards in attendance. No assistants or ministers or parents or brothers hovering nearby. She felt freer than she ever had and she didn't want to waste a moment of it. Already, her excitement had a bittersweet tinge to it because Alex knew this time away from home couldn't last.

All too soon, she would have to go back to Cadria. Duty was far too ingrained in her to allow for a permanent vacation. Another week was probably all she could manage before she would have to return and be Princess Alexis again. At the thought, she almost heard the palace doors close behind her. Almost sensed the weight of her crown pressing against her forehead. *Poor little rich girl,* she thought wryly and briefly remembered Garrett's tiny cousin wistfully dreaming of being a princess.

If only the little girl could realize that what she already had was worth so much more. A ripple of regret washed through Alex as she turned her gaze on the busy street.

She wondered how many of the people laughing, talking, planning a lazy day at the beach were like her—on holiday and already dreading the return to their real world.

"Alex?"

She turned her head to look at him and found his gaze locked on her. "Sorry. Must have been daydreaming."

"Didn't look like much of a daydream. What's got you frowning?"

He was far too perceptive, she thought and warned herself to guard her emotions more closely. "Just thinking that I don't want my holiday to end."

"Everything ends," he said quietly. "The trick is not to worry about the ending so much that you don't enjoy what you've got while you've got it."

Nodding, she said, "You're absolutely right."

"I usually am," he teased. "Ask anybody."

"You're insufferable, aren't you?"

"Among many other things," he told her, and she felt a tug of something inside her when his mouth curved just the slightest bit.

Then he turned his back on the busy street and looked out at the water. She followed his gaze, and nearly sighed at the perfection of the view. Tiny, quick-footed birds dashed in and out of the incoming tide. Lovers walked along the shore and children built castles in the sand.

Castles.

She sighed a little at the reminder of her daydream, of the world waiting for her return.

"So no big plans for today then?" he asked.

"No," she said with a suddenly determined sigh, "just to see as much as I can. To enjoy the day."

"Sounds like a good idea to me. How about we explore the town a little then take a drive along the coast?"

Relief sparkled inside her. She had been sure he'd have to leave. Go to work. Do whatever he normally did when not spending time with a runaway princess. "Really? That sounds wonderful. If you're sure you don't have to be somewhere…"

"I'm all yours," he said, spreading his arms as if offering himself to her.

And ooh, the lovely sizzle that thought caused. "You don't have to be at work?"

"Nope. I'm taking a few days off."

"Well, then, lucky me."

The waitress approached with the check, Garrett pulled a few bills from his wallet and handed them to her.

"Hmm, that reminds me," Alex said when the woman was gone again. "You owe me five dollars."

His eyebrows lifted. "For what?"

She folded her arms on the table. "We had a wager yesterday and you never did guess where I'm from."

He nodded, gaze locked on hers, and warmth dazzled her system. Honestly, if he were to reach out and touch her while staring at her as he was, Alex was sure she'd simply go up in flames.

"So we did," he said and reached into his wallet again.

"You don't have to actually pay me," she said, reaching out to stop him. Her hand touched his and just as she'd suspected, heat surged through her like an out of control wildfire. She pulled her hand back quickly, but still the heat lingered. "I just wanted you to admit you lost. You did buy breakfast after all."

"I always pay my debts," he said and pulled out a five. Before he could hand it over, though, Alex dug into her purse for a pen and gave it to him. "What's this for?"

"Sign it," she said with a shrug and a smile. "That way I'll always remember winning my first wager."

He snorted an unexpected laugh. "That was your first bet?"

No one but her brothers—and they didn't count—ever made bets with a princess. It would be considered tacky. A tiny sigh escaped her before she could stop it. How much she had missed just because of how things might "look." "You're my first—outside my family of course. And I did pretty well, I think, don't you? I did earn five dollars."

"So you did," he said, clearly amused. "Okay then…" He took her pen, scrawled a message, signed it and handed both the pen and the money to her.

Alex looked down and read, "Payment in full to Alex from Garrett." She lifted her gaze, cocked her head and said, "I still don't know your last name."

He nodded. "Don't know yours, either."

"Seems odd, don't you think?" Her gaze dropped to his signature. It was bold, strong and she had no doubt that a handwriting analyst would say that Garrett was confident, powerful and even a little arrogant.

"I'll tell you my name if you tell me yours," he taunted.

Her gaze snapped to his. Tell him her last name? She considered it for a second or two. Wells was common enough; maybe he wouldn't think anything of it. But then again, if he put her first name with her last, it might ring a familiar bell that she'd rather remain silent.

She was having too much fun as "just Alex" to want to give it up this early in her holiday. So why risk it? Why insist on last names when it didn't really matter anyway? After all, when her holiday was over, they'd never see each other again. Wasn't it better for both of them to keep things light? Superficial?

He was still watching her. Waiting. She couldn't read his expression and she really wished she could. Alex would have loved to know what he was thinking about this…whatever it was between them. If he was as intrigued, as filled with a heightened sense of anticipation as she was.

"So?" he asked, a half smile curving his mouth as he waited for her decision.

"First names only," she said with an emphatic nod. "It's more fun that way, don't you agree?"

"I think," Garrett said as he stood up and held one hand out to her, "the fun hasn't even started yet."

"Is that a promise?" she asked, slipping her hand into his and relishing the rush of heat and lust that immediately swamped her.

"It is," he said, "and I always keep my promises."

Garrett looked down at their joined hands then lifted his gaze to hers as the buzz between them sizzled and snapped like sparks lifting off a bonfire. "Fun. Coming right up."

They spent a couple of hours in Laguna, wandering down the sidewalks, drifting in and out of the eclectic mix of shops lining Pacific Coast Highway. There were art galleries, handmade ice cream parlors, jewelry stores and psychics. There were street performers, entertaining for the change dropped into open guitar cases and there were tree-shaded benches where elderly couples sat and watched the summer world roll by.

Alex was amazing. She never got tired, never got bored and absolutely everything caught her attention. She talked to everyone, too. It was as if she was trying to suck up as much life as possible. And he knew why. Soon she'd be going back behind palace walls and the freedom she was feeling at the moment would disappear.

Hard to blame her for wanting to escape. Who the hell didn't occasionally think about simply dropping off the radar and getting lost for a while? He'd done it himself after—Garrett shut that thought down fast. He didn't want to relive the past. Had no interest in wallowing in the pain and guilt that had ridden him so hard for so long. There was nothing to be gained by remembering. He'd learned his lesson, he assured himself, and that was why he was sticking to Alex like glue.

It had nothing to do with how she looked in those mile-high heels. Or the brilliance of her smile or the damn sparkle in her eyes.

He could tell himself whatever he wanted to, he thought, but even *he* didn't believe the lies.

"You're frowning," she said, snapping him out of his thoughts. He was pitifully grateful for the distraction.

"What?"

"Frowning," she repeated. "You. Do I look that hideous?"

He shook his head at the ridiculousness of the question, but dutifully looked at the drawing the caricature artist was doing of Alex. The guy had an easel set up under one of the trees along the highway and boxes of colored pastels sat at his elbow. Garrett watched him drawing and approved of the quick, sure strokes he made.

Alex was coming alive on the page, her smile wider, her eyes bigger and brighter and her long blond hair swirling in an unseen wind.

"So?" she asked.

"It looks great," he muttered, not really caring for how the artist had defined Alex's breasts and provided ample cleavage in the drawing.

"Thanks, man," the guy said, layering in a deeper blue to Alex's eyes. "I love faces. They fascinate me. Like you," he said to Alex, "your face is familiar, somehow. Like I've seen you before. But with that accent no way you're from around here."

Garrett's gaze snapped to her in time to see her face pale a bit and her eyes take on a wary sheen.

"I'm sure I've just got one of 'those' faces," she said, trying to make light of the guy's statement. "You know they say we all have a double out there, wandering the world."

"Yeah," the artist murmured, not really listening. "But you're different. You're..."

"You done?" Garrett asked abruptly.

"Huh?" The guy glanced up at him and whatever he saw in Garrett's eyes convinced him that he was indeed finished. "Sure. Let me just sign it."

A fast scrawl with a black chalk and he was tearing the page off the easel and handing it to Alex. She looked at it and grinned, obviously pleased with the results. In fact, she was so entranced by the drawing, she didn't notice the artist's eyes suddenly widen and his mouth drop open in shock.

Apparently, Garrett thought grimly, he'd finally remembered where he had seen Alex before. Moving fast, Garrett caught the other man's eye and gave him a warning glare that carried threats of retribution if he so much as said a single word.

His meaning got across with no problem. The tall, thin man with the straggly beard closed his mouth, wiped one hand across the back of his neck and nodded in silent agreement.

Garrett pulled out his wallet and handed over a wad of cash. Way more than the price of the drawing, this was also shut-the-hell-up-and-forget-you-ever-saw-her money. When the guy whistled low and long, Garrett knew the bribe was successful.

"Thank you!" Alex said and finally looked at the artist. "It's wonderful. I know just where I'll hang it when I get home."

"Yeah?" The artist grinned, obviously loving the idea that one of his drawings would soon be hanging in a castle.

"Well, cool. Glad you like it, Pr—" He stopped, shot a look at Garrett and finished up lamely, *"Miss."*

Alex missed the man's slipup. She reached into her purse. "How much do I owe you?"

"It's taken care of," Garrett said, stepping up beside her and dropping one arm around her shoulders. He shot another warning look at the artist. "Isn't it?"

"You bet," the guy said, nodding so hard Garrett half expected the man's head to fly off his neck. "All square. We're good. Thanks again."

Garrett steered her away from the artist, and got her walking toward where he'd parked his car. Best to get out of here before the guy forgot just how threatening Garrett could be and started bragging about how he had drawn the portrait of a princess.

"You didn't have to buy this for me, Garrett," she said, with a quick glance up at him. "I appreciate it, but it wasn't necessary."

"I know that. I wanted to."

"Well, I love it." She turned her head to study the portrait. "Whenever I look at it, I'll think of today and what a lovely time I had. I'll remember the ocean, the ice cream, the tide pools, the shops…"

She came to a stop and the people on the sidewalk moved past them like water rushing around a rock in a fast moving stream. She looked at him, reached up and cupped his cheek in her palm. He felt her touch all the way to his bones.

Her blue eyes shone with the glitter of promises when she said, "And I'll remember *you* most of all."

He knew with a soul-deep certainty that he'd never forget her, either.

Five

Decker King looked more like a beach bum than a successful businessman. And that was just how he liked it.

Garrett only shook his head while Decker flirted like crazy with Alex. Decker wore board shorts, flip flops and a T-shirt that read, Do it With a King.

And in smaller letters, King's Kustom Krafts.

The man might be annoying, but his company built the best luxury pleasure crafts in the world. His specialty was the classic, 1940s style wooden powerboats. Decker had customers all over the world sitting on waiting lists for one of his launches.

"You sure you want Garrett to take you out?" Decker was saying, giving Alex a smile meant to seduce.

"Yeah," Garrett interrupted. "She's sure."

Decker glanced at him and smirked. "Okay, then. My personal boat is moored at the dock out back." He tossed the keys to Garrett. "Don't scratch it."

"Thank you, Decker," Alex said with a smile as Garrett grabbed her hand and headed for the dock.

"My pleasure, Alex," he called back as she was hustled away. "Anytime you get tired of my dull cousin, just call me!"

"I don't think you're dull," Alex said on a laugh, her hand tightening around his.

"Decker thinks anyone with a regular job is dull. He's talented but he's also a flake."

"But he runs this business…"

"Yeah, like I said, talented. He's like a savant."

Alex laughed again as they stepped out into the sunlight, leaving the airy boat-building warehouse behind. "Oh, come on. He's very sweet."

"All women like Decker." Garrett looked down at her and smiled. "None of the cousins have figured out why, yet."

"None of you? How many cousins do you have?"

"I can't count that high," he said with a half laugh. "We're all over California. Like a biblical plague."

She laughed and Garrett let the sound ripple over him like sunlight on the water.

"Must be nice, having that much family."

"It can be," he admitted. "It can also be a pain in the ass from time to time."

They stopped at the end of the dock, and Garrett helped her into the sleek boat waiting for them. He untied the rope, tossed it aside then jumped in beside her. The wood planks of the hull gleamed a dark red-brown from layers of varnish and careful polishing. The red leather bench seats were soft and the engine, when Garrett fired it up, sounded like the purr of a mighty beast.

Alex laughed in delight and Garrett couldn't help grinning in response. In a few minutes, he was out of the harbor and headed for open water.

"I love this boat," she shouted over the engine noise. "It's like the ones in that Indiana Jones movie!"

"I love that you know that!" He grinned and gunned the engine harder, bringing the bow up to slap at the water as they careened across the surface.

When they were far enough out that Garrett was convinced that Alex was perfectly safe, he eased back on the throttle. The roar of the engine became a vibrating purr as the sleek powerboat shifted from a wild run into a lazy prowl.

Garrett slanted a look at her. "So, action movie fan are you?"

"Oh, yes." She turned her face up to the sun, closed her eyes and smiled. "It's having three brothers, I think. They had no time for comedies or romance, so movie night at our house meant explosions and gunfire."

"Sounds like my house," he said, remembering the many nights he and his brothers had spent reveling in movie violence. Garrett and Griffin especially had enjoyed the cops and robbers movies. The good guys tracking down the bad guys and saving the day in the end. Maybe that was why he and his twin had both ended up in the security business.

"You have brothers?"

"Four—one of them is my twin."

"A twin! I always thought it would be wonderful to be a twin. Was it?"

"Wonderful?" He shook his head. "Never really thought about it, I guess. But yeah, I suppose so. Especially when we were kids. There was always someone there to listen. To play with and, later, to raise hell with."

Being a twin was such a part of who and what he was

that he'd never really considered what it must look like from the outside. Griffin and he had done so much together, always right there, covering each other's backs that Garrett couldn't imagine *not* being a twin.

"Did you? Raise a lot of hell?"

"Our share," he mused, lost briefly in memories of parties, football games and women. "When we were kids, being identical was just fun. Swapping classes, tricking teachers. As we got older, the fun got a little more…creative."

"Identical?" She took a long look at him. "You're exactly alike?"

He shook his head and gave her a half smile. "Nah. I'm the good-looking one."

She laughed as he'd hoped she would.

"Must have been nice," she said, "raising a little hell once in a while. Having someone to have fun with."

"No hell-raising in your house?" he asked, though he couldn't imagine her and her brothers throwing any wild parties when the king and queen were out of town.

"Not that you'd notice," she said simply, then changed the subject. "Decker seemed very nice." She ran her fingertips across the small brass plaque on the gleaming teak dashboard. *King's Kustom Krafts.*

"Decker King is his name?"

"Yeah." He hadn't even considered that she would learn Decker's last name. And what kind of thing was that for a man like him to admit? Hell, he made his living by always thinking three steps ahead. By knowing what he was going to do long before he actually did it. By being able to guess at what might happen so that his clients were always safe. But around Alex, his brain wasn't really functioning. Nope, it was a completely different part of his body that was in charge now.

And it was damned humbling to admit he couldn't seem to get his blood flowing in the direction of his mind.

"Yeah. Decker's okay."

"He builds lovely boats."

"He really does," Garrett said, relaxing again when she didn't comment on Decker's last name. "So, you've heard about my family, tell me about these brothers of yours."

She looked at him and he read the wary suspicion in her eyes. "Why?"

"Curiosity." He shrugged and shifted his gaze to the sea. No other boats around. But for the surfers closer to shore, they were completely alone. Just the way he preferred it. Giving her a quick glance he saw her gaze was still fixed on him as if she were trying to make up her mind how much to say.

Finally, though, she sighed and nodded. "I've already told you I've got three brothers. They're all older than me. And very bossy." She turned her face into the wind and her long blond hair streamed out behind her. "In fact, they're much like my father in that regard. Always trying to order me about."

"Maybe they're just looking out for you," he said, mentally pitying the brothers Alex no doubt drove nuts. After all, the king himself had told Garrett that Alex managed to lose whatever bodyguards were assigned to her. He could only imagine that she made the lives of her brothers even crazier.

"Maybe they should realize I can look after myself." She shook her head and folded her arms over her chest in such a classic posture of self-protection that Garrett almost smiled.

But damned if he didn't feel bad for her in a way, too. He hated the idea of someone else running his life. Why should she be any different? Still, every instinct he possessed had him siding with her brothers and her father. Wasn't he here, protecting her, because he hadn't been able to stand the idea of her being on her own and vulnerable?

"Guys don't think like that," he told her. "It's got nothing to do with how capable they think you are. Men look out for our families. At least the decent guys do."

"And making us crazy while you do it?"

"Bonus," he said, grinning.

Her tense posture eased as she gave him a reluctant smile. "You're impossible."

"Among many other things," he agreed. Then, since he had her talking, he asked more questions. Maybe he could get her to admit who she was. Bring the truth out herself. *And then what?* Was he going to confess that he already knew? That her father was now *paying* him to spend time with her? Yeah, that'd go over well. How the hell had he gotten himself into this hole anyway?

Disgusted, he blew out a breath and asked, "So, you've got bossy brothers. What about your parents? What're they like?"

She frowned briefly and shifted her gaze back to the choppy sea, focusing on the foam of the whitecaps as if searching for the words she needed. Finally, on a sigh, she said, "They're lovely people, really. And I love them terribly. But they're too entrenched in the past to see that their way isn't the only way."

"Sound like normal parents to me," he mused. "At least, sounds like my dad. He was always telling us how things had been in his day, giving us advice on what we should do, who we should be."

She tucked her hair behind her ears and, instantly, it blew free again. Garrett was glad. He was getting very fond of that wild, tangled mane of curls.

"My parents don't understand that I want to do something different than what they've planned for me."

He imagined exactly what the royal couple had in mind for their only daughter and he couldn't picture it having anything to do with boat trips, ice cream and Disneyland. He knew enough about the life Alex lived to know that she would be in a constant bubble of scrutiny. How she dressed, what she said and who she said it to would be put under a microscope. Reporters would follow her everywhere and her slightest slip would be front page news. Her parents no doubt wanted her safely tucked behind palace walls. And damned if he could blame them for it.

"Give me an example," he said, steering the boat along the coastline. More surfers were gathered at the breakers and, on shore, towels were scattered across the sand like brightly colored jewels dropped by a careless hand.

"All right," she said and straightened her shoulders as if preparing to defend her position. Her voice was stronger, colored with the determination she felt to run her own life. "At home, I volunteer with a program for single mothers."

Her expression shifted, brightening, a smile curving her mouth. Enthusiasm lit up her eyes until they shone like a sunlit lake. When she started talking, he could hear pride in her voice along with a passion that stirred something inside him.

"Many of the women in the program simply need a little help in finding work or day care for their children," she said. "There are widows or divorcées who are trying to get on their feet again." Her eyes softened as she added, "But there are others. Girls who left school to have their babies and now don't have the tools they'll need to support themselves. Young women who've been abused or abandoned and have nowhere to turn.

"At the center, we offer parenting classes, continuing

education courses and a safe day care for the kids. These young women arrive, worried about the future and when they leave, they're ready to take on the world. It's amazing, really."

She turned on the bench seat, tucked one leg beneath her and rested one arm along the back of the seat. Facing him, she looked him in the eye and said, "The program has grown so much in the past couple of years. We've accomplished so many things and dozens of women are now able to care for their children and themselves. A few of our graduates have even taken jobs in the program to give back what they've received."

"It sounds great."

She smiled to herself and he saw the well-earned pride she felt. "It is, and it feels *good* to do something to actually help, you know? To step outside myself and really make a difference."

"Sounds like you're doing a good thing," Garrett said quietly.

"Thank you." She shrugged, but her smile only brightened. "I really feel as though I'm doing something important. These women have taught me so much, Garrett. They're scared and alone. But so brave, too. And being involved with the program is something I've come to love. On my own."

She sighed then and beneath the pride in her voice was a wistfulness that tore at him. "But my parents, sadly, don't see it that way. They're happy for me to volunteer—organizing fundraisers and writing checks. But they don't approve of me donating my time. They want me in the family business and don't want me, as they call it, 'splitting my focus.'"

"They're wrong," he said and cut back enough on the throttle so that they were more drifting now than actually motoring across the water. "You are making a difference. My mom could have used a program like that."

"Your mother?"

Garrett gave her a small smile. "Oh, my mom was one of the most stubborn people on the face of the planet. When she got pregnant with my brother Nathan, she didn't tell our father."

"Why ever not?"

"Always told us later that she wanted to be sure he loved *her.*" He smiled to himself, remembering the woman who had been the heart of their family. "She was alone and pregnant. No job skills. She supported herself working at In and Out Burgers. Then, a week before Nathan was born, my father showed up."

"Was he angry?"

"You could say that." Garrett laughed. "Mom insisted later that when he walked into the burger joint and shouted her name, there was steam coming out of his ears."

Alex laughed at the image.

"Dad demanded that she leave with him and get married. Mom told him to either buy a burger or get out of line and go away."

"What did he do?"

"What any man in my family would do," Garrett mused, thinking about the story he and his brothers had heard countless times growing up. "He demanded to see the owner and when the guy showed up, Dad bought the place."

"He bought the *restaurant?*"

"Yep." Grinning now, Garrett finished by saying, "He wrote the guy a check on the spot and the first thing he did as new owner? He fired my mother. Then he picked her up, carried her, kicking and screaming the whole way, to the closest courthouse and married her."

He was still smiling to himself when Alex sighed, "Your father's quite the romantic."

"More like hardheaded and single-minded," Garrett told her with a rueful shake of his head. "The men in our family know what they want, go after it and don't let anything get in their way. Well, except for my uncle Ben. He didn't marry *any* of the mothers of his kids."

"Any?" she asked. "There were a lot of them?"

"Oh, yeah," Garrett said. "That branch of the family still isn't sure they've met all of the half brothers that might be out there."

"I don't even know what to say to that," she admitted.

"No one does."

"Still, passion is hard to ignore," she told him, then asked, "are your parents still that way together?"

"They were," he said softly. "They did everything together. Even dying. We lost them about five years ago in a car accident. Drunk driver took them out when they were driving through the south of France."

"Garrett, I'm so sorry." She laid one hand on his arm and the touch of her fingers sent heat surging through him as surely as if he'd been struck by lightning.

He covered her hand with his and something…indefinable passed between them. Something that had him backing off, fast. He let her go and eased out from under her touch. "Thanks, but after the shock passed, all of us agreed that it was good that they had died together. Neither of them would have been really happy without the other."

"At least you have some wonderful memories. And your family."

"Yeah, I do. But you're lucky to still have your parents in your life. Even if they do make you nuts."

"I know," she said with a determined nod. "I just wish I could make them understand that—" She broke off and laughed. "Never mind. I'm wasting a lovely day with complaints. So I'm finished now."

Whatever he might have said went unspoken when he heard the approach of another boat. Garrett turned to look and saw a speedboat seemingly headed right for them. As casually as he could manage, he steered their boat in the opposite direction and stepped on the gas, putting some distance between them.

"What's wrong?"

He glowered briefly because he hadn't thought she was paying close attention to what he was doing. "Nothing's wrong. Just keeping my distance from that boat."

She looked over her shoulder at the boat that was fading into the distance. "Why? What're you worried about?"

"Everything," he admitted, swinging the little boat around to head back toward shore.

"Well, don't," she said and reached out to lay one hand on his forearm again. The heat from before had hardly faded when a new blast of blistering warmth shot through him. Instantly, his groin tightened and he was forced to grind his teeth together and clench his hands around the wheel to keep from shutting the damn engine off and grabbing her.

Seriously, he hadn't been this tempted by a woman in years.

Maybe never.

Shaking his head at the thought, he said, "Don't what?"

"Don't *worry,* Garrett." She released him and even with the heat of the sun pouring down on them, his skin felt suddenly cool now at the loss of her touch. "I'm taking a holiday from worry and so should you."

That wasn't going to happen. Garrett made his living worrying about possibilities. About danger around every corner. Possible assassins everywhere. Not an easy thing to turn off, and he wasn't sure he would even if he could.

"And what do you usually worry about?" he asked.

"Everything," she said, throwing his own word back at him. "But as I said, I'm taking a holiday. And so are you."

Then she laughed and tipped her face up to the sky. Closing her eyes, she sighed and said, "This is wonderful. The sea, the sun, this lovely boat and—"

"And—?"

She looked over at him. "You."

He nearly groaned. Her blue eyes were wide, her lush mouth curved and that off-the-shoulder blouse of hers was displaying *way* too much off-the-shoulder for his sanity's sake. Now it had dipped low over her left shoulder, baring enough of her chest that he could only think about getting the damn fabric down another two or three inches.

For God's sake, she was killing him without even trying. Garrett was forced to remind himself that he was on a job here. He was working for her father. It was his job to *guard* her luscious body, not *revel* in it.

Besides, if she knew the truth, knew who he was and that her father was paying him to spend time with her… hell, she'd probably toss his ass off the boat and then drive it over him just for good measure.

Knowing that didn't change a damn thing, though. He still wanted her. Bad.

"Alex…"

"I've been thinking." She slid closer. Their thighs were brushing now and he felt the heat of her through the layers of fabric separating them.

He almost didn't ask, but he had to. "About what?"

"That kiss."

Briefly, he closed his eyes. Throttling back, he cut the engine and the sudden silence was overwhelming. All they heard was the slap of water against the hull, the sigh of the wind across the ocean and the screech of seagulls wheeling in air currents overhead.

That kiss.

Oh, he'd been thinking about it, too. About what he would have done if they'd been alone in the dark and not surrounded by laughing kids and harassed parents. In fact, he'd already invested far too much time indulging his fantasies concerning Alex. So much so that if she moved another inch closer…pressed her body even tighter to his…

"Garrett?"

He turned his head to look at her and knew instantly that had been a mistake. Desire glittered like hard diamonds in her eyes. He recognized it, because the same thing was happening to him. He felt it. His whole damn body was on fire, and he couldn't seem to fight it. More, he didn't want to.

He hadn't asked for this. Hadn't expected it. Didn't need it, God knew. But the plain truth was he wanted Alex so badly he could hardly breathe.

The worst part?

He couldn't have her.

He was working for her father. She was a princess. He was responsible for her safety. In the real world, a holiday romance was right up his alley. No strings. No questions. No complications. But *this* woman was nothing *but* complications. If he started something with Alex, regret would be waiting in the wings.

All good reasons for avoiding this situation. For brushing her off and steering this damn boat back to Decker's yard as fast as possible. For dropping her at her hotel and keeping an eye on her from a distance.

And not one of those reasons meant a damn thing in the face of the clawing need shredding his insides.

"Not a good idea, Alex," he managed to say.

"Why ever not?" She smiled and the brilliance of it was blinding. She leaned in closer and he could smell the soft, flowery scent of her shampoo.

Her question reverberated in his mind. *Why not?* He couldn't give her any of the reasons he had for keeping his hands to himself. So what the hell was he supposed to say?

That he was actually a monk? That he didn't find her the least bit attractive? She wouldn't buy either of those.

"It's a beautiful day," she said, pressing her body along his on the bench seat. "We're both on holiday—" She stopped suddenly and looked at him. "Unless you're involved with someone already and—"

"No." One word, forced through clenched teeth. He took a breath. "If I were, I wouldn't be here with you."

"Good. Then Garrett…kiss me again."

He ground his teeth in a last ditch effort to hang on to his rampaging desires, or at least his professionalism. Then her scent came to him again on a soft wind and he knew he was lost. Maybe he'd *been* lost since the moment he met her.

Alex the princess might be easy enough to ignore, but Alex the woman was an entirely different story.

He grabbed her, pulled her onto his lap as he moved out from under the steering wheel and looked down into her eyes. "This isn't a good idea."

"I think it's a brilliant idea," she countered with a smile, then lifted her face to his.

Her eyes were bright, her mouth so close he could almost taste it and her hair flew about them like a blond cloud, drawing him in. He didn't need any more encouragement. Right or wrong, this was inevitable.

He took what she offered, what he needed more than

he'd like to admit. He'd curse himself later for surrendering. For now, there was Alex, a soft sea breeze and the gentle lap of water against the hull of the boat. They were alone and damned if he'd waste another minute.

Six

His mouth came down on hers and the first taste of her sent Garrett over the edge. The kiss they'd shared at Disneyland had haunted him until he had damn near convinced himself that no kiss could be as good as he remembered it.

He was wrong.

It was better.

He knew the contours of her mouth now, how her body folded into him, the sigh of her breath on his cheek. She wrapped her arms around his neck and pressed herself more tightly to him. Her hands swept up into his hair, and each touch of her fingers was like lightning through his bloodstream.

He parted her lips with his tongue and she met him eagerly, stroking, tasting, exploring. Mouths fused, breaths mingling, hearts hammering in time, they came together with a desperate need that charged the air around them.

Garrett set his hands at her hips and lifted her up, shifting her around until she was straddling him, her pelvis pressed to his hard, aching groin. It wasn't enough, but it was a start. She groaned into his mouth as his hips arched up against her.

Alex moved with him, rocking her body against his, as demanding as he felt. She slanted her head, giving as well as taking, tangling her tongue with his, losing herself in the heat that seemed to be searing both of them.

His hands swept up, beneath the hem of that red shirt that had been making him crazy all morning. He skimmed his fingers across her skin until he could cup her lace-covered breasts in his palms. Then he swept his thumb back and forth across her erect nipples until she was twisting and writhing against him, grinding her hips against his.

Her kiss grew hungrier, more desperate.

He knew the feeling.

Her moans enflamed him. Her touch, the scrape of her short, neat fingernails over the back of his neck, felt like accelerant thrown onto a bonfire. He was being engulfed and he welcomed it.

It was as if everything in his life had come down to this moment with her. As if his hands had always ached for the touch of her. His body hard and ready, all he wanted was to peel her out of her white slacks and panties and bury himself inside her.

The ocean air slid around them like a cool caress, keeping the heat at bay and adding new sensations to the mix. Hair rippled, clothing was tugged as if even nature wanted them together in the most basic way.

"You're killin' me," he muttered, tearing his mouth from hers long enough to drag in a deep breath of the salt-stained air.

"No," she said with a sigh and a grin as she licked her lips. "Not interested in killing you at all, Garrett."

He returned that smile, and slowly lifted the hem of her shirt, baring her abdomen and more to his gaze. When her lace-covered breasts were revealed, he reached behind her, unhooked her bra with a flick of his fingers then lifted the lacy cups for his first good look at her breasts.

Round and full, with dark pink, pebbled nipples, they made his mouth water. He lifted his gaze to hers and saw passion glazing her eyes. She licked her bottom lip, drew a shallow breath and leaned into him.

"Taste me," she whispered.

And it would have taken a stronger man than Garrett to turn down that offer. He bent his head and took first one nipple, then the other into his mouth. Moving back and forth between them, he licked and nibbled at her sensitive skin until she was a jangle of need, practically vibrating against him.

Finally, he suckled at her left breast while tugging at the nipple of her right with his fingers. His tongue traced damp circles around her areola and his mouth worked at her, sucking and pulling, drawing as much of her as he could into him.

"Garrett, yes," she whispered, holding his head to her, as if afraid he might stop.

But he had no intention of stopping. Now that they had crossed the barrier keeping them apart, nothing would keep him from having her completely.

"That feels so good." She was breathless, her body moving of its own accord, looking for the release she needed.

And as she moved on him, his groin tightened to the point of real pain and he wouldn't change anything. He dropped one hand to the juncture of her thighs and through the material of her white slacks, he felt her heat. Felt the dampness gathering there at her core.

He rubbed her, pressing hard against the nub of sensation he knew would be aching as he ached. She groaned again, louder this time, and moved restlessly on him. Dropping her hands to the snap and zipper, she undid them, giving him a view of the pale, ivory lace panties she wore before going up on her knees on the bench seat.

Garrett released her nipple, looked up into her eyes and lost himself in their passion-filled depths. He lifted one hand and deliberately, slowly dipped his fingers beneath the elastic band of her panties. She took a breath, let her head fall back and tensed, waiting for his first touch.

She looked like a pagan goddess.

Breasts bared to the sun, face lifted to the sky, hair flying in the wind and her center, open and waiting. He was rocked right down to his soul. She was magnificent. And the need clamoring inside him whipped into a churning frenzy.

He cupped her heat with his palm and was rewarded by a soft sigh of pleasure that slid from her elegant throat. Garrett's hand moved lower, his fingers reaching. She moved with him, giving him easier access. Her hands dropped to his shoulders to steady herself and when his thumb stroked over that one bud of passion, she jolted and gasped in a breath.

"Garrett...Garrett..." It was both plea and temptation.

He watched her, gaze fixed on her expressive face as he dipped first one finger, then two, inside her damp heat. He worked her body, making her rock and twist as she climbed that ladder of need to the climax that was waiting for her. His thumb moved over that nub again and again until she was practically whimpering. Her fingers dug into his shoulders, her sighs came fast and furious.

He stroked her, inside and out, until her body was bowed with building tension, until she was so blindly wrapped up in her own need, he, too, felt the gathering storm. When the first shocking jolt of release hit her, Garrett steadied her with one hand while with the other he pushed her higher, and higher, demanding more, always more.

"I can't," she whispered brokenly. "No more…"

"There's always more," he promised and then delivered—another orgasm, crashing down on her right after the first.

She wobbled on unsteady knees and finally dropped to his lap. Only then did she open her eyes and look into his. Only then did she lean forward and kiss him with a long, slow passion that left him as breathless as she felt.

Never before had he taken so much pleasure from his partner's climax. Never before had he been willing to put his own needs on hold for the simple joy of watching a woman shatter in his arms.

Dragging his hand free of her body, he reached up and smoothed her tangled hair back from her face. Then he cupped her cheek and drew her in close. He kissed her then, relishing the slow slide of her tongue against his.

Alex's mind splintered under the assault of too many sensations at once. His hands, his mouth, his breath. He was everything. The center of the universe, and she was left spinning wildly in his orbit. This moment, this touch, this kiss, was everything.

And in the aftermath of two amazing orgasms, it was all she could do to breathe.

She had thought she knew what it was to kiss Garrett. Truthfully, though, she'd had no idea. This was so much *more* than she had experienced before, there was no way she could have been prepared for what she would feel when it was more than a kiss. When his touch lit up her insides like the firework-lit skies over the palace on Cadria's Coronation Day.

Alex stared into his blue eyes, suddenly as dark and mysteriously hypnotic as the deepest seas, and tried to gather up the frayed threads of her mind. A useless endeavor.

Her brain had simply shut down. Her body was in charge now and all she knew was that she needed him. Needed to feel his skin against hers. Though she was still trembling with the reaction of her last orgasm, she wanted more. She wanted his body locked inside hers.

She traced her fingertips across his cheek, smiled and whispered, "That was amazing. But we're not finished… are we?"

"Not by a long shot," he told her before he gave her a quick, hard kiss that promised so much more.

"Thank heaven," she answered and dropped her hands to the hem of his shirt. As she went to tug it up, though, a deep, throaty noise intruded. A noise that was getting closer. They both turned to see the speedboat, racing toward them again.

Instantly, Alex pulled her shirt down, fastened her bra and quickly did up her pants. The other boat was too far away still for anyone to get a glimpse of bare skin, but the intimacy of the moment had been shattered anyway, and she didn't want to risk a stranger getting a peek at her.

Garrett's gaze narrowed on the approaching craft and his mouth firmed into a grim line. In seconds, he went from ravaging lover to alert protector. He lifted her off his lap, slid behind the wheel of the boat and fired up the engine. The throaty roar pulsed out around them and still, the racing boat's motor screamed loud enough that Alex wanted to cover her ears.

They watched as the speedboat came closer, its hull bouncing and crashing over the surface of the water. A huge spray of water fantailed in its wake as the driver swung in their direction.

"What's he doing?" Alex shouted.

"I don't know," Garrett called out, focus locked on the fast-approaching watercraft.

The boat was close enough now that Alex could see a couple up near the front of the boat and a child standing alone in the back. She whipped her head around, but saw no one else nearby. Just the far away surfers and the jet boat coming ever closer.

"Guy's an idiot," Garrett told her as the boat swung into a sharp turn. "If he doesn't throttle back, someone's going to—"

Before he could finish the sentence, the child flew off the back of the boat, hit the water hard and promptly sank. The boat kept going, the two other people on board apparently unaware they had lost the child.

"Oh, my God!" Alex stood up, frantically waving both arms at the driver to get his attention, but she went unnoticed. "The boy! He hasn't surfaced!"

Garrett shut off the engine, yanked his shirt over his head and tossed it to the deck then shouted, "Stay on the boat!" before he dove into the water.

His body knifed below the surface so cleanly he hardly made a splash. Terrified, Alex watched as he swam with swift, sure strokes, tanned arms flashing in and out of the water as he headed for the spot where the boy had gone under.

Alex's stomach jumped with nerves. With outright fear. She threw a glance at the jet boat, still flying across the water then looked back to where Garrett was swimming purposefully toward the child in trouble. She felt helpless. Useless. She had to *do* something.

Sliding behind the wheel, she fired up the engine and carefully eased the throttle forward, inching the boat closer to Garrett. She'd never driven a boat before and the power at her hands terrified her. One wrong move and she could endanger both Garrett and the child. Too much gas, she could run over them—if she didn't hit them outright. And there was the damage the propellers below the surface could do.

Tension gripping her, Alex's hands fisted on the steering wheel as she fought her own fears and her sense of dread for both the boy and Garrett. She kept her gaze locked on Garrett's sleek figure slicing through the water. Where was the boy? Why hadn't he come up? How could Garrett find him?

Fear ratcheted up another notch or two inside her as she inched ever closer. She risked another glance around; she was still alone out here. The jet boat hadn't returned.

"Do you see him?" she shouted.

Garrett shook his head, water spraying from the ends of his hair just before he suddenly dived deep, disappearing beneath the water entirely.

Alex cut the engine and stood up, watching the ever-churning water, hoping, waiting. What felt like *hours* ticked past.

"Come on, Garrett," she chanted, studying the water, looking for any sign of him. "Come back up. Come on!"

How could he hold his breath that long? What should she do? If she jumped in as well, would she make it that much more dangerous? One more person flailing about? She wasn't a strong swimmer anyway.

She heard a roar of sound and turned her head to see the jet boat hurtling toward them. If they didn't slow down…

"Stop!" Waving her arms and jumping up and down like a crazy woman, Alex screamed and shouted to get their attention. Idiots. Complete idiots. Didn't they realize that they could run over both Garrett and the child they must have finally realized was missing?

The boat slowed and when the engine cut off, the silence was deafening.

"Tommy!" The woman yelled as the man on board dived off the stern of his boat. Hanging over the railing, the woman was oblivious to Alex's presence, her focus concentrated solely on the dark water and what might be happening below.

Alex felt the same.

She didn't know how long Garrett had been underwater. She'd lost track of time. Couldn't think. Could hardly breathe. Dimly, she was aware that prayers were whipping through her mind at a furious rate and she hoped that someone upstairs was listening.

Apparently, they were. *"There!"*

Alex pointed at the shadow of movement in the dark water as it headed toward the surface. The woman on the boat behind her was still screaming and wailing. Alex hardly heard her.

Garrett shot out of the water, shaking his hair back from his face. In his arms, a boy of no more than five or six lay limply, eyes closed. A moment later, the man from the jet boat popped up beside Garrett and tried to take the boy.

Garrett ignored him and swam toward the jet boat. Alex followed his progress, her gaze locked on him and on the pale, young face he towed toward safety.

"Oh, God. Oh, God." The woman was babbling now,

tears streaming down her face, voice breaking on every word. "Is he breathing? Is he breathing?"

Garrett laid the boy on the cut out steps at the back of the boat and tipped the child's head back. While Alex watched, Garrett blew into the boy's mouth once. Twice. The waiting was the worst part. The quiet, but for the water continually slapping the hull and the now quiet weeping from the woman who had to be the boy's mother.

Again, Garrett breathed air into the boy's lungs and this time, there was a reaction.

Coughing, sputtering, retching what seemed a gallon of sea water, the little boy arched up off the deck of the boat, opened his eyes and cried, "Mommy!"

Instantly, the woman was on her knees, gathering her son to her chest. Rocking him, holding him, murmuring words only he could hear between the sobs racking her.

Tears streaked down Alex's cheeks, too, as she watched the man in the water grab Garrett and give him a hard hug. "Thanks, man. Seriously, thank you. I don't know what— If you hadn't been here—"

Garrett's gaze drifted to Alex and she felt his fury and relief as surely as she felt her own. But mixed in with those churning emotions, pride in what Garrett had done swelled inside her. He'd saved that child. If not for him, the boy would never have been recovered. His parents might have spent hours looking, wondering exactly where the boy had fallen in, having no idea where to search for him.

"Glad I could help," Garrett said tightly. "Next time slow down. And give that kid a life vest when you're on a damn boat."

"Right. Right." The man swiped one hand across his face, looked up at his family and Alex saw him pale at the realization of what might have happened.

"Yeah," he said. "I will. I swear it."

"Thank you," the woman said, lifting her head long enough to look first at Garrett and then at Alex. "Thank you so much. I don't know what else to say—"

She broke off, her gaze narrowing as she stared at Alex, a question in her eyes. "Aren't you…"

A knot of panic exploded in Alex's stomach. Would this woman recognize her? Say something?

"You'd better get him to a doctor," Garrett blurted. "Have him checked out."

"Yes," the woman said, tearing her gaze away from Alex long enough to nod, then stare down at her son again. "Good idea. Mike?"

"Coming," the man said, pushing himself out of the water and onto the boat. "Thanks again. It's not enough but it's all I can say."

Relieved that not only the boy was safe, but her secret as well, Alex watched Garrett swim toward her. She paid no attention when the speedboat owners fired up their powerful engine and took off—at a slower pace than they had been going previously. She was just glad to see them gone. Of course she was happy the child had survived. Happy that Garrett had been able to save him. But she was also grateful that her identity was still a secret. What were the odds, she wondered, of being in the middle of an ocean with a child near drowning and that boy's mother recognizing her?

She shoved those thoughts away as Garrett braced his hands on the edge of the boat and hoisted himself inside. Then he just sat there, holding his head in his hands. Alex sat down beside him, uncaring about the water sluicing off his clothes, soaking into hers.

Alex wrapped her arms around him and leaned her head on his shoulder.

"You were wonderful," she said softly.

"I was lucky," he corrected, lifting his head to look at her. "Saw a flash of the kid's white T-shirt and made a blind grab for him."

"You saved him," Alex said, cupping his cheek in her palm. "You were wonderful, Garrett."

A slow smile curved his mouth. "If you say so."

She smiled too. "I do."

"I learned a long time ago—never argue with a beautiful woman." He caught her hand in his, squeezed it briefly then leaned in to give her a fast kiss. "But, I think our boating trip is over."

Her heart tumbled in her chest. She didn't want the day to end. It had been filled with emotional ups and downs and moments of sheer terror. A boy's life had been saved and her own life had taken a wild turn in a direction she hadn't expected.

Alex looked at Garrett and couldn't even imagine *not* being with him. She'd known him only two days and he had touched her more deeply than anyone she had ever known. He was strong and capable and funny. He kissed her and her body exploded with need. He caressed her and the world fell away. She had never felt more alive than she did when she was with Garrett.

So no, she didn't want this day to end because every day that passed put her one day closer to leaving—and never seeing him again.

"Hey," he asked, brow furrowing, "what is it? What's wrong?"

"Nothing," she said. "It's nothing. I just…didn't want today to be over, I suppose."

He brushed a kiss across her mouth and eased back. "Day's not over, Alex. Just the boat ride."

"Really?"

"Really. Dress codes in five-star restaurants are a

lot looser in California than anywhere else, but…" He slapped one hand against his jeans and looked ruefully at his sodden boots. "I think they'll draw the line at soaking wet. I need to change clothes before I take you to dinner."

What he was saying made sense, but the look in his eyes told a different story. It was as if in saving the child, he'd closed a part of himself off from her, and Alex wanted to know why. He was pulling back, even sitting here beside him. She could feel a wall going up between them and wasn't sure what to do about it.

So for now, she let it go and gave him the answer she knew he was expecting.

"In that case," she told him, "we'd better get going."

Seven

The King Security company building was quiet. Halls were dark, phones silent and Garrett appreciated the peace. The light on his desk shone like a beam of sunlight in the darkness as he added his signature to a stack of papers Griffin had already signed in his absence.

The puddle of light from his desk lamp was bright and golden and threw the rest of the room into deep shadow. But Garrett didn't need light to find his way around. This place had pretty much been his life for the past ten years. He and Griffin had adjoining offices with a shared bathroom complete with shower separating them. There were plenty of times they had to leave fast for a job and having a shower and a change of clothes around came in damn handy.

There were bookcases on two of the walls and floor-to-ceiling windows overlooking the ocean on another. Family photographs and paintings hung on the remaining wall, and plush leather furniture completed the room. There was a fireplace, wet bar and a long couch comfortable enough to have served as Garrett's bed more than once.

This was the company he and Griffin had built with a lot of hard work, tenacity and the strength of their reputation. He was proud of it and until recently, hadn't so much as taken a day off. Garrett King lived and breathed the job. At least he *had,* until Alex came into his life.

And just like that, she was at the forefront of his thoughts again.

Instantly, his mind turned back to the afternoon on Decker's boat. His body reached for the sense memory of Alex trembling against him, but his brain went somewhere else. To the child falling into the water and nearly drowning. To Garrett's split-second decision to leave Alex alone and unprotected while he saved the child.

He couldn't have done it differently and he knew that, but still the decision haunted him. She had been alone. What if it had all been a setup? Some cleverly disguised assassination or kidnapping attempt on a crown princess? Sure, chances were slim, but they were *there.* The boy could have been a champion swimmer, doing exactly what he had been paid to do.

Absurd? he asked himself. Maybe. Paranoid? Absolutely. But stranger things had happened, and he'd been around to see a lot of them. Gritting his teeth, Garrett silently fumed at his complete lack of professionalism. He'd saved the boy but risked Alex and that was not acceptable.

He could still feel the slide of her skin beneath his fingers. Hear her whispered cries and the catch in her breath as her climax took her. His body went hard and tight as stone and he told himself the pain was only what he deserved.

Never should have let any of it happen, he told himself.

Hell, he knew better. Years ago, he'd learned the hard way that putting your own wants before the job was a dangerous practice that could end up costing lives.

Garrett threw the pen and swiped one arm across his desk, sending the stack of papers flying like a swarm of paper airplanes. Releasing his temper hadn't helped, though, and he pushed back from his desk, swiping one hand across his face. His eyeballs felt like sand-crusted rocks. He couldn't sleep for dreams of Alex.

That was why he was here, in the middle of the night. He had hoped that focusing his mind on work would keep thoughts of Alex at bay. So far he'd been there for two hours and it wasn't working.

Instead his brain insisted on replaying that scene in the boat over and over again. Those few, stolen, amazing moments that even now, he couldn't really regret. How the hell could he?

He had tried to tell himself that Alex was no different than any other celebrity or royal needing protection. That being with her didn't really mean a damn thing. But then she would laugh and his calm reason flew out the window.

The woman had a hell of a laugh.

It was just part of what he'd noticed about Alex at Disneyland. What set her apart from every other female Garrett had ever known.

She threw herself into life—she held nothing back. Even there in his arms, she had been open and vulnerable, offering him everything. It was damn sexy to watch, and every minute with her was a kind of enjoyable misery. His body was so tight and hard, he could hardly walk. He felt like a damn teenager again. No woman had ever affected him like this. Which was a big problem. She wasn't his. Not even temporarily.

She was a damn princess, and he was lying to her every

minute he was around her. She thought she was free and on her own, and he was being paid by her father to look out for her.

How much deeper was this hole he was in going to get?

Shaking his head, Garrett bent to scoop up the fallen papers and shuffle them back into some kind of order. Griffin had been right when he had ragged on Garrett for being practically monklike for months. Garrett had long ago burned out on women who were more interested in what being seen with a King could do for them than they were in him. And frankly, the women he knew were all the damn same. They all talked about the same things, thought the same way and, in general, bored the hell out of him.

Not Alex.

Nothing about her was ordinary. Or boring.

He never should have called the king. Never should have agreed to this bodyguard gig. Hell, he never should have gone to Disneyland.

Yeah, he told himself wryly. It was all Jackson's fault. If he'd never gone with his cousin and his family, if he'd never met Alex at all…he didn't like the thought of that, either.

"Son of a bitch." He tossed the papers to his desktop and glared at them hard enough to start a fire.

"Problem?"

Garrett snapped a look at the open doorway where his twin stood, one shoulder braced against the doorjamb. The shadows were so thick, he couldn't see Griffin's face, but the voice was unmistakable.

"What're you doing here in the middle of the night?" Garrett leaned back in his black leather chair and folded his hands atop his flat abdomen.

"Funny," Griffin said, pushing away from the doorway

to wander into his brother's office, "I was going to ask you the same thing." He dropped into one of the visitor's chairs opposite Garrett. "Was headed home from Amber's place and imagine my surprise when I spotted a single light on in the office. I figured it was either you or a really stupid burglar."

Garrett looked at his twin. His tuxedo was wrinkled, the collar of his shirt opened halfway down his chest and the undone bow tie was hanging down on both sides of his neck. Apparently at least *one* of them had had a good night.

"How is Amber?"

Griffin snorted and shoved one hand through his hair. "Still talking about getting that modeling job in Paris. I heard all about her packing tips, what she'll be wearing in the runway show and what kind of exfoliant will leave her skin—and I quote here—'shimmery.'"

He had to laugh. Shaking his head, he studied his brother and asked, "Why do you insist on dating women who don't have two active brain cells?"

"There are…compensations," Griffin said with a grin. "Besides, you date women who can walk and talk at the same time and you don't look happy."

"Yeah, well." What the hell could he say? He wasn't happy. Things with Alex were more complicated than ever.

He was tangled up in knots of hunger and frustration. Torn by his sense of duty and responsibility. For two days, he'd fought his every urge and instinct. All he wanted to do was get Alex naked and have her to himself for a few hours. Or weeks.

Instead, he'd made damn sure that the scene in the boat or anything remotely like it, hadn't happened again. For those few moments with Alex, Garrett had allowed himself to forget who and what she was. To put aside the reality of the situation. He'd indulged himself—putting her in a potentially dangerous situation—and now he was paying for it.

Every cell in his body was aching for her. He closed his eyes to sleep and he saw her. He caught her scent in his car, on his clothes. He was being haunted, damn it, and there didn't seem to be a thing he could do about it.

Disgusted, he said, "I'm happy."

"Yeah, I'm convinced." Griffin scowled at him.

He was really not in the mood to listen to his twin. He didn't want to hear about how he should let go of the past. Stop blaming himself for what had happened so long ago. He didn't want to talk. Period.

"Go away," he said, snatching up his pen again and refocusing on the papers in an attempt to get Griffin moving. Of course, it didn't work.

"Princess giving you problems?"

Garrett's gaze snapped to his twin's.

"Whoa. Quite the reaction." Griffin's eyebrows lifted. "So she's getting to you, huh?"

He dropped the pen, scraped both hands across his face and then shoved them through his hair. When that didn't ease his tension, he pushed out of his chair and stalked to the window overlooking the ocean. The moon was out, shining down on the water, making its surface look diamond studded. It was a scene that had soothed him many times over the years. Now, all it did was remind him of Alex. Of being on that boat in the sunshine. Of holding her while she—

"She's not getting to me. Everything's fine. Leave it alone, Griff."

"I don't think so." His twin stood up and walked to join him at the window. "What's going on, Garrett?"

"Nothing. Absolutely *nothing.* That's the problem."

Griffin studied him for a long minute or two and even in the shadowy light, Garrett saw amusement flicker in his twin's eyes. "You've got it bad, don't you?"

"You don't know what you're talking about."

"Right. Everything's great with you. That's why you're here. In the middle of the night, sitting alone in the dark."

"My desk light's on."

"Not the point."

"What *is* the point, Griffin?"

His twin gave him a half smile. "The point is, the mighty Garrett King is falling for a princess."

"You're out of your mind."

"Sure I am."

"She's a job. Her father hired us, remember?"

"Uh-huh."

"She's a princess. And God knows I'm no prince."

"Rich as one," Griffin pointed out helpfully.

"It's not enough and you know it." He shook his head. "Royalty hangs with royalty. Period."

"Not lately." When Garrett glared at him, Griffin shrugged. "I'm just sayin'…

He shifted his gaze away from his twin and stared unseeing at the ocean. Alex's face swam into his mind and as much as he tried to ignore it, she wouldn't go away. He was getting in too deep here and he knew it. But damned if he could see a way out.

"She's a job," he repeated, and which of them he was trying harder to convince, Garrett wasn't sure.

"Sure she is." Griffin slapped him on the shoulder. "Look, making yourself nuts over this just isn't worth it, Garrett. Why not just tell her the truth? Tell her who you are, that you're working for her father."

He'd thought about it. But confessing all wouldn't solve

anything. He'd still want her. And he still wouldn't be able to have her. And as a bonus, she'd be hurt.

"Can't do that."

"Fine, then let me take over," Griffin said.

Garrett just stared at him. "What?"

"Wouldn't be the first time we twin-switched somebody."

"You can't be serious," Garrett said with a snort of laughter.

"Why not? If she's just a job, I'll show up as you, spend some time with her…"

"Stay the hell away from her, Griffin."

His twin grinned. "So I'm right. She *does* mean something to you."

Blowing out a breath, Garrett frowned and turned his face back to the window. His own reflection stared back at him.

"Yeah, guess she does," he murmured, talking to his brother but somehow hoping to reassure the man in the glass as well. "Damned if I know what, though. But in another week or so she'll be gone. Problem solved."

"You think so?"

"I know it." All he had to do was find a way to keep his hands off her. Then she'd be back behind palace doors and his life would go back to normal. If the man in the glass didn't look reassured at all, Garrett ignored it.

Glancing at his twin, he deliberately changed the subject. "As long as you're here, bring me up to speed on what's going on with the business."

"Garrett…"

"Drop it, Griff," he said tightly. "Just, drop it."

"The most stubborn son of a—fine. Okay then, we've got a new client." Griffin moved back to the chair and sat down, stretching out his legs and crossing them at the ankle. "He's opening a luxury resort in Georgia and apparently he's having trouble with some local protestors."

"What're they protesting?"

Griffin snorted. "He's building a golf course and apparently threatening the home ground of the three-legged-gnat-catcher-water-beast-frog or some damn thing. Anyway, to protect the insects, they're threatening our client, and he wants to hire us to protect his family."

"It's a weird world, brother," Garrett muttered. "Protect the gnats by killing people."

"You got that right. Still, upside is, the weirdness is good for business. Anyway..."

Garrett nodded and listened while his brother outlined his plans for their latest client. This was better. Work. Something definable. Something he could count on. All he had to do was keep his focus centered. Remember who he was and why it was so important to keep a hard demarcation line between him and Alex.

He took a seat behind his desk, picked up the pen and began making notes. King Security was his reality.

Not a runaway princess looking for a white knight.

Three days.

It had been three days since they were together on that boat. Three days since Garrett had touched her in any but the most impersonal way. Three days that Alex had spent in a constant state of turmoil, waiting for it all to happen again and then being crushed when *nothing* happened.

Which was making her insane.

"Honestly," she demanded out loud of the empty room, "what is he waiting for?"

She knew he wanted her as much as she did him. When they were together, she felt the tension rippling off him in waves. So *why* was he working so hard at keeping her at arm's length? And why was she allowing it? For heaven's sake, this wasn't the nineteenth century. If she wanted him, she should go after him. No subtlety. No more waiting. He was determined to ignore what was between them, and she was just as determined that he be unable to.

Time was running out for her, Alex thought grimly. Soon enough, she would be on a plane headed back to Cadria and all of this would be nothing but a memory. And damn it, if memories were all that was going to be left of her, then she wanted as many of them as she could make.

With that thought firmly in mind, she checked her mirror and gave herself an objective once-over. Garrett had had some business to take care of that morning and so she'd had a couple of hours to herself and hadn't wasted them. A cab had taken her to the nearest mall where she had shopped until her feet gave out.

It had been good, walking through the Bella Terra mall, just another woman shopping. The freedom she felt was still thrilling, and she didn't know how she would get used to being under the palace microscope once her bit of freedom had ended. Being just one of a crowd was so liberating. She'd laughed with salesgirls, had a hamburger in the food court and then spent a lovely hour in a bookstore.

In fact, it would have been a perfect morning but for the fact that she'd had the oddest sensation that she was being watched. Ridiculous really and probably her own nerves rattling around inside her. No one here knew who she was so why would anyone be interested in what she was doing? She simply wasn't totally accustomed to being alone, that was all. Since leaving her guards behind her, she had been with Garrett almost every moment. Of course she would feel a touch uncomfortable. But it meant nothing.

Brushing off those thoughts, she returned to studying her reflection with a critical eye.

Hair good, makeup perfect and the slinky black dress she'd purchased just that morning clung to her like a second skin. The neckline was deep, displaying cleavage that should surely catch Garrett's eye. And the hemline was just barely legal. Paired with a pair of four-inch black heels, she looked, if she had to say so herself, hot.

Which was her intention, after all.

Her insides swirled with anticipation as she imagined the look on Garrett's face when he saw her. "Let him try to ignore me *now.*"

A smile curved her mouth as she let her mind wander to all sorts of interesting places. Damp heat settled at her core and a throbbing ache beat in time with her pulse. She needed him as she had never needed anyone before. And tonight, she was going to make sure he knew it.

An extremely vivid memory rose up in her mind. In a flash, she recalled just how it felt to have Garrett kissing her, touching her. Showering her body with the kinds of sensations she'd never known before. And she wanted it again, blast it.

"What's missing in this holiday romance," she told her reflection sternly, "is *romance.*"

Her time here was almost over. She couldn't very well put off her return indefinitely. First of all, she wouldn't do that to her family. But secondly, even if she *tried,* her father would never stand for it. If she didn't go home soon, the king would have an army of investigators out searching for her and they *would* find her. Her father was nothing if not thorough.

Now that she considered it actually, she was a little surprised her father hadn't already sent a herd of search dogs after her. It wasn't like him to let her minirebellion stand.

Frowning at the girl in the mirror, Alex shifted her gaze to the telephone on the bedside table. Guilt gnawed at her as she thought about calling home. At least letting her mother know that she was safe. The problem was, reaching her mother wouldn't be easy. The queen didn't have an email account. And she refused to get a cell phone, despite the palace and the king's insistence, so Alex would have to go through the palace phone system. Then she would have to talk to who knew how many ladies-in-waiting, assistants and secretaries before finally reaching her mother.

And during that interminable wait, everyone she talked to could spill the beans to her father the king, and Alex was in no mood to hear another lecture on the evils of selfishness.

"No," she said, staring at the phone, "I'm sorry, Mother, but I'll be home soon enough."

Just thinking about home had Alex imagining the castle walls closing in around her. She took a deep breath and reminded herself that she was still free. Still on her own. She still had time to enjoy life in the real world. To enjoy her time with Garrett.

Garrett.

She frowned again and turned to the laptop computer sitting on the desk near the terrace. She still didn't know Garrett's last name. They'd never discussed it again after that first time when they had decided to keep their identities a mystery. But…she did know his *cousin's* last name.

Garrett had kept her so busy the past couple of days, she'd hardly had a moment to think about the possibilities that knowledge provided. Every day had been so filled with activities and rushing about that when he brought her back to the hotel at night, she was so exhausted she usually just fell into bed.

But tonight…

She chewed at her bottom lip and wondered. What if there was a reason Garrett hadn't made any further moves?

Maybe he had lied when he said he wasn't involved with someone. Maybe he had a *wife.* That thought jolted and rocked through her on an equal tide of disappointment and righteous indignation.

For the first time, she considered the fact that she actually had a *reason* for keeping her last name a secret. Perhaps Garrett did, too.

"Right, then," she told herself. "Time to find out more about Garrett."

Decision made, she walked quickly to the computer, booted it up and took a chance. She entered the name Garrett King in the search engine and hit Enter.

In seconds, her world tilted and her stomach dropped. The first listing read *King Security, Garrett and Griffin King.*

King Security?

She couldn't believe it. Mouth dry, heart pounding, she clicked on the link and watched as their website opened up. She clicked on the About Us tab and there he was.

Her Garrett.

Garrett King.

Security expert.

"Bloody hell."

Garrett waited outside the penthouse door. He shot his cuffs, smoothed the lapels of his tailored, navy blue suit and wondered what the hell was taking Alex so long. Damn, hadn't taken him much time to get used to her being painfully punctual. Now that she was taking a few seconds to open the door, he was both bothered and worried.

Was she safe?

He knocked again and the door flew open. Alex was there and she looked…amazing.

The misery of the past couple of days gathered into a twist of knots in his gut. Just looking at her was pure, unadulterated torture. How the hell was he supposed to not touch her?

Garrett took a breath and reminded himself *again* of just what had happened the last time he'd allowed his dick to make his decisions for him. He had thrown professionalism aside in favor of his own wants and someone else had paid the price.

He'd be damned before he'd do the same damn thing again and have Alex paying for it.

When she just stared at him, he finally said, "You're so beautiful, you're dangerous."

She inclined her head in what he could only call a "regal" gesture. "Thank you." Grabbing her black bag from a nearby table, she hooked her arm through his and stepped out of the suite. "Shall we go?"

"Sure." Frowning to himself, Garrett felt the first stirrings of unease creep through him.

If he were out in the field, he'd be checking for snipers or some other bad guy sneaking up on him. It was just a feeling, but it had never let him down before.

Something was wrong.

Damian's was the hottest new restaurant on the coast. Designed to mimic the lush, noir atmosphere of the forties, the restaurant boasted a view of the ocean, a teakwood dance floor, linen-draped tables dusted with candlelight and the best seafood in California.

The place had struck a solid chord with the public—older people loved coming here to remember their youth and the younger crowd seemed to enjoy the romance and elegance of another era. It was easier to get a private audience with the pope than it was to land a reservation at

Damian's. Not a problem for Garrett, of course. It paid to be related to the owner.

A singer on stage, backed by a small orchestra working to evoke the feel of the big band era crooned about apple trees and lost loves. Dancers swayed to the music, bathed in spotlights that continually swept the floor.

Garrett wasn't surprised this place was a rousing success. Damian King was known for running restaurants that became legendary. At the moment, Damian was in Scotland, brokering a deal for a new "ghost" theme club to be opened in Edinburgh.

Jefferson King was happily living in Ireland. Garrett's brother Nash called London home and now Damian was in Scotland. He smiled to himself as he realized the Kings of California were slowly but surely starting to take over the world.

"It's lovely," Alex said and he turned to look at her.

Those were the first words she'd spoken to him since they'd left her hotel. She'd been polite, cool and completely shut off from him. The complete opposite of the Alex he had come to know over the last several days. There was no joy in her eyes, no easy smile and her spine was so straight, her shoulders so squared, it was as if she were tied to her chair.

"Yeah," he said warily. "Damian did a nice job of it. But then he always does."

"This isn't his only restaurant?"

"No, he's got a string of 'em up and down California."

"Interesting."

Okay, this was not right. She couldn't have made it plainer that something was chewing at her insides. He studied her and tried to figure out what the hell was going on. It was his *business,* after all, to be able to read people.

But for the first time since he'd known Alex, he didn't have a clue what was going on in her mind.

Her eyes were cool, dispassionate. Her luscious mouth was curved in a half smile that didn't reach her eyes. She was the epitome of the kind of sophisticated, aloof woman he usually avoided. Who was she and what had she done with Alex?

"Your cousin. That would be Damian *King?*"

"Yeah."

She nodded again, letting her gaze slide from his briefly. When she looked back at him again it was as if she was looking at a stranger.

That eerie-ass feeling he'd had earlier rose up inside him again. This whole night had been off from the jump. Something was up with Alex, and she wasn't even trying to hide it. He watched her. Waited. And had the distinct sensation that he wasn't going to like what was coming. She stroked her fingertips along the stem of the crystal water glass, and he was damn near hypnotized by the action.

A waitress approached and Garrett waved her away. Whatever was coming, he didn't want an audience for it. Keeping his gaze locked on the woman opposite him, he asked, "What's going on, Alex?"

"I was just wondering," she said, icicles dripping from her tone, "how many lies you've told me since the day we met."

A sinking sensation opened up in the pit of his stomach. A dark, yawning emptiness that spread throughout his system as the seconds ticked past.

"How long have you known?" she demanded quietly, her blue gaze frosty as it locked with his. "How long have you known who I am, Mr. *King?*"

The proverbial crap was about to hit the fan. He

shouldn't have been surprised. Alex was a smart woman. Sooner or later she was going to figure things out. Put two and two together and, any way you added it up, he was going to look like an ass.

No wonder everything had felt off to him tonight, Garrett thought grimly.

The woman sitting opposite him wasn't the Alex he knew.

This was Princess Alexis.

Eight

He didn't say anything.

Alex watched him, saw the flicker of an emotion dart across his eyes, but it came and went so quickly she couldn't identify it. Why wasn't he talking? Explaining? Because there was nothing he could say? Because if he tried to explain, it would only result in *more* lies?

The anger that had filled her since she had found his website spiked and roiled inside her. It had cost her every ounce of her self-control to keep what she was feeling locked within. She'd waited, half hoping that he would tell her the truth spontaneously. But then, why would he, when he was such a consummate liar?

King Security.

Alex felt like an idiot.

She'd believed everything.

Had *trusted* him, when all along, it had been nothing more than a game. He'd pretended to *like* her. Pretended to be attracted to her. When all along, he had known that she was a princess. God, she was a fool.

Garrett and his company had actually *been* to the palace. Had done work for her father. She hadn't recognized him because when he was in Cadria to provide security for the crown jewel celebration, Alex had avoided the whole situation. At the time, she and her father had been feuding over her involvement with the women's shelter. She'd been so furious with her father that she'd refused to have anything to do with the palace goings-on. Including, it seemed, meeting the security man brought in for the occasion.

If she had, she would have noticed Garrett. Looking at him even now, she could admit that he was most definitely a hard man to ignore. And if she'd met him then, she would have recognized him at Disneyland.

None of this would have happened. Her heart wouldn't be bruised, her feelings wouldn't be battered and she wouldn't now be wrapped in what felt like an icy blanket from head to toe.

She never would have found something with him that she could convince herself was real. She never would have believed that she, too, had discovered the same kind of magic her mother had found at the famous amusement park.

Instead she was left feeling the fool and staring into the eyes of a man she had thought she knew.

"How long?" she demanded, keeping her voice low enough that no one but him could hear her.

The strains of the music rose up and swelled around them, and the irony of the slow, romantic sound wasn't lost on her. She had hoped for so much from tonight. She'd wanted to seduce Garrett. Now all she could hope for was that she wouldn't get angry enough to cry.

She *hated* crying when she was furious.

Tilting her head to one side, she watched him. “Did you know at Disneyland?”

“Not right away,” he admitted, and the iron bands around her chest tightened another inch or so until every breath was a minor victory.

That statement told her that at least part of what she had thought of as a magical day had been colored with lies.

Betrayal slapped at her. Was it before he’d kissed her in the dark during the pirate ride? While they laughed with his nieces on the carousel?

She looked into his blue eyes and searched for the man who had been with her on his cousin’s boat a few days ago. The man who had touched her, shown her just how amazing two people could be together. But Alex didn’t see him. Instead, she saw a cool-eyed professional, already pulling back from her. A part of her wondered how he could turn his emotions on and off so easily. Because right at that moment, she’d like nothing better than to be able to do the same.

“I didn’t know you at first,” he was saying. “Not until you and Molly were standing at the castle, talking about being a princess.”

She nodded, swallowed hard and said, “So that’s why you insisted on taking me home that night.”

“Partly,” he admitted.

She laughed shortly, the sound scraping against her throat. “Partly. It wasn’t about me that night, Garrett. Not *me,* Alex. It was about protecting a princess. And you’ve been with me every day since for the same reason, haven’t you?”

Scraping one hand across the back of his neck, he said, “I called your father that first night.”

"Oh, God..." Just when she thought the icy cold enveloping her couldn't get worse...it did.

"I told him where you were. That you were alone and that I was...concerned."

"You had no right."

"I had a responsibility."

"To *whom?*" she demanded.

"To myself," he snapped. "I couldn't walk away leaving you unprotected once I knew who you really were."

"No one asked for your help."

"Your father did."

She shook her head, not wanting to hear any more. But she knew that was a futile hope.

"That's wonderful. Really. Your responsibility. Your decision. Your phone call." She narrowed her gaze on him. "But *my* life. This was never about you, Garrett. This was about me. What I wanted. And it never mattered, did it? Not to you. Not to anyone."

"Alex—"

She looked around the restaurant as if searching for an exit. But all she saw were couples sitting at tables, laughing, talking, easy with each other. They were enjoying the restaurant, the music, the romance of the place, and Alex suddenly envied them all so much it choked her.

"I never intended to hurt you."

"How nice for you then," she said, looking back at him. "Because you haven't hurt me. You've enraged me."

"Now who's lying?"

That snapped her mouth shut and all she could do was glare at him. Yes, she was lying because she *was* hurt. Devastated, in fact, but damned if she would show him how much his lies had cut at her.

"There's more," he said.

"Of course there is."

"Like I said before, your father hired me to protect you."

His words sunk into her consciousness like a rock tossed to the bottom of a lake. The sense of betrayal she had felt before was *nothing* compared to this. Her mouth opened and closed a few times as she struggled to speak past the hard knot of something bitter lodged in her throat. Finally, though, she managed to blurt, "Yes, he's *paying* you to spend time with me."

Garrett huffed out a breath and glanced to each side of him before he spoke again and a small part of Alex's brain chided her for dismissing just how careful he was. For thinking that he was simply a cautious man. She remembered thinking not long after they met that he was acting a lot like one of the palace guards. Foolish of her not to realize just what that actually might mean.

Then she pushed those thoughts aside and concentrated solely on what he was saying.

"Your father hired me as a personal bodyguard. We were both worried about what might happen if you were on your own."

"Yes," she said tightly, amazed that she could form thoughts, let alone *words*. "Can't have Alex out and about behaving like an actual person. No, no. Can't have *that*."

"Damn it, Alex, you're deliberately misunderstanding."

"I don't think so," she snapped. "And you know? Maybe you and my father were right. Maybe poor Alex doesn't have a brain in her head. After all, she was foolish enough to think a handsome man wanted to know her better when, in reality, he was on her father's payroll." Her fingers clenched into useless fists. She wanted to throw something. To surrender to the temper frothing and boiling inside her. Unfortunately, her breeding and training had been too thorough. Duty and dignity ran through her veins along with the blood.

Circumspection was another watchword of the royal family and she was too steeped in its tradition to give rein to what she was feeling now. Still, she couldn't continue sitting across from him as if this were a date. She couldn't look at him now without feeling like a complete idiot. She couldn't watch his eyes, cool and dark, without remembering the heat and passion that had flared there so briefly.

At that thought, she gaped at him, horrified. "What about the boat? What happened there? Are you getting a bonus?"

"What?"

She leaned in toward him, pushing the flickering candle to one side. "Was that on the agenda? Show the princess a good time? Or did you just want bragging rights? Want to be able to tell your friends how you got a princess naked? Is that it?"

He leaned in, too, and the flare of the candle flame threw dancing patterns across his features. His eyes were more shadowed, his cheekbones more pronounced. "You know damn well that's not true."

"Do I?" she countered. "Do I really? I know! I should trust you on this because you've been so honest with me from the first, I suppose."

"You kept secrets, too," he argued.

That stopped her for a second. But only a second. "I did, but I wasn't *spying* on you."

"I'm not a damn spy!" His voice pitched a little too loud just as the song ended and several people turned to look. He glared them away before staring back at her. "I told your father I wouldn't be an informer, and I haven't been."

"Again," she said coolly, "with your sterling reputation, I should just take your word?"

His mouth worked furiously as though he were fighting an inner battle to keep his temper in check and angry words from spilling free. Well, she knew just how he felt.

Finally, he managed to say, "You're angry, I get it."

"Oh, I'm well beyond angry, Mr. King," she snapped and stood up. "Fury is a good word and still it doesn't capture exactly what I'm feeling. But thankfully, neither of us has to suffer the other's presence any further."

"Where do you think you're going?" he asked, standing up to look down at her.

Her body lit up inside and Alex silently cursed her response to him. What was it about this man that he could get to her even when she was more furious than she had ever been in her *life?* That simply wasn't right. "Anywhere but here. This *is* a free country, isn't it?"

"Alex, don't do anything foolish just because you're mad."

"I'll do what I please, Garrett King, and I'll thank you to stay away from me." She turned to go, but he caught her arm and held on to her.

She glared down at his hand and then lifted her gaze to his. "You know, when we first met, I thought you were a hero. Now I know you're the villain in the piece."

The muscle in his jaw twitched, and she knew he was grinding his teeth into powder. Good to know that she wasn't the only one feeling as if the top of her head was about to blow off.

"I'm not a hero. Never claimed to be. But I'm not a damn villain, either, Alex. I'm just a man."

"Doing his *job,*" she finished for him and jerked her arm free of his grasp. "Yes, I know."

Head up, chin lifted in a defiant tilt, she headed for the bar. He was just a step or two behind her. "What're you doing?"

"I think I need a drink."

"Don't be an idiot. Come back to the table. We'll talk about this."

"Now I'm an idiot, am I?"

"I didn't *say* that," he muttered.

"Well, you're right on one score. I have *been* an idiot. But not any longer." She hissed in a breath. "I don't want to talk to you, Garrett. Go away."

"Not a chance," he whispered, close to her ear.

His deep voice rumbled along her spine and lifted goose bumps across her flesh. She so wanted to be unaffected by him. But it looked as though *that* wasn't going to happen anytime soon.

The worst part of all of this? Beyond the humiliation of her father going behind her back and the man she was... involved with selling her out to the palace?

She still wanted Garrett.

Mingled in with the anger and the hurt were the underlying threads of desire that still had her wrapped up in knots. How could she still want him, knowing what she did now?

Alex stalked into the bar and gave a quick glance around. There were a dozen or so tall tables with singles and couples gathered at them. A long, gleaming bar snaked around the room in a semicircle. Three bartenders in World War II military uniforms hurried back and forth filling drink orders. Mirrors behind the bar reflected the candlelight and the stony face of the man standing behind her.

The face that had haunted her dreams from the day they met. Their gazes locked in the mirror and Alex felt a jolt of something hot and wicked sizzle through her system in spite of everything.

Deliberately, she tore her gaze from his and walked to

the bar, sliding onto one of the black leather stools. She crossed her legs, laid her bag on the bar top and ordered a gin and tonic.

In the bar mirror, she watched Garrett take a seat a few stools down from her. Not far enough, she thought, but better than nothing. She was only surprised that he was giving her this small amount of space.

"Hello, gorgeous." A deep voice spoke up from just behind her and Alex lifted her gaze to the mirror.

A tall, blond man wearing a black suit and a wide smile stood watching her. "You are way too beautiful to be alone," he said and sat down without waiting for an invitation.

"Thank you, that's very kind." She saw Garrett's reaction from the corner of her eye and seeing him fume made her smile a welcome at the man beside her.

"An accent, too?" He slapped one hand to his heart in a dramatic gesture that had Alex smiling. "You're going to fuel my dreams for weeks."

"That's a lovely thing to say," she told him, though truthfully she thought he was a little on the ridiculous side. With his glib lines, and over-the-top reactions, he was nothing like Garrett with his quiet, deadly, sexy air. Ordinarily, in fact, she wouldn't have been the slightest bit interested in the blond. Still, she caught a glimpse of Garrett's face in the mirror and noted the abject fury on his features. So she leaned toward her new admirer and asked, "What's your name, love?"

"I'm Derek. Who're you?"

"Alexis," she said, "but you can call me Alex."

"You're no 'Alex,' babe," he said with a wink. "So Alexis it is."

In the other room, the music started up again and Derek stood, holding out one hand. "Dance?"

From the corner of her eye, Alex saw Garrett stand up as if he was going to try to stop her. So she quickly took Derek's hand and let him lead her to the floor.

Damn woman.

She was doing this on purpose. Letting that slick guy give her a lame line and then sweep her off to the dance floor. Well, fine, if that's what she wanted, she could have the plastic blond guy. But she wouldn't be alone with him. Garrett was still working for her father and damned if he was going to leave a woman like Alex to the likes of *that* guy.

He followed them into the other room and stood to one side as the blond pulled Alex into his arms and started moving to the music. Alex looked like a vision. That wild mane of blond hair, those heels that made her legs look ten miles long and where the hell had she gotten that dress, anyway? Didn't she know he could practically see her *ass?*

Alex laughed at something Blondie had to say and Garrett's teeth crushed together. He'd known from the start that his lies would eventually catch up with him. Maybe, he told himself, he should have listened to Griffin and confessed the truth to Alex himself. Then at least he would have had the chance to smooth things over with the telling.

But how much smoothing could he have done, realistically? She would still have been hurt. Still have been pissed. And he'd *still* end up standing here watching as some other guy made moves on her.

Moves, he told himself, that she wasn't deflecting.

Irritated beyond belief, Garrett stood like a statue, arms crossed over his chest, feet braced wide apart in a fighting stance. His gaze never left the couple as he watched Blondie ooze his way across the dance floor. Surely, Alex wasn't buying this guy's lines? Any minute now in fact, she'd probably step out of the dance and walk away.

Any minute.

Walking.

Damn it, Alex.

The music slid around the room and the singer's voice wrapped them all in a sensual web. His arms ached to hold her. His hands warmed at the thought of touching her again and his mouth craved the taste of her.

His eyes narrowed as Blondie steered Alex off the dance floor and out onto the dark balcony overlooking the ocean. While the music played and couples danced, Garrett moved through the crowd with a quiet intensity. Focused on his target, he was aware of his surroundings in a heightened way, but all he could think about was reaching Alex.

He stepped onto the polished wood balcony and heard the rush of the sea pushing into shore. Moonlight washed the whole scene in a silvery glow and the wind sweeping across the ocean was nearly icy. Voices came to him and he turned his head in response. That's when he spotted them, at the end of the deck, in a puddle of darkness that lay between the more-decorative-than-useful balcony lights.

Alex was facing the water, and Blondie was plastered up behind her, as close as he could get. Garrett's mind splintered a little and he actually *saw* red around the edges of his vision.

Then his eyes nearly popped from his head in an onslaught of pure fury. Blondie had one hand on Alex's ass and was giving it a rub—and Alex wasn't even trying to stop him.

What the hell?

It only took a few, long strides to carry him to Alex's

side, where he dropped one hand on Blondie's shoulder and squeezed. Blondie looked up, annoyed at the interruption, but annoyance faded fast when he got a good look at Garrett's expression.

"Dude, we're having some private time here."

"Dude," Garrett corrected through gritted teeth. "You're done. Take off."

Alex whipped her windblown hair out of her face and glared at him. "Go away, Garrett."

Astonished, the handsome guy stared at her. "You know this guy?"

"Yes, but pay no attention to him," Alex said.

Garrett's hand on Blondie's shoulder tightened as he silently convinced the other man it would be a much better idea to disappear. Fast.

Message received.

"Yeah, right. Okay. Outta here." He hunched away from Garrett's grip, gave Alex a wistful look and shrugged. "Sorry, babe. I don't do violence. I think *he* does."

"Damn straight," Garrett assured him.

"Oh, for—" Alex set her hands at her hips and glared at Garrett as Blondie hurried back to the restaurant, in search of easier prey. "What do you think you're doing?"

"Hah!" Garrett backed her up against the railing, looming over her as he planted his hands at either side of her. His grip on the cold, damp, iron railing tightened as he looked down into her eyes. "What am I doing? I'm keeping you from getting mauled in public."

"We were hardly in public and what if I *liked* being mauled?" she snapped, her eyes flashing with the kind of heat that any sane man would accept as a warning.

Garrett, though, had passed "sane" a couple of exits back. He was too close to her, bodies aligned, that damn dress of hers displaying way too much beautiful, smooth skin. Heat seared his insides and his dick went to stone. Just the scent of her was enough to drive him insane. He fought for clarity. Fought for control.

"Damn it, Alex. I get that you're pissed at me. And fine. I can deal with it."

"Oh, how very gracious of you."

"But," he continued, leaning close enough that her breasts were pillowed against his chest. That she could feel his erection pressing into her abdomen. Her eyes widened and her lips parted on a sigh. "I'm not going to stand around and watch you make a mistake."

"Another one, you mean?"

In the background, the music was soft, tempting; the singer's voice a lure, drawing them into a world where it was just the two of them, locked together. He felt every inch of her luscious body aligned along his. And in a heartbeat, control and focus went out the window, and Garrett found he couldn't even give a good damn.

"You didn't want that guy's hands on you, Alex."

She let her head fall back. Her eyes met his and a long sigh slid from her throat. "Is that right? And how do you know that?"

"Because you want *my* hands on you," he muttered, his gaze raking over her features before settling on her eyes. "You want *me* touching you and no one else."

She opened her mouth to say something, but Garrett didn't let her speak. Instead, he cupped her face in his hands, leaned down and took her mouth with his.

Pissed or not, Alex wanted him, too. He felt it in her instant surrender. She wrapped her arms around his neck, held his head to her and gave him everything she had. Their tongues entwined, caressing, stroking. The cool air swept past them, and danced across their heated skin.

She shivered, and he wrapped his arms around her,

holding her closer, tighter, until he felt her frenzied heartbeat racing in time with his own. Every inch of his skin hummed with anticipation.

He knew they had been headed for this moment since the day they had met. It didn't matter that he had fought it. This was inevitable. Pulling his head back, he looked down into her glassy eyes and whispered, "Your hotel's only a few minutes from here."

Dragging in a breath, she shivered again and leaned into him. "Then why are we still standing here?"

A fierce grin split his face briefly. Then he took her hand and headed around the edge of the balcony toward the front of the place. Now he was glad he hadn't bothered with valet parking. He didn't have the patience to hang around while some kid ran to bring him his car.

No more waiting.

That first taste of her pushed him over the edge. Touching her wouldn't be enough this time.

This time, he had to have it all.

Nine

It was minutes that felt like hours.

Desire pumping in the air around them, making each heartbeat sound like a gong in their heads, the drive to Alex's hotel was bristling with sexual heat. Somehow, Garrett got the car parked, and Alex through the lobby into the private elevator. Somehow, they managed to walk through the door of the penthouse and slam it closed behind them.

And then all bets were off.

Hunger was king here and neither of them had the strength or the will to fight it any longer.

Garrett tore off his jacket and tossed it aside. Alex's hands fumbled at the buttons on his shirt while he ripped his tie off and discarded it, as well. The moment his shirt was undone, her hands moved over his chest and every one of her fingers felt as if it were imprinting itself on his skin. Heat sizzled back and forth between them, leaving each of them struggling for air. Sighs and groans were the only sounds as they kissed again, hungrily, frantically.

He stabbed his fingers through her wild mane of hair and let the silkiness slide across his skin like cool water. She opened her mouth under his, offering him everything and he took it. Garrett was through pretending that their relationship was strictly business.

At least for this one night, he wanted everything that he had been dreaming of, thinking of, for the past several days. He couldn't touch her enough. Couldn't kiss her enough. He wanted more. Wanted all. Had to have her.

"Now, Alex," he muttered, tearing his mouth from hers to drag his lips and tongue and teeth along the elegant sweep of her neck.

She sighed and tipped her head to one side, as she held his head to her throat. "Yes, Garrett. Yes, please, *now*."

He unzipped the back of her dress and pushed the slender straps down her arms, letting it fall to the floor at her feet. She stepped out of the puddle of fabric and kicked it to one side.

"You're amazing," he whispered, gaze moving over her as she stood there, naked but for those high heels she loved and a tiny scrap of black lace panties. She looked like every man's fantasy and she was his. All his.

Garrett caught her, pulled her in close, then bent his head to take first one then the other erect, pink nipple into his mouth. Her fingers threaded through his hair and pressed his head to her breasts as if afraid he would stop.

He had no intention of stopping.

The taste of her filled him. Her scent surrounded him. A haze settled over his mind, shutting out everything but the present. All there was in the world was this woman.

His hands moved over her skin, up and down her back, around and across her abdomen to the tiny scrap of black lace she wore. His fingers gave a sharp tug and she was naked, open for his touch.

Still suckling at her, he dropped one hand to the juncture of her thighs and sighed against her when she parted her legs for him. He stroked that single bud of pleasure until she was whimpering and rocking against his hand. Her hips twisted and moved in time with his touch, and he smiled against her breast as he felt her climax build.

Lifting his head, he stared at her as his fingers worked her body into a frenzy. She licked her lips, tossed her hair back and took breath after greedy breath.

Her gaze locked with his and her voice was soft as she said, "I want you inside me this time, Garrett. I need to feel you inside me."

He wouldn't have thought he could get any harder. But he did. Reluctantly, he let her go just long enough to strip out of his clothes. He paused only long enough to take a condom from his wallet and sheathe himself. When she made to kick off her high heels, though, he shook his head. "Leave 'em on."

She gave him a slow, wide smile, then dropped her gaze to take in all of him. Her eyes widened and when she looked up at him again, she was even more eager for him. "Now, Garrett. Be with me. Be *in* me."

They were still in the damn living room of the suite and Garrett knew that they'd never make it to the bedroom. Neither of them was willing to wait that long.

He swept her close to him and when his erection pushed at her, she moaned and moved into him, feeding the fires that were already swallowing him. "That's it. Right here, right now. We'll do it slow next time."

"Next time," she agreed.

He carried her a few short steps to the couch, set her on the high back and stepped in between her thighs. She opened herself wider for him and when he entered her, Alex groaned aloud.

Garrett gritted his teeth to keep from shouting as his body invaded hers in one hard thrust. Her damp heat enveloped him, a tight glove, squeezing. When he was seated to the hilt, Alex held him even closer. She moved on the precarious edge of the couch as much as she could. Now she did kick off those heels so she could lock her legs around his hips and hold on as he set a fast, dizzying pace that pushed them both as high as they could go.

They raced to the edge together. Gazes locked, bodies joined, two halves of the same whole. Again and again, his hips pistoned against her and she took everything he had, urging him on.

As the first crash of her orgasm slammed into her, she called out his name and Garrett felt her body spasm around his. He watched her shatter, felt the strength of her climax shaking her. And Garrett realized he'd never known this before. Never been this connected to any woman before. He watched her pleasure and felt it as his own.

He heard her sighs and wanted to capture them forever. Heard his name on her lips and felt both humbled and victorious. Possession raged through him and his only thought as his own release finally claimed him was: *mine*.

Seconds ticked past, became minutes, and those could have been hours for all Alex knew. Or cared.

With Garrett's body still locked with hers, she had everything she had been craving for days. The incredible feel of him deep inside her. The dazzling orgasm that was so much better than anything she had ever felt before. The sweet sensation of his arms wrapped around her. It was all…perfect.

As if she really had found the magic she had been looking for when she first began this holiday.

But even as that thought flitted through her mind, she

knew it wasn't true. Despite what she was feeling, she knew now that Garrett didn't share it.

Want wasn't romance.

Desire wasn't love.

Love? Now where had that thought come from? She stiffened in his arms as the word circled round and round in her mind. She didn't want to believe it, but how could she not? What she felt for Garrett was so far beyond what she had ever known with anyone else.

What else could it be, but love?

Which put her in a very uncomfortable position.

She was in love with a man who was only with her because he had been hired by her father.

"Alex..." Garrett's voice thundered down around her, sounding like a summer storm, and she knew that their moment was over.

She looked up at him, watching his face as he spoke again.

"I'm sorry."

She blinked. "You're *sorry?*"

He pulled away from her and she instantly missed the feeling of his body pressed into hers. And she wanted to kick herself for it. How could she possibly love such a Neanderthal?

"It shouldn't have happened," he muttered, raking one hand through his hair and stepping back so she could slide off the back of the couch. "I let myself be distracted and allowed you to do the same."

"Allowed?" she echoed. "You *allowed* me?"

He didn't pick up on the temper in her voice, or if he did, he wasn't paying attention. His mistake.

"I take full responsibility for this, and I want you to know, it won't happen again."

"You...you..." She opened and closed her mouth several times, but nothing came out. Well, who knew that "stunned speechless" could actually happen? Her bare toes curled into the rug beneath her feet as if she needed all the help she could get just to keep her balance.

"I know what you're going to say," he told her, with a small, brief smile. "And you don't have to. I know you regret this as much as I do."

Oh, she wanted to do something to wipe that "understanding" expression off his face. But once again, her breeding rang true and she settled for quietly seething instead. When she could speak again, she did so quietly. "So you're writing my dialogue for me as well, are you?"

"What?"

Fury flashed inside her like an electrical storm. She actually *felt* bolts of white-hot anger stabbing through her system, and it was all she could do to keep from screaming. Looking up at him, Alex shook her head and said, "You pompous, arrogant, dim-witted, ego-maniacal… *twit!*"

He scowled at her. "What the hell?"

"Oh," she said, eyes widely innocent. "Weren't expecting that, were you?"

"What are you so pissed about *now?*"

"The very fact that you could even ask me that proves your twit-dom!"

"That's not even a word."

"It is now," she told him, stalking a few paces away because she was simply so furious she couldn't stand still. She should have been embarrassed, or, at the very least, uncomfortable, walking about her suite stark naked. But truthfully, she was too angry to care.

"I'm trying to do the right thing," he said, each word grinding out of his throat.

"For the both of us, it seems," she snapped. Her gaze

fixed on him, she said, "Did it even occur to you that what I might regret most is your ridiculous attitude?"

"Ridiculous? I'm taking responsibility for this mess. How is that ridiculous?"

"How is this a *mess?*" she countered.

"You know damn well how," he muttered. "Because I'm here to protect you."

"But not from pompous asses, apparently," she said.

"Okay, that's enough."

"Have you decided that, as well?" she asked, a sugary sweet tone to her voice.

"What the hell, Alex? We both know this shouldn't have happened."

"So sayeth the almighty arbiter of everything sexual."

"You're starting to piss me off."

"Well, join the bloody club!" Walking back to him, she stopped within a foot of his gorgeous body, tipped her head back and glared into those eyes that only moments ago had been glazed with passion. Now there were ice chips in those depths and damned if she didn't find them just as attractive. "I'm not a naive young virgin out for her first romp in the hay, you know. You're not the first man in my bed. You're simply the first to regret it the moment it was over. Well, thank you very much for that, Garrett King.

"Now, why don't you take your sense of responsibility and leave?"

"I'm not going anywhere until we settle this."

"Then I hope you packed a lunch," she quipped, "because I don't see that happening anytime soon."

"Maybe if you'd be reasonable…"

She sucked in a gulp of air and gave him a shove. He didn't budge an inch. Like shoving a bloody wall. "Reasonable? You think I'm *not* being reasonable? It's only my exceptional breeding and the training of my mother, not to mention countless governesses, that's keeping me from punching you in the nose!"

He laughed at the very idea, which infuriated her enough to curl her hand into a fist and take a wild swing at him, just as her brothers had taught her to. Garrett, though, was too fast for her and caught her hand in his before she could make contact.

"Nice 'breeding,'" he said with a half smile.

"You're insufferable."

"You've said that before."

"Then clearly I'm an astute human being."

He sighed. "Alex, look me in the eye and tell me you think this was a good thing. I'm not looking for a relationship. This is going nowhere."

His words slapped her, but she wouldn't let him see it. She wouldn't be the needy one while he tried to make light of something that had shaken her to her very foundations. So she took a page from his book…she lied. "What makes you think I'm looking for a future with you? Are you really that egotistical? Do you think one night in bed with you is enough to make a woman immediately start craving white picket fences? Start scribbling her name next to yours surrounded by lacy hearts?

"I'm a *princess,* Garrett. I may have run off for a holiday but I know what my duties are. I know what my life will be. God knows, it was planned for me practically from the moment I drew my first breath! And nowhere in that plan does it say *fall in love with a Neanderthal, move to California and remain barefoot and pregnant.*"

Her breath was coming fast, in and out of her lungs. Her heartbeat was racing and her blood was pumping. Being this close to him was feeding more than her anger. In spite of everything, she wanted him.

He was stupid and clueless and impossibly arrogant—and, he was the most intriguing man she had ever known. Even the fact that he had lied to her from the beginning wasn't enough to cool off the fires licking at her insides. And Alex had the distinct feeling that thirty years from now, when he was nothing more than a hazy memory, she would *still* want him.

"Neanderthal?"

Her fury abated for the moment, she only asked, "How would you describe yourself at this moment?"

"Confused, angry—" he paused, tucked his fingers beneath her chin and lifted her face, her eyes, up to his "—and more turned on than I was before."

He felt it, too. That soul-deep stirring. He didn't want it, either, but it seemed as though neither of them had a choice when it came to what lay sizzling between them. Arguments didn't matter. Differences didn't matter.

All that mattered was the next touch. The next kiss.

"Oh," she admitted on a sigh, "me, too."

He kissed her and the rest of the world fell away. Alex let go of her anger and gave herself up to the wonder of what he could make her feel.

His arms came around her as his mouth took hers. He carried her into the bedroom and laid her down atop the silk duvet. The slide of the cool fabric against her skin was just another sensation to pile onto the rest.

Sliding his hands up and down her body, Alex arched into him, allowing her mind to drift free so that she could concentrate solely on the moment. Every stroke was a benediction. Every caress a promise of more to come.

Her body felt alive in a way it never had before. His touch was magic…kindling sparks of flame at every spot he touched. He leaned over her, kissing her, then sliding along her body, nibbling his way down. Then he stopped, pulled back and slid off the bed.

"Where are you going?"

"Right back," he swore, his eyes fixed on hers.

True to his word, he was gone only moments and she saw that he had another condom with him, sheathing himself as he came closer.

A smile tugged at the corner of her mouth. "You always carry those in your wallet?"

"I have since I met you," he admitted, kneeling back on the bed, dropping his head for a quick kiss. "Just in case."

"Always prepared?" she asked.

"Babe, those are the Boy Scouts. And trust me when I say I'm no Boy Scout."

"No," she whispered as he moved down the length of her body again, letting his mouth and tongue blaze the trail, "you're really not."

Alex sighed deeply and stared up at the ceiling. Moonlight poured through the windows, along with a chill ocean breeze that ruffled the white sheers and sent them into a sensual dance that mimicked her own movements beneath Garrett's talented hands.

"You're torturing me," she whispered and arched into him as his lips crossed over her abdomen.

"That's the plan," Garrett assured her.

"You're an evil man," she said on a sigh. "Don't stop."

"Not a chance," he promised.

Then he moved, shifting down to kneel between her thighs and Alex looked at him. Slowly he scooped his hands beneath her bottom and lifted her from the bed. Everything in her tensed in expectation. Her gaze locked with his as he lowered his mouth to her center and—

She groaned at the first sweep of his tongue across a bud of flesh so sensitive it felt as if it had a life of its own.

Electric-like jolts of sensation shot through her, coiling the tension within her even tighter. Alex moved into him, loving the feel of his mouth on her.

Reaching down, she pushed her fingers through his hair as he pushed her higher and faster than she had gone before. This intimacy was so overwhelming; her system was flooded with emotions tangling together. She felt so much, wanted so much, *needed* so much.

It was close. She felt it. The orgasm hovering just out of reach was almost on her and she wanted him inside her when it hit. “Garrett, please.”

Instantly, he pulled away from her, sat back on his thighs and lifted her onto his lap. Alex went up onto her knees and slowly, deliberately, lowered herself onto him. It was delicious. The tantalizingly slow slide of his hard thickness pushing into her depths. She gloried in every inch of him. She let her head fall back as she wrapped her arms around his neck and swiveled her hips against him, taking him even higher and deeper than she had before.

Until she was sure he was touching the tip of her heart.

“You feel so good,” he whispered, kissing the base of her throat, locking his lips against her pulse point. His breath hot against her skin, he whispered words she couldn’t hear—could only *feel.*

And then she moved on him and his hands settled at her hips, guiding her motions, helping her set a rhythm they both kept time with. Again and again, she rocked her body onto his, and, over and over, they tore apart and came together. They moved as one. Breathed as one.

And at last, they shattered as one.

Ten

In the dark, when it was quiet, reality crashed down on top of them again, and Alex was the first to feel its sharp tugs at the edges of her heart.

Grabbing up her short, blue silk robe, she slipped it on, then crossed her bedroom, opened the French doors leading to the balcony that wrapped around the entire penthouse suite and stepped outside. The stone floor was cool and damp beneath her feet and the wind off the ocean lifted her hair and teased her heated skin.

Staring out at the moonlit sea, Alex tried to get a handle on the rampaging emotions crashing through her. Her mind was alive with careening thoughts that rushed up to be noticed then were swallowed and replaced by the next one. In fact, the only thing she was truly sure of was that she did love Garrett King. Infuriating as he was, she loved him.

They'd known each other such a short time, it was hard

to believe. But the simple fact was, as her mother had always told her, love didn't come with a timetable. It was either there or it wasn't and no amount of waiting would change that.

Her heart ached and her mind whirled. There was misery along this road and she knew it. Garrett had made no secret of the fact that he wasn't interested in a relationship. And even if he were, their lives were so different. They didn't even live on the same *continent!* What possible chance was there for anything more than what they had already shared?

Taking hold of the iron railing in front of her, she squeezed tightly in response to the tension within.

A moment later, Garrett joined her, and her heart sped into a gallop. She glanced at him. He was wearing the slacks he'd abandoned what felt like hours ago, but he was barefoot and shirtless and his broad, sculpted chest seemed to be begging for her touch. She gripped the handrails to keep from giving in to that urge.

"Alex, we really need to talk."

"That never bodes well," she replied, deliberately turning her gaze on the ever-shifting surface of the water below.

He stood beside her. Close, but not touching and still, she felt the heat from his body sliding into hers.

"It's too late to do a damn thing about it, but none of that should have happened, Alex."

She stiffened. He still regretted being with her. How would he react, she wondered, if he knew she loved him? She glanced over the railing to the sand ten stories below. He'd probably jump.

"No doubt you're right."

"Huh." She felt more than saw him turn his gaze on her. "You surprise me. I expected a different reaction."

Alex steeled herself then turned to look up into his eyes. "What were you thinking? Keening? Gnashing of teeth?" She gave him a smile that felt stiff and wooden. "Sorry to disappoint."

"Not disappointed. Just surprised."

"Well, you shouldn't be," she said, silently congratulating herself on how calm and cool she sounded. Honestly, if she weren't a princess, she should think of going on the stage. "You'd already made yourself quite clear on the subject, and, as I've mentioned, I'm not an idiot, Garrett. I know that we don't suit. I know we mean nothing to each other and that this isn't going anywhere…."

Those words ripped a new hole in the fabric of her heart, but better *she* say them than him.

"I didn't say you mean nothing to me, Alex," he said, laying his hands on her shoulders and turning her so that she faced him.

God, she didn't want to look into his eyes. Didn't want to feel the heat of him spearing through her body. Didn't want to think about the pain she would feel when she was gone and back in the palace.

The only way to get through any of it was to pretend none of it mattered.

So she gave him that forced smile again and hoped he wouldn't notice. "Ah, yes, I forgot," she quipped. "I do mean something to you after all. Quite a hefty paycheck, I'm guessing."

"I didn't say that, either," he ground out.

"You haven't said much, Garrett," she told him. "What else am I to think?"

"That you're an amazing, smart, funny, incredibly sexy *princess*."

"It always comes back to that, doesn't it?" she mused, stepping out of his grip and turning to face the sea again.

"If I'd known how you would focus on that, I would have worn my crown while we were in bed together."

"I don't give a damn for your crown, Alex," he snapped, voice near growling now. "In fact this would all be a hell of a lot easier if you *weren't* a princess. You think your father would be thrilled to know that I'm here with you?"

"What's my father got to do with any of this?"

Clearly exasperated, he snapped, "I've done security work for royalty all over the globe. You know what's the *one* thing they all have in common? They don't get involved with non-royals. Hell, I've got more money than a lot of them, but I'm still a 'commoner.' You think your father feels any different?"

"Probably not."

"Exactly." Garrett shook his head. "It all comes down to that, Princess."

"Story of my life," she murmured, sliding a glance at him.

"What's that supposed to mean?"

"Please," she scoffed. "Do you think you're the only man who has run screaming into the night trying to escape the glare of the palace? You're not." Shaking her head she added, "And for all of those that run away, dozens more run *toward* the crown. None of them see me, Alex. They see the princess. Some hate the very idea of royalty and others covet it. People on the outside look at the royal family and think, *Isn't it wonderful? All the pomp and pageantry. How nice to shop wherever you like and not worry about the price.*

"Well," she continued, "there's *always* a price, Garrett. It's just one that most people never see. It's a lack of privacy. A lack of freedom and imagination. It's being locked into centuries of tradition whether you like it or not, and it's duty."

Her gaze narrowed, her breath coming fast and furious, she hurried on before he could say a word. She looked up into his eyes and watched them flash with emotion, but she didn't let that stop her.

"You think I don't understand your 'duty' to protect me? Trust me when I say that's the one thing I am all too aware of. Duty is the first thing I was taught. Duty to my country, to the citizens of Cadria and to my king. My family has ruled for centuries. Yes, Cadria is a small country, but she's proud and it's *our* duty to protect her. Keep her safe. So, yes. I understand your self-imposed duties, but it doesn't mean I like them any more than I like the golden chains linking me to my own set of duties."

He studied her for a long minute before speaking. When he did, he said only, "Quite a rant."

She huffed out a short laugh. "Apparently, I have what you Americans refer to as 'issues.'"

"I never use that word," he assured her, and reached out for her again.

Smiling, she let herself be held. Probably another monumental mistake, but she needed the comfort of his arms. The strength of him, wrapped around her. If she had one more thing to regret in the morning, then so be it.

"Why'd your father have to be a *king?*"

She laughed a little and linked her arms at the small of his back. "Your father was a King, too."

He gave her a squeeze. "Funny."

Tipping her head back, she looked up at him and whispered, "You may be willing to pretend that everything that happened tonight was a mistake, but I for one, enjoyed myself immensely."

"So did I, Alex. That's the problem."

"Doesn't have to be."

He shook his head. "I'm here to do a job and that doesn't include bedding *you*."

That barb hit home with a staggering force she didn't even want to admit to herself. So much for tender makeup scenes in the moonlight. "Yes," she said softly. "I wonder if you'll get a raise in pay for this? Maybe if I tell my father how very good you were?"

"Cut it out, Alex."

She felt like a fool. She'd spilled her heart out to him, laid it at his feet and he chose that moment to remind her that he was being paid by her father. How could she possibly *love* a man who only saw her as a job? How could she have forgotten, even for a minute, that he had lied to her from their first day together? That her father was paying him to watch over her?

Well, fine. If he wanted to turn his back on what they had together, then she wouldn't stop him. She might be fool enough to love him, but she wasn't so big a fool that she didn't know when to pull back from the edge of a very steep cliff. Releasing him, she steeled herself for the soul-deep cold that slipped inside her the instant she left the circle of his arms.

"You're the one who brought this up again," she reminded him.

"I just want you to understand is all. I didn't want to say yes to your dad, but he's a hard man to refuse."

"That much I know from personal experience."

He took a breath. "When I realized who you were, I was worried. I called your father and told him I was uncomfortable with you out on your own with no protection. And so was he. I talked to your mother, too."

She closed her eyes briefly and he felt the tension in her body tighten. "So they double-teamed you."

"Yeah," he said with a sharp nod. "Guess you could say that."

"They're very good at it," she mused, a half smile blooming and disappearing from her mouth in a fraction of a second. "It's how they deal with my brothers and me, as well."

"Then you can see why—"

"I can see why you said yes to my father," she cut him off neatly and speared him with a glance that had gone icy. "What I don't see is why you *lied* to me."

"I lied because I had to. Your father told me you're adept at escaping your guards."

"And because you lied, I never even tried to escape you," she whispered.

"I couldn't risk you escaping me, Alex. I had to keep you safe. As for fighting what was happening between us..." He paused and shook his head again as if he couldn't believe they were in this situation. "In my job, when I get distracted, people tend to *die.* I won't let that happen to you, Alex."

"Garrett, if you don't *live,* you might as well be dead already. Don't you see that?"

"What I see is that I let you get to me," he said, gaze moving over her face. "Didn't mean to. Didn't want you to. But you did anyway."

A part of her thrilled to hear it. But the more rational voice in her mind warned against it. The look in his eyes was far from warm and fuzzy. The set of his jaw and the tension in every line of his body screamed that he was a man who'd made his decision. Alex had come in second to his sense of honor. What he said next only defined it.

"As much as I want you, I can't let this happen again, Alex. Not while I'm responsible for your safety."

There it was. Duty first. She should respect that sentiment, seeing as she had been raised to believe the same. But somehow, that didn't make her feel any better.

A chill swept over her that had nothing at all to do with the cold wind still flying toward them. Garrett couldn't have made himself clearer.

"No worries, Garrett," she told him, keeping her voice light in spite of the knot of pain clogging her throat. "You're absolutely safe from me now as I'm just not interested anymore."

"Liar."

She laughed shortly. "Amazing that you even feel comfortable using that word against someone else."

"Amazing that you can be so pissed at me for doing something you're pretty good at yourself."

She ignored that and turned for the bedroom, suddenly more than ready for this conversation to be over. "Before you go, want to check the bathroom for hidden assassins?"

"Funny."

Stepping into the bedroom, she walked to the dressing table, picked up her hairbrush and started drawing the bristles through her tangled hair. Staring into the mirror, she caught his reflected gaze. "You're making far too much of this situation. You're assuming I want this 'relationship' to continue. But I don't."

"Lying again."

She tossed the brush down. "Stop telling me when I'm lying. It's rude."

"Then stop lying."

"Same to you."

"I'm not lying now," he said. "I still want you."

"Me, too."

"Damn it, Alex."

"Shut up and kiss me, Garrett."

He did and Alex's brain went on hiatus again. Soon,

she would be able to sit back and regret this at her leisure. But at the moment, all she could think was how right it felt. How good it was to be in his arms again. To have his mouth fused to hers.

He lifted her and carried her to the bed and when he set her down onto the mattress, she looked up into icy-blue eyes that sparked and shone with the kind of need that shook her to the bone.

For now, that was enough.

Three days later, Garrett was on the edge with no way out.

Now that she knew who he was, Alex seemed to delight in making him nuts. She insisted on walking down crowded sidewalks, going shopping through packed malls and even driving to San Diego to visit SeaWorld. It was as if she had determined to make him earn every dime of his paycheck from her father.

It was a security expert's nightmare.

Garrett knew damn well it was only a matter of time before her identity was revealed. Someone, somewhere, was going to recognize her and then he'd be hip-deep in paparazzi, reporters and general nutcases, all trying to get close to the visiting princess.

But short of locking her into her penthouse, he didn't have a clue how to keep her from being noticed. A woman like Alex got people's attention. She was tall, gorgeous and had a perpetual smile on her face that seemed to welcome conversations with strangers. He hovered as closely as he could and still it wasn't enough.

His mind filled with ugly possibilities. He'd seen enough damage done over the years to be prepared for the absolute worst—his brain dredging up any number of horrific scenarios. And it killed him to think of anything happening to Alex.

Which was only natural, he assured himself. After all, she was in his care. Of course he'd be worried about her—that was his *job*. And that was all it was.

Garrett's trained gaze swept the room as he deliberately tried to become invisible, as any good bodyguard would. But, being the only man in a homeless shelter that catered to women and kids made Garrett's job harder. He stood out like Death at the Party. He caught the glances tossed his way and was sorry to know he was making some of the women here really uncomfortable. But damned if he was going to let Alex out of his sight.

The woman continued to press her luck and push him closer and closer to the ragged edge of control. Today, she had insisted on visiting a women's shelter to compare their setup with the program she knew at home.

Jane, the woman in charge, hadn't had a problem with his presence—but she had asked him to stay out of the way and that he was willing to do. Better all the way around for a protection detail to blend into the background as much as possible. It gave him eyes and ears to the place without attracting attention himself.

Watching Alex move around the room with the director, Garrett felt his admiration for her grow. She wasn't here as a princess. She had introduced herself as a fellow volunteer, visiting from Europe. And in a few short minutes, she and Jane had been chatting like old friends.

While Alex looked at the facility and met a few of the residents, Garrett watched *her*. She fit in any damn where, he thought and wondered at how easily Alex dismissed *what* she was in favor of *who* she was. She was so much more than some dilettante royal. She was eager and involved and she *cared* for people and what she might do to help. It had nothing to do with her crown. This was her soul he was watching, and damned if he could look away.

"You a cop?"

Garrett jolted out of his daydreams, gave himself a mental kick for being caught unaware and then looked down at the little boy staring up at him with wide brown eyes. "No, I'm not a cop."

"Look like one," the boy said, giving Garrett a gap-toothed smile. "You're all straight and stiff like one."

Great. He was doing such a good job being invisible that a five-year-old had made him. Alex really was throwing him off his game.

One corner of his mouth lifted in a smile. "You stand up straight, you get taller."

Those brown eyes went as big as saucers. "Tall as you?"

"Taller," Garrett assured him and instantly, the kid squared his shoulders, straightened his spine and lifted his chin. All forty pounds of him.

"Is she your girlfriend?"

That question came unexpectedly, though why it had, he didn't know. He'd spent enough time around his cousin's kids to know that they said pretty much whatever popped into their heads. "No," he said, shifting his gaze back to Alex. "She's a friend."

"She's nice," the boy said. "Pretty, too, and she smells good."

"Yeah," Garrett said, still watching Alex. "You're right."

"You should make her your girlfriend."

Intrigued, he shot the kid a look and asked, "Yeah? Why's that?"

"Because she smiles when she looks at you and that's nice. Besides, she's *pretty*."

"Timmy!" A woman shouted from across the room and the little boy trotted off, leaving Garrett staring after him.

Out of the mouths of babes, he mused. He looked up, caught Alex's eye and she flashed him one of those smiles that seemed designed to knock him off balance. In a flash, he remembered her under him, over him. The feel of her skin, the taste of her mouth, the scent of her, surrounding him.

As if she knew exactly what he was thinking, her smile slipped into something more private. More…intimate. And Garrett was once again hit with the knowledge that he'd fallen into a hole that just kept getting deeper.

Alex very much enjoyed watching Garrett go quietly insane at the beach. It was a lovely day to sit on the sand and enjoy the last of summer. There were only a handful of people there, including a few children busily building sand walls in an attempt to hold back the inexorable rush of the tide. Sandpipers and seagulls strutted along the shoreline and surfers sat atop their boards waiting for the perfect ride.

Everyone was having a good time, she thought. Everyone, that is, but Garrett King.

Honestly, it was simply too easy to push the man's buttons. And Alex had discovered just how much fun it could be. The man was determined to keep her at a distance. He hadn't touched her since that one night they'd spent together. Her heart hurt and her body ached for his and so, she had decided to make him as uncomfortable as possible with his decision to leave her alone.

If she was going to be miserable, then she would do everything she could to make sure he was, too. She challenged him, worried him and in general made his time with her as difficult as possible. She flirted with him outrageously and watched him fight his own desires to keep his professionalism at the fore.

With his serious "bodyguard" expression, he kept most people at bay. But those who weren't the least bit intimidated slipped past him, much to Alex's delight. Because then she flirted with other men, just to watch Garrett's instant, infuriated response.

Take for example the surfer who was right now giving her a wink and a smile before heading for the water. If she weren't in love with a perfectly infuriating man, she would very well be tempted to take the other man up on his not-so-subtle offer.

"He's short," Garrett muttered from behind her.

She smiled to herself, nodded at the surfer and said, "He's at least six feet tall."

"Shorter than me, then," Garrett said tightly.

"Most people are," she returned. "Hardly a crime."

"He's at least thirty and he's at the beach in the middle of the week."

"So are you," she pointed out, glancing over her shoulder at the man in black who was glowering at the rest of humanity. Honestly, he looked like the Grim Reaper. No wonder most people tended to give her a wide berth.

"Yes, but I'm *working,*" he told her.

"And you never let me forget that, do you?" Alex gritted her teeth and turned her head back to watch the handsome surfer carry his board out to the water. His black wet suit clung to a fairly amazing body and his long, light brown hair was sun-streaked, telling her he spent most of his days in the sun. Perhaps Garrett was right and he was a layabout. She frowned at the thought.

"Alex, don't start that again."

"I didn't start it, Garrett," she told him, now ignoring the surfer to concentrate on the conversation she was having with the man who refused to get close to her. "I never do. You're the one who consistently reminds me that I'm your *responsibility.* And I simply can't tell you how flattering that is."

He sighed. She heard it even from three feet away.

"But, even though it's your *job* to watch over me," she added, not for the first time, "it doesn't give you the right to chase away any man who dares to look at me."

"It is if I think they're dangerous."

She laughed outright at that comment and turned to stare at him. "Like the college student yesterday at the art gallery? That sweet young man who was so nervous he dropped his bottle of water?"

Garrett frowned. "He kept touching you."

"It was *crowded* in that shop."

"That's what he wanted you to think. He wasn't nervous, Alex. He was on the prowl. He kept bumping into you. *Touching* you." Scowling, he picked up a handful of sand and let it drift through his fingers. "It wasn't that crowded."

"Well, certainly not after you threw the poor soul up against a wall and frisked him!"

He smiled at the memory. "Did discourage him quick enough, didn't it?"

"And half the gallery," she pointed out. "People scattered, thinking you were a crazy person."

"Yeah..." He was still smiling.

"You're impossible. You know that, don't you?"

"If I hadn't known it before I met you, I do now. You tell me often enough."

"And yet you don't listen." Pushing up from the sand, Alex dusted off the seat of her white shorts and snatched up the sandals she had kicked off when they first arrived. Walking to him, she looked down into Garrett's eyes and said, "You might want to ask yourself why you take it so personally when another man looks at me. Or talks to me."

"You know why," he muttered, keeping his gaze fixed on hers.

"Yes, the job." She went down to one knee in front of him. "But I think it's more than that, Garrett. I think it's much more, but you're too much of a coward to admit it."

His features went like granite, and Alex knew she'd struck a nerve. Well, good. Happy to know it.

So quickly she hardly saw him move, he reached out, grabbed her and pulled her close. Then he gave her a brief, hard kiss before letting her go again. Shaking his head, he stood up, then took her hand and drew her to her feet as well.

"You keep pushing me, Alex, and you never know what might happen."

"And that, Garrett," she said, licking her lips and giving him a small victory smile, "is the fun part."

Eleven

"I quit."

"I beg your pardon?"

Garrett winced at the snooty tone the King of Cadria could produce. He had known going in that this phone call wouldn't go well, but there was nothing to be done about it. Garrett was through working for the king, and Alex's father was just going to have to deal with it.

"You heard me correctly, your majesty," he said, leaning back in his desk chair. The study in his home was dark, filled with shadows in every corner. A single lamp on his desk wasn't enough to chase them away—seemed like a pretty good metaphor for his life at the moment, he thought, surprised at the poetic train his mind was taking. But there were shadows in Garrett's past, too. Always there. Always ready to pounce. And the light that was Alex—though damn brighter than anything he'd ever known—still couldn't get rid of all those dark places.

So there was really only one thing to do. "I quit as your daughter's bodyguard."

The king blustered and shouted and Garrett let him go. He figured he owed it to the man to let him get it all out of his system. And while a royal father thousands of miles away ranted and raged, Garrett's mind turned to that afternoon on the beach. The look in Alex's eyes. The taste of her.

These past few days had been torturous. He couldn't be with her without wanting her and he couldn't have her as long as he was responsible for her safety. But the whole truth was, he couldn't have her, *period.*

Even if he gave in to what he wanted, what would it gain either of them? Soon she'd be going home to a damn palace. He would be here, in California running his business. He wasn't looking to be in love or to be married. But even if he were, she was a princess and there was just no way Garrett could compete with that. Oh, he was rich enough to give her the kind of house and servants she was used to. But he didn't have the pedigree her family would expect of a man wanting to be with Alex.

He was a King, and he was damn proud of it. The problem was, she was the daughter of a *king.*

No. There was nothing ahead for them but more misery and, thanks very much, but he'd rather skip that part of the festivities.

Sitting forward, he braced his elbow on the desktop and only half listened to the king on the other end of the line. Whatever the man said wouldn't change Garrett's mind. He already knew he was doing the only thing possible. For both of them.

"Mr. King," Alex's father was sputtering, "you cannot simply walk away from my daughter's safety without so much as a warning. I will need time to—"

Enough was enough.

"Sir, I won't take money from you to watch over Alex," Garrett finally interrupted the king and the other man's abrupt silence told him the king wasn't used to that kind of treatment. Just one more nugget of proof that Garrett King and royalty were never going to be a good mix. "But, that said," he continued into the quiet, "I won't leave her out there alone, either. On my own, I'll watch out for her until she's on a plane headed home."

"May I ask *why* you've decided to leave my employ?"

Touchy question, Garrett told himself. He could hardly confess to the king that he didn't want to be taking money from the father of the woman he wanted in his bed. That might be enough for a beheading in Cadria, for all Garrett knew.

"Let's just say, Alex and I have become friends. And I feel badly taking money from her father."

There was a long silence, and then the king gave a tired sigh. Garrett sympathized. Couldn't be easy being thousands of miles away from someone you worried about. "Fine then. I appreciate your help in this, Mr. King, and it won't be forgotten."

Long after the king hung up, Garrett sat in his darkened study and stared at nothing. No, he thought. None of this would be forgotten.

Ever.

The late-night knock on Alex's door startled her.

She tossed the book she had been reading to the sofa cushion beside her. Jumping up from the couch, she tugged at the belt of her blue silk robe and crossed the room with hesitant steps. She wasn't expecting anyone and the desk always called before they disturbed her. And just who would have been able to get onto the penthouse elevator besides… She looked through the peephole and saw Garrett staring back at her.

Her heart did a slow roll in her chest as her nerves drained away and an entirely different emotion charged to the surface. She leaned her forehead on the cool, painted surface of the door and took a breath. Would the man always have this effect on her? Would one look at him always be enough to turn her knees to water?

Shaking her head, she steadied herself, then fumbled with the locks and opened the door to him. "Garrett. I didn't expect to see you until tomorrow."

"Yeah," he muttered, stepping past her to enter the suite. "Something's come up."

She frowned as he walked into the room, careful not to get close enough to brush against her. Alex noticed that his features were grim, his cheeks shadowed by beard stubble and his hair looked as if he'd been running his fingers through it for hours.

"Garrett? Is something wrong?"

He laughed shortly and turned to look at her. His eyes were dark and filled with charged emotions too deep to name. Shoving his hands into the back pockets of his worn jeans, he just looked at her for a long minute before saying, "Just came to tell you something. You win."

"What?"

Shaking his head, he blew out a breath and said, "I talked to your father a while ago. Told him I quit."

"You did?" All right, she should be pleased, and yet, the look on his face told her that more was coming and that she wasn't going to like it.

"Told him I couldn't take money from him for keeping you safe."

She took a single step toward him. "Why, Garrett? Why would you do that?"

"You know why." His gaze swept her up and down before settling on her eyes again. "But that doesn't mean I'm backing off, Alex. I'm still going to be there. Every day. Making sure nothing happens to you."

"Garrett." She reached up and cupped his cheek in her palm. "Nothing's going to happen to me."

He caught her hand in his and held on. His shadow-filled eyes locked with hers and flashed with steely determination. "Damn straight, it's not."

Her hand trapped in his tight grip, she could only stare up at him. "Garrett, you're even more crazed about protecting me than the palace guards. Why?"

"Because I won't fail again."

"Fail? Fail how?"

He released her, turned and walked to the couch and looked down at the book, spine up on the cushions. He snorted. "Romance novel?"

"There's nothing wrong with a happy ending," she said.

"Happy endings are fictional, Alex."

"They don't have to be."

He turned back to face her. "You don't get it." A choked off laugh shot from his throat. "No reason why you should."

Alex was standing not two feet from him and yet she felt distance stretching out between them. The pale light of her reading lamp was a golden circle in the darkness, reaching for Garrett and not quite making it. Absently she noted the soft roar of the ocean, like an extra heartbeat in the room.

"Then explain it to me, Garrett. Tell me what's driving you."

He reached up, scraped both palms across his face and then shoved them through his hair. When he'd finished, he looked at her and his eyes were bleak, sending a thread of worry sliding through Alex's body.

When he spoke, his voice was rough and low, as if he regretted saying the words even before they were out of his mouth. "About ten years ago, I was hired to be a bodyguard for the daughter of a very wealthy man."

Alex held her breath and stayed perfectly still. Finally, she was going to get to the heart of the problem and she didn't want to risk interrupting him. Yet at the same time, she couldn't fight the notion that once he said what he had to, nothing would be the same. For either of them.

"Her name was Kara." A smile briefly twisted his mouth and was gone again in a blink. "She was beautiful and stubborn and smart. A lot like you, really."

A trickle of cold began to snake down her spine and still, she remained quiet.

"I got…distracted," he said and once again shoved a hand through his hair as if somehow he could wipe away the memories swarming in his mind. "I fell in love with her—"

Pain was swift and sharp. Jealousy dug its talons into her heart and twisted. And just as quickly, it all faded away. He had loved, but it was ten years ago and obviously it hadn't ended well. She forced herself to ask, "What happened?"

"I quit my job," he said, and swept the room with his troubled gaze before looking back at her. "Knew I couldn't protect Kara with my focus splintered. Told her father I wouldn't be responsible for her life anymore and I left. Two days later, Kara ditched her new guard and ran away. The letter she left behind said she was running to me. She never got there. She was kidnapped and killed."

"God, Garrett…"

"I won't let that happen to you."

Sympathy briefly warred with frustration inside her. Frustration won. "What makes you think it would? One tragedy doesn't always signal another."

"I know. But even getting past that, it's not just Kara. It's you and me. We're too different, Alex. Our worlds are light years apart." He shook his head and she felt the finality of that one single action. His features were tight, implacable. His voice a promise as he added, "I'm not looking to fall in love, Alex. What would be the point?"

Her heart gave a sudden lurch in her chest, and it felt as if a ball of lead had dropped into the pit of her stomach. He was walking away from her. Without even trying. Without a backward glance. Tears filled her eyes but she furiously blinked them back. She wasn't about to let him see her *cry*. What would be the point anyway?

Whatever she had convinced herself they shared, in reality, it was no more than a holiday fling. A summer romance doomed to die at the end of the season. She loved a man determined to not love her back, and there didn't seem to be a thing she could do to change it.

And would she if she could?

She had her pride after all. And that emotion was leading the charge when she snapped, "I never said anything about love, Garrett."

"Please." He gave her a patient, tired smile that made her want to kick something. "I can see it in your face, feel it in your touch. Alex, you're looking for something I can't give you."

She felt the sting of those words, and actually swayed in place when they hit her. But she kept her chin lifted and her eyes defiant as she corrected, "Not can't. *Won't*."

"Same thing," he said, folding his arms across his chest and glaring down at her.

"For a man who prides himself on seeing every possible angle of every possible situation, you're surprisingly blind."

"Is that right?"

"It is," she answered and took a step closer to him. Her gaze fixed with his. "This isn't even about *me,* Garrett. It's about you and how you look at your life. I'm sorry about Kara. But that wasn't your fault. Bad things happen. You can't stop them. You can only live your life in spite of them."

"She left her guards because of me," he told her flatly. "If I hadn't gotten involved with her, she'd be alive today."

"You don't know that," she told him and saw denial in his eyes. "You're not God, Garrett. You don't have the power of life and death, and you can't personally protect everyone you care about."

"But I can limit those I care about," he said softly.

"So rather than love and risk the pain of losing it, you would make your own world smaller so maybe danger won't notice you? Maybe your circle of loved ones will be tiny enough that nothing bad will touch you?"

He didn't say anything to that, but then, he didn't have to. Alex knew now for certain that what they had was over. He could stay and watch over her as he'd said he would, but there would be no more lovemaking. No more flirtatious fun. No more laughter. There would be only Garrett, in his role of knight errant ready to do battle in defense of his charge.

And that wasn't enough for Alex. Not nearly enough.

Sadly, she shook her head and said, "The difference between you and me is, I won't deny myself something wonderful for fear of losing it."

"That's because you've never lost."

"Wrong again," she said, a half smile curving her mouth. "I just did."

"Alex—"

"I think you should go," she said, though the words tore at her.

This was over. He couldn't have made himself plainer. He didn't want her—he saw her only as his responsibility—and she wanted the magic.

The gulf lying between them was wider than ever.

"Fine. I'll go. But I'll be back in the morning," he said. "Don't leave the hotel without me."

She didn't answer because an order didn't require one. She simply stood, alone in the dim light and listened to the door close behind him.

First thing in the morning, though, the plan changed.

Griffin needed some backup with a client and Garrett had already dumped so much of the company work on his twin lately, he couldn't turn him down. Besides, he figured it might do both he and Alex some good to have some space.

He'd been up half the night, reliving that scene in her penthouse suite. He could still feel the chill in the room when he told her he wouldn't love her. Could still see her eyes when she told him to leave. A low, deep ache settled in his chest, but Garrett accepted it as the price he had to pay for screwing this up so badly.

And he knew that the pain was going to be with him a long, damn time. He was halfway to San Diego when he thought it was late enough that he could call Alex without waking her up. Punching in the phone number, Garrett steered his car down the 405 freeway and waited for what seemed forever for Alex to answer the damn phone. The moment she did, the sound of her voice sent another ping of regret shooting through him.

Mentally, he explained it away. Of course he regretted

that she'd be leaving. Why the hell wouldn't he? He'd spent practically every day with her for more than a week. Why wouldn't he be accustomed to her smile, her laughter? It was only natural that he'd listen for the sound of her accent and get a buzz when he knew he was going to see her.

Didn't mean he cared. Didn't *mean* anything. When she was gone, things would settle down. Get back to normal, he assured himself. Which was all he wanted. The regular world that didn't include runaway princesses.

"Alex, it's me," he said shortly, changing lanes to pass an RV moving at a snail-like speed in the sun-washed morning.

"What is it, Garrett?"

Her voice was clipped now, as if anger was churning just below the surface. He hated to hear it, but it was probably best, he told himself. If she was mad, then she wasn't hurting. He'd never meant to hurt her, God knew. But it had happened anyway and now the best thing he could do was keep up the wall he'd erected between them the night before.

"I won't be able to come over this morning," he said tightly. "Griffin needs some help on a case, and I—"

"No need to explain. I'm sure you're very busy."

The words might be right, but her tone said differently. He scowled at the phone. "Yeah. Well, anyway. You won't be alone. I sent one of our best agents over there. Terri Cooper. She's in the lobby now, waiting for a call from you to the front desk. She's the best in the business, so I know she'll keep you safe."

"Garrett, I don't need a babysitter."

"She's a bodyguard, Alex, and until I get back, she's sticking to you like glue."

"And I've no say in it."

He frowned to himself and downshifted as the flow of

traffic picked up a bit. "If you don't want to see Terri, don't leave the hotel. I'd prefer that anyway. I should be able to be back before dinner."

"I see," she said, her accent a little sharper, "and I'm to await you at your convenience, is that it?"

He punched the accelerator and swung around another car, which had no business driving in the fast lane. "Alex, don't start with me. We've been over this. You know it's not safe."

"No, Garrett," she argued, "*you* know it's not safe. But I've a mind of my own and am in no way burdened with your overwhelmingly cautious nature."

"Damn it, Alex." He thought about hitting the first off-ramp and heading back. Then he realized his twin was in La Jolla waiting for him, and Garrett was stuck between the proverbial rock and a hard place.

And he did *not* have a cautious nature.

Made him sound like some old lady afraid to leave her house. Nothing could be further from the truth. He faced down danger every damn day of his life. It was *Alex* facing danger he couldn't bear the thought of.

"I'm in charge of your safety."

"No, you're not. You said yourself last night that you're no longer working for my father. That makes you nothing more than a bossy ex-bed partner. And I don't take orders from my exes."

"You're making me crazy, Alex. Terri will be with you if you leave the hotel."

Someone cut him off and Garrett honked at them. Didn't do any good, but made him feel a little better.

"I won't promise anything. And if that makes you crazy, then I'll admit to enjoying your misery as a side benefit."

She was enjoying it, too. He heard it in her voice. God knew what she would do today just to prove to him that she could take care of herself. He didn't even want to think about it.

The stream of traffic was slowing down. Brake lights flashed ahead and cars were stacked up behind him, too. Just another day on Southern California's freeways. Once he was stopped dead, he muttered, "I'll be back as soon as I can. Just—be careful, okay?"

There was a long pause and, for a moment, he half wondered if she'd hung up on him and he hadn't noticed. Then finally, she said only, "Goodbye, Garrett."

Car horns blared, the radio in the car beside him was set to a volume probably audible in space and the only sound Garrett really noticed was the hum of the dial tone, telling him she was gone.

"She's making me nuts."

"In her defense," Griffin said helpfully, "she didn't have far to go."

"Thanks for that." Garrett gave his twin a dark look. "You're supposed to be on my side, remember? Blood thicker than water and all that?"

"Yeah, we're family, blah, blah," Griffin said, kicking back in the leather booth seat and pausing long enough to take a long pull on his bottle of beer. "But if the princess is getting to you this badly, then I'm all for it."

Garrett stared down at his own beer and then lifted his gaze to look around the half-empty pub. It was supposed to look Irish, but Garrett had seen the real thing not long ago when he did a job for his cousin Jefferson. Still, it wasn't bad, just touristy. Lots of dark wood, flags of Ireland all over the place and even a bronze leprechaun crouched on the bar.

He and Griffin had finished with their client early and had stopped in here for some lunch before facing the long drive home again. He was still worried about Alex, but she'd been on her own for hours already, doing God knew what—because the damn woman wouldn't answer her damn phone. All Terri sent him was a brief text saying everything was fine. So him taking a half hour for lunch wasn't going to make that much difference at this point.

"And did I mention," Griffin said with a knowing leer, "you look like *hell?*"

He had known that talking to Griffin about all of this wouldn't get him any sympathy. And maybe he didn't need any. What he needed was somebody to talk to.

He should have picked someone smarter.

"Doesn't matter if she's 'getting' to me or not—which she isn't," he added, after a pause for a sip of beer. "The point is she's a princess, Griff. Would never work."

"Man, I really did get all the brains," Griffin mused with a slow shake of his head. "The way you talk about her, she seems damn near perfect. And you don't want her because she's a princess? What is that?"

"It's not a question of want."

"Then what is it?"

"Even if I did admit to wanting Alex, the fact that she's a princess pretty much cools that whole idea."

"Because…"

Irritated, Garrett glared at his twin. "You think her family would want her with a security expert?"

"Who better?"

"Nice try. But royals prefer royals, and everyone knows that. Her father's probably got her future husband all picked out for her." The thought of that made him want to break something.

"Uh-huh. And what else?" Griffin shook his head. "There's more here, Garrett."

"Kara." He'd loved once and lost her. He wasn't sure he was willing to go through that again.

"Here we go," Griffin muttered. "You know, I've been hearing that excuse for years, and I'm just not buying it anymore."

"What the hell's that mean?"

"It means, that you've been hiding behind Kara. Yeah, it was terrible what happened to her. But you know damn well it wasn't your fault."

Garrett shifted in his seat, took a swig of beer and set the bottle down again.

"You loved her, and she died."

"Thanks for the news flash. But I don't need you to tell me that. I lived it."

Griffin ignored him. Leaning on the tabletop, he said, "Somewhere along the way, though, you died, too. Or at least you stopped living, which amounts to the same thing."

Garrett glared at his twin again, but it didn't do any good. Nothing could shut Griffin up if he had something to say and clearly he did. Seemed he'd been building up to this little speech for years.

"Now along comes the princess, shakes you up, makes you notice, *hey, not a bad world out here,* and *boom.*" He clapped both hands together for emphasis. "You shut down. Start pulling Kara out of the past and using her as a shield or some damn thing. The problem isn't Kara, Garrett. Never was. The problem is *you.*"

The waitress arrived with their lunch and while Griffin flirted and got an extra order of fries for his trouble, Garrett did some fast thinking. His twin might actually have a point. He had been enjoying his time with Alex. Had been relaxing the guard around his heart and the minute she got close, he'd pulled back. So was he using Kara as a shield? If that was true, then Alex had been right the night before when she'd accused him of making sure his world was small enough that tragedy would have a harder time striking.

When it was just the two of them again, Griffin noted, "Hmm. Looks like a lightbulb might have gone off in your head."

"Maybe," Garrett admitted, then added, "but even if you're right—"

"Can't hear that often enough," Griffin said with a grin just before popping a French fry into his mouth.

"—it doesn't change the fact that Alex is a princess and lives in a palace for God's sake. I live in a condo at the beach—"

"No, you don't," Griffin interrupted.

"Excuse me?" Seriously, he knew where he *lived.*

Taking another pull of his beer, Griffin said, "You don't live there. You live out of suitcases. Hell, you spend more time on King Jets than you do in that condo."

"What's that supposed to mean?"

"Means you don't live anywhere, Garrett. So what's keeping you here?"

He just stared at his twin. Was he the only one who could see the problems in this? Alex was oblivious and now Griffin, too? "Our *business?*"

"More excuses." Griff waved one hand at his brother, effectively dismissing him, then picked up his burger and took a bite. After chewing, he said, "We can run our place from anywhere. If you wanted to, you could set up a European branch and you damn well know it."

His chest felt tight. The noise in the pub fell away. All he could hear was himself, telling Alex that he wouldn't love her. That he couldn't. The problem was, he *did* love her.

A hell of a thing for a man to just be figuring out. But

there it was. He'd had to quit working for her father because he couldn't take money for protecting the woman he loved. He had kept his distance from her because he couldn't sleep with her knowing that he'd have to let her go.

But did he have to?

What if he was wrong? What if there was a chance a commoner might have a shot with a princess? Was he really ready to let Alex go without even *trying* to make it work? His brain raced with possibilities. Maybe he had been short-sighted. Stupid. But he didn't have to stay that way.

His phone rang, and he glanced at the readout. Instantly, he answered it and fought the sudden hot ball of worry in his guts. "Terri? What is it?"

"Boss, I'm sorry, but you *did* tell me to stick to her and—"

"What happened?" In his mind, he was seeing car wrecks, holdups, assassins…

"She had me drive her to L.A. and—"

"Uh, Garrett…"

"Shut up," he muttered, then to Terri he said, "L.A.? Why L.A.?"

"Garrett!"

His gaze snapped to Griffin.

Pointing to the bar, his twin said, "You need to see this."

He turned to look. Terri was still talking in his ear, but he hardly heard her. There was a flat screen TV above the bar, the sound muted. But he didn't need the sound. What he saw opened a hole in his chest. He snapped the phone shut and stared.

Alex was on the TV. But an Alex he hardly knew. Her long, thick hair was twisted into a complicated knot at the top of her head. Diamonds winked at her ears and blazed at the base of her throat. She wore a pale green dress that was tailored to fit her beautifully and she looked as remote as a…well, a *princess.*

Garrett pushed out of his seat, crossed the room and ordered the bartender to, "Turn it up, will you?"

The man did and Garrett listened over the roaring in his own ears. Someone shoved a microphone at Alex and shouted, "Princess, how long have you been here and why the big secret?"

She smiled into the camera, and Garrett could have sworn she was looking directly at him. His hands curled around the edge of the polished wood bar and squeezed until he was half afraid he was going to snap the thick wood in two.

"I've been in America almost two weeks," she said, her voice low, moderate, regal. "As for the secrecy of my visit, I wanted the opportunity to see the *real* America. To meet people and get to know them without the barriers of my name and background getting in the way."

People in the bar were listening. Griffin had moved up alongside him, but Garrett hardly noticed. His gaze was fixed on Alex. She looked so different. And already so far away.

"Did it work?" someone else shouted.

"It did," she said, her gaze still steady on the camera, staring directly into Garrett's soul. "I've enjoyed myself immensely. This is a wonderful country, and I've been met with nothing but kindness and warmth."

"You're headed home now, Princess," a reporter called out. "What're you going to miss the most?"

There was a long, thoughtful pause before Alex smiled into the camera and said, "It's a difficult question. I loved Disneyland, of course. And the beach. But I think what

I loved most were the people I met. *They* are what I'll miss when I go home. *They* are what will stay with me. Always."

She was leaving.

And maybe, he told himself darkly, it was better this way. But even he didn't believe that.

The camera pulled away and an excited news anchor came on to say, "Princess Alexis of Cadria, speaking to you from the Cadrian Consulate in Los Angeles. I can tell you we were all surprised to get the notice of her brief press conference. Speculation will be rife now, as to just where the princess has been for the last week or more.

"But this afternoon, a private jet will be taking her back to her home country. A shame we didn't get to see more of the lovely Princess Alexis while she was here."

Garrett had already turned away when the woman shifted gears and launched into another story. Walking back to their booth, Garrett sat down, picked up his burger and methodically took a bite. There was no reason to hurry through lunch now.

"Garrett—"

He glared his twin into silence and concentrated on the burger that suddenly tasted like sawdust.

Twelve

Everything was just as she'd left it.

Why that should have surprised Alex, she couldn't have said. But it did. Somehow, she felt so…changed, that she had expected to find the palace different as well.

Standing on the stone terrace outside the morning room, she turned to look up at the pink stone walls of the palace she called home. The leaded glass windows winked in the early morning sunlight and the flag of Cadria, flying high atop the far turret, snapped in the breeze.

She was both comforted and irritated that life in Cadria had marched inexorably on while she had been gone. But then, her emotions were swinging so wildly lately, that didn't surprise her, either. Since coming home a week ago, she had slipped seamlessly back into the life she had so briefly left behind. She had already visited two schools and presided over the planting of new trees in the city's park.

The papers were still talking about her spontaneous visit to the U.S. and photographers still haunted her every step.

Now, when she wanted to go shopping, she couldn't just walk to the closest mall or wander down to the neighborhood shops. A shopping excursion became more of a battle strategy. There were guards, which she told herself, Garrett would thoroughly approve of, there were state cars and flags flying from the bumpers. There were stores closed to all other shoppers and bowing deference from shopkeepers.

God, how she missed being a nobody.

Of course, her family didn't see it that way. They were all delighted to have her back. Her oldest brother was about to become engaged, and the other two were doing what they did best. Immersing themselves in royal duties with the occasional break for polo or auto racing. Her parents were the same, though her father hadn't yet interrogated her about her holiday and Alex suspected she had her mother to thank for that.

And she appreciated the reprieve. She just wasn't ready to talk about Garrett yet. Not to anybody. She was still hoping to somehow wipe him out of her mind. What was the point in torturing herself forever over a man who saw her as nothing more than an anvil around his neck?

"Bloody idiot," she muttered and kicked the stone barrier hard enough to send a jolt of pain through her foot and up her leg. But at least it was *physical* pain, which was a lot easier to deal with.

"Well," a familiar voice said from behind her, "that's more like it."

Alex looked over her shoulder at her mother. Queen Teresa of Cadria was still beautiful. Tall and elegant, Alex's mother kept her graying blond hair in a short cut that swung along her jawline. She wore green slacks, a white silk blouse and taupe flats. Her only jewelry was her wedding ring. Her blue eyes were sharp and fixed on her daughter.

"Mom. I didn't know you were there."

"Clearly," Teresa said as she strolled casually across the terrace, "care to tell me who the 'bloody idiot' is? Or will you make me guess?"

The queen calmly hitched herself up to sit on the stone parapet and demurely crossed her feet at the ankles. Alex couldn't help but smile. In public, Teresa of Cadria was dignified, elegant and all things proper. But when the family was alone, she became simply Teresa Hawkins Wells. A California girl who had married a king.

She had bowed to some traditions and had livened up other staid areas of the palace with her more casual flair. For instance, when she became queen, Teresa had made it clear that the "old" way of raising royal children wouldn't be happening anymore. She had been a hands-on mother and had remained that way. Naturally, there had also been governesses and tutors, but Alex and her brothers had grown up knowing their parents' love—and there were many royals who couldn't claim that.

None of Teresa's children had ever been able to keep a secret from her for long. And not one of them had ever successfully lied to their mother. So Alex didn't even bother trying now.

"Garrett King," she said.

"As I suspected." Teresa smiled as encouragement.

Alex didn't need much. Strange, she hadn't thought she wanted to talk about him, yet now that the opportunity was here, she found the words couldn't come fast enough. "He's arrogant and pompous and bossy. Always ordering me about, as bad as Dad, really. But he made me laugh as often as he made me angry and—"

"You love him," her mother finished for her.

"Yes, but I'll get over it," Alex said with determination.

"Why would you want to?"

The first sting of tears hit her eyes and that only made Alex more furious. She swiped at them with impatient fingers and said, "Because he doesn't want me." She shook her head and looked away from her mom's sympathetic eyes to stare out over the palace's formal gardens.

She focused on the box hedge maze. The maze had been constructed more than three hundred years ago, and Alex smiled, remembering how she and her brothers used to run through its long, twisting patterns at night, trying to scare each other.

The maze was so famous it was one of the most popular parts of the castle tour that was offered every summer. But the most beautiful part of the garden was the roses. They were Alex's mother's pride and joy. Teresa had brought slips of California roses with her when she'd given up her life to be queen. And she still nurtured those plants herself, despite grumblings from the head gardener.

Their thick scent wafted to them now, and Alex took a deep breath, letting the familiar become a salve to her wounded pride.

"Alex," her mother said, reaching out to lay one hand on her daughter's arm, "of course he wants you. Why else would he refuse to take money for protecting you?"

"Stubbornness?" Alex asked, shifting her gaze to her mother.

Teresa smiled and shook her head. "Now who's being stubborn?"

"You don't understand, Mom." Alex turned her back on

the garden and pushed herself up to sit beside her mother. The damp cold from the stones leached into her black slacks and slid into her bones, but she hardly noticed. "It was different for you. You met Dad at Disneyland, and it was magic. He fell in love and swept you off your feet and—"

She stopped and stared when her mother's laughter rang out around her. "What's so funny?"

"Oh, sweetie," Teresa said as she caught her breath again. "I didn't mean to laugh, but…maybe your father was right. When you were a little girl, he used to tell me I was spinning too many romantic stories. Filling your head with impossible expectations."

Confused, Alex just looked at her mother. "But you did meet at Disneyland. And you fell in love and became a queen."

"All true," her mother said, "but, that's not *all* of the story."

Intrigued, Alex let her own troubles move to the background as she listened to her mother.

"I did meet Gregory at Disneyland," she said, a half smile on her face. "I was working at the Emporium and he came in and bought half the merchandise at my station just so he'd have an excuse to keep standing there talking to me."

Alex could enjoy the story even more now that she had been to the famous park and could imagine the scene more clearly.

"We spent a lot of time together in the two weeks he was in California and, long story short, we fell in love." She smiled again, then picked up Alex's hand and gave it a squeeze. "But it wasn't happily ever after right away, sweetie."

"What happened?"

"Your dad left. He came back here, to the palace." She swept her gaze up to take in the pink castle and its centuries of tradition. "He told me he was going to be a king and that he couldn't marry me. That we couldn't possibly be together. His parents wouldn't have allowed it, and his country wouldn't stand for it."

"What? That's ridiculous!" Alex immediately defended her. "Cadria *loves* you."

"Yes," her mother said with a laugh. "*Now.* Back then, though, it was a different story. I was heartbroken and furious that he would walk away from love so easily."

She and her mother had more in common than Alex knew, she thought glumly. But at least her mom had eventually gotten a happy ending. But how? "What happened?"

"Your father missed me," Teresa said with a grin. "He called, but I wouldn't speak to him. He sent me gifts that I returned. Letters that went back unopened." Nudging Alex's shoulder with her own, Teresa admitted, "I drove him crazy."

"Good for you. I can't believe Dad walked away from you!"

"Centuries of tradition are hard to fight," Teresa said. "And so was your grandfather who had no interest in a commoner daughter-in-law."

"But—"

"I know, sweetie. Your grandfather loved me. Once he met me, everything was fine." She sighed a little. "But, your dad actually had to threaten to abdicate before his father would listen to reason."

"Dad was willing to give up the throne for you?"

"He was," Teresa said with another sigh of satisfaction. "Thankfully, it didn't come to that, since he's a very good king. But once his father saw how serious Gregory was, he promised to make it work. He went to the Law Chambers himself to see that the country's charter was rewritten to allow for a commoner as queen."

"Wow." She didn't know what else to say. Alex had had no idea of the intrigue and passion and clashes that had been involved in her parents getting together.

"Yes, wow," Teresa said, laughing again. "When it was all settled, in a record amount of time, thanks to your father being an impatient soul, Gregory came back to California with his grandmother's ring in hand and the rest, as they say, is history."

Holding up her left hand as proof, Teresa wiggled her fingers, letting the ancient diamond wink and glitter in the sunlight.

"I had no idea."

"Of course you didn't, and I should have told you the whole truth sooner. But, Alex, I had a point in telling you this now," her mother said and reached out to give her a one-armed hug. "And that is, don't give up on your young man. Love is a powerful thing and, once felt, it's impossible to walk away from. If your Garrett is anything like my Gregory…" She smiled again. "There's always hope."

"Excuse me, your majesty."

Teresa looked to the open doorway into the morning room. A maid stood in the shadows. "Yes, Christa?"

"I've laid the tea out, ma'am, for you and her highness."

"Thank you, Christa," Teresa said, "we'll be right in."

A quick curtsy and the maid was gone again. A moment later, Teresa scooted off the parapet, dusted off the seat of her slacks and said, "I'll pour the tea. You come in when you're ready, okay?"

Nodding, Alex watched her mother go, as her mind

whirled with possibilities. Was her mom right? Was there hope? Yes, her parents' love story had turned out well in the end, but the King of Cadria had been in love.

Whereas Garrett King *refused* to be in love with her.

She turned her head to stare out over the gardens, to the ocean beyond and to the man on the other side of the world. Hope, she thought wistfully, could be a both a blessing and a curse.

"She sent it back."

"What?" Griffin looked up as Garrett stormed into his office.

Tossing a small package onto his brother's desk, Garrett complained, "The necklace I sent to Alex two days ago. She returned it!"

"And this is my problem because…"

"You're my brother, and it's your job to listen to me," Garrett told him as he stalked the perimeter of his brother's office.

"Actually, it's my job to look into the file we just got on our Georgia client and—"

"Why would she return it?" Garrett asked no one in particular, thinking of the platinum and onyx piece he'd had commissioned just for her. He hadn't asked himself why it was so important for him to give her a memento of their time together. It simply was. He couldn't have her, but damned if he could entirely let go, either.

These past two weeks without her had nearly killed him. Nothing felt right to him anymore. Without Alex in his life, everything else was just white noise. He kept as busy as possible and *still* her absence chewed at him, widening the black hole inside him every damn day.

His fingers closed around the box that had been returned to him just a few minutes ago. Shaking it for emphasis, he blurted, "It was a trinket. Sort of a souvenir. You know, help her remember her holiday."

Griffin gave up and sat back in his chair. "Maybe she doesn't *want* to remember."

Garrett stopped dead and glared at his twin. "Why the hell wouldn't she want to remember? She had a great time."

"Yeah, but it's over, and she's back home at the palace."

"So, close the door? That's it?" Could she really cut him out of her life, her memories, that easily?

"Aren't you the one who closed the door?" Griffin asked.

"Not the point." Hell, Garrett knew he wasn't making any sense. He didn't need his twin stating the obvious.

Two weeks without her. Didn't seem to matter that he knew he'd done the right thing. Didn't matter that he knew there was no way they could have worked out anything between them. He missed her like he would an arm. Or a leg.

She was as much a part of him as his damn heart and without her, it was like he didn't have one.

This had not been a part of the plan. He'd expected to miss her, sure. But he hadn't counted on not being able to sleep or keep his mind on his damn work. He hadn't counted on seeing her everywhere, hearing her voice, her laugh in his mind at odd moments during the day.

"You're just going to prowl around my office, is that it?" Griffin asked.

Garrett stopped and glared at him. "What the hell am I supposed to do?"

"You know what I think you should do. Question is, what are you *going* to do?"

"If I knew that," he muttered darkly, "I'd be doing it."

"Well then, maybe this will help you decide," Griffin said and pulled the morning paper out from under a stack of files. "Wasn't going to show you this—but maybe you should see it after all."

"What?" Garrett took the paper, glanced at the picture on the front page and felt his heart stop.

Front and center, there was a photo of Alex, dressed in a flowing gown and a crown, holding on to the arm of an impossibly handsome man in a tux, wearing a damn sash across his chest that was loaded down with medals. The tagline above the photo screamed, Royal Engagement In The Wind?

"Oh, *hell* no," Garrett muttered.

"Looks to me like you'd better go get your woman back before it's too late," Griffin said, clearly amused at Garrett's reaction.

Garrett's vision fogged at the edges until all he could see was Alex's face staring up at him from the paper. He was about to really lose her. Permanently. Unless he took a chance.

Clutching the newspaper tight in one fist, Garrett grabbed the returned package and said, "Call the airport for me. Have one of the King Jets fueled up and ready to go when I get there."

Griffin was laughing as he made the call, but Garrett was already gone.

"Where is he?" Garrett stormed past the footman at the door to the castle and stomped loudly across the marble flooring. His head turned as if on a swivel as he scanned every hallway for signs of the king.

"If you'll follow me," the butler said, "his majesty is in the library."

Garrett hadn't slept in nearly twenty-four hours. He felt ragged and pushed to the edge of his endurance, but damned if he was going to wait another minute to talk to Alex's father. He'd gotten past the palace guards on the strength of his having done work for the crown before. But getting an audience with the king this easily was a plus.

The air smelled of roses and beeswax, and Garrett took a deep breath to steady himself for the coming confrontation. The sound of his footsteps as he followed after his guide rang out hollowly in the air, thudding like a heartbeat. He had a plan, of course. Wasn't much of one, but he'd use whatever he could. Alex was here, somewhere, and no matter what happened between him and the king in the next few minutes, he wasn't leaving until he spoke to her.

He stepped into the library and the butler left him with the king. The room was imposing, as it was meant to be. Dark paneling, bloodred leather furniture and floor-to-ceiling windows with a view of the sea. The man standing before a crackling fire was just as imposing. King Gregory was tall, muscular and the gray in his hair only made him look more formidable.

"Garrett, this is a surprise."

About to be an even bigger one, he thought and cut right to the chase. "Your majesty, Alex can't marry Duke Henrik."

"Is that right?" One eyebrow lifted.

Hell, Garrett couldn't believe the man would allow Alex *near* the duke. A quick online search had been enough to show Garrett that the man was more known for his string of women than for any work done in the House of Lords.

Well, the king might be okay with that, but damned if Garrett would let Alex end up with someone who didn't deserve her.

"How is this any of your business, Garrett?"

"It's my business because there's a good chance Alex is pregnant with my child."

Risky move, he told himself, since there was no way Alex was pregnant. But it was the one sure way he knew to delay any kind of wedding but for the one Garrett now wanted more than anything.

The king's face went red. "You—"

"Pregnant?"

Garrett whirled around at the deep voice behind him and was just in time to watch Alex's older brother Prince Christopher's fist collide with his face. Pain exploded inside his head, but he ducked before the prince could land another one.

Then he threw a fast right himself and watched the prince stagger backward. The other man recovered quickly and came at Garrett again, still furious.

The king was shouting, "Pregnant? *Pregnant?*"

Two more men ran into the room. They took in the scene at a glance and immediately joined their older brother in the fray.

"Perfect," Garrett muttered, turning a slow circle so he could keep an eye on all three of them. Seemed he wasn't going to come out of this without a few bruises. But he'd give as good as he got, too.

He blocked another blow, threw a punch himself and smiled when the youngest of the princes was laid out flat on his back. The king pushed past one of his sons and threw a punch of his own that Garrett managed to avoid.

He wasn't about to hit a king, either, so he focused on protecting himself and doing a lot of dodging.

As Garrett avoided another blow, he yelled, "Just let me talk to Alex and we can straighten this out."

"You stay away from my sister." This from the prince pushing up from the floor.

"No one is talking to anyone until I have some answers," the king shouted again.

"Why is everyone yelling?" Alex called into the mix.

Garrett turned at the sound of her voice and Christopher landed another solid jab on his jaw. "Damn it!"

Hands clapped loudly, followed by a sharp, feminine command. "Stop this at once! Christopher, no more fighting. Help Henry off the floor, and Jonathon, get your father some water."

The king was sputtering in rage, but everyone else moved to follow the queen's orders. Everyone but Alex. She just stood there in the doorway, staring at him as if she'd never seen him before. Her hair was tidy, her elegant dress and tasteful jewelry made her seem unapproachable. But somewhere beneath that cool exterior was *his* Alex. And Garrett wasn't leaving until he'd had a chance to reach her.

The capper for Garrett, though, was seeing the damn duke standing right behind her. That settled everything. No way in hell was Garrett letting his woman go. And she *was* his. Had been from that first day at Disneyland.

"Who's pregnant?" Alex demanded.

"Apparently, *you* are," Christopher told her.

"I'm *what?*" She fired a furious look on Garrett and he just glared right back.

"I said you could be."

"Pregnant?" Henrik repeated from behind her. "You're *pregnant?* I'll be leaving."

"Henrik!" The king's shout went unanswered as the duke scuttled out the door to disappear. Probably forever.

"What is going on here? I could hear the shouts all the way to the garden." The queen looked from one face to the next, her silent, accusatory stare demanding answers.

"Garrett King claims Alexis is pregnant with his child," the king managed to say through gritted teeth.

"And I was just about to beat him to a pulp," Christopher said helpfully.

"In your dreams," Garrett muttered, never taking his eyes off Alex.

"Well, it's a lie," she snapped. "I'm not pregnant."

No one was listening. The princes were arguing among themselves, the queen and the king were locked into battle and Alex was looking at Garrett through furious eyes. When she turned to leave, he bolted across the room, grabbed her hand and tugged her into the hall, away from her arguing family.

"Don't," she said, pulling her hand free. Looking up at him, she said, "You don't belong here, Garrett. Go home."

"No."

"You had your choice, and you made it. Now it's time we both live with it."

He grabbed her again, holding on to her shoulders half worried that she'd run if he let her go. It could take him *weeks* to find her again in this place. "Why did you return the package I sent you?"

"Because what we had is over. Now please, just *go*."

"I'm not going anywhere," he murmured and pulled her in close. Wrapping his arms around her, to hold on tight when she started to squirm, Garrett kissed her. He poured everything he'd been feeling for the last two weeks into that kiss. The longing. The pain. The regret. The joy at being with her again. For the first time in too damn long, he felt whole. As if the puzzle pieces of his life had fallen into place.

Her tongue tangled with his, her breath slid into his lungs and her heartbeat clamored in time with his own. Everything was right. He just had to convince her that he was a changed man.

Finally, he broke the kiss, stared down into those amazing eyes of hers and said, "Alex, I don't give a damn about your crown. I don't care that you're a princess. Don't care that our worlds are so different. I'll convince your father to let us be together. We can make it work, Alex. We *will* make it work."

"Garrett…" She sighed, and said, "I want to believe you. But you made yourself perfectly clear before. You didn't want me in California. So why now? What's changed?"

"Me," he told her, lifting his hands to cup her face. His thumbs moved over her cheekbones and just the feel of her soft, smooth skin beneath his eased the pain that had been tearing at him for what seemed forever. "I've changed. And I did want you in California, Alex. I always wanted you. From the first time I saw you in Disneyland, I wanted you. I was just too busy looking for trouble to see what I'd already found."

She shook her head, and Garrett's heart stopped briefly. But a King never backed away from a challenge. Especially one that meant more to him than his life.

"Alex, I know now what's really important." God, he had to make her believe him. Those eyes of hers were so deep, so rich with emotion, with *love.* Seeing it gave him enough hope to continue. To tell her everything he wanted her to know.

And he still hadn't even said the most important thing. "I love you. I *love* you, Alex, Princess Alexis Morgan Wells. I really do."

Her breath caught and a single tear rolled from the corner of her eye. He caught it with his thumb as if it were precious. Sunlight speared in from an overhead window and lay on her beautiful hair, now tightly controlled in a twist on top of her head.

"I love your laugh." His gaze moved over her and then he reached up to tug a few pins loose, letting her hair fall down around her shoulders. "And I love your hair, all wild and tangled. I love the way you find something beautiful in everything. I love your clever brain and your smart-ass mouth. I love that you're willing to call me out when you think I'm being an idiot."

Her lips quirked.

"And I love that you want to help women in need and I'd like to be a part of that."

She took a sharp breath.

"I want to be with you, Alex. Always. I want to build a life with you. In California *and* Cadria."

"How—"

"I'm opening a branch of King Security right here in Cadria. We'll be the European division."

"Garrett—" She shook her head sadly. "You're not used to this kind of life. I'm followed by reporters and photographers. We wouldn't be able to just buy a house in town and move in. We would have to live here in a wing of the palace. You'd hate that, you know you would."

He laughed shortly. "First off, you forget. I'm one of the Kings of California. We've got paparazzi following us all the damn time looking for a story. I'm used to life in a fishbowl. It's not always pretty, but if you want to badly enough, you can carve out a private life."

"But—"

"And it doesn't matter where we live, Alex," he said, "as long as we're together." He gave a glance around the wide hallway, with its priceless art hanging on the walls and the gleam of marble shining up at them. "I could learn to love the palace."

She laughed, and God, it sounded like music to him.

"I'll miss good Thai food at one in the morning, but if the craving gets bad, I'll have Griffin send me some on a King Jet."

"Oh, Garrett," she said on a chuckle.

"It'll work, Princess," he said quickly, giving her a quick kiss as if to seal a promise. "We'll blend our lives and build one together that will suit both of us."

Alex's breath caught in her chest. Everything she had ever dreamed of was right here, in front of her. All she had to do was reach out and take it. Returning the package he had sent her hadn't been easy, but she'd hoped that he would come to her, repeating family history. Now, here he was and Alex was half afraid to believe in it.

"I love you, Alex," he said softly. "Marry me. Love me back."

She sighed and lifted both arms to wrap them around his neck. "I do love you, Garrett King."

"Thank God," he said on a laugh, dropping his forehead to hers. "When you returned the necklace…"

"It was a necklace?"

"I brought it with me." He dipped one hand into his pocket and pulled out a flat, dark green jeweler's box.

Alex took it, opened the lid and sighed with pleasure.

"It's a seagull," he told her unnecessarily. "I had it made to remind you of the ocean. Of all the time we spent at the beach."

Tears stung her eyes as she lifted the beautifully crafted piece free of the box. She turned and lifted her hair so that he could put it around her neck and when it was lying against the base of her throat, she touched it and whispered, "I love it, Garrett, though I don't need a reminder. I'll never forget a moment of my time with you."

She had everything she had ever dreamed of, right there in her arms. Garrett King was looking at her with more love than she could have imagined possible. She felt the truth of it in his touch. Saw it plainly in his beautiful eyes that were no longer shadowed with old pain. Her heart felt full and yet…

"I'm still a princess, Garrett," she warned. "That won't change, ever. There will still be the chance of danger surrounding me and my family. It will still drive you crazy."

"Yeah," he said solemnly. "I know. But I'll be here to make sure you're safe. All of you." A small smile crooked one corner of his mouth. "King Security can be the palace's personal protection detail.

"Marry me, Alex. Together, you and I can do anything."

"I know we can," she said and went up on her toes to kiss him. "So yes, Garrett, I'll marry you."

He grinned and blew out a relieved breath. "Took you long enough."

Shaking her head, she said, "I can't believe you told my father I was pregnant."

"It was the only thing I could come up with on short notice."

She smiled up at him. "You used to be a much better liar, Mr. King."

"It's all in the past, Princess. No more lies. Not between us."

"Agreed," she said, a grin she felt might never go away curving her mouth.

"So," he asked as he leaned in to kiss her, "how do you feel about Disneyland for a honeymoon?"

"I think that sounds perfect."

Then he kissed her, and the world righted itself again. Alex reveled in the sensation of everything being just as it should be. She gave herself up to the wonder and the joy and wasn't even aware when her brothers and father burst into the hall to see why things had gotten so suddenly quiet.

And she didn't see when her mother ushered her men back into the study to allow her daughter time to enjoy the magic of a lifetime.

* * * * *

ROYAL RESCUE

LISA CHILDS

To Philip Tyson for proving to me that heroes really do exist! Thank you for being my white knight!

Chapter One

Goose bumps of dread rising on her arms, Josie Jessup slipped into a pew in the back of church. She hated funerals, hated saying goodbye to anyone but most especially to someone who had died too soon. And so senselessly and violently—shot down just as his adult life was beginning.

The small church, with its brilliantly colored stained-glass windows, was filled with her former student's family and friends. Some of them nodded in polite acknowledgment; others glared at her. They probably blamed her for the career he had pursued, the career that had cost him his life. At the local community college where she taught journalism courses, she had recognized the kid's talent. She had even recommended he cover the story that had killed him, because it had been killing her that she couldn't cover it herself.

But she couldn't risk anyone recognizing her. Even though her appearance had changed, her writing style hadn't. If she had written the story, certain people would have recognized it as hers no matter whom the byline claimed had authored it. And Josie couldn't risk anyone realizing that she wasn't really dead.

That was her other reason for hating funerals—

because it reminded her of her own, of having to say goodbye to everyone she loved. She actually hadn't attended her funeral; her ashes hadn't been in the urn as everyone else had believed. But still she'd had to say goodbye to the only life she'd known in order to begin a new life under a new identity.

But apparently she wasn't making any better choices in this life than she had in her last, since innocent people were still getting hurt. She hadn't pulled the trigger and ended this young man's promising life. But she blamed herself nearly as much as some of these people blamed her. If only she hadn't mentioned her suspicions regarding the private psychiatric hospital and the things that were rumored to take place there…

The gnawing pangs of guilt were all too familiar to her. The first story she'd covered, back in college, had also cost a young man his life. But then she'd had someone to assure her that it wasn't her fault. Now she had no one to offer her assurances or comfort.

Chatter from the people in front of her drifted back. "Since Michael was hoping to sell the Serenity House story to one of Jessup Media's news outlets, I heard Stanley Jessup might attend the funeral."

Josie's breath caught with hope and panic. She wanted to see him. But she couldn't risk his *seeing* her. For his own protection, her father had to go on believing that his only child was dead.

"Not anymore," the other person responded. "He's in the hospital. They don't even know if he'll make it."

Josie leaned forward, ready to demand to know what had happened to her father. But before she could, the other person had already asked.

"He was attacked," the gossiper replied. "Someone tried to kill him."

Had all the sacrifices she'd made been for naught? Had her father been attacked because of her? And if so, then she'd done nothing to protect him except deprive him of what mattered most to him. She had already been guilt-ridden. Now that guilt intensified, overwhelming her.

If her father didn't make it, he would die never knowing the truth. She couldn't let that happen.

"JESSUP...HOSPITALIZED in critical condition..."

The breaking news announcement drew Brendan O'Hannigan's attention to the television mounted over the polished oak-and-brass bar of O'Hannigan's Tavern. At 9:00 a.m. it was too early for the establishment to be open to the public, but it was already doing business. Another kind of business than serving drinks or sandwiches. A dangerous kind of business that required his entire focus and control.

But Brendan ignored the men with whom he was meeting to listen to the rest of the report: "Nearly four years ago, media mogul Stanley Jessup's daughter died in a house explosion that authorities ruled arson. Despite her father's substantial resources, Josie Jessup's murder has never been solved."

"Josie Jessup?" one of the men repeated her name and then tapped the table in front of Brendan. "Weren't you dating her at one time?"

Another of the men snorted. "A reporter? Brendan would never date a reporter."

He cleared his throat, fighting back all the emotions just the sound of her name evoked. And it had been more than three years....

Wasn't it supposed to get easier? Weren't his memories of her supposed to fade? He shouldn't be able to see her as clearly as if she stood before him now, her pale green eyes sparkling and her long red hair flowing around her shoulders. Brendan could even hear her laughter tinkling in his ear.

"At the time I didn't know she was a reporter," he answered honestly, even though these were men he shouldn't trust with the truth. Hell, he shouldn't trust these men with anything.

He leaned back against the booth, and its stiff vinyl pushed the barrel of his gun into the small of his back. The bite of metal reassured him. It was just one of the many weapons he carried. That reassured him more.

The first man who'd spoken nodded and confirmed, "It wasn't common knowledge that the girl wanted to work for her father. All her life she had seemed more intent on spending his money, living the life of an American princess."

An American princess. That was exactly what Josie had been. Rich and spoiled, going after what she wanted no matter who might get hurt. She had hurt others—with the stories Brendan had discovered that she'd written under a pseudonym. Her exposés had started before she'd even graduated with her degree in journalism.

Brendan should have dug deeper until he'd learned the truth about her before getting involved with her. But the woman had pursued him and had been damn hard to resist. At least he had learned the truth about her before she'd managed to learn the truth about him. Somehow she must have discovered enough information to have gotten herself killed, though.

The news report continued: "The death of his daughter nearly destroyed Jessup, but the billionaire used his work to overcome his loss, much as he did when his wife died twenty years ago. The late Mrs. Jessup was European royalty."

"So she was a real princess," Brendan murmured, correcting himself.

"She was also a reporter," the other man said, his focus on Brendan, his dark eyes narrowed with suspicion.

It had taken Brendan four years to gain the small amount of trust and acceptance that he had from these men. He had been a stranger to them when he'd taken over the business he'd inherited from his late father. And these men didn't trust strangers.

Hell, they didn't trust anyone.

The man asked, "When did you learn that?"

Learn that Josie Jessup had betrayed him? That she'd just been using him to get another exposé for her father's media outlets?

Anger coursed through him and he clenched his jaw. His eyes must have also telegraphed that rage, for the men across the booth from him leaned back now as if trying to get away. Or to reassure themselves that they were armed, too.

"I found out Josie Jessup was a reporter," Brendan said, "right before she died."

It's too great a risk... She hadn't been able to reach her handler, the former U.S. marshal who had faked Josie's death and relocated her. But she didn't need to speak to Charlotte Green to know what she would have told her. *It's too great a risk...*

After nearly being killed for real almost four years ago, Josie knew how much danger she would be in were anyone to discover that she was still alive. She hadn't tried to call Charlotte again. She'd had no intention of listening to her anyway.

Josie stood outside her father's private hospital room, one hand pressed against the door. Coming here was indeed a risk, but the greater risk was that her father would die without her seeing him again.

Without him seeing her again. And…

Her hand that was not pressed against the door held another hand. Pudgy little fingers wriggled in her grasp. "Mommy, what we doin' here?"

Josie didn't have to ask herself that question. She knew that, no matter what the risk, she needed to be here. She needed to introduce her father to his grandson. "We're here to see your grandpa," she said.

"Grampa?" The three-year-old's little brow furrowed in confusion. He had probably heard the word before but never in reference to any relation of his. It had always been only the two of them. "I have a grampa?"

"Yes," Josie said. "But he lives far away so we didn't get to see him before now."

"Far away," he agreed with a nod and a yawn. He had slept through most of the long drive from northwestern Michigan to Chicago; his soft snoring had kept her awake and amused. His bright red curls were matted from his booster seat, and there was a trace of drool that had run from the corner of his mouth across his freckled cheek.

CJ glanced nervously around the wide corridor as if just now realizing where he was. He hadn't awakened until the elevator ride up to her father's floor. Then with protests that he wasn't a baby but a big boy now, he had wriggled out of her arms. "Does Grampa live here?"

"No," she said. "This is a hospital."

The little boy shuddered in revulsion. His low pain threshold for immunizations had given him a deep aversion to all things medical. He lowered his already soft voice to a fearful whisper. "Is—is Grampa sick?"

She whispered, too, so that nobody overheard them. A few hospital workers, men dressed in scrubs, lingered outside a room a few doors down from her father's. "He's hurt."

So where were the police or the security guards? Why was no one protecting him?

Because nobody cared about her father the way she did. Because she had been declared dead, he had no other next of kin. And as powerful and intimidating a man as he was, he had no genuine friends, either. His durable power of attorney was probably held by his lawyer. She'd claimed to be from his office when she'd called to find out her father's room number.

"Did he falled off his bike?" CJ asked.

"Something like that." She couldn't tell her son what had really happened, that her father had been assaulted in the parking garage of his condominium complex. Usually the security was very high there. No one got through the gate unless they lived in the building. Not only was it supposed to be safe, but it was his home. Yet someone had attacked him, striking him with something—a baseball bat or a pipe. His broken arm and bruised shoulder might not hurt him so badly if the assault hadn't also brought on a heart attack.

Would her showing up here as if from the dead bring on another one? Maybe that inner voice of hers, which sounded a hell of a lot like Charlotte's even though she hadn't talked to the woman, was right. The risk was too great.

"We shoulda brought him ice cream," CJ said. "Ice cream makes you feel all better."

Every time he had been brave for his shots she had rewarded him with ice cream. Always shy and nervous, CJ had to fight hard to be brave. Had she passed her own fears, of discovery and danger, onto her son?

"Yes, we should have," she agreed, and she pulled her hand away from the door. "We should do that…"

"Now?" CJ asked, his dark bluish-green eyes brightening with hope. "We gonna get ice cream now?"

"It's too late for ice cream tonight," she said. "But we can get some tomorrow."

"And bring it back?"

She wasn't sure about that. She would have to pose as the legal secretary again and learn more about her father's condition. Just how fragile was his health?

Josie turned away from the door and from the nearly overwhelming urge to run inside and into her father's arms—the way she always had as a child. She had hurled herself at him, secure that he would catch her.

She'd been so confident that he would always be there for her. She had never considered that he might be the one to leave—for real, for good—that he might be the one to really die. Given how young she was when her mother died, she should have understood how fragile life was. But her father wasn't fragile. He was strong and powerful. Invincible. Or so she had always believed.

But he wasn't. And she couldn't risk causing him harm only to comfort herself. She stepped away from the door, but her arm jerked as her son kept his feet planted on the floor.

"I wanna see Grampa," he said, his voice still quiet but his tone determined. Afraid to draw attention to himself, her son had never thrown a temper tantrum. He'd never even raised his voice. But he could be very stubborn when he put his mind to something. Kind of like the grandfather he'd suddenly decided he needed to meet.

"It's late," she reminded him. "He'll be sleeping and we shouldn't wake him up."

His little brow still furrowed, he stared up at her a moment as if considering her words. Then he nodded. "Yeah, you get cranky when I wake you up."

A laugh sputtered out of her lips. Anyone would get cranky if woken up at 5:00 a.m. to watch cartoons. "So we better make sure I get some sleep tonight." That meant postponing the drive back and getting a hotel. But she needed to be close to the hospital…in case her father took a turn for the worse. In case he needed her.

"And after you wake up we'll come back with ice cream?"

She hesitated before offering him a slight nod. But instead of posing as the lawyer's assistant again, she would talk to Charlotte.

Someone else had answered the woman's phone at the palace on the affluent island country of St. Pierre where Charlotte had gone to work as the princess's bodyguard after leaving the U.S. Marshals. That person had assured Josie that Charlotte would be back soon to return her call. But Josie hadn't left a message—she couldn't trust anyone but Charlotte with her life. Or her father's. She would talk to Charlotte and see what the former marshal could find out about Josie's father's condition and the attack. Then she would come back to see him.

Her son accepted her slight nod as agreement and finally moved away from the door to his grandfather's room. "Does Grampa like 'nilla ice cream or chocolate or cookie dough or…"

The kid was an ice-cream connoisseur, his list of flavors long and impressive. And Josie's stomach nearly growled with either hunger or nerves.

She interrupted him to ask, "Do you want to press the elevator button?"

His brow furrowing in concentration, he rose up on tiptoe and reached for the up arrow.

"No," she said. But it was too late, he'd already pressed it. "We need the down arrow." Before she could touch it, a hand wrapped around her wrist.

Her skin tingled and her pulse leaped in reaction. And she didn't need to lift her head to know who had touched her. Even after more than three years, she recognized his touch. But she lifted her head and gazed up at him, at his thick black hair that was given to curl, at his deep, turquoise-green eyes that could hold such passion. Now they held utter shock and confusion.

This was the man who'd killed her, or who would have killed her had the U.S. marshal and one of her security guards not diffused the bomb that had been set inside the so-called *safe* house. They had set it off later to stage her death.

Since he had wanted her dead so badly, he was not going to be happy to find her alive and unharmed—if he recognized her now. She needed for him *not* to recognize her, as she wasn't likely to survive his next murder attempt. Not when she was unprotected.

If only she'd listened to that inner voice…

The risk had been too great. Not just to her life but to what would become of her son once she was gone.

Would her little boy's father take him or kill him? Either way, the child was as doomed as she was.

Chapter Two

For more than three years, her memory had haunted Brendan—her image always in his mind. This woman didn't look like her, but she had immediately drawn his attention when he'd stepped out of the stairwell at the end of the hall. Her body was fuller and softer than Josie's thin frame had been. And her chin-length blond bob had nothing in common with Josie's long red hair. Yet something about her—the way she tilted her jaw, the sparkle in her eyes as she gazed down at the child—reminded him of her.

Then she'd spoken to the boy, and her soft voice had hit him like a blow to the stomach. While he might not have recognized her body or face, he could not mistake that voice as anyone's but hers. Her voice had haunted him, too.

Before he could recover, he turned his attention to the child and reeled from another blow. With his curly red hair and bright green eyes, the child was more recognizable than the woman. Except for that shock of bright hair, he looked exactly like the few childhood photos of Brendan that his stepmother hadn't managed to *accidentally* destroy.

He didn't even remember closing the distance between them, didn't remember reaching for her. But now he held her, his hand wrapped tightly around her delicate wrist.

She lifted her face to him, and he saw it now in the almond shape and silvery-green color of her eyes. What he didn't recognize was the fear that widened those eyes and stole the color from her face.

"Josie…?"

She shook her head in denial.

She must have had some cosmetic work done, because her appearance was different. Her cheekbones weren't as sharp, her chin not as pointy, her nose not as perfectly straight. This plastic surgeon had done the opposite of what was usually required; he'd made her perfect features imperfect—made her look less movie-star gorgeous and more natural.

Why would she have gone to such extremes to change her identity? With him, her effort was wasted. He would know her anywhere, just from the way his body reacted—tensing and tingling with attraction. And anger. But she was already afraid of him and he didn't want to scare the child, too, so he restrained his rage over her cruel deception.

"You're Josie Jessup."

She shook her head again and spoke, but this time her voice was little more than a raspy whisper. "You're mistaken. That's not my name."

The raspy whisper did nothing to disguise her voice, since it was how he best remembered her. A raspy whisper in his ear as they'd made love, his body thrusting into hers, hers arching to take him deep. Her nails digging into his shoulders and back as she'd screamed his name.

That was why he'd let her fool him once, why he'd

let her distract him when he had needed to be focused and careful. She had seduced and manipulated him with all her loving lies. She'd only wanted to get close to him so she could get a damn story. She hadn't realized how dangerous getting close to him really was. No matter what she'd learned, she didn't know the truth about him. And if he had anything to say about it, she never would. He wouldn't let her make a fool of him twice.

"If you're not Josie Jessup, what the—" He swallowed a curse for the child's sake. "What are you doing here?"

"We were gonna see my grampa," the little boy answered for her, "but we didn't wanna wake him up."

She was the same damn liar she had always been, but at least she hadn't corrupted the boy.

His son...

JOSIE RESISTED THE urge to press her palm over CJ's mouth. It was already too late. Why was it *now* that her usually shy son chose to speak to a stranger? And, moreover, to speak the truth? But her little boy was unfailingly honest, no matter the fact that his mother couldn't be. Especially now.

"But we got out on the wrong floor," she said. "This isn't where your grandfather's room is."

CJ shook his head. "No, we watched the numbers lighting up in the el'vator. You said number six. I know my numbers."

Now she cursed herself for working with the three-year-old so much that he knew all his numbers and letters. "Well, it's the wrong room."

"You said number—"

"Shh, sweetheart, you're tired and must not remember correctly," she said, hoping that her son picked up the warning and the fear in her voice now. "We need to leave. It's late. We need to get you to bed."

But those strong masculine fingers were still wrapped tight around her wrist. "You're not going anywhere."

"You have no right to keep me," she said.

With his free hand, he gestured toward CJ. "He gives me the right. I have a lot of rights you've apparently denied me."

"I—I don't know what you're talking about." Why the hell would she have told the man who'd tried to kill her that she was pregnant with his baby? If his attempts had been successful, he would have killed them both.

"You know exactly what I'm talking about, Josie."

CJ tugged on her hand and whispered loudly, "Mommy, why does the man keep calling you that?"

Now he supported her lie—too late. "I don't know, honey," she said. "He has me mixed up with someone else he must have known."

"No," Brendan said. "I never really knew Josie Jessup at all."

No. He hadn't. Or he would have realized that she was too smart to have ever really trusted him. If only she'd been too smart to fall for him...

But the man was as charming as he was powerful. And when he'd touched her, when he'd kissed her, she had been unable to resist that charm.

"Then it's no wonder that you've mistaken me for her," Josie said, "since you didn't really know her very well."

She furrowed her brow and acted as if a thought had just occurred to her. "Josie Jessup? Isn't that the daughter of the media mogul? I thought she died several years ago."

"That was obviously what she wanted everyone to believe—that she was dead," he said. "Or was it just me?"

She shrugged. "I wouldn't know." *You. Just you.* But unfortunately, for him to accept the lie, everyone else had had to believe it, too. "I am not her. She must really be gone."

And if she'd had any sense, she would have stayed gone. Well away from her father and this man.

"Why are *you* here?" she asked. "Are you visiting someone?"

Or knowing all this time that she wasn't really dead, had he set a trap for her? Was he the one who had attacked her father? According to the reports from all her father's media outlets, there was no suspect yet in his assault. But she had one now.

She needed to call Charlotte. But the phone was in her purse, and she had locked her purse in her vehicle so that if anyone was to recognize her, they wouldn't be able to find her new identity.

"It doesn't matter why I'm here—just that I am," he said, dodging her question as he had so many other questions she had asked him during the months they'd been together. "And so are you."

"Not anymore. We're leaving," she said, as much to CJ as to Brendan. As if on cue, the elevator ground to a stop, and the doors slid open. She moved to step into the car, but her wrist was clutched so tightly she couldn't move.

"That one's going up," Brendan pointed out.

"As I said, we got off on the wrong floor." She tugged hard on her wrist, but his grip didn't ease. She didn't want to scream and alarm her already trembling son, so through gritted teeth she said, "Let go of me."

But he stepped closer. He was so damn big, all broad muscles and tension. There were other bulges beneath the jacket of his dark tailored suit—weapons. He had always carried guns. He'd told her it was because of the dangerous people who resented his inheriting his father's businesses.

But she'd wondered then if he'd been armed for protection or intimidation. She was intimidated, so intimidated that she cared less about scaring her son than she did about protecting him. So she screamed.

HER SCREAM STARTLED Brendan and pierced the quiet of the hospital corridor. But he didn't release her until her son—*their* son—launched himself at Brendan. His tiny feet kicked at Brendan's shins and his tiny fists flailed, striking Brendan's thighs and hips.

"Leggo my mommy! Leggo my mommy!"

The boy's reaction and fear startled Brendan into stepping back. Josie's wrist slipped from his grasp. She used her freed hand to catch their son's flailing fists and tug him close to her.

Before Brandon could reach for her again, three men dressed in hospital scrubs rushed up from the room they'd been loitering near down the hall. Brendan had noted their presence but had been too distracted to realize that they were watching him.

Damn! He had been trained to constantly be aware of his surroundings and everyone in them. Only Josie had ever made him forget his training to trust no one.

"What's going on?" one of the men asked.

"This man accosted me and my son," Josie replied, spewing more lies. "He tried to grab me."

Brendan struggled to control his anger. The boy—his boy—was already frightened of him. He couldn't add to that fear by telling the truth. So he stepped back again in order to appear nonthreatening, when all he wanted to do was threaten.

"We'll escort you to your car, ma'am," another of the men offered as he guided her and the child into the waiting elevator.

"Don't let her leave," Brendan advised. Because if she left, he had no doubt that he would never see her and his son again. This time she would stay gone. He moved forward, reaching for those elevator doors before they could shut on Josie and their son.

But strong hands closed around his arms, dragging him back, while another man joined Josie inside the elevator. Just as the doors slid shut, Brendan noticed the telltale bulge of a weapon beneath the man's scrubs. He carried a gun at the small of his back.

Brendan shrugged off the grasp of the man who held him. Then he whirled around to face him. But now he faced down the barrel of his gun. Why were he and at least one of the other men armed? They weren't hospital security, and he doubted like hell that they were orderlies.

Who were they? And more important, who had sent them?

The guy warned Brendan, "Don't be a hero, man."

He laughed incredulously at the idea of anyone considering *him* a hero. "Do you know who I am?"

"I don't care who the hell you are," the guy replied, as he cocked the gun, "and neither will this bullet."

Four years ago Brendan's father had learned that it didn't matter who he was, either. When he'd been shot in the alley behind O'Hannigan's early one morning, that bullet had made him just as dead as anyone else who got shot. Even knowing the dangerous life his father had led, his murder had surprised Brendan.

As the old man had believed himself invincible, so had Brendan. Or maybe he just remembered being fifteen, running away from the strong, ruthless man and never looking back.

But Dennis O'Hannigan's death had brought Brendan back to Chicago and to the life he'd sworn he'd never live. Most people thought he'd come home to claim his inheritance. Even now he couldn't imagine why the old man had left everything to him.

They hadn't spoken in more than fifteen years, even though his father had known where Brendan was and what he'd been doing. No one had ever been able to hide from Dennis O'Hannigan—not his friends or his family and certainly not his enemies.

Which one had ended the old man's life?

Brendan had really returned to claim justice. No matter how ruthless his father had been, he deserved to have his murder solved, his killer punished.

Some people thought Brendan had committed the murder—out of vengeance and greed. He had certainly had reasons for wanting revenge. His father had been as cruel a father and husband as he'd been a crime boss.

And as a crime boss, the man had acquired a fortune—a destiny and a legacy that he'd left to his only blood relative. Because, since his father's death, Brendan was the only O'Hannigan left in the family. Or so he'd thought until he'd met his son tonight.

He couldn't lose the boy before he even got to know him. No matter how many people thought of him as a villain, he would have to figure out a way to be the hero.

He had to save his son.

And Josie.

Four years ago she must have realized that she was in danger—that must have been why she'd staged her own death. Had she realized yet that those men in the elevator with her were not orderlies or interns but dangerous gunmen? Had she realized that she was in as much or more danger now than she'd been in before?

Chapter Three

Fear gripped Josie. She was more scared now than she'd been when Brendan wouldn't let go of her. Maybe her pulse raced and her heart hammered just in reaction to his discovering her. Or maybe it was because she wasn't entirely certain she had really gotten away from him…even as the doors slid closed between them.

"Thank you," she told the men. "I really appreciate your helping me and my son to safety."

"Was that man threatening you?" one of them asked.

She nodded. More threatening than they could possibly understand. Brendan O'Hannigan could take even more from her now than just her life. He could take away her son.

"H-he's a b-bad man," CJ stammered. The little boy trembled with fear and the aftereffects of his physical defense of his mother.

"Are you okay?" she asked him, concerned that he'd gotten hurt when he'd flung himself at Brendan. She couldn't believe her timid son had summoned that much courage and anger. And she hated that she'd been so careless with their safety that she'd put him in such a dangerous predicament. Dropping to her knees in front of her son, she inspected him to see if he had been harmed.

His little face was flushed nearly as bright red as his tousled curls. His eyes glistened with tears he was fighting hard not to shed. He blinked furiously and bit his bottom lip. Even at three, he was too proud to cry in front of strangers. He nodded.

Her heart clutched in her chest, aching with love and pride. "You were so brave." She wound her arms tightly around him and lifted him up as she stood again. Maybe a good parent would have admonished him for physically launching himself at a stranger. But it was so hard for him to be courageous that she had to praise his efforts. "Thank you for protecting Mommy."

She hadn't been able to shake Brendan's strong grip. But CJ's attack had caught the mobster off guard so that he'd released her and stepped back. She released a shuddery breath of relief that he hadn't hurt her son.

CJ wrapped his pudgy little legs around her waist and clung to her, his slight body trembling against her. "The bad man is gone?"

"He's gone."

But for how long? Had he just taken the stairs to meet the elevator when it stopped? CJ had pushed the up arrow, so the car was going to the roof. She doubted Brendan would waste his time going up. Instead he would have more time to get down to the lobby and lay in wait for her and CJ to leave for the parking garage.

And if he followed her there, she would have no protection against him. Unlike him, she carried no weapons. Just a can of mace and that was inside her purse, which she had locked in her vehicle.

But these men had promised to see her safely to her car. Surely they would protect her against Brendan…

But who would protect her from them?

The thought slipped unbidden into her mind, making her realize why her pulse hadn't slowed. She didn't feel safe yet.

Not with them.

Balancing CJ on her hip and holding him with just one arm, she reached for the panel of buttons. But one of the men stepped in front of it, blocking her from the lobby or the emergency call button. Then the other man stepped closer to her, trapping her and CJ between them.

She clutched her son more closely to her chest and glanced up at the illuminated numbers above the doors. They were heading toward the roof. Why hadn't they pushed other buttons to send the car back down? These men would have no patients to treat up there. But then, just because they wore scrubs didn't mean that they actually worked at the hospital.

When Charlotte had relocated her more than three years ago, she'd taught Josie to trust no one but her. And her own instincts. She should have heeded that warning before she'd stepped inside the elevator with these men. She should have heeded that warning before she'd driven back to Chicago.

"My son and I need to leave," she said, wishing now that she had never left her safe little home in Michigan. But she'd been so worried about her father that she'd listened to her heart instead of her head.

"That's the plan, Miss Jessup," the one standing in front of the elevator panel replied. "To get you out of here."

Somehow she suspected he wasn't talking about just getting her out of the hospital. And, like Brendan, he had easily recognized her.

She should have heeded Charlotte's other advice all those years ago to have more plastic surgery. But Josie had stopped when she'd struggled to recognize her own face in the mirror. She hadn't wanted to forget who she was. But maybe she should have taken that risk. It was definitely safer than the risk she'd taken in coming to see her father.

She feared that risk was going to wind up costing her everything.

"COME ON, GUY, just walk away," the pseudo-orderly advised Brendan.

"You don't want to shoot me," Brendan warned, stepping closer to the man instead of walking away. That had always been his problem. Once he got out of trouble, the way he had when he'd run away nearly twenty years ago, he turned around and headed right back into it—even deeper than before.

The other man shrugged. "Doesn't matter to me. The security cameras are not functioning up here."

Brendan suspected that had been intentional. While he had been completely shocked to see Josie, these men had been expecting her. They had actually been waiting for her...with disabled security cameras and weapons.

So Stanley Jessup's assault hadn't been such a random act of violence. It was the trap that had been used to draw Josie out of hiding.

Was he the only one who hadn't known that she was really alive?

"And Jessup, who's heavily drugged, is the only patient in a room near here. So by the time someone responds to the sound of the shot," the man brazenly bragged, "I'll be gone. We planned our escape route."

Brendan needed to plan his, too. But he didn't intend to escape danger. He planned to confront it head-on and eliminate the threat.

"In fact," the man continued, his ruddy face contorting with a smirk, "it would be better to kill you than leave you behind as a potential witness." He lifted the gun, so there was no way the bullet would miss. Then he cocked the trigger.

Brendan had a gun, too, holstered under his arm. And another at his back. And one strapped to his ankle. But before he could pull any of them, he would have a bullet in his head. So instead of fighting with a weapon, he used his words.

"I'm Brendan O'Hannigan," he said, "and that's why you don't want to shoot me."

First the man snorted derisively as if the name meant nothing to him. Then he repeated it, "O'Hannigan," as if trying to place where he'd heard it before. Then his eyes widened and his jaw dropped open as recognition struck him with the same force as if Brendan had swung his fist at him. "Oh, shit."

That was how people usually reacted when they learned his identity—except for Josie. She had acted as if she'd known nothing of his family or their dubious family business. And she had gotten close to him, with her impromptu visits to the tavern and her persistent flirting, before he'd realized that she had been doing just that: acting.

She had known exactly who he was or she would have never sought him out. She'd been after a scoop for her father's media outlets. Even after all those other stories she'd brought to him, she'd still been trying to prove herself to *Daddy*.

Brendan had devoted himself to just the opposite, trying to prove himself as unlike his father as possible.

Until the old man had died, drawing Brendan back into a life that he had been unable to run far enough away from when he was a kid.

"Yeah, if you shoot me, you better hope the police find you before any of my family does," Brendan warned the man. But it was a bluff.

He really had no idea what his "family" would do or if they would even care. He was the only one who cared about his father's murder—enough to risk everything for justice. Hell, his "family," given the way they'd resented his return and his inheritance, would probably be relieved if he died, especially if they knew the truth about him.

The man stepped back and lifted his gun so that the barrel pointed toward the ceiling, waving it around as if there were a white flag of surrender tied to the end of it. "I don't want any trouble—any of *your* kind of trouble."

Brendan didn't want that kind of trouble, either. But it was too late. He was in too deep now—so deep that he hadn't been able to get out even after he'd thought Josie had been killed. But then her death had made him even more determined to pursue justice.

"If you didn't want trouble," Brendan said, "then you shouldn't have messed with my son and his mother." Now he swung his fist into the man's face.

The guy fell back, but before he went down, Brendan snapped the gun from his grasp and turned it on him. There was no greater power play than turning a man's own gun on him. His father had taught him that, starting his lessons when Brendan was only a few years older than his son was now.

"What the hell do you want with her?" he demanded.

"I just got paid to do a job, man," the man in scrubs said, cringing away from the barrel pointed in his face.

"What's the job?"

The man opened his mouth but hesitated before speaking, until Brendan cocked the trigger. Then he blurted out, "To kill Josie Jessup!"

"Damn it!" he cursed at having his suspicions confirmed.

He had only just discovered that she was alive and that she'd given birth to his son. He didn't want to lose the boy before he'd gotten the chance to claim him. And he didn't want Josie to die again. He glanced back at the elevator, at the numbers above the doors that indicated it had stopped—on the top floor.

"You're not going to make it," the man advised. "You're not going to be able to save her."

Brendan cursed again because the guy was probably right. But still he had to try. He turned the gun and swung the handle at the man's head.

One down. Two to go...

THE WIND ON the roof was cold, whipping through Josie's light jacket and jeans. She slipped the side of her unzipped jacket over CJ's back to shield him from the cold bite of the breeze. He snuggled against her, his face pressed into her neck. Her skin was damp from the quiet tears he surreptitiously shed. He must have felt the fear and panic that clutched at her, and he trembled with it while she tensely held herself together.

She had to do something. She had to make certain these men didn't hurt her son. But since she hadn't reached Charlotte, earlier, the former U.S. marshal couldn't come to her rescue as she had last time. Josie had only herself—and the instincts she'd previously ignored—to help her now.

The two men were huddled together just a few feet away from them, between her and CJ and the elevator. There was no way to reach it without going through them. And with the bulges of weapons at their backs, she didn't dare try to go through them. Nor did she want to risk turning her back on them to run, for fear that they would shoot. And since they were on the roof, where could she go? How far could she run without falling over the side?

One of the men spoke into a cell phone about the change in plans: *CJ.*

While they had somehow discovered that she was really alive, they must not have been aware that she was pregnant when she'd gone into hiding.

Despite the fact that he'd lowered his voice, it carried on the wind, bringing the horrifying words to her.

"…never agreed to do a kid."

"…someone else knows she's alive and hassled her in the hall."

Because Brendan wasn't any happier she was alive than these men apparently were. Of course he hadn't seemed as eager to rectify that as they were.

"Okay, I understand," said the man holding the phone before he clicked it off and slid it back into his pocket. Then he turned to his co-conspirator and nodded. "We have to eliminate them both."

A shudder of fear and revulsion rippled through Josie. Thankfully CJ wouldn't understand what they meant by "eliminate." But eventually he would figure it out, when he stared down the barrel of a gun.

"I don't know what you're getting paid to do this," she addressed the men as they turned toward her. "But

I have money. Lots of money. I can pay you more than you're getting now."

The man who'd been on the phone chuckled bitterly. "We were warned you might make that offer. But you forfeited your access to that money when you faked your death, lady."

They were right. Josie Jessup's bank accounts and trust fund had closed when she'd *died*. And JJ Brandt's salary from the community college was barely enough to cover her rent, utilities and groceries. She had nothing in her savings account to offer them.

"My father would pay you," she said, "whatever you ask." But first they would have to prove to him that she was really alive. She hadn't dared step inside his room. What would happen if gunmen burst inside with her? The shock would surely bring on another heart attack—maybe a fatal one.

The men shared a glance, obviously debating her offer. But then one of them shook his head. "This is about more than money, lady."

"What is it about?" she asked.

As far she knew, Brendan was the only one with any reason to want her dead. If these men worked for him, they wouldn't have held him back from boarding the elevator with her. If they worked for him, they wouldn't have dared to touch him at all. She still couldn't believe that she had dared to touch him, that she'd dared to go near him even to pursue her story. The police had been unable to determine who had killed his father, the legendary crime boss, so she had vowed to find out if there was any truth to the rumors that Dennis O'Hannigan's runaway son had killed him out of revenge and greed.

She had found something else entirely. More than the story, she had been attracted to the man—the complex man who had been grieving the death of his estranged father while trying to take over his illicit empire. She had never found evidence proving Brendan was the killer, but he must have been worried that she'd discovered something. Why else would he have tried to kill her?

Just because he'd learned she'd been lying to him about what she really was? Maybe. He'd been furious with her—furious enough to want revenge. But if he wasn't behind this attempt to eliminate her, had he been behind that bomb planted more than three years ago?

Could she have been wrong about him?

"I have a right to know," she prodded, wanting the truth. That was her problem—she always wanted the truth. It was what had made her such a great reporter before she'd been forced to give it all up to save her life. But since it was probably her last chance to learn it, she wanted this truth more than she'd ever wanted any other. If not Brendan, who wanted her dead?

"It doesn't matter what it's about," one of the men replied.

She suspected he had no idea, either, that he was just doing what he had been paid to do.

"It's not going to change the outcome for you and your son," the fake orderly continued as he reached behind him and drew out his gun.

What about her father? Had he only been attacked to lure her out of hiding? Was he safe now?

If only her son was safe, too…

She covered the side of CJ's cold, damp face with her hand so that he wouldn't see the weapon. Then she turned, putting her body between the boy and the men. Her body wouldn't be enough to protect her son, though. Nothing could protect him now. "Please…"

But if the men wouldn't respond to bribes, they would have no use for begging, either. So she just closed her eyes and prayed as the first shot rang out.

Chapter Four

Was he too late?

As the elevator doors slid open, a shot rang out. But the bullet ricocheted off the back of the car near his head. Both men faced *him* with their guns raised. Maybe this had nothing to do with Josie.

Maybe the woman wasn't even really her and the boy not really even his son. Maybe it had all been an elaborate trap to lure him here—to his death. Plenty of people wanted him dead. That was why he usually had backup within gunshot range. But he hadn't wanted anyone to be aware of his visit to the bedside of a man he didn't really know but with whom he'd thought he'd shared a tragedy: Josie's death.

So nobody had known he was coming here. These men weren't after him, because the suspects he knew wouldn't have gone to such extremes to take him out; they wouldn't have had to. Whenever they dared to try to take him out, as they had his father, they knew where to find him—at O'Hannigan's. Inside the family tavern was where Josie had found him. He'd thought the little rich girl had just wandered into the wrong place with the wrong clientele, and he'd rescued her before any of his rough customers could accost her.

Just as he had intended to rescue her now. But both times he was the one who wound up needing to be rescued. Maybe he should have had backup even for this uncomfortable visit. With the elevator doors wide open, Brendan was a damn sitting duck, more so even than the woman and the boy. They might be able to escape. Seeing the fear on their faces, pale and stark in the light spilling out of the elevator, it was clear that they were in real danger and they knew it.

"Run!" he yelled at them.

She sprinted away, either in reaction to his command or in fear of him as well as the armed men. With her and the kid out of the line of fire, he raised the gun he'd taken off their co-conspirator.

But the men had divided their attention now. Standing back-to-back, one fired at him while the other turned his gun toward Josie.

The boy clutched tightly in her arms, she ran, disappearing into the shadows before any bullets struck her. But maybe running wasn't a good thing, given that the farther away she went, the thicker the shadows grew. The light from the elevator illuminated only a small circle of the rooftop around the open doors. The farther she ran, the harder it would be for her to see where the roof ended and the black abyss twenty stories above the ground began.

He ducked back into the elevator and flattened himself against the panel beside the doors. He could have closed those doors to protect himself. But then he couldn't protect Josie and the child. *His son...*

These men weren't just trying to kill the woman who was supposed to already be dead. They were trying to kill a helpless child.

An O'Hannigan.

His father would be turning over in his grave.

Despite his occasional violent behavior toward them, Dennis O'Hannigan had never really wanted his family harmed—at least not by anyone but him. Brendan didn't want his family harmed at all. He kept one finger on the button to hold open the doors. Then he leaned out and aimed the gun. And squeezed the trigger.

His shots drew all the attention to him. Bullets pinged off the brass handrail and shattered the smoky glass of the elevator car. The glass splintered and ricocheted like the bullets, biting into his skin like a swarm of bees.

His finger jerked off the button, and the doors began to close. But he couldn't leave Josie and the child alone up here with no protection. Despite the other man's warning, he had to play the hero. But it had been nearly four years since he'd been anything but the villain.

Had he gotten rusty? Would he be able to protect them? Or had his arrival put them in even more danger?

"THEY'RE ALL BAD men," CJ said, his voice high and squeaky with fear and panic. "They're bad! Bad!"

He was too young to have learned just how evil some people were. As his mother, Josie was supposed to protect him, but she'd endangered his life and his innocence. She had to do her best to keep her little boy a little boy until he had the time to grow into a man.

"Shh..." Josie cautioned him. "We need to be very quiet."

"So they don't find us?"

"First we have to find a hiding place." Which wouldn't be easy in a darkness so enveloping she could barely see the child she held tightly against her.

She had been able to see the shots—those brief flashes of gunpowder. She'd run from those flashes, desperate to keep her son safe. But now those shots were redirected toward Brendan, and running wouldn't keep CJ safe since she couldn't see where she was going. She moved quickly but carefully, testing her footing before she stepped forward.

"Are they shooting real bullets?" he asked.

To preserve that innocence she was afraid he was losing, she could have lied. But that lie could risk his life.

"They're real," she replied, aware that they'd come all too close to her and CJ. "That's why we need to find a place to hide until the police come."

Someone must have heard the shots and reported them by now. Help had to be on the way. Hopefully it would arrive in time to save her and her son. But what about Brendan? He had stepped into the middle of an attempted murder—a double homicide, actually. And he hadn't done it accidentally. He had tracked her to the roof, maybe to kill her himself. But perhaps he'd be the one to lose his life, since the men were now entirely focused on him.

She shuddered, the thought chilling her nearly as much as the cold wind that whipped around the unprotected rooftop.

"Let's go back there, Mommy," CJ said, lifting his hand, which caught her attention only because she felt the movement more than saw it.

"Where?" she asked.

"Behind those big metal things."

She peered in the direction he was pointing and finally noted the glint of some stray starlight off steel vents, probably exhaust pipes for the hospital's heating or cooling system. If only they could escape inside them…

But she could barely move around them, let alone find a way inside them. The openings were too high above the rooftop, towering over her. As she tried to squeeze around them, her hip struck the metal. She winced and swallowed a groan of pain. And hoped the men hadn't heard the telltale metallic clink.

"Shh, Mommy," CJ cautioned her. "We don't want the bad men to hear us."

"No, we don't," she agreed.

"They might find our hiding place."

"I'm not sure we can hide here," she whispered. She couldn't wedge them both between the massive pipes. The metal caught at her clothes and scraped her arms. "We can't fit."

"Let me try," he suggested. Before she could agree, he wriggled down from her arms and squeezed through the small space.

She reached through the blackness, trying to clutch at him, trying to pull him back. What if he'd fallen right off the building?

She had no idea how much space was on the other side of the pipes. A tiny ledge? None?

A scream burned in her throat, but she was too scared to utter it—too horrified that in trying to protect her son she may have lost him forever.

But then chubby fingers caught hers. He tugged on her hand. "Come on, Mommy. There's room."

"You're not at the edge of the roof?" she asked, worried that he might be in more danger where he was.

"Nooo," he murmured, his voice sounding as if he'd turned away from her. "There's a little wall right behind me."

"Don't go over that wall," she advised. It was probably the edge of the roof, a small ledge to separate the rooftop from the ground far below. A curious little boy might want to figure out what was on the other side of that wall.

"Okay, Mommy," he murmured again, his voice still muffled. Was he trying to peer over the side?

She needed to get to him, needed to protect him, from the men and from himself. She turned sideways and pushed herself against the space where CJ had so effortlessly disappeared. But her breasts and hips—curves she'd barely had until her pregnancy with him—caught. She sucked in her stomach, but it made no difference. She couldn't suck in her breasts or hips. "I can't fit."

CJ tugged harder on her hand. "C'mon, Mommy, it's a good hiding place."

"No, honey," she corrected him, her pulse tripping with fear that he'd go over the wall, "you need to come back out. We'll find another one."

But then she heard it. She tilted her head and listened harder. And still it was all she heard: silence. The shooting had stopped.

What did that mean?

Was Brendan dead? Were the men? Whoever had survived would be searching for her next—for her and her son. The silence broke, shattered by the scrape of a shoe against the asphalt roofing.

She sucked in a breath now—of fear. But it didn't make it any easier for her to squeeze through the small space. And maybe pulling CJ out wasn't the best idea, not when he was safe from the men.

She dropped his fingers. "You stay here," she said. "In the best hiding place."

"I wanna hide with you."

"I'll find a bigger hiding place," she said. "You need to stay here and play statue for me."

She had played the game as a kid when she'd pretended to be a statue, completely still and silent. On those mornings that CJ had woken her up at five, she'd taught him to play statue so she could sleep just a little longer. Now acting lifeless was perhaps the only way for CJ to stay alive.

The footfalls grew louder as someone drew closer. She had to get out of here, had to distract whoever it was from CJ's hiding place. But first she had to utter one more warning. "Don't come out for anyone but me."

Her son was such a good boy. So smart and so obedient. She didn't have to worry that anyone else would lure him out of hiding. She just had to make sure that she stayed alive, so that he would come out when it was safe. So she drew in a deep breath and headed off, moving as fast as she dared in the darkness. She glanced back, but night had swallowed those metal vent pipes and had swallowed her son. Would she be able to find him again, even if she eluded whoever had survived the earlier gun battle?

She would worry about finding him after she found a hiding spot for herself. But it was so dark she could barely see where she was going. So she wasn't surprised when she collided with a wall.

But this wasn't a short brick wall like the one CJ had found behind the pipes. This wall was broad and muscular and warm. Her hands tingled in reaction to the chest she touched, her palms pressed against the lapels of a suit. The other men had been wearing scrubs, which would have been scratchy and flat.

And she wouldn't have reacted this way to them. Her skin wouldn't tingle; her pulse wouldn't leap. And she wouldn't feel something very much like relief that he was alive. No matter what threat he posed to her, she hadn't wanted him dead.

"Brendan...?"

IT WAS HER. Despite her physical transformation, he'd recognized her. But now he had not even a fraction of a doubt. That voice in the darkness...

Her touch...

He recognized all that about her, too.

But more importantly, *she* had recognized *him*. If she was truly a stranger that he had mistaken for his former lover and betrayer, she wouldn't know his name. Or, if by some chance, she had just recognized him as the son of a notorious mobster, she wouldn't have been comfortable and familiar enough to call him by his first name.

"Yes, Josie, it's me," he assured her.

She shuddered and her hands began to tremble against his chest. "You—you," she stammered. "You're..."

He was shaking a little himself in reaction to what had nearly happened. Adrenaline and fear coursed through him, pumping his blood fast and hard through his veins. "You know who I am. You just said my name," he pointed out. "And I damn well know who you are. So let's cut the bullshit. We don't have time for it. We need to get the hell out of here!"

She expelled a ragged sigh of resignation, as if she had finally given up trying to deny her true identity. Her palms patted his chest as if checking for bullet holes. "You didn't get shot?"

"No." But he suspected he had come uncomfortably close. If either of the gunmen, who were probably hired assassins, had been a better shot than he was, Josie would be in an entirely different situation right now.

As if she sensed that, she asked, "And those men?"

Brendan flinched with a pang of regret. But he had had no choice. If he hadn't shot the men, they would have killed him. And then they would have found Josie and the boy and killed them, too.

"They're not a threat. But the guy I left on the floor by your father's room could be."

Her breath audibly caught in a gasp of fear. "You left him there? He could hurt my father."

The assailant was in no condition to hurt anyone. Unless he'd regained consciousness…

"I don't think your father is their target," Brendan pointed out.

"They hurt him already," she said, reminding him of the reason the media mogul was in the hospital in the first place. Because he'd been attacked.

"That must have been just to lure you out of hiding." Someone had gone to a lot of trouble to track her down, and that someone was obviously very determined to do what Brendan had thought had been done almost four years ago. Kill Josie Jessup. If only he had had more time to interrogate the man downstairs, to find out who had hired him.

"They have no reason to hurt your father now," Brendan assured her before adding the obvious. "It's you they're after."

"And my son," she said, her voice cracking with emotion. "They were going to hurt him, too."

"Where is he?" he asked. His eyes had adjusted

to the darkness enough to see her before him now. "Where's my son?"

She shuddered again. "He's not your son."

"Stop," he impatiently advised her. "Just stop with the lies." She'd told him too many four years ago. "You need to get the boy and we need to get the hell out of here."

Because the bad men weren't the only threat.

Sirens wailed in the distance. Maybe just an ambulance on its way to the emergency room. Or maybe police cars on their way to secure a crime scene. He couldn't risk the latter. He couldn't be brought in for questioning or, worse, arrested. The local police wouldn't care that it had been self-defense; they were determined to arrest him for something. Anything. That was why Brendan had used the other fake orderly's gun. No bullets could be traced back to him. He'd wiped his prints off the weapon and left it on the roof.

"I'm not leaving with you," she said. "And neither is *my* son."

"You're in danger," he needlessly pointed out. "And you've put him in danger."

She sucked in a breath, either offended or feeling guilty. "And leaving with you would put us both in even more danger."

Now he drew in a sharp breath of pure offense. "If I wanted you gone, Josie, I could have just let those men shoot you."

"But they weren't going to shoot just me."

He flinched again at the thought of his child in so much danger. Reaching out, he grasped her shoulders. "Where is my son?" he repeated, resisting the urge to shake the truth out of her. "Someone wants you both dead. You can't let him out of your sight." And he couldn't let either of them out of his.

"I—I…"

"I won't hurt you," he assured her. "And I sure as hell won't hurt him."

Her head jerked in a sharp nod as if she believed him. He felt the motion more than saw it as her silky hair brushed his chin. She stepped back and turned around and then around again in a complete circle, as if trying to remember where she'd been.

"Where did you hide him?" he asked, hoping like hell that she had hidden him and hadn't just lost him.

"It was behind some exhaust pipes," she said. "I couldn't fit but he squeezed behind them. I—I just don't remember where they were."

"What's his name?"

She hesitated a moment before replying, as if his knowing his name would make the boy more real for Brendan. "CJ."

Maybe she was right—knowing the boy's name did make him more real to Brendan. His heart pounded and his pulse raced as he reeled from all the sudden realizations. He had a son. He was a father. He was continuing the "family" of which *he* had never wanted to be part.

"CJ," he repeated, then raised his voice and shouted, "CJ!"

"Shh." Josie cautioned him.

"He might not hear me if I don't yell," he pointed out. And Brendan needed to see his boy, to assure himself that his child was real and that he was all right.

"He won't come out if he hears *you,*" she explained. "He thinks you're a bad man."

Brendan flinched. It didn't matter that everyone else thought so; he didn't want his son to believe the lie, too.

"Is that what you told him?" he asked. It must have been what she'd believed all these years, because no matter how determined a reporter she'd been, she hadn't learned the truth about him.

"It's what you showed him," she said, "when you grabbed me by the elevator."

Dread and regret clenched his stomach muscles. His own son was afraid of him. How would he ever get close to the boy, ever form a relationship with him, if the kid feared him?

He flashed back so many years ago to his own heart pounding hard with fear as he cowered from his father, from the boom of his harsh voice and the sting of his big hand. Brendan hadn't just feared Dennis O'Hannigan. He'd been terrified of the man. But then so had everyone else.

"I'll be quiet," he whispered his promise. "You find him."

She called for the boy, her voice rising higher with panic each time she said his name. "CJ? CJ?" Then she sucked in a breath and her voice was steadier as she yelled, in a mother's no-nonsense tone, what must have been his full name, "Charles Jesse Brandt!"

Brandt? The boy's last name should have been O'Hannigan. But maybe it was better that it wasn't. Being an O'Hannigan carried with it so many dangers.

But then danger had found the boy no matter what his mother called him. CJ didn't respond to that maternal command only the rare child dared to disobey. Brendan certainly never would have disobeyed.

Panic clutched at his chest as worst-case scenarios began to play out in his mind. He had seen so many horrible things in his life that the possibilities kept coming. Had the man from the sixth floor somehow joined them on the roof without Brendan noticing? Had he found the boy already?

Another scenario played through his head, of Josie lying to him again. Still. Had she hidden the child and told him not to come out for Brendan? She'd hidden his son from him for three years—a few more minutes weren't going to bother her.

"Where is he?" he asked, shoving his hands in his pockets so that he wouldn't reach for her again. He had already frightened her, which was probably why she'd hidden their son from him.

She shook her head. "I don't know." The panic was in her voice, too.

Brendan almost preferred to think that she was lying to him and knew where the boy was, having made certain he was safe.

Her hand slapped against a metal pipe. "I thought he was behind here. CJ! CJ!"

"Then why isn't he coming out?" Brendan had stayed quiet and now kept his voice to a whisper despite the panic clutching at him.

"No, it can't be..." she murmured, her voice cracking with fear and dread.

"What?" He demanded to know the thought that occurred to her, that had her trembling now with fear.

"He's at the edge of the roof," she said. "He told me there was a short wall behind him. I—I told him not to go over it..."

Because there would have been nothing but the ground, twenty stories below, on the other side. If the boy was still on the roof with them, he would answer his mother. Even if he heard Brendan, he would come out to protect her, as he did before.

Oh, God!

Had Brendan lost his son only moments after finally finding him?

Chapter Five

Tears stung Josie's eyes, blinding her even more than the darkness. And sobs clogged her throat, choking her. She had been trying to protect her son, but she'd put him in more danger. She clawed at the pipes, trying to force them apart, trying to force her way back to where her son had been last.

"CJ! CJ!" she cried, her voice cracking with fear she could no longer contain.

She hadn't made sacrifices only to protect her father; she had made them to protect her baby, too. If she hadn't learned she was pregnant, she wouldn't have agreed to let her father hire bodyguards after the first attempt on her life—a cut brake line. And if she hadn't realized that no one could keep them truly safe, she wouldn't have agreed to fake her death and disappear.

Everything she'd done, she'd done for her son. Maybe that was why she'd brought him to see her father—not just so the two could finally meet, but so that her father would understand why she'd hurt him so badly. As a parent himself, he would have to understand and forgive her.

"CJ..." The tears overtook her now.

"Shh," a deep voice murmured, and a strong hand grasped her shoulder.

But the man didn't offer comfort.

"Shh," he said again, as a command. And his hand squeezed. "Listen."

Since Brendan was alive, she had just assumed that the men who'd wanted to kill her and CJ were not. But maybe he had just scared them off. And now they had returned. Or maybe that other gunman, the one he'd left near her father's room, had joined them on the roof.

She sucked in a breath, trying to calm herself. But if her child was truly gone, there would be no calming her—not even if the men had come back for them. They would need their guns—to defend themselves from her attack. This was their fault because they'd forced her to hide her son to protect him. But it wasn't their fault that she hadn't hidden him in a safe spot.

That was all on her.

"Shh," Brendan said again.

And she managed to control her sobs. But she heard their echo—coming softly from behind the metal pipes.

"CJ?" He wasn't gone. But why hadn't he come out? "Are you hurt?"

Perhaps there were more dangers behind the pipes than just that short wall separating him from a big fall. Maybe the pipes were hot. Or sharp.

"Listen," Brendan advised again.

The sobs were soft but strong and steady, not broken with pain, not weak with sickness. He was scared. Her little boy was too scared to come out, even for his mother.

"Tell him I'm not going to hurt him," Brendan said, his voice low but gruff. "Or you."

She nearly snorted in derision of his claim. When

he'd realized she had been working on a story about his father's murder, he'd been furious with her. Too furious to let her explain that even though the story was why she'd sought him out, she had really fallen in love with him.

Despite his difficult life, losing his mother, running away at fifteen, he'd seemed such a charming, loving man that she'd thought he might have fallen for her, too. But then his anger had showed another side of his personality, one dangerously similar to his merciless and vengeful father.

As if he'd heard the snort she'd suppressed, he insisted, "I'm not going to hurt either of you."

"Did you hear him, CJ?" she asked. "You don't have to be afraid." Then she drew in another breath to brace herself to lie to her son. "Mr. O'Hannigan is not a bad man."

She had actually been foolish enough to believe that once, to think that he was not necessarily his father's son. She'd thought that given all the years he'd spent away from the old man, he might have grown up differently. Honorably. That was why she'd fallen for him.

But when he'd learned she had actually been working on a story…

He hadn't been her charming lover. He had been cold and furious. But he hadn't been *only* furious. If he'd cut her brake line, he'd been vengeful, too. But she hadn't really meant anything to him then; she had been only a lover who'd betrayed him. Now he knew she was the mother of his child.

"He saved us from the bad men, CJ. The bad men are gone now." She turned back toward Brendan. He was just a dark shadow to her, but she discerned that his head jerked in a sharp nod.

She pushed her hand between the pipes, but no pudgy fingers caught hers. "CJ, you can come out now. It's safe."

She wasn't sure about that, but her son would be safer with her than standing just a short wall away from a long fall.

"It is safe." Brendan spoke now, his voice a low growl for her ears only. "But it may not stay that way. We need to get out of here before more *bad* men show up."

She shivered, either over his warning or his warm breath blowing in her ear and along her neck. Memories rushed back, of his breath on her neck before his lips touched her skin, skimming down her throat. His tongue flicking over her pulse before his mouth moved farther down her body…

Her pulse pounded faster, and she trembled. Then she forced the memories back, relegating them to where they belonged as she'd done so many times before. If she hadn't been able to keep the past in the past, she wouldn't have survived the past four years.

"CJ, why won't you come out?" she asked.

The boy sniffed hard, sucking up his tears and his snot. Josie flinched but resisted the urge to admonish him and was grateful she had done so when he finally spoke. "Cuz I—I was bad."

"No," Josie began, but another, deeper voice overwhelmed hers.

"No, son," Brendan said.

Josie gasped at his brazenness in addressing her child as his. Technically, biologically, it was true. But CJ didn't know that. And she never wanted him to learn the truth of his parentage. She never wanted him to know that he was one of *those* O'Hannigans.

"You weren't bad," Brendan continued. "You were very brave to protect your mother. You're a very good kid."

The boy sniffled again and released a shuddery breath.

"Now you have to be brave again," Brendan said. "And come out. There might be more bad men and we have to leave before they can be mean to your mother."

"You—you were mean to Mommy," CJ said. Her son was too smart to be as easily fooled by Brendan's charm as she had been. And as if compelled to protect her again, the little boy wriggled out from behind the pipes. But instead of confronting Brendan as he had inside the hospital, he ducked behind Josie's legs.

Brendan dropped to his haunches as if trying to meet the child's eyes even though it was so dark. "I shouldn't have been mean to her," he said. "And I'm sorry that I was. I thought she was someone else." His soft tone hardened. "Someone who lied to me, tricked me and then stole from me."

Josie shuddered at his implacable tone. He had saved her from the gunmen, but he hadn't forgotten her betrayal. Over the years it had apparently even been exaggerated in his mind, because she had never stolen anything from him. Judging by the anger he barely controlled, it seemed as if he would never forgive her.

"I don't like it when people lie to me," Brendan said. "But I would never hurt anyone."

"Who's lying now?" she murmured.

"Unless I had to in order to protect someone else," he clarified. "I will protect you and your mommy."

"I will p-tect Mommy," CJ said, obviously unwilling to share her with anyone else. But then, he'd never had to before. He had been the most important person—the only person, really—in her life since the day he was born.

Josie turned and lifted him in her arms. And she finally understood why he'd been so reluctant to come out of his hiding place. He was embarrassed, because his jeans were wet. Her little boy, who'd never had an accident since being potty-trained almost a year ago, had been so scared that he'd had one now. She clutched him close and whispered in his ear. "It's okay."

Brendan must have taken her words as acceptance. He slipped his arm around her shoulders. Despite the warmth of his body, she shivered in reaction to his closeness. Then he ushered her and CJ toward the elevator. He must have jammed the doors open, because it waited for them, light spilling from it onto the rooftop.

As she noticed that the armed men were gone, fear clutched at her. Brendan must not have injured them badly enough to stop them. They could be lurking in the shadows, ready to fire again. She covered CJ's face with her hand and leaned into Brendan, grateful for his size and his strength.

But then as they crossed the roof to the open doors, she noticed blood spattered across the asphalt and then smeared in two thick trails. Brendan had dragged away the bodies. Maybe he'd done it to spare their son from seeing death. Or maybe he'd done it to hide the evidence of the crime.

It hadn't actually been a crime though. It had been self-defense. And to protect her and their son. If she believed him…

But could she believe him? No matter what his motives were this time, the man was a killer. She didn't need to see the actual bodies to know that the men were dead. Her instincts were telling her that she shouldn't trust him. And she damn well shouldn't trust him with their son.

BRENDAN HELD HIS son. For the first time. But instead of a fragile infant, the boy was wriggly and surprisingly strong as he struggled in his grasp. He had taken him from Josie's arms, knowing that was the only way to keep her from running. She cared more about their son's safety than her own.

Maybe she really wasn't the woman he'd once known. Josie Jessup had been a spoiled princess, obviously uncaring of whom she hurt with her exposés and her actions. She had never run a story on Brendan though—she'd just run.

Brendan wouldn't let that happen again. So he held his son even though she reached for him, her arms outstretched. And the boy wriggled, trying to escape Brendan's grasp.

"Come on," he said to both of them. "We need to move quickly."

"I—I can run fast," CJ assured him.

Not fast enough to outrun bullets. Brendan couldn't be certain that the guy from the sixth floor hadn't regained consciousness and set up an ambush somewhere. He couldn't risk going through the hospital, so he pressed the garage express button on the elevator panel. It wouldn't stop on any other floors now. It would take them directly from the roof to the parking level in the basement.

"I'm sure you can run fast," Brendan said. "But we all have to stay together from now on to make sure we stay safe from the bad men."

But the little boy stopped struggling and stared up

at him, his blue-green eyes narrowed as if he was trying to see inside Brendan—to see if he was a bad man, too. He hoped like hell the kid couldn't really see inside his soul.

It was a dark, dark place. It had been even darker when he'd thought Josie had been murdered. He had thought that she'd been killed because of him—because she'd gotten too close, because she'd discovered something that he should have.

From the other stories she'd done, he knew she was a good reporter. Too good. So good that she could have made enemies of her own, though.

At first he hadn't thought this attack on her had anything to do with him. After all, he hadn't even known she was alive. And he'd certainly had no idea he had a child.

But maybe one of *his* enemies had discovered she was alive. She stared up at him with the same intensity of their son, her eyes just a lighter, smokier green. No matter how much her appearance had been altered and what she'd claimed before, she was definitely Josie Jessup. And whoever had discovered she was really alive knew what Brendan hadn't realized until he heard of her death—that he'd fallen for her. Despite her lies. Despite her betrayal.

He had fallen in love with her, with her energy and her quick wit and her passion. And he'd spent more than three years mourning her. Someone might have wanted to make certain that his mourning never ended.

Josie shook her head, rejecting his protection. "I think we'll be safer on our own."

She didn't trust him. Given his reputation, or at least the reputation of his family, he didn't necessarily blame her. But then she should have known him better. During those short months they'd spent together before her "death," he had let her get close. He may not have told her the truth about himself, but he'd shown her that he wasn't the man others thought he was. He wasn't his father.

He wasn't cruel and indifferent. "If I'd left you alone on the roof..."

SHE AND CJ would already be dead. She shuddered in revulsion at the horrible thought. She could not deny that Brendan O'Hannigan had saved their lives. But she was too scared to thank him and too smart to trust him.

Despite her inner voice warning her to be careful, she had thought only of her father when she'd risked coming to the hospital. She hadn't considered that after spending more than three years in hiding someone might still want to kill her. She hadn't considered that someone could have learned that she was still alive. "I was caught off guard."

Brendan stared down at the boy he held in his arms. "I can relate."

He had seemed shocked, not only to find her alive but also to realize that he was a father. Given that they had exactly the same eyes and facial features, Brendan had instantly recognized the child as his. There had been no point for her to continue denying what it wouldn't require a DNA test to prove.

"Are you usually on guard?" he asked her.

"Yes." But when she'd learned of the assault on her father, she had dropped her guard. And it had nearly cost her everything. She couldn't take any more risks. And trusting Brendan would be the greatest risk of all. "I won't make that mistake again."

"No," he said, as if he agreed with her. Or supported her. But then he added, "I won't let you."

And she tensed. She lifted her arms again and clasped her hands on her son's shoulders. After nearly losing him on the rooftop, she should have held him so tightly that he would never get away. But he'd started wriggling in the elevator, and she'd loosened her grip just enough that Brendan had been able to easily pluck him from her.

A chill chased down her spine as she worried that he would take her son from her just that easily. And permanently.

Josie's stomach rose as the elevator descended to the basement. Panic filled her throat, choking her. Then the bell dinged, signaling that they had reached their destination. They had gone from one extreme to another, one danger to another.

"We'll take my car," Brendan said as the doors slowly began to slide open.

We. He didn't intend to take her son and leave her alone, or as he'd left the men on the rooftop. Dead. But she and her son couldn't leave with him, either. She shook her head.

"We don't have time to argue right now," he said, his deep voice gruff with impatience. "We need to get out of here."

"Do you have a car seat?" she asked. She had posed the question to thwart him, thinking she already knew the answer. But she didn't. As closely as she followed the news, she hadn't heard or read anything about Brendan O'Hannigan's personal life. Only about his business. Or his *alleged* business.

He'd kept his personal life far more private than his professional one. But she had been gone for more than three years. He could have met someone else. Could even have had another child, one he'd known about, one with whom he lived.

He clenched his jaw and shook his head.

"CJ is too little to ride without a car seat."

"I'm not little!" her son heartily protested, as he twisted even more forcefully in Brendan's grasp. Her hands slipped from his squirming shoulders. "I'm big!"

If CJ had been struggling like that in her arms, she would have lost him, and just as the doors opened fully. And he might have run off to hide again.

But Brendan held him firmly, but not so tightly that he hurt the boy. With his low pain threshold, her son would have been squealing if he'd felt the least bit of discomfort.

"You are big," Josie assured him. "But the law says you're not big enough to ride without your car seat."

Arching a brow, she turned toward Brendan. "You don't want to break the law, do you?"

A muscle twitched along his clenched jaw. He shook his head but then clarified, "I don't want to risk CJ's safety."

But she had no illusions that if not for their son, he would have no qualms about breaking the law. She had no illusions about Brendan O'Hannigan anymore.

But she once had. She'd begun to believe that his inheriting his father's legacy had forced him into a life he wouldn't have chosen, one he'd actually run from when he was a kid. She'd thought he was better than that life, that he was a good man.

What a fool she'd been.

"Where's your car?" he asked as he carried their son from the elevator.

She hurried after them, glancing at the cement pillars, looking at the signs.

"What letter, Mommy?" CJ asked. He'd been sleeping when she'd parked their small SUV, so he didn't know. She could lie and he wouldn't contradict her as he had earlier.

But lying about the parking level would only delay the inevitable. She wasn't going to get CJ away from his father without a struggle, one that might hurt her son. Or at least scare him. And the little boy had already been frightened enough to last him a lifetime.

"A," she replied.

CJ pointed a finger at the sign. "That's this one."

"What kind of car?" Brendan asked.

"A—a white Ford Escape," she murmured.

"And the plate?"

She shook her head and pointed toward where the rear bumper protruded beyond two bigger sport utility vehicles parked on either side of it. "It's right there."

Because CJ had been sleeping, she'd made certain to park close to the elevators so she wouldn't have far to carry him. As he said, he was a big boy—at least big enough that carrying him too far or for too long strained her arms and her back.

She shoved her hand in her jeans pocket to retrieve the keys. She'd locked her purse inside the vehicle to protect her new identity just in case anyone recognized her inside the hospital. She was grateful she'd taken the precaution. But if she'd had her cell phone and her can of mace, maybe she wouldn't have needed Brendan to come to her rescue.

Lifting the key fob, she pressed the unlock button. The lights flashed and the horn beeped. But then another sound drowned out that beep as gunshots rang out. The echo made it impossible to tell from which direction the shots were coming.

But she didn't need to know where they were coming from to know where they were aimed—at her. Bullets whizzed past her head, stirring her hair.

A strong hand clasped her shoulder, pushing her down so forcefully that she dropped to the ground. Her knees struck the cement so hard that she involuntarily cried out in pain.

A cry echoed hers—CJ's. He hadn't fallen; he was still clasped tightly in Brendan's arms. But one of those flying bullets could have struck him.

Now she couldn't cry. She couldn't move. She could only stay on the ground, frozen with terror and dread that she had failed her son once again.

Chapter Six

Vivid curses reverberated inside Brendan's head, echoing the cries of the woman and the child. Those cries had to be of fear—just fear. He'd made certain that they wouldn't be hit, keeping them low as the shots rang out. If only he'd had backup waiting…

But just as he had taken on the gunmen inside the hospital, he also had to confront this one alone—while trying to protect people he hadn't even known were alive until tonight. So he didn't utter those curses echoing inside his head, not only because of his son but also because he didn't have time.

He'd taken the gun off the guy he'd left alive. But that didn't mean the man hadn't had another one on him, as Brendan always did. Or maybe if he'd come down to ambush them in the garage he'd retrieved a weapon from his vehicle.

Where the hell were the shots coming from? Since they ricocheted off the cement floor and ceiling and pillars, he couldn't tell. So he couldn't fire back—even if he'd had a free hand to grab one of his concealed weapons.

His hands were full, one clasping his son tightly to his chest while his other wrapped around Josie's arm.

He lifted her from the ground and tugged her toward the car she'd unlocked. Thankfully, it was next to two bigger SUVs that provided some cover as he ushered them between the vehicles.

"Do you still have the keys?" he asked.

Josie stared at him wide-eyed, as if too scared to comprehend what he was saying, or maybe the loud gunshots echoing throughout the parking structure had deafened her. Or she was just in shock.

Brendan leaned closer to her, his lips nearly brushing her ear as her hair tickled his cheek. Then he spoke louder. "Keys?"

She glanced down at her hand. A ring of keys dangled from her trembling fingers.

He released her arm to grab the keys from her. Then, with the keys jamming into his palm, he pulled open the back door and thrust her inside the vehicle.

"Stay low," he said, handing their son to her. As he slammed the door shut behind them, a bullet hit the rear bumper. The other vehicles offered no protection if the shooter was behind them now.

Brendan let a curse slip out of his lips. Then he quickly pulled open the driver's door. As he slid behind the steering wheel, he glanced into the rearview mirror. He couldn't see anyone in the backseat. Josie had taken his advice and stayed low.

But he noticed someone else. A dark shadow moved between cars parked on the other side of the garage, rushing toward Josie's SUV. In the dim lighting, he couldn't see the guy's face, couldn't tell if this was the supposed orderly from the sixth floor. He couldn't risk the guy getting close enough for Brendan to recognize him.

He shoved the keys in the ignition. As soon as

the motor turned over, he reversed. He would have slammed into the cars behind them, would have tried to crush the shooter. But Josie and the boy were not buckled in, so he couldn't risk their being tossed around the vehicle.

And Brendan couldn't risk the gunman getting close enough to take more shots. If these guys were all hired professionals, they were bound to get an accurate shot. So he shifted into Drive and pressed his foot down on the accelerator. If only he could reach for one of his weapons and shoot back at the shadow running after them…

But he needed both hands on the wheel, needed to carefully careen around the sharp curves so he didn't hit a concrete pillar, or fling Josie and his son out a window. He had to make sure that he didn't kill them while he tried so desperately to save them.

Josie didn't know what would kill them first: the gunshots or a car accident. Since Brendan was driving so fast, he must have outdistanced the gunman so no bullets could fly through the back window and strike CJ. She quickly strapped him into his booster seat. As short as he was, his head was still beneath the headrest.

"Stay down," Brendan warned her from the front seat as he swerved around more sharp corners and headed up toward the street level and the exit. "There could be more—"

Hired killers? That was probably what he'd intended to say before stopping himself for their son's sake, not wanting to scare the boy.

"Bad men?" she asked. She hadn't expected any of them or she never would have brought her son to the hospital. She wouldn't have put him at risk. How the hell had someone found out she was alive?

He had acted surprised. Had he really not known until tonight?

She had so many questions, but asking Brendan would have been a waste of time. He had never told her anything she'd wanted to know before. And she wasn't certain that he would actually have any answers this time. If he really hadn't known she was alive, he would have no idea who was trying to kill her.

She needed to talk to Charlotte.

Leaning forward, she reached under the driver's seat and tugged out the purse she'd stashed there earlier. She hadn't left only her identification inside but also her cell phones. Her personal phone and that special cell used only to call her handler. But Josie couldn't make that confidential call, not with Brendan in the vehicle.

"What are you doing?" he asked, with a quick glance in the rearview mirror. He probably couldn't see her, but he'd felt it when she'd reached under his seat. Was the man aware of everything going on around him? Given his life and his enemies, he probably had to be—or *he* wouldn't be alive still.

"Getting my purse," she said.

"Do you have a weapon in it?" he asked.

"Why?" Did he want her to use it or was he worried that she would? She reached inside the bag and wrapped her fingers around the can of mace. But even if he wasn't driving so fast, she couldn't have risked spraying it and hurting her son.

His gaze went to the rearview mirror again. "Never mind. I think we lost him," he said. But he didn't stop at the guard shack for the parking garage. Instead he crashed the SUV right through the gate.

CJ cried, and Josie turned to him with concern. But his cry was actually a squeal as his teal-blue eyes twinkled with excitement. What had happened to her timid son?

She leaned over the console between the seats. “Be careful.”

“Are you all right?” he asked. “And CJ?”

“We’re both fine. But is the car all right?” she asked. One of the headlamps wobbled, bouncing the beam of light around the street. “I need to be able to drive it home.”

But first she had to get rid of Brendan.

“You can’t go home,” he told her. “The gunman was coming up behind the vehicle. He could have gotten your plate and pulled up your registration online. He could already know where you live.”

She didn’t know what would be worse: the gunman knowing where she lived or Brendan knowing. But she wouldn’t need to worry about either scenario. Charlotte had made certain of that. “The vehicle isn’t registered to me.”

JJ Brandt was only one of the identities the U.S. marshal had set up for her. In case one of those identities was compromised, she could assume a new one. But for nearly four years, she had never come close to being recognized. Until tonight, when no one had been fooled by her new appearance or her new name.

Thanks to Brendan’s interference, JJ Brandt hadn’t died tonight. Literally. But she would have to die figuratively since Brendan might have learned that name. And she would have to assume one of the other identities.

But she couldn’t do anything until she figured out how to get rid of him. Maybe she needed to ask him how to do that. He was the one around whom people tended to disappear.

First her.

But according to the articles she'd read, there had been others. Some members of his "family" and some of his business rivals had disappeared over the past four years. No bodies had been found, so no charges had been brought against him. But the speculation was that he was responsible for those disappearances.

She'd believed he was responsible for hers, too, blaming him for those attempts on her life that had driven her into hiding. Since he'd saved her on the roof and again in the garage, she wanted to believe she'd been wrong about him.

But what if she'd been right? Then she'd gotten into a vehicle with a killer. Was she about to go away for good?

THE FARTHER THEY traveled from the hospital, the quieter it was. No gunshots. No sirens. He'd made certain to drive away from the emergency entrance so that he wouldn't cross paths with ambulances or, worse yet, police cars. It wasn't quiet only outside, but it was eerily silent inside the vehicle, too.

Brendan glanced at the rearview mirror, his gaze going first to his son. He still couldn't believe he had a child; he was a *father*.

The boy slept, his red curls matted against the side pad of his booster seat. Drool trickled from the corner of his slightly open mouth. How had he fallen asleep so easily after so much excitement?

Adrenaline still coursed through Brendan's veins, making his pulse race and his heart pound. But maybe it wasn't just because of the gunfire and the discovery that Josie was alive and had given birth to his baby.

Maybe it was because of her. She was so close to

him that he could feel the warmth of her body. Or maybe that was just the heat of his own attraction to her. She didn't look exactly the same, but she made him feel the same. Just as before, she *made* him feel when he didn't want to feel anymore.

She leaned over the console, her shoulder brushing against his as she studied the route he was taking. Did she recognize it? She'd taken it several times over those few months they had gone out. But then that was nearly four years ago.

Four years in which she'd been living another life and apparently not alone. And not with only their son, either.

"This isn't your vehicle?" Brendan asked, unable to hold back the question any longer. It had been nagging at him since she'd said the plate wasn't registered to her.

"What?" she asked.

"You borrowed it from someone else?" Or had she taken it from a driveway they shared? Was she living with someone? A boyfriend? A husband?

And what would that man be to CJ? His *uncle?* Stepfather? Or did he just have CJ call him *Daddy?*

Had another man claimed Brendan's son as his?

"Borrowed what?" she asked, her voice sounding distracted as if she were as weary as their son. Or maybe she was wary. Fearful of telling him too much about her new life for fear that he would track her down.

"This vehicle. You borrowed it?" Maybe that was the real reason she had worried about him wrecking it—it would make someone else angry with her.

"No," she said. "It's mine."

Had someone given it to her? Gifted her a vehicle? It might have seemed extravagant to the man. But to

Stanley Jessup's daughter? She was able to buy herself a fleet of luxury vehicles on her weekly allowance.

"But it's not registered to your name?" he asked. "To your address?"

"No, it's not," she said. And her guard was back up.

His jealousy was gone. The vehicle wasn't a gift; it was registered under someone else's name and address to protect her, to prevent someone running her plates and finding where she and her son were living.

"You do usually have your guard up," he observed. "You are very careful."

"Until tonight," she murmured regretfully. "I never should have come here."

"No," he agreed. "Not if you wanted to stay in hiding."

"I *have* to stay in hiding."

"Why?" he asked.

She gasped. "I think, after tonight, it would be quite obvious why I had to..." Her voice cracked, but she cleared her throat and added, "Disappear."

Brendan nodded in sudden realization of where she had been for almost four years. "You've been in witness protection."

Her silence gave him the answer that he should have come to long ago. He was painfully familiar with witness protection. But he couldn't tell her that. Her identity might have changed, but he suspected at heart she was still a reporter. He couldn't tell her anything without the risk of it showing up in one of her father's papers or on one of his news programs.

So he kept asking the questions. "Why were you put in witness protection?"

What had she seen? What did she know? Maybe

she'd learned, in those few short months, more than he'd realized. More than he had learned in four years.

"What did you witness?" he asked.

She shrugged and her shoulder bumped against his. "Nothing that I was aware of. Nothing I could testify about."

"Then why would the marshals put you in *witness* protection?"

Her breath shuddered out, caressing his cheek. "Because someone tried to kill me."

"Was it like tonight?" he asked.

She snorted derisively. "You don't know?"

So she assumed he would know how someone had tried to kill her. But he didn't. "You were shot at back then?"

"No," she said. "The attempts were more subtle than that. A cut brake line on my car." She had driven a little sports car—too fast and too recklessly. He remembered the report of her accident. At the time he had figured her driving had caused it. She was lucky that the accident hadn't killed her. "And then there was the explosion."

"That was subtle," he scoffed. The explosion had destroyed the house she'd been staying in, as well as her "remains," so that she'd only been identifiable by DNA. "It wasn't just a ploy the marshals used to put you into witness protection?"

She shook her head and now her hair brushed his cheek. His skin tingled and heated in reaction to her maddening closeness. He should have told her to sit back and buckle up next to their son. Or pulled her over the console into the passenger's seat.

But she was closer where she was, so he said nothing.

"No," Josie replied. "Someone found the supposedly *safe* house where I was staying after the cut brake line and set the bomb to try again to kill me."

No wonder she'd gone into protection again. Faking her death might have been the only way to keep her alive. But he might have come up with another way… if she'd told him about the attempts.

But they hadn't been talking then. He'd been too furious with her when he'd discovered that she'd been duping him—only getting close for a damn exposé for her father's media organizations. Once Brendan had figured out her pen name, he'd found the stories she'd done. No one had been safe around her, not even her classmates when she'd been at boarding school and later at college.

None of her friends had been safe from her, either. Maybe that was why she'd had few when they'd met. Maybe that was why it had been so easy for her to leave everyone behind.

Including him.

Except her father. That was why she'd come to the hospital after he'd been assaulted. Perhaps they hadn't actually severed contact, as she had with Brendan—never even letting him know he'd become a father.

She probably didn't know the identity of her would-be killer or she wouldn't have had to stay in hiding all this time. But he asked anyway. "Who do you think was trying to kill you?"

She answered without hesitation and with complete certainty, "You."

Chapter Seven

Maybe Josie was as tired as her son was. Why else would she have made such an admission? Moreover, why else would she have let him drive her here—of all places?

She should have recognized the route, since her gaze had never left the road as he'd driven them away from the hospital. She had driven here so many times over those months when they had been seeing each other. She'd preferred going to his place, hoping that she would find something or overhear something the police didn't know that could have led her to a break in his father's murder investigation.

And she hadn't wanted him to find anything at her apartment that would have revealed that she was so much more than just the empty-headed heiress so many others had thought she was. Things like her journalism awards or her diploma or the scrapbook of articles she'd published under her pseudonym.

But it didn't matter that he had never found any of those things. Somehow he'd learned the truth about who she was anyway. And after the ferocious fight they'd had, the attempts on her life had begun.

"How could you think I would have tried to kill

you?" he asked, his voice a rasp in the eerie silence of the vehicle. Even CJ wasn't making any sounds as he slept so deeply and quietly.

Brendan had pulled the SUV through the wrought-iron gates of the O'Hannigan estate, but they had yet to open the car doors. They remained sealed in that tomblike silence he'd finally broken with his question.

"How could I *not* think it was you?" she asked, keeping her voice to a low whisper so that she didn't wake her son. He didn't need to know that tonight wasn't the first time a bad man had tried to hurt his mommy. Even the authorities had suspected Brendan O'Hannigan was responsible. That was why they'd offered her protection—to keep her alive to testify against him once they found evidence that he'd been behind the attempts. "Who else would want me dead?"

He turned toward her, and since she still leaned over the console, he was close. His face was just a breath away from hers. And his eyes—the same rare blue-green as her son's—were narrowed, his brow furrowed with confusion as he stared at her. "Why would *I* want you dead?"

"I lied to you. I tricked you," she said, although she doubted he needed any reminders. And given how angry he'd been with her, she shouldn't have reminded him, shouldn't have brought back all his rage and vengeance. He might forget that she was the mother of his son. Of course he had earlier mentioned those things to their son. He'd included stealing, too, although she'd stolen nothing from him but perhaps his trust.

Despite how angry he'd been, Brendan literally shrugged off her offenses, as if they were of no consequence to him. His broad shoulder rubbed against hers, making her skin tingle even beneath her sweater and jacket. "I've been lied to and tricked before," he said.

She doubted that many people would have been brave enough to take on Dennis O'Hannigan's son—the man that many people claimed was a chip off the block of evil. She still couldn't believe that she had summoned the courage. But then she'd been a different woman four years ago. She'd been an adrenaline junkie who had gotten high on the rush of getting the story. The more information she had discovered the more excited she had become. She hadn't been only brave—she'd been fearless.

Then she had become a mother, and she had learned what fear was. Now she was always afraid, afraid that her son would get sick or hurt or scared. Or that whoever had tried to kill her would track them down and hurt him.

And tonight that fear, her deepest, darkest fear, had been realized. She shuddered, chilled by the thought. But the air had grown cold inside the car now that Brendan had shut off the engine. His heavily muscled body was close and warm, but the look on his ridiculously handsome face was cold. Even colder than the air.

"And," he continued, "I never killed any of those people."

With a flash of that old fearlessness, she scoffed, "Never?" All the articles about Brendan O'Hannigan alleged otherwise. "That's not what I've heard."

"You, of all people, should know better than to believe everything you hear or read," he advised her.

Growing up the daughter of a media magnate, she'd heard the press disparaged more than she'd heard fairy tales. Fairy tales. What was a bigger lie than a fairy tale? Than a promise of happily-ever-after?

"If it's coming from a credible source, which all of my father's news outlets are, then you should believe the story," she said.

He snorted. "What makes a source *credible?*"

As the daughter of a newsman, she'd grown up instinctively knowing what a good source was. "An insider. Someone close to the story."

"An eyewitness?" He was the one scoffing now.

She doubted anyone had witnessed him committing any crime and lived to testify. She shivered again and glanced at their son. She shouldn't have put his life in the hands of a killer. But the gunman in the garage had given her no choice. Neither had Brendan.

"Even grand juries rarely issue an indictment on eyewitness testimony," he pointed out, as if familiar with the legal process. "They need evidence to bring charges."

Had he personally been brought before a grand jury? Or was he just familiar with the process from all the times district attorneys had tried to indict his father? But she knew better than to ask the questions that naturally came to her. He had never answered any of her questions before.

But he kept asking his own inquiries. "Is there any evidence that I'm a—" Brendan glanced beyond her, into the backseat where their son slept peacefully, angelically "—a bad man?"

She hadn't been able to find anything that might have proven his guilt. She'd looked hard for that evidence—not just for her story but also for herself. She'd wanted a reason not to give in to her attraction to him, a reason not to fall for him.

But when, as a journalist, she hadn't been able to come up with any cold, hard facts, she'd let herself, as a woman, fall in love with an incredibly charming and smart man. And then he'd learned the truth about her.

What was the truth about him?

BRENDAN WAITED, but she didn't answer him. Could she really believe that he was a killer? Could she really believe that he had tried to kill *her?*

Sure, he had been furious because she'd deceived him. But he'd only been so angry because he'd let himself fall for her. He'd let himself believe that she might have fallen for him, too, when she'd actually only been using him.

He wasn't the only one she'd used. There were the friends in boarding school she'd used as inside sources to get dirt on their famous parents. Then there was the Peterson kid in college with a violence and drug problem that the school had been willing to overlook to keep their star athlete. She'd used her friendship with the kid to blow the lid off that, too. Hell, her story had probably started all the subsequent exposés on college athletic programs. It had also caused the kid to kill himself.

"You really think that I'm the only one who might want you dead?" Josie Jessup had been many things but never naive.

She gasped as if shocked by his question. Or maybe offended. How the hell did she think he felt with her believing he was a killer?

He was tempted, as he'd been four years ago, to tell her the truth. But then he'd found out she was really a reporter after a story, and as mad as he'd been, he'd also been relieved that he hadn't told her anything that could have blown his assignment.

Hell, it wasn't just an assignment. It was a mission. Of justice.

She didn't care about that, though. She cared only about exposés and Pulitzers and ratings. And her father's approval.

But then maybe his mission of justice was all about his father, too. About finally getting his approval—postmortem.

"Who else would want me dead?" she asked.

"Whoever else might have found out that you wrote all those stories under the byline Jess Ley." It was a play on the name of her father, Stanley Jessup. Some people thought the old man had written the stories himself.

But Brendan had been with her the night the story on her college friend had won a national press award. And he'd seen the pride and guilt flash across her face. And, finally, he'd stopped playing a fool and really checked her out, and all his fears had been confirmed.

She sucked in a breath and that same odd mixture of pride and guilt flashed across her face. "I don't even know how you found out...."

"You gave yourself away," he said. "And anyone close to you—close to those stories—would have figured out you'd written them, too."

She shook her head in denial, and her silky hair skimmed along her jaw and across his cheek. No matter how much she'd changed her appearance, she was still beautiful, still appealing.

He wanted to touch her hair. To touch her face...

But he doubted she would welcome the hands of the man she thought was her would-be killer. "If I wanted you dead, I wouldn't have helped you tonight," he pointed out.

She glanced back at their sleeping son. "You did it for him. You know what it's like to grow up without a mother."

So did she. That was something that had connected them, something they'd had in common in lives that had been so disparate. They'd understood each other intimately—emotionally and physically.

He shook his head, trying to throw off those memories and the connection with her that had him wanting her despite her lies and subterfuge.

"That was sloppy tonight and dangerous," he said, dispassionately critiquing the would-be assassins, "trying to carry off a hit in a hospital."

His father and his enemies would have been indicted long ago if they had operated their businesses as sloppily. Whoever had hired the assassins had not gotten their money's worth.

Neither had the U.S. Marshals. Like the local authorities, they must have been so desperate to pin something on him that they'd taken her word that he was behind the attempts on her life. They'd put her into protection and worried about finding evidence later. Like her, they had never come up with any. No reason to charge him.

If only they knew the truth…

But the people who knew it had been kept to a minimum—to protect his life and the lives of those around him. So it might not have been his fault that someone had tried to kill Josie, yet he felt responsible.

JOSIE REALIZED THAT he was right. Even if he hadn't been with her tonight, in the line of fire on the roof and in the garage, it was possible that he had nothing to do with the attempts on her life.

Brendan O'Hannigan was never sloppy.

If he was, there would have been evidence against him and charges brought before a grand jury that would have elicited an indictment. No. Brendan O'Hannigan was anything but sloppy. He was usually ruthlessly controlled—except in bed. With her caresses and her kisses, she had made him lose control.

And that one day that had her shivering in remembrance, she'd made him lose his temper. The media hadn't been wrong about her being spoiled. Her father had never so much as raised his voice to her. So Brendan's cold fury had frightened her.

If only it had killed her attraction to him, as he had tried to kill her. Not tonight, though. She believed he hadn't been behind the attempt at the hospital.

If he'd wanted her gone, he would have brought her someplace private. Someplace remote. Where no one could witness what he did to her.

Someplace like the O'Hannigan estate.

"You're cold," he said. As close as they were he must have felt her shiver. And the windows were also steaming up on the inside and beginning to ice on the outside. It was a cold spring, the temperature dropping low at night.

And it was late.

Too late?

"Let's go inside," he said.

It would be too late for her if she went inside the mansion with him. She still clutched her purse, her hand inside and still wrapped around her cell phone—the special one she used only to call Charlotte. But she released her grip on it.

It wouldn't help her against the immediate threat he posed. She didn't even know where Charlotte was, let alone if she could reach her in time to help.

"I'll get CJ," he offered as he opened the driver's door. But she hurried out the back door, stepping between him and their sleeping son.

"No," she said.

"He's getting cold out here."

Brendan tried to reach around her, but she pushed him back with her body, pressing it up against his. Her pulse leaped in reaction to his closeness.

"You can't bring him inside," she said, "not until you make sure it's safe."

He gestured toward the high wrought-iron fence encircling the estate. "The place is a fortress."

"You don't live here alone," she said.

"You really shouldn't believe everything you read," he said.

So obviously if there had been something in the news about a live-in girlfriend, it hadn't been from a credible source. Despite her fear of him, she felt a flash of relief.

"You don't take care of this place yourself," she pointed out. "You have live-in staff."

He nodded in agreement and leaned closer, trying to reach around her. "And I know and trust every one of them."

She clicked her tongue against her teeth in admonishment. "You should know that you can't trust anyone."

He stared at her and gave a sharp nod of agreement before stepping back. "You're right."

She held in a sigh of relief, especially as he continued to stare at her. Then he reached inside the open driver's door and pulled out the keys. Obviously she was the one he did not trust—not to drive off without him. He knew her too well.

"I'll check it out." He slid the keys into his suit pocket. "And come back for you."

With a soft click, she closed the back door. "I'll go with you."

As they headed up the brick walk toward the front door, she reached inside her bag for the can of mace. She would spray it at him and retrieve the keys while he was coughing and sputtering.

She could get away from him. She could protect her son and herself.

"Remember the first time you walked up this path with me?" Brendan asked, his deep voice a warm rasp in the cold.

She shivered as a tingle of attraction chased up her spine. Their fingers had been entwined that night. They had been holding hands since dinner at a candlelit restaurant.

"I teased you about playing the gentleman," he reminisced. "And you said that you were no gentleman because you just wanted to get me alone."

Her face heated as she remembered what a brazen flirt she'd been. But she'd acted that way only with him. And it hadn't been just for the story. It had been for the way his gorgeous eyes had twinkled with excitement and attraction. And it had been for the rush of her pulse.

Brendan chuckled but his voice was as cold as the night air. "You really just wanted to get inside."

That wasn't the situation tonight. Inside his house, with its thick brick walls and leaded-glass windows to hold in her screams, was the last place Josie wanted to be. Maybe he hadn't been a bad man four years ago, but he'd only just begun taking over his father's business then. Now that business was his. And he'd been leaving his own legacy of missing bodies.

"You just wanted to search my stuff," he angrily continued, "see what secrets you could find to shout out to the rest of the world through one of your father's publications."

"You're so bitter over my misleading you," she remarked. "Can't you see why I would think you're the one who wants me dead?"

He sighed and dragged out a ring of keys from his pants pocket. She recognized them because she'd tried so often to get them away from him—so she could make copies, so she could come and go at will in his house, business and offices.

"If you would realize why I am so bitter," he said, "you would also understand why the last thing I want is for you to be gone."

He turned away from the door and stared down at her, as he had that first night he'd brought her home with him. His pupils had swallowed the blue-green irises then, as they did now. "I wanted you with me that night…and all the nights that followed."

There was that charm that had given her hope that he was really a good man. That charm had distracted and disarmed her before.

But she hadn't had CJ to worry about and protect then. So now she kept her hand wrapped tightly around the can of mace. And when he lowered his head toward hers, she started to pull it from her purse.

But then his lips touched hers, brushing softly across them. And her breath caught as passion knocked her down as forcefully as he had earlier in the parking garage.

He had saved her tonight. He had saved her and her son. And reminding herself of that allowed her to kiss him back. For just a moment though…

Because he pulled away and turned back toward the door. And she did what she should have done as he'd lowered his head—she pulled out the can of mace and lifted it toward him.

Then she smelled it. The odor lay heavy on the cold air, drifting beneath the door of the house. She dragged in a deep breath to double-check.

Maybe she was just imagining it, as she had so often the past four years, waking in the middle of the night shaking with fear. She had to check the stove and the furnace and the water heater.

And though she never found a leak, she never squelched those fears. That this time no one would notice the bomb before it exploded.

This time the fire wouldn't eat an empty house. It would eat hers, with her and CJ trapped inside. But this wasn't her house.

It was Brendan's, and he was sliding his key into the lock. Would it be the lock clicking or the turning of the knob that would ignite the explosion?

She dropped the damn can and reached for him, screaming as her nightmare became a fiery reality.

Chapter Eight

Flames illuminated the night, licking high into the black sky. The boy was screaming. Despite the ringing in his ears, Brendan could hear him, and his heart clutched with sympathy for the toddler's fear.

He could hear the fire trucks, too, their sirens whining in the distance. Ambulances and police cars probably followed or led them—he couldn't tell the difference between the sirens.

Despite the slight shaking in his legs, he pressed harder on the accelerator, widening the distance between Josie's little white SUV and the fiery remains of the mansion where he'd grown up.

It had never been home, though. That was why he'd run away when he was fifteen and why he'd intended never to return. If not for feeling that he owed his father justice, he would have never come back.

"Are—are you sure you want to leave?" Josie stammered, wincing as if her own voice hurt her ears. She was in the front seat but leaning into the back this time, her hand squeezing one of their son's flailing fists. She'd been murmuring softly to the boy, trying to calm him down since they'd jumped back into the vehicle and taken off.

The poor kid had been through so much tonight, it was no wonder he'd gotten hysterical, especially over how violently he'd been awakened from his nap.

"Are you sure?" Josie prodded Brendan for an answer, as she always had.

He replied, this time with complete honesty, "I have no reason to stay."

"But your staff..."

Wouldn't have survived that explosion. Nothing would have. If he hadn't noticed the smell before he'd turned that key, if Josie hadn't clutched his arms...

They would have been right next to the house when a staff member inside, who must have noticed the key rattling in the door, had opened it for them and unknowing set off the bomb. Instead he and Josie had been running for the SUV, for their son, when the bomb exploded. The force of it had knocked them to the ground and rocked her vehicle.

"Are you all right?" he asked again.

She'd jumped right up and continued to run, not stopping until she'd reached their screaming son. The explosion had not only awakened but terrified him. Or maybe he felt the fear that had her trembling uncontrollably.

She jerked her chin in an impatient nod. "Yes, I—I'm okay."

"Maybe we should have stayed," he admitted. But his first instinct had been to get the hell away in case the bomber had hung around to finish the job if the explosion hadn't killed them.

While Brendan wished he could soothe his son's fears, his first priority was to keep the boy and his mother safe. And healthy. "We should have you checked out."

She shook her head. "Nobody can see me, in case they recognize me like you did. And those other men..." She shuddered, probably as she remembered the ordeal those men had put her and CJ through. "We can't go back to the hospital anyway."

"There are urgent-care facilities that are open all night," he reminded her. Maybe her new location wasn't near a big city and she'd forgotten the amenities and conveniences of one.

She shook her head. "But someone there might realize we were at this explosion..." The smell of smoke had permeated the car and probably her hair. "And they might call the police," she said. "Or the media."

He nearly grinned at the irony of her wanting to avoid the press.

"And it's not necessary," she said, dismissing his concerns. "I'm okay."

He glanced toward the backseat. CJ's screams had subsided to hiccups and sniffles. Brendan's heart ached with the boy's pain and fear. "What about our son?"

"He's scared," Josie explained. And from the way she kept trembling, the little boy wasn't the only one.

"It's okay," she assured the child, and perhaps she was assuring herself, too. "We're getting far away from the fire."

Not so far that the glow of the fire wasn't still visible in the rearview mirror, along with the billows of black smoke darkening the sky even more.

"It won't hurt us," she said. "It won't hurt us...."

"We're going someplace very safe," Brendan said, "where no bad men can find us."

He shouldn't have brought them back to the mansion. But the place was usually like a fortress, so he hadn't thought any outside threats would be able to get to them. He hadn't realized that the greatest danger was already inside those gates. Hell, inside those brick walls. Had one of his men—one of the O'Hannigan family—set the bomb?

He'd been trying to convince her that he'd had nothing to do with the attempts on her life, years ago or recently. And personally, he hadn't. But that didn't mean he still wasn't responsible…because of who he was.

As if she'd been reading his mind, she softly remarked, "No place, with you, is going to be safe for us."

But he wasn't only the head of a mob organization. He had another life, but, regrettably, that one was probably even more dangerous.

"WHERE ARE WE?" she asked, pitching her voice to a low whisper—and not just because CJ slept peacefully now in his father's arms, but also because the big brick building was eerily silent.

There had been other vehicles inside the fenced and gated parking lot when they'd arrived. But few lights had glowed in the windows of what looked like an apartment complex. Of course everyone could have been sleeping. But when Brendan had entered a special code to open the doors, the lobby inside looked more commercial than residential.

Was this an office building?

He'd also needed a code to open the elevator doors and a key to turn it on. Fortunately, he'd retrieved his keys from the lock at the mansion…just before the house had exploded.

Her ears had finally stopped ringing. Still, she heard nothing but their footsteps on the terrazzo as they walked down the hallway of the floor on which he'd stopped the elevator. He'd been doing everything with one hand, his arms wrapped tight around their sleeping son.

At the hospital she'd suspected that Brendan had held their son so that she wouldn't try to escape with him. Now he held him almost reverently, as if he was scared that he'd nearly lost him in the explosion.

If he had parked closer to the house…

She shuddered to think what could have happened to her son.

"It'll be warmer inside," Brendan assured her, obviously misinterpreting her shudder as a shiver.

She actually was cold. The building wasn't especially well heated.

"Inside what? Where are we?" she asked, repeating her earlier question. When he'd told her to grab her overnight bag, which she had slung over her shoulder along with her purse, she'd thought he was bringing them to a hotel. But this building was nothing like any hotel at which she'd ever stayed, as Josie Jessup or as JJ Brandt.

"This is my apartment," he said as he stopped outside a tall metal door.

"Apartment? But you had the mansion…" And this building was farther from the city than the house had been, farther from the businesses rumored to be owned or run by the O'Hannigan family. But maybe that was why he'd wanted it—to be able to get away from all the responsibilities he'd inherited.

"I already had this place before I inherited the house from my father," he explained as he shoved the key into the lock.

She wanted to grab her son and run. But she recognized she could just be having a panic attack, like the ones the nightmares brought on when they awakened her in a cold sweat. And those panic attacks, when she ran around checking the house for gas leaks, scared CJ so much that she would rather spare him having to deal with her hysteria tonight.

So she just grabbed Brendan's hand, stilling it before he could turn the key. "We can't stay here!"

Panic rushed up on her, and she dragged in a deep breath to control it and to check the air for that telltale odor. She smelled smoke on them, but it was undoubtedly from the earlier explosion. "Someone could remember you lived here and find us."

"No. It's safe here," he said. "There's no bomb."

"Bu—"

Rejecting her statement before he even heard it, he shook his head. "Nobody knows where I was living before I showed up at my father's funeral."

Some had suspected he hadn't even been alive; they'd thought that instead of running away, he might have been murdered, like they believed his mother was. Some had refused to believe that he was his father's son, despite his having his father's eyes. The same eyes that her son had.

His stepmother had still demanded a DNA test before she had stopped fighting for control of her dead husband's estate. She hadn't stopped slinging the accusations though. She had obviously been the source of so many of the stories about him, such as the one that Brendan had killed his father for vengeance and money. She had even talked to Josie back then to warn her away from a dangerous man.

Given the battle with his stepmother and the constant media attention, Josie could understand that Brendan would need a quiet place to get away from it all.

And it might have occurred to someone else that he would need such a place.

"But they can find out." Somehow, someone had found out she was alive.

"They didn't," he assured her. "It's safe." And despite her nails digging into the back of his hand, he turned the key.

She held her breath, but nothing happened. Then he turned the knob. And still nothing happened, even as the door opened slightly. She expelled a shaky sigh, but she was still tense, still scared.

Perhaps to reassure her even more, he added, "My name's not on the lease."

Just as her name was not on the title of her vehicle or the deed to her house…

Did Brendan O'Hannigan have other identities as well? But why? What was he hiding?

All those years ago she had suspected plenty and she had dug deep, but had found nothing. *She* had never found this place. Back then she would have been elated if he'd brought her here, since he was more likely to keep his secrets in a clandestine location. But when he pushed the door all the way open and stepped back for her to enter, she hesitated.

There was no gas. No bomb. No fire. Nothing to stop her from stepping inside but her own instincts.

"You lost your can of mace," he said. "You can't spray me in the face like you intended."

She gasped in surprise that he'd realized her intentions back at the mansion. "Why didn't you take it from me?"

He shrugged. "By the time I noticed you held it, I was distracted."

He must have smelled the gas, too.

"And then you were saving me instead of hurting me," he reminded her with a smile. "If you were really afraid of me, if you really wanted me gone from your life, you could have just let me blow up."

She glanced down at the child he held so tenderly in his arms. "I—I couldn't do that."

No matter how much she might fear him, she didn't hate him. She didn't want him dead.

"Why?" he asked, his eyes intense as he stared at her over the child in his arms.

"I—I..."

Her purse vibrated, the cell phone inside silently ringing.

"You lost the mace but you didn't lose your phone," he remarked. "You can answer it."

She fumbled inside and pulled out the phone. *That* phone, so it had to be Charlotte. Earlier Josie had wanted desperately to talk to the former marshal. But now she hesitated, as she paused outside his secret place.

"You need to talk to your handler," Brendan advised. "Tell him—"

"Her," she automatically corrected him. But she didn't add that technically she no longer had a handler. When the marshals had failed to find any evidence of his involvement in the attempts on her life, they'd determined they no longer needed to protect her. "Her name is Charlotte Green." Despite neither of them really being associated with the marshals any longer, the woman continued to protect Josie—if only from afar.

"Tell her that you're safe," he said. And as if to give her privacy, he carried their son across the threshold and inside the apartment.

Josie followed him with her gaze but not her body. She hesitated just inside the doorway, but finally she clicked the talk button on the phone. "Charlotte?"

"JJ, I've been so worried about you!" the other woman exclaimed.

That made two of them. But Josie hadn't been worried about just herself. She watched Brendan lay their child on a wide, low sofa. It was a darker shade of gray than the walls and cement floor. But the whole place was monochromatic, which was just different shades of drab to her.

Despite what he'd said, the space didn't look much like an apartment and nothing like a home. As if worried that the boy would roll off the couch and strike the floor, Brendan laid down pillows next to him. He might have just discovered that he was a father, but he had good paternal instincts. He was a natural protector.

And no matter what she'd read or suspected about him, Josie had actually always felt safe with him. Protected. Despite thinking that she should have feared him or at least not trusted him, she'd struggled to come up with a specific reason why. She had no proof that he'd ever tried to hurt her.

Or anyone else.

Maybe all those stories about him had only been stories—told by a bitter woman who'd been disinherited by a heartless and unpitying man.

"JJ?" the female voice emanated from her phone as Charlotte prodded her for a reply.

"I'm okay," she assured the former marshal and current friend.

"And CJ?" Charlotte asked after the boy who'd been named for her.

She had been in the delivery room, holding Josie's

hand, offering her support and encouragement. She hadn't just relocated Josie and left her. Even after she'd left the U.S. Marshals, she had remained her friend.

But the past six months Charlotte hadn't called or emailed, hadn't checked in with Josie at all, almost as if she'd forgotten about her.

"Is CJ okay?" Charlotte asked again, her voice cracking with concern for her godson.

"He had a scare," Josie replied, "but he's safe." While she wasn't entirely sure how safe she really was with him, she had no doubt that Brendan would protect his son.

The other woman cursed. "They found you? That was part of the reason I haven't been calling."

Betrayal struck Josie with all the force of one of the bullets fired at her that evening. "You knew someone was looking for me?"

If Josie had had any idea, she wouldn't have risked bringing CJ to meet his grandfather. Maybe Josie had trusted the wrong person all these years.…

"I only just found that out a few weeks ago," Charlotte explained. "Before that I had been unreachable for six months."

"Unreachable?" Her journalistic instincts told her there was more to the story, and Josie wanted to know all of it. "Why were you unreachable?"

"Because I was kidnapped."

She gasped. "Kidnapped?"

"Yes," Charlotte replied, and the phone rattled as if she'd shuddered. "I was kidnapped and held in a place you know about. You mentioned it to Gabby."

"Serenity House?" It was the private psychiatric hospital where Josie's former student had been killed pursuing the story she'd suggested to him. She had known there were suspicious things happening there. She just hadn't imagined how dangerous a place it was. Guilt churned in her stomach; maybe Brendan had had a good reason for being so angry with her. Her stories, even the ones she hadn't personally covered, always caused problems—sometimes even costing lives.

"I'm fine now," Charlotte assured her. "And so is Gabby."

"Was she there, too?" Princess Gabriella St. Pierre was Charlotte's sister and Josie's friend. Josie had gotten to know her over the years through emails and phone calls.

"No, but she was in danger, too," Charlotte replied.

And Josie felt even guiltier for doubting her friend. "No wonder I haven't heard from either of you." They'd been busy, as she had just been, trying to stay alive.

"We think we've found all the threats to our lives," Charlotte said. "But in the process, we found a threat to yours. My former partner—"

Josie shuddered as she remembered the creepy gray-haired guy who had called himself Trigger. Because Josie hadn't felt safe around him, Charlotte had made certain that he wasn't aware of where she had been relocated.

"He was trying to find out where you are."

She hadn't liked or trusted the older marshal, and apparently her instincts had been right. "Why?"

Charlotte paused a moment before replying, "I think someone paid him to learn your whereabouts."

"Who? Did he tell you?"

"No, Whit was forced to kill him to protect Aaron."

Whit and his friend Aaron had once protected Josie. They were the private bodyguards her father had hired after the accident caused by the cut brake lines. But then Whit had discovered the bomb and involved the marshals. He had helped Charlotte stage Josie's death and relocate her. But no one had wanted to put Aaron in the position of lying to her grieving father, so he'd been left thinking he had failed a client. He and Whit had dissolved their security business and their friendship and had gone their separate ways until Charlotte had brought them back together to protect the king of St. Pierre.

"I would have called and warned you immediately," the former marshal said, "but I didn't want to risk my phone being tapped and leading them right to you."

So something must have happened for her to risk it. "Why have you called now?"

"I saw the news about your father," Charlotte said, her voice soft with sympathy. She hadn't understood how close Josie had been to her father, but she'd commiserated with her having to hurt him when she'd faked her death. "I wanted to warn you that it's obviously a ploy to bring you out of hiding."

"Obviously," Josie agreed.

Charlotte gasped. "You went?"

"It was a trap," Josie said, stating the obvious. "But we're fine now." Or so she hoped. "But please check on my dad." The man who had fired at them in the garage was probably the one Brendan had left alive on the sixth floor. He could have gone back to her father's room. "Make sure my dad is okay. Make sure he's safe."

"I already followed up with the hospital," she said. "He's recovering. He'll be fine. And I think he'll stay fine as long as you stay away from him."

Pain clutched Josie's heart. But she couldn't argue

with her friend. She never should have risked going to the hospital.

"You're in extreme danger," Charlotte warned her. "Whoever's after you won't stop now that they know you're alive."

They wouldn't stop until she was dead for real.

"You have no idea who it could be?" Josie asked. She'd never wanted the facts more than she did now.

"It has to be someone with money," Charlotte said, "to pay off a U.S. marshal."

Josie shivered. It wasn't any warmer in Brendan's apartment than it was in the hall. But even if it had been, her blood still would have run cold. "And hire several assassins."

Charlotte gasped. "Several?"

"At least three," she replied. "More if you count whoever set the bomb."

"Bomb!" Charlotte's voice cracked on the exclamation.

"We're fine," Josie reminded her. "But whoever's after me must have deep pockets."

"It's probably O'Hannigan," Charlotte suggested. And she'd no sooner uttered his name than the phone was snapped from Josie's hand.

Brendan had it now, pressed to his ear, as the former U.S. marshal named him as suspect number one. Charlotte hadn't been wrong about anything else. She probably wasn't wrong about this, either.

Chapter Nine

"If you hurt her, I will track you down—"

He chuckled at the marshal's vitriolic threat. And *he* had been accused of getting too personally involved in his job.

Of course, this time he had. But then no one else had been able to take on the assignment. Maybe that was why his father had left him everything. Because Dennis O'Hannigan had known that if anyone ever dared to murder him, Brendan would be the only person capable of bringing his killer to justice.

He couldn't share any of this with Josie though, not with the risk that she would go public with the information. Risk? Hell, certainty. It would be the story of her career. So he stepped inside his den and closed the door behind him, leaving her standing over their sleeping son.

"I'll be easy to find," he assured the marshal. "And I suspect that if anyone gets hurt in my involvement with Josie, it'll be me." Just like last time. And he began to explain to her why he couldn't trust the journalist but why she could trust him.

Of course the marshal was no fool and asked for names and numbers to verify his story. Her thoroughness gave him comfort that she'd been the one protecting Josie all these years. But then she made an admission of her own—that she was no longer on the job.

"What the hell!" he cursed, wishing now that he'd checked her out before he'd told her what so few other people knew. "I thought you had clearance—"

"I do. Through my current security detail, I still have all my clearances and contacts," she assured him. "But as you know, that doesn't mean I couldn't be corrupted like so many others have been."

She was obviously suggesting that he may have been.

"Call those numbers," he urged her.

"I will," she promised. "I will also keep protecting Josie. I can't trust anyone else. That's why I insisted she stay in hiding even after the marshals deemed she wasn't really a witness and withdrew their protection. I had to make certain she stayed safe."

"Why?" he wondered. Then he realized why she'd threatened him, why she cared so much: Josie had become her friend. Hell, the *C* of CJ's name, for Charles, was probably for her.

But her answer surprised him when she replied, "Because of you."

"Because of me?"

"You're part of a powerful family," she reminded him needlessly. "You have unlimited resources of both money and manpower. Josie said several gunmen came after her tonight and someone had set a bomb."

"And those gunmen were shooting at me, too," he said. "And the bomb was set at *my* house."

She sucked in an audible breath of shock.

"I would *never* hurt her," Brendan promised. "I can't

believe she thought that I would." After everything they'd shared...

He hadn't given her a declaration of his feelings, but he had shown her over and over how he felt. Despite his tough assignment, he'd let her distract him. Of course his superiors had authorized it, saying his having a relationship helped establish his cover—that he would have been more suspicious had he remained on his own.

But hell, he'd been on his own most of his life. He was used to that.

"I protected her and CJ tonight," he said. "Hell, I would have died for her—for them." He had wound up having to kill for them instead.

Silence followed his vehement declaration. It lasted so long that he thought he might have lost the connection. Maybe the marshal had hung up on him.

Then she finally spoke again. "I think I know why you wouldn't hurt her, and it has nothing to do with what you've just told me and everything to do with what you *haven't* told me."

Maybe the cell connection was bad, because the woman seemed to make no sense. "What?"

"You love her."

He'd thought so. Once. But then he'd learned the truth about her and why she'd tried so hard to get close to him. "I can't love someone I can't trust."

She laughed now. "I thought that once, too."

"But you fell anyway?"

"No," she said. "My husband did—once Aaron understood my reasons for keeping things from him. He realized that I was only doing my job. Josie will understand when you tell her the truth."

"I can't trust her with the truth," he said.

Charlotte's sigh rattled the phone. "Then you won't be able to make her trust you, either."

"Tell her that she can," Brendan implored her. "She trusts you."

"For a good reason," Charlotte said. "I tell her the truth. And I need to call these people you've given me numbers for and check out your story. Once I do, I'll call Josie back, but I'm not sure she'll take my word without proof. She's been afraid of you for a long time."

Brendan's heart clutched at the thought of the woman he'd once loved living in fear of him, thinking that he would kill her if he found out she was still alive. Maybe he was more like his old man than he'd realized. He clicked off the cell phone and opened the door to his den, half expecting to find Josie listening outside.

But the apartment was eerily silent. Charlotte was right. He couldn't make Josie trust him. And now he didn't have the chance because she'd taken their son and run.

JOSIE WASN'T AS strong as Brendan. She couldn't carry her son, her purse and the backpack with their overnight clothes and toys, and struggle with the special locks and security panels. So she had awakened CJ for an impromptu game of hide-and-seek.

But she hoped Brendan never found them.

CJ was too tired to play though. The poor child had had such a traumatic day that he was physically and emotionally exhausted. He leaned heavily against Josie's legs, nearly knocking her over as she stood near the elevator panel.

She realized that even if she had picked up the code Brendan had punched in, she didn't have the key to work the elevator. He had shoved it back into his pocket.

So she abandoned the elevator and searched for the door to a stairwell. But they were all tall metal doors that looked the same. They could have been apartments. If this place were really an apartment complex…

Its austereness had Josie imagining what Serenity House must have been like. It had her feeling the horror that Charlotte must have felt when she'd been held hostage for six months.

Did Brendan intend to keep her here that long? Longer?

She kept pressing on doors but none of them opened. All were locked to keep her out. Or to keep other people inside?

"Mommy, I wanna go to bed," CJ whined.

"I know, sweetheart." Josie was exhausted, too. She wished she were under the covers of her soft bed and that this whole night had been a horrible nightmare.

But the smoke smell clung to her clothes and hair, proving that it hadn't been a dream. It had happened—every horrible moment of it had been real. She lifted the sleepy child in her arms. For once he didn't protest being carried but laid his head on her shoulder.

"I'm scared, Mommy."

"I know." *Me, too.* But she couldn't make that admission to him. She had to stay strong for them both.

"I wanna go home!"

Me, too. Finally one of the doors opened, and she nearly pitched forward, down the stairs. She'd found the stairwell. Her feet struck each step with an echoing thud as she hurried down. Her arms ached from the weight of the child she carried, and her legs began to tremble in exhaustion.

A crack of metal echoed through the stairwell as a door opened with such force it must have slammed against the wall. Then footsteps, heavier than hers, rang out as someone ran down the steps above her. She quickened her pace. But with CJ in her arms, she couldn't go too fast and risk tumbling down the stairs with him.

Finally she reached the bottom and pushed open the door to the lobby. There was no desk. No security. Nothing but the door with its security lock. She pressed against the outside doors, but they wouldn't open.

Footsteps crossed the lobby behind her. With a sigh of resignation, she turned to face Brendan.

"ARE YOU GOING to stop running from me now?" he asked as she stepped from his den and rejoined him and CJ in the living room. He hated seeing that look on her face, the one he'd seen at the hospital and again in the lobby—that mixture of fear and dread swirling in her smoky-green eyes.

Because of his last name, a lot of people looked at him with fear and he'd learned to not let it bother him. But he didn't want her or their son looking at him that way.

While she'd been on the phone with the former marshal, he had made progress with CJ. Before she'd made her call, she'd given the boy a bath and changed him into his pajamas for bed. So Brendan had told the child a bedside story that his mother used to tell him. The story had lulled the boy to sleep in his arms.

Of course the kid had been totally exhausted, too. But even as tired as he'd been, CJ had kept fighting to keep his eyes open and watchful of Brendan. If a three-year-old couldn't trust him, he probably had no hope of getting a woman, who'd actually witnessed him losing his temper, to trust him.

He eased CJ from his arms onto the couch and then stood up to face the boy's mother. His son's mother. She'd been carrying his baby when she'd disappeared. If only she could have trusted him then…

Obviously still distrustful, Josie narrowed her eyes with suspicion. "What did you tell Charlotte?"

He expelled a quick breath of relief. He hadn't known if he could trust the former U.S. marshal to keep his secrets. Out of professional courtesy she should have. But then, obviously, there wasn't always any communication or respect between the different agencies. And she was no longer with the marshals.

Unable to suppress a slight grin, he innocently asked, "What do you mean?"

She moved her hand, beckoning him inside the den with her so that they wouldn't awaken the child. At this point, Brendan wasn't sure anything—even another explosion—could wake the exhausted boy. But he stepped away from the couch and joined her.

She closed the door behind her and leaned against it with her hands wrapped around the handle, as if she might need to make a quick getaway. After her last attempt, she should have realized she wouldn't easily escape this complex.

He should have brought her and his son here immediately. But since she'd already been in witness protection, he'd worried that she might recognize a "safe" house and question, as she questioned everything, why he had access to one.

"You know what I mean," she said, her voice sharp

with impatience. "What did you say to make Charlotte Green trust you?"

The truth. But that wasn't something with which he could trust Stanley Jessup's daughter. He shrugged as if he wasn't sure. "What I told her doesn't really matter. I think it would take a lot more to make you trust me than her."

"True." She nodded in agreement. "Because I know you better than Charlotte does."

Images flashed through his mind, of how she knew him. She knew how to kiss him and touch him to make him lose control. She knew how to make love with him so that he forgot all his responsibilities and worries, so that he thought only of her. And even during all the years she was gone, he'd thought of her. He'd mourned her.

He stepped closer so that she pressed her back against the door. He only had to lean in a few more inches to close the distance between them, to press his body against hers, to show her that she still got to him, that he still wanted her.

His voice was husky with desire when he challenged, "Do you?"

Her pupils darkened as she stared up at him and her voice was husky as she replied, "You know I do."

Were those images of their entwined naked bodies running through her mind, too? Was she remembering how it felt when he was inside her, as close as two people could get?

She cleared her throat and emphatically added, "I know you."

"No." He shook his head. "If you did, you would have known I wasn't the one who tried to kill you three years ago."

"But you were so angry with me...."

"I was," he agreed. "You were lying to me and tricking me."

"But I didn't steal from you." She defended herself from what he'd told their son earlier.

She had stolen from him; she just didn't know it. She'd stolen his heart.

But he just shrugged. "My trust..."

"I guess that went both ways," she said.

"You never trusted me," he pointed out. "Or you would have known you wouldn't find the story you were after, that I'm not the man my father was."

She leaned wearily against the door, as if she were much older than she was. "I never found the story," she agreed. "And I gave up so much for it."

She had given up the only life she'd known. Her home. Her family. Brendan could relate to that loss.

Then a small smile curved her lips and she added, "But I got the most important thing in my life."

"Our son?"

She nodded. "That's why I have to be careful who I trust. It's why I have to leave here."

"You're safe here," he assured her. Only people who knew what he really was knew about this place. Until tonight, when he'd taken her here.

She shook her head. "Not here. CJ and I need to go home. We've been safe there. I know I can keep him safe."

He appreciated that she was a protective mother. "You don't have to do that alone anymore."

"I haven't," she said. "I had Charlotte. She was even in the delivery room with me."

That was why Josie had named their son after the U.S. marshal.

"She's too far away to help you now," he pointed out. "That's why she told you to—" he stepped closer and touched her face, tipping her chin up so she would meet his gaze "—let me."

She stared up at him, her eyes wide as if she were searching. For what?

Goodness? Honor?

He wasn't certain she would find them no matter how hard she looked. In his quest for justice for his father, he had had to bury deep any signs of human decency—at least when he was handling business. When he'd been with her, he'd let down his guard. He'd been himself even though he hadn't told her who he was.

"What would I have to say to you," he asked, "to make you trust me?"

"Whatever you told Charlotte," she said. "Tell me what you told her."

He shook his head. "I can't trust you with that information."

She jerked her chin from his hand as if unable to bear his touch any longer. "But you expect me to trust *you*—not with just my life, but CJ's, too."

She had a point. But he'd worked so long, given up so much.

If only she hadn't lied to him…

He flinched over her disdainful tone. "Why would I be more untrustworthy than anyone else?"

"Like you don't know why," she said.

"Because of who I am?"

"Because of *what* you are."

Charlotte had definitely not told her anything that he had shared with the former U.S. marshal.

"What am I?"

"I never got my story about you," she said, "because

you never answered my questions. But I need you to answer at least one if you expect me to stay here."

He nodded in agreement. "I'll answer one," he replied. "But how do you know I'll tell you the truth?"

"Swear on your mother's grave."

He wouldn't need to tell her the truth then, because his mother wasn't dead. Like everyone else, he had believed she'd been murdered when he was just a kid. But she was actually the first person he'd known who'd entered witness protection. The marshals hadn't let her take him along, forcing her to leave a child behind with a man many had considered a psychopath as well as her killer.

If Brendan hadn't run away when he was fifteen, he might have never learned the truth about either of his parents.

"Do you swear?" she prodded him. "Will you answer me honestly?"

"Yes," he agreed, and hoped like hell he wouldn't have to lie to her. But no matter what he'd promised her, he couldn't tell her what he really was. "What do you want to know?"

"Before tonight, before those men on the roof—" she shuddered as though remembering the blood and the gunshots "—have you killed anyone else?"

He had promised her the truth, so he answered truthfully. "Yes."

Chapter Ten

He was a killer. Maybe she should have believed everything she had heard and read about him—even the unsubstantiated stories.

"But just like tonight, it was in self-defense," he explained, his deep voice vibrating with earnestness and regret, as though killing hadn't been easy for him. "I have only killed when there's been no other option, when it's been that person's life or mine, or the life of an innocent person." He flinched as if reliving some of those moments. "Like you or our son."

"You've been in these life-and-death situations before tonight," she said.

He nodded.

"How many times?" she asked. "Twice? Three times?"

"I agreed to answer only one question," he reminded her.

She swallowed hard, choking on the panic she felt just thinking of all the times he'd been in danger, all the times he could have died. "And you were trying to say I was responsible for what happened tonight. And for the attempts on my life years ago. You're the one leading the dangerous life."

He stepped back from her and sighed. “You’re right.”

She appealed to him. “So you need to let us leave, to let me go home.”

“I can’t do that.”

“How can you expect to keep me and CJ safe when you’re always fighting for your own life?” she asked.

He stripped off his suit jacket. Despite the crazy night they’d had, it was barely wrinkled, but he carelessly dropped it on the floor. And in doing so, he revealed the holsters strapped across his broad shoulders, a gun under each heavily muscled arm. She’d already known about the concealed weapons; she’d already seen all of his guns. Then he reached up and pulled one of those guns from its holster and pointed it toward her.

She gasped and stepped back, but she was already against the door and had no place else to go. Unless she opened the door, but then her son might see that the man he didn’t even realize yet was his father was holding a gun on his mother.

“What—what are you doing?” she stammered. “I—I thought you wanted me to trust you.”

“That’s why I’m giving you this gun,” he said. The handle, not the barrel, was pointed toward her. “Take it.”

She shook her head. “No.”

“Don’t you know how to shoot one?”

“Charlotte taught me.” The marshal had taken her to the shooting range over and over again until Josie had gotten good at it. “She tried to give me one, too. But I didn’t want it.”

“You don’t like guns?”

Until tonight, when they’d been shooting at her, Josie hadn’t had any particular aversion to firearms. “I don’t want one in the same house with CJ.”

"You can lock it up," Brendan said, "to make sure he doesn't get to it."

"So if I take this gun, you'll let us leave?" she asked, reaching for it. The metal was cold to the touch and heavy across her palms. She identified the safety, grateful it was engaged.

He shook his head. "Until we find out who's trying to kill you, I can't let you or our son out of my sight."

"Then why give me this?"

"So you'll trust me," he said. "If I wanted to hurt you, I wouldn't give you a gun to protect yourself."

She expelled a ragged sigh, letting all her doubts and fears of Brendan go with the breath from her lungs. A bad man wouldn't have given her the means to defend herself from him. Had she been wrong about him all these years?

Had she kept him from his son for no reason?

Guilt descended on her, bowing her shoulders with the heavy burden of it she already carried. For her student, and for that other young man's death she'd inadvertently caused. She hadn't needed Brendan to remind her that there were other people with reason to want to hurt her, as she'd hurt them. She hadn't meant to.

She'd only been after the truth. But sometimes the truth caused more pain than letting secrets remain secret. If only she'd understood that sooner…

"Are you okay?" he asked, his deep voice full of concern.

How could he care about her—after everything she'd thought of him, everything she'd taken from him? He had been right that she'd stolen from him. She had taken away the first three years of his son's life.

Her hands trembled so much that she quickly slid the

gun into her purse so that she wouldn't drop it. "I—I'm fine," she said. "I'm just overwhelmed."

"You're exhausted," he said.

And he was touching her again, his hands on her shoulders. He led her toward the couch. Like the one in the living room, it was wide and low, and as she sank onto the edge of it, it felt nearly as comfortable as a mattress.

Her purse dropped to the floor next to the couch, but she let it go. She didn't need the gun. She didn't need to protect herself from Brendan, at least not physically. But emotionally she was at risk of falling for him all over again.

"You can lie down here," he said. "And I'll keep an eye on CJ."

"He's out cold," she said. Her son wouldn't awaken again before morning. But regrettably that was only a few hours off.

Brendan shook his head. "I can't sleep anyway."

"I can't sleep, either." She reached up and grabbed his hand, tugging him down beside her.

He turned toward her, his eyes intense as he stared at her. The pupils dilated, and his chest—his massively muscled chest—heaved as he drew in an unsteady breath. "Josie..."

"You gave me a gun," she murmured, unbelievably moved by his gesture.

"Most women would prefer flowers or jewelry."

The woman she'd once been would have, but that woman had died nearly four years ago. The woman she was now preferred the gun, preferred that he'd given her the means to protect herself...even from him.

"I'm not most women," she said.

"No," he agreed. "Most women I would have been able to put from my mind. But I never stopped thinking about you—" he reached for her now, touching her chin and then sliding his fingers up her cheek "—never stopped wanting you."

Then his mouth was on hers as he kissed her deeply, his tongue sliding between her lips. She moaned as passion consumed her, heating her skin and her blood.

Her fingers trembled, and she fumbled with the buttons on his shirt. She needed him. After tonight she needed to feel the way he had always made her feel—*alive*.

He caught her fingers as if to stop her. Josie opened her eyes and gasped in protest. But then he replaced her hands with his. He stripped off his holsters and then his shirt, baring his chest for her greedy gaze.

He was beautiful, the kind of masculine perfection that defied reality. That weakened a woman's knees and her resolve. Josie leaned forward and kissed his chest, skimming her lips across the muscles.

Soft hair tickled her skin.

His fingers clenched in her hair, and he gently pulled her back. Then his hands were on her, pulling her sweater over her head and stripping off her bra.

"You're beautiful," he said, his voice gruff.

She wasn't the woman she'd once been, emotionally or physically. She'd worried that he wouldn't look at her as he once had—his face flushed with desire, his nostrils flaring as he breathed hard and fast. But he was looking at her that way now.

"You're even more beautiful," he murmured, "than you once were."

She didn't know whether to be offended, so she

laughed. “Then the marshals didn’t get their money’s worth from the plastic surgeon.”

“It’s not an external thing,” he said. “You have a beauty that comes from within now.”

“It’s happiness,” she admitted.

“Despite all you had to give up?” His hands skimmed along her jaw again. “Even your face?”

“I have my son,” she said, “our son…”

“Our son,” he said.

“I’m sorry I didn’t tell you I was pregnant,” she said, “that I didn’t tell you when he was born.”

“You didn’t trust me,” he said. “You thought I wanted to kill you.”

“I was wrong.” She knew that now. She didn’t know everything. He was keeping other things from her—things that he’d shared with Charlotte but wouldn’t tell her. But maybe it was better that she didn’t know. Maybe the secrets kept her safer than the gun.

He kissed her again, as he had before. Deeply. Passionately. His chest rubbed against her breasts, drawing her nipples to tight points.

She moaned again and skimmed her hands over his back, pressing him closer to her. As she ran her palms down his spine, she hit something hard near his waistband. Something cold and hard.

Another gun.

How many did he have on him?

He stood up and took off that weapon, as well as another on his ankle. Then his belt and pants came off next.

And Josie gasped as desire rushed over her. She had never wanted anyone the way she’d wanted Brendan. Because she’d known she never would, she hadn’t gotten involved with anyone else the past four years. She’d focused on being a mother and a teacher and had tried to forget she was a woman.

She remembered now. Her hands trembling, she unclasped her jeans and skimmed them off along with her simple cotton panties. Brendan reached between them and stroked his fingers over her red curls.

Her breath caught. And she clutched his shoulders as her legs trembled.

"You haven't changed completely," he murmured.

He continued to stroke her until she came, holding tight to him so that she didn't crumple to the floor. But then he laid her down on the couch. And he made love to her with his mouth, too, his fingers stroking over her breasts, teasing her nipples until she completely shattered, overcome with ecstasy. But there was more.

She pulled him up her body, stroking her hands and mouth over all his hard, rippling muscles…until his control snapped. And he thrust inside her, filling the emptiness with which she'd lived the past four years.

Their mouths made love like their bodies, tongues tangling, lips skimming, as he thrust deep and deeper. She arched to take all of him. A pressure wound tightly inside her, stretching her, making her ache. She gasped for breath as her heart pounded and her pulse raced.

Then Brendan reached between them; his fingers stroked through those curls and his thumb pressed against that special nub. And she came. So she wouldn't scream, she kissed him more deeply as pleasure pulsed through her.

He groaned deeply into her mouth as his body tensed and he joined her in ecstasy. Pleasure shook his body, just as hers still trembled with aftershocks. But even once their bodies relaxed, he didn't let her go. He wrapped his arms tightly around her, holding her close to his madly pounding heart.

And she felt safe. Protected. For the first time in nearly four years.

FOR THE FIRST time in nearly four years, Brendan didn't feel so alone. Josie had had their son; he had had no one. No one he dared get close to. No one he dared to trust.

Part of that had been her fault. After her subterfuge, he'd been careful to let no other woman get to him. But he suspected that even if he hadn't been careful, no other woman could have gotten to him.

Only Josie…

Maybe Charlotte Green was right. Maybe he did love Josie. And maybe he should trust her. He hadn't noticed any articles she'd written showing up in her father's papers. Maybe she'd stepped away from the media world. Not that her articles had been sensationalized. They had been brutally honest, stripping the subject bare. That was why he would have recognized anything she'd written—her style was distinctive.

But maybe becoming a mother had changed her priorities. Maybe she cared more about keeping CJ hidden than exposing others.

He stroked his fingers over her shoulder and down her bare back. "Your skin is so soft." He'd thought it was because of fancy spa treatments she would have had as American princess Josie Jessup. But with the new lifestyle the marshals would have set up for her, she wouldn't have been able to go to expensive spas.

She would have had to live modestly and quietly, or else she would have been found before now. Because someone was looking for her.

Why?

To get to him?

She was his only weakness. Hurting her would draw him out, and maybe make him careless enough for someone to get the jump on him.

Had she had to give up everything—her home, family and career—because of him? Then she deserved to know the truth.

"Josie…"

"Hmm…" she murmured sleepily.

He looked down at her face and found her eyes closed, her lashes lying on the dark circles beneath. And her body was limp in his arms, relaxed. He couldn't wake her. After everything she'd been through that night, she needed to rest and recuperate. Because their ordeal wasn't over yet. It wouldn't be over until he discovered who was trying to kill her.

But they were safe now, here, wrapped in each other's arms, so he closed his eyes.

He didn't know how long he'd been asleep when the alarm sounded. No, the piercing whistle was not from a clock but from the security panel in the den.

"What!" Josie exclaimed as she jerked awake in his arms. "What is that?"

"Security has been breached," he said, already reaching for his clothes and his weapons.

There were other apartments inside the building, other witnesses or suspects or agents the intruder could have been after. But Brendan knew the alarm was for them—the danger coming for them.…

He had just one question for her. "How well do you know how to shoot?"

Chapter Eleven

While she'd held the gun when he'd handed it to her, the weight of it was still unfamiliar in her hands. Before tonight she hadn't held one in years, let alone fired one. And when she had fired one, it had only been at targets—not people.

Could she pull the trigger on a person?

"Mommy, the 'larm clock is too loud," CJ protested with his tiny hands tightly pressed against his ears.

Brendan scooped him up and headed toward the apartment door. "Grab your stuff," he told her over his shoulder. He carried the boy with one arm while he clutched a gun in his other hand.

"Sh-shouldn't we stay here?" she asked. "And just lock the door?"

His turquoise eyes intense, he shook his head. "We don't know if the breach was someone getting inside or *putting* something inside."

A bomb.

Josie gasped and hurried toward the door. But she slammed into Brendan's back as he abruptly stopped.

"We have to be very quiet," he warned them.

"CJ, you have to play statue," she told their son. "No matter what happens, you have to be quiet."

"Like on the roof?"

Not like that. She wouldn't dare leave her little boy alone in the dark again. "Well…"

"We're all staying together," Brendan said, "and we're staying quiet."

She released a shaky sigh.

"Mommy, shh," the little boy warned her.

A corner of Brendan's mouth lifted in a slight grin. Then he slowly opened the door. He nodded at her before stepping into the hall. It was clear. He wouldn't have brought their son into the line of fire.

But they needed to get out of the building. Fast.

She breathed deep, checking for the telltale odor of gas. But she smelled nothing but Brendan; the scent of his skin clung to hers. While they'd been making love, someone had gotten inside the building.

What if that person had gotten inside the apartment? He or they could have grabbed CJ before his parents had had a chance to reach him.

Her heart ached with a twinge of guilt more powerful than any she'd felt before. And she'd felt plenty guilty over the years.

She followed after Brendan, watching as he juggled the boy and his gun. "If we're taking the elevator…"

He would need to give her the code to punch into the security panel. But he shook his head and pushed open the door to the stairwell.

Of course they wouldn't want to be in the elevator. If the building exploded, they would be trapped. But wouldn't they be trapped inside the stairwell, too? If the gunmen were heading up, they would meet them on the way down—and CJ would be caught in the crossfire.

Brendan didn't hesitate though. He hurried down the first flight and then the second.

"Brendan…"

Over his father's shoulder, their little boy pressed a finger to his lips, warning her again to be quiet.

They had stopped, but their footsteps echoed. Then she realized it wasn't their footsteps that were echoing. It was someone else's—on their way up, as she'd feared. But Brendan continued to go down.

"No," she whispered frantically. "They're coming!"

He stopped on the next landing and pushed open the door to the hall. "Run," he told her.

"To the elevator?" They could take it now. The men wouldn't have come inside if they'd set a bomb.

"No," he said. "Door at the end of the hall. Go through it." He pushed her ahead of him and turned back as the door to the stairwell opened. But he kept his back toward that door, his body between their son and whoever might exit the stairwell. Before anyone emerged, he fired and kept firing as he ran behind Josie.

She pushed through that door he'd pointed at and burst onto a landing with such force that she nearly careened over the railing of the fire escape. Brendan, CJ clutched tight against his chest, exited behind her.

He momentarily holstered his gun, even though the men had to be right behind him, and he grabbed up a pipe that lay on the landing and slid it through the handle, jamming the door shut.

How had he known the pipe was there? Had he planned such an escape before?

The door rattled as another body struck it.

"Go," he told her. "Run!"

She nearly stumbled as she hurried down the dimly illuminated metal steps. But gunfire rang out again—shots fired against that jammed door.

Brendan, still holding their son, who was softly sobbing, rushed down the stairs behind her. The shots, the urgency, the danger had her trembling so uncontrollably that she slipped, her feet flying from beneath her.

She would have fallen, would have hit each metal step on the long way to the ground. But a strong hand caught her arm, holding her up while she regained her footing.

When they neared the bottom of the fire escape, the gun was back in his hand, the light from the parking lot lamps glinting off the metal.

She hadn't lost the gun she'd carried. She hadn't used it, either, and wasn't even sure that she could. But then she heard a car door open and a gun cock.

And she knew that someone had a clear shot at them. So she slid off the safety and turned with the gun braced in both hands. But before she could squeeze the trigger, a shot rang out and she heard a windshield shatter.

"Come on," Brendan urged her. "Your car's over here. Hurry."

"But—"

There was a shooter in the lot. Or had Brendan already shot him? The gun was in his free hand while his other hand clasped their son to his chest.

"Do you have the keys?" he asked.

She pulled them out of her purse and clicked the key fob. Lights flashed on the SUV, guiding them to it and also revealing it to the gunmen as they erupted from the lobby of the building.

This time she squeezed the trigger, shooting at the men pointing guns at her son and the man she loved. The weapon kicked back, straining her wrist.

"Get in!" Brendan yelled as he put their boy into the backseat. "Buckle him up!"

She dropped the gun into her bag and jumped into the passenger's seat. As she leaned over the console and buckled up their son, Brendan was already careening out of the lot.

"Stay down!" he yelled at her, just as more shots rang out. Bullets pinged and tires squealed.

And their son continued to play statue, staying silent in the backseat. "You're so brave," she praised him, reaching back to touch his face.

His chin quivered and she felt moisture on her fingers—probably his tears. But he had his eyes squeezed tightly shut, trying not to cry. She pulled back her hand and studied what was smeared across her fingers. It wasn't tears. It was something red and sticky. Blood.

"Brendan! He's hurt!" she exclaimed, fear and dread clutching her heart in a tight vise. "Get to the hospital! Call the police!"

"NO," HE CORRECTED her as blood trickled down his temple. "CJ wasn't hit." He'd made damn certain of that.

"Th-there's blood on his face," she said, her voice shaking with fear and anger.

Brendan tipped the rearview mirror and studied their son in the backseat. The little boy scrubbed at his face and held up a hand sticky with blood. "It's not mine, Mommy. It came off..." His son didn't know what to call him, didn't know who he was to him.

"Your daddy," Brendan answered the boy. "I'm your daddy."

Josie gasped, probably at his audacity for telling their child who he was. But then she was reaching across the console and touching his head. "Where are you hit?"

"Daddy?" CJ asked.

Brendan's head pounded. He wanted to pull off the road, wanted to explain to his son who he was, wanted to let Josie touch him. But he had to tip the mirror back up and check the road behind them. Had anyone followed them?

He'd thought he'd been vigilant on his way from the estate to the complex, that he hadn't been followed. Had he missed a tail?

With blood trickling into his eyes, he was more likely to miss one now, so he asked Josie, "Do you see anything?"

Her fingers stroked through his hair. "No. Where were you hit?"

He shook his head, and the pain radiated, making him wince. "I wasn't hit," he replied, lifting his fingers to his left temple. "I was grazed. It's just a scratch." A scratch that stung like a son of a bitch, but he ignored the pain and focused on the road. "Is there anyone behind us?"

"What?" She must have realized what he was referring to, because she turned around and peered out the rear window. "I don't see any other lights."

The roads were deserted this early in the morning. He passed only a garbage truck going the other direction. No one was behind him. No one had been behind him earlier, either. He blinked back the trickle of blood and remarked, "I was not followed to the complex."

"So how did they find us?" she asked.

"Daddy?" CJ repeated from the backseat, interrupting them. "You're my daddy?"

Josie sucked in an audible breath as if just noticing

that Brendan had told their son who he was. He waited to see if she would deny it now, if she would call him a liar for claiming his child. If she did, he would call her on the lie. After his close call with that bullet, he wanted his son to know who he was…before it was too late. Before he never got the chance to tell him.

Josie turned toward the backseat and offered their son a shaky smile. "Yes, sweetheart, he's your daddy."

"I—I thought he was a bad man."

Josie shook her head. "No, sweetheart, he's a good man. A hero. He keeps saving us from the bad men."

Was she saying that for the boy's sake? To make CJ feel better? Safer? Or did she believe it? Had she finally really come to trust Brendan, even though he hadn't told her the truth?

"My daddy…" the little boy murmured, as if he were falling back to sleep. Given that his slumber kept getting violently interrupted, it was no wonder that the little boy was still tired.

"Well, we know who I am," Brendan said. A hero? Did she really see him that way? "What about who's after us?"

She kept staring into the backseat as if watching her son to make sure that the blood really wasn't his. Or that the news of his parentage hadn't affected him.

"Whoever it is," he said, "appears to want us both dead."

"They're gone," she murmured. Apparently she'd been watching the back window instead. "We're safe now."

"We should have been safe where we were," he replied. It was a damn *safe* house.

"We need to go home," she murmured, sounding as dazed as their son. But she wasn't just tired; she was probably in shock. She'd fired her gun at people. If that had been the first time, she was probably having an emotional reaction. She was trembling and probably not just because the car had yet to warm up. "We need to go home," she repeated.

She wasn't talking about his home. Neither the mansion where he'd grown up nor the apartment where he'd spent much of his adult life was safe. But she couldn't be talking about her place, either.

Maybe her father's? But if the news reports were correct, he'd been attacked in the parking garage of his condominium complex.

"We can't," he said. "It's not safe at your dad's, either."

"We have to go home," she said, her voice rising slightly now, as if with hysteria. "To what CJ and I call home, where we've been living."

"Don't you get it?" he asked. "The only one who could have tracked down where we were was your *friend*."

She leaned forward and peered into his face as if worried that the bullet had impaired his thinking. "Friend?"

"The former marshal," he said. "She must have traced the call to where we were staying. She sent those people." It couldn't have been anyone else. Damn! Why had he trusted the woman?

Josie sucked in an audible breath of shock. "Charlotte? You think Charlotte is behind the attempts on my life?"

"No." He knew she considered the woman a friend, at one point maybe her only friend. And she had to be devastated. But she also had to know the truth. "But she must have sold out to whoever wants you dead."

Josie chuckled. Maybe she'd given over completely to hysteria and shock. "You think Charlotte Green sold out?"

He nodded, and his head pounded again. "It had to be her. You can't trust her."

"She told me to trust you," she reminded him. "So now you're saying that I shouldn't?"

"No, no," he said. "You should trust me but not her. Remember what you told our son—I'm not a bad man. I've saved you."

Something jammed into his ribs, and he glanced down. She held the gun he'd given her, not just on him but nearly in him as she pushed the barrel into his side. After the night she'd had, he could understand her losing it. But was she irrational enough to pull the trigger?

Had she slid off the safety? If he hit a bump in the road, she might squeeze the trigger. She might shoot him and then he might crash the SUV and take them all out.

He hadn't realized that he might need to protect Josie from herself.

HE WAS LOOKING at her nervously, as if he worried that she'd lost her mind. Maybe she had.

Could she do it? Could she pull the trigger? If she had to… If killing Brendan was necessary to save her life or CJ's.

But she believed what she'd told their son. He was a hero—at least he had been their hero—time and time again the past night. Moreover, she believed in him.

She had the safety on the gun, in case there were any bullets left in it. She hoped like hell there were none. But with Brendan looking as nervous as he was, he obviously thought there could be.

And he thought she could fire the gun.

Good. That was the only way she was going to coerce him to take her where she wanted to go. Where she needed to go. Home.

"We're doing things my way now," she said. Since the shoot-out at the hospital, he had brought her from one place to another and neither had been safe.

"You're not going to pull the trigger," he said. "You're not a killer."

She flinched, hoping that was true. She'd fired the gun back at the complex. Had she hit anyone?

She shot back at him with a smart remark. "Guess that makes one of us."

"Then why pull the gun on me if you don't intend to use it?" he asked, his body pressed slightly against the barrel of her gun as if he were beginning to relax. Had he realized that she hadn't gone crazy? That she was just determined?

"I don't want to use it," she admitted, "but I will if you don't take me where I want to go."

"It's too dangerous," he protested. "Since Charlotte gave up our safe house, she sure as hell gave up the place where she relocated you."

"Why?" she asked.

"I told you—for money."

She laughed again. "Do you have any idea who Charlotte Green is?"

He glanced at her with that look again, as if he thought she belonged in a place like Serenity House. "A former U.S. marshal."

"Her father is king of a wealthy island country near Greece," she shared. The last thing Charlotte needed was money. "She's a princess."

"What?" He definitely thought she was crazy now.

"She's Princess Gabriella St. Pierre's sister," she explained. "They're royal heiresses." Of course Charlotte had spent most of her life unaware that she was royalty. Only upon her mother's death had she learned the woman had been the king's mistress and herself his illegitimate heir.

"So are you."

She snorted over the miniscule amount of royal blood running in her veins. Her mother had been a descendent of European royalty, but she'd given up her title to marry Josie's father. "Not anymore," she reminded him. "I gave up that life."

And she shouldn't have risked coming back to it, not even to see her father, because her arrival had only put him in more danger. God, she hoped he was safe. She had asked Charlotte to check on him, to protect him. What if Brendan was actually right about her?

No, that wasn't possible. Charlotte would never betray her.

"I have a *new* home," she said. "And we're going there. It might be the only safe place we have left to go."

"Or it could be a trap," he said. "They could be waiting for us there."

"Charlotte wouldn't have given us up," she said. "She's CJ's godmother. My friend. She wouldn't have given us up."

She barked out directions, and he followed them. She suspected it wasn't because of the gun she pressed into his side but because he had no place else to take her. He'd tried the O'Hannigan mansion and what had probably been some type of safe house. Why had no other tenants come out into the halls when the alarm had sounded? Why had it only been them and the gunmen?

"What if you're wrong about her?" he asked. "What if she's not really who you think she is?"

Then Charlotte wouldn't be the only one she'd misjudged. Brendan O'Hannigan wasn't who she'd thought he was, either. She had been wrong about him for so long. What if she was wrong about Charlotte, too? What if the marshal had been compromised?

She wouldn't have sold out Josie for money, but she might have sold her out if there was a threat against someone she loved, such as her sister. Or Aaron…

The closer they got to her home, the more scared Josie became that Brendan might be right. They could be walking right into the killer's trap.

Chapter Twelve

Brendan could have taken the gun away from her at any time. He could have snapped it out of her hand more easily than he had taken the weapon off the faux orderly who'd grabbed him on the sixth floor. But he hadn't wanted to hurt her. She had already been hurt enough. And if he was right, she was about to be hurt a hell of a lot more.

He intimately knew how painful it was to be betrayed by someone you loved. As a friend, as a lifeline to her old life, she had loved Charlotte Green. And he'd been fool enough to trust the woman with the truth about himself.

But he'd wanted her to convince Josie to trust him. Now Josie held a gun on him, forcing him to bring her back to a trap. Should he trust her?

Was she part of it? Was this all a ploy to take him down? If not for the boy, he might have suspected her involvement in a murder plot against him. But she loved her son. She wouldn't knowingly endanger him.

As he drove north, light from the rising sun streamed through her window, washing her face devoid of all color. Her eyes were stark, wide with fear, in her pale face.

"Are you sure you want to risk it?" he asked.

"You're trying to make me doubt myself," she said. "Trying to make me doubt Charlotte."

"Yes," he admitted.

She looked at him, her eyes filling with sadness and pity. "You don't trust anyone, do you?"

"I shouldn't have," he said. "But I trusted you."

She pulled the gun slightly away from his side. "You gave me this gun."

"The one you're holding on me."

"I wouldn't really shoot you," she assured him, and with a sigh, she dropped the gun back into her purse.

"I know."

"Then why did you come here?" She sat up straighter as they passed a sign announcing the town limits of Sand Haven, Michigan. Another sign stood beyond that, a billboard prompting someone named Michael to rest in peace.

Josie flinched as she read the sign.

"Do you know Michael?" he asked.

She jerked her chin in a sharp nod. "I knew him."

"I'm sorry." Had her recent loss explained why she'd been so desperate to see her father that she'd risked her safety and CJ's?

She hadn't been in contact with her father, as he'd initially expected. The man, who'd looked so sad and old at her funeral, had believed she was dead just as Brendan had.

"You hadn't seen your dad until—" he glanced at the sun rising high in the sky "—last night?"

"I didn't see him last night, either," she said.

"But you were on the right floor," he said, remembering the lie she'd told him.

She bit her lip and blinked hard, as if fighting tears,

before replying, "The assault brought on a heart attack. I didn't want his seeing me to bring on another one."

"So he has no idea that you're really alive?"

She shook her head. "I thought it would be better if he didn't know. I thought he'd be safer."

"You and your father were close," he said. "It must have been hard to leave him."

"Harder to deceive him," she said.

But she'd had no problem deceiving him when she'd been trying to get her story. But then she hadn't loved him.

He drew in a deep breath and focused on the road. She'd given him directions right to her door. Giving her the gun had made her trust him. But she had placed her trust in someone she shouldn't have.

"Let me go in first," he suggested as he drove past the small white bungalow where she lived now. "Let me make sure that it's not a trap."

She shuddered as if she remembered the bomb set at his house. There had been very little left of the brick Tudor; it wouldn't take a very big bomb to totally decimate her modest little home.

He turned the corner and pulled the SUV over to the curb on the next street. After shifting into Park, he reached for the door handle, but she clutched his arm.

Her voice cracking, she said, "I don't want you to go alone."

"You can't go with me," he said. "You have to protect our son."

"If you can't?" She shook her head. "It's not a trap. It can't be a trap." She had been on her own so long that she was desperately hanging on to her trust for the one person who'd been there for her.

He forced a reassuring smile for her sake. “Then I’ll be right back.”

She stared at him, her eyes wide with uncertainty. She wanted to believe him as much as she wanted to believe that Charlotte hadn’t betrayed her.

“I’ll be back.” He leaned across the console and clasped her face in his hands, tipping her mouth up for his kiss. He lingered over her lips, caressing them slowly and thoroughly. “Wait here for me.”

She opened her mouth again, but she made no protest. He opened the driver’s door and then opened the backseat door. She turned and looked over the console as he leaned in and pressed a kiss against his son’s mussed red curls. The boy never stirred from his slumber.

“Thank you,” he said. “Thank you for telling him that I’m his father.”

“You told him.”

“But you didn’t contradict me,” he said. “He would have believed what you told him over whatever I told him.” Because he loved and trusted his mother. Brendan was a stranger to him. And if he was right about the trap, he may forever remain a stranger to him.

The little boy might grow up never knowing his father.

BRENDAN HAD BEEN gone too long. Longer than he needed to check out the house and make sure it was as safe as she was hoping it was.

But what if it wasn’t?

The keys dangled from the ignition. He hadn’t taken them this time, because he wasn’t sure he’d be coming back. Josie’s heart rate quickened, pounding faster with each second that passed.

She needed to go to her house. Needed to check on him.

Or perhaps she should call Charlotte for backup. But he wouldn't need backup unless Charlotte had betrayed them. Panic and dread clutched her heart. Not Charlotte. Not her friend, her son's godmother.

Charlotte couldn't have revealed Josie's new location, not even to protect someone else. But maybe someone had found out anyway. Josie needed to learn the truth.

She wriggled out of the passenger's seat, over the console and behind the steering wheel. Then she turned the keys in the ignition.

CJ murmured as the engine started. He was waking up. She couldn't leave him in the car and she couldn't bring him with her—in case Brendan was right about her house being a trap now.

So she brought her son where she brought him every morning, where she would have brought him that morning if she hadn't taken a leave from work. She drove him to day care. It was only a few blocks from her house, at the home of a retired elementary schoolteacher.

Mrs. Mallory watched CJ and two other preschool children. The sixty-something woman opened the door as Josie carried him up the walk. And the smile on her face became tight with concern the closer Josie came.

"Are you all right?" the older woman anxiously asked.

How awful did she look?

A glance in the mirror by the door revealed dark circles beneath her eyes, and her hair was tangled and mussed, looking as though she'd not pulled a comb through it in days. She probably hadn't.

"I'm fine," Josie assured her. "I'm just in a hurry."

Mrs. Mallory reached out for the sleepy child. "I wasn't even expecting you. I thought you were taking some time off." As she cradled the boy in one arm, she squeezed Josie's shoulder with her other hand. "You really should. Let this whole tragic situation with Michael die down."

"So people are blaming me?"

Mrs. Mallory bit her lip and nodded. "It's not your fault, though, honey. That boy wanted to be a reporter since he wasn't much older than CJ here."

"But I suggested the story...."

"But you didn't pull the trigger," the older woman pointed out. "People are blaming the wrong person and they'll realize that soon enough. Just give them some time. Or take some for yourself."

She had no time to lose—not if Brendan had walked into a trap. "Even though you weren't planning on it, would you mind watching him for a little while?"

"'Course not," the older woman assured her, and she cuddled him close in her arms. She was wearing one of the velour tracksuits that CJ loved snuggling into. "I was just starting to miss him."

CJ lifted his head from Mrs. Mallory's shoulder as if just realizing where he was. "Daddy? Where's my daddy?"

Mrs. Mallory's eyes widened with shock. The boy had never mentioned him before. Of course, before last night he hadn't even known he had a father. Or a grandfather.

"You have to stay here with Mrs. M," Josie told him, leaning forward to press a kiss against his freckled cheek, "and be a good boy, okay?"

His bottom lip began to quiver and his eyes grew

damp with tears he fought back with quick blinks. "What if the bad men come here?"

"Bad men?" Mrs. Mallory asked, her brow wrinkling with confusion and uneasiness.

Josie shrugged off the question. "He must have had a bad dream."

If only that had been all it was…

Just a bad dream.

The little boy vehemently shook his head. "The bad men were real and had guns. They were shootin' at us and then there was a big bang!"

Josie shook her head, too, trying to quiet the boy's fears and Mrs. Mallory's. "It must have been quite the dream," she said, "and his imagination is so vivid."

Mrs. Mallory glanced from the boy to Josie and back. "He does have quite the imagination," she agreed, his story, although true, too fanciful for the older woman to believe. "He's a very creative boy. Did you watch a scary movie with him last night—something that brought on such a horrible dream?"

"No," Josie replied. She touched her little boy's trembling chin. "You have no reason to be afraid," she told him. "You're perfectly safe here."

Not buying her assurances in the least, CJ shook his head and wriggled out of Mrs. Mallory's arms. "I need my daddy to p'tect me."

Brendan had gone from bad man to hero for his son. He needed to know that; hopefully he was alive for her to share that news with him. She needed to get to her house. If it had blown up, she would have heard the explosion—or at least the fire trucks.

He had to be okay….

Josie knelt in front of her son and met his gaze. "I

am going to go get your daddy," she promised, "and he will come back here with me to get you, okay?"

"I can get Daddy, too," he said, throwing his arms around her neck to cling to her.

Her heart broke, but she forced herself to tug him off and stand up. He used to cling to her like this every morning when she'd first started bringing him to Mrs. Mallory, but today was the first time he'd had a reason for his fears. Not only because of the night he'd had, but also because she might not be able to come back—if she walked into the same trap his father might have. But then his godmother would take him....

Charlotte. She wouldn't have endangered them. Brendan must have had another reason for not returning to the SUV. Maybe that injury to his head was more severe than he'd led her to believe.

"No, honey," she said, and it physically hurt her, tightened her stomach into knots, to deny his fervent request. The timid boy asked her for so little that she hated telling him no. "I have to talk to Daddy alone first, and then we'll come get you."

Mrs. Mallory had always helped Josie escape before when her son was determined to cling. But now the older woman just stood in the foyer, her jaw hanging open in shock. As Josie stared at her, she pulled herself together. But curiosity obviously overwhelmed her. "His—his father? You've never mentioned him before."

With good reason. She had thought he wanted her dead. "We haven't been in contact in years," she honestly replied.

"But he's here?"

She nodded. "At my house."

Or so she hoped. Maybe he'd come back to where

he'd parked the SUV and found her gone. What would he think? That she'd tricked him again?

Hopefully she wasn't the one who'd been tricked. Hopefully he wasn't right about Charlotte.

"I—I have to go," she said. It had been too long. Now that she'd stood up, CJ was clinging to her legs.

Finally Mrs. Mallory stepped in and pried the sniffling child off her.

"I'll be back," she promised her son.

"With Daddy?"

She hoped so. But when she parked in the alley behind her house moments later, her hope waned. She hadn't seen him walking along the street. And while the house wasn't in pieces or on fire, it looked deserted.

She opened the driver's door and stepped out into the eerie quiet. Her neighbors would have already left for work, their kids for school. Josie was rarely home this time of day during the week. Maybe that was why it felt so strange to walk up to her own back door.

The glass in the window of the door was shattered. Of course, since Brendan had left her keys in the car, he would have had to break in to gain entrance. She was surprised he would have done it with such force, though, since the wooden panes were broken and the glass shattered as if it had exploded.

She sucked in a breath of fear. But she smelled no telltale odor of gas or smoke. The glass may have exploded, but a bomb had not.

Could a gunshot have broken the window?

If so, her neighbors would have called the police. There would have been officers at her home, crime scene tape blocking it off from the street. But there was nothing but a light breeze blowing through her broken window and rattling the blind inside.

The blind was broken, like the panes and the glass. Had Brendan slammed his fist through it? Or had someone else?

Gathering all her courage, she opened that door and stepped inside the small back porch. Glass crunched beneath her feet, crushed between the soles of her shoes and the slate floor. As she passed the washer and dryer on her way to the kitchen, she noticed a brick and crumpled paper sitting atop the washer.

Someone had thrown a brick through her window?

Brendan?

Or was he the one who'd found it and picked it up? She suspected the latter, since there had obviously been a note secured to the brick with a rubber band. The broken band lay beside the brick and the crumpled paper.

She picked up the note and shivered with fear as she read the words: *You should have been the one who died.*

Oh, God. She was too late. Brendan had walked into a trap meant for her.

Chapter Thirteen

The scream startled Brendan, chilling his blood. He'd lost all sense of time and place. How long ago had he left Josie and their son? Had someone found them?

He'd left them alone and defenseless but for the gun he'd given Josie. Had she even had any bullets left?

He reached for the weapon at his back, pulling the gun from under his jacket. Then he crept up the stairs from the room he'd found in the basement, the one that had answered all the questions he'd had about ever trusting Josie Jessup.

The old steps creaked beneath his weight, giving away his presence. A shadow stood at the top of the stairwell, blocking Brendan's escape. The dim bulb swinging overhead glinted off the metal of the gun the shadow held, the barrel pointed at Brendan. He lifted his gun and aimed. But then he noticed the hair and the figure. "Josie!"

"Brendan? You're alive!" She launched herself at him, nearly knocking him off the stairs. "I thought you were dead!"

He caught himself against the brick wall at his back. "Now you know how it feels," he murmured. Despite his bitterness, his arms closed around her, holding her against him.

Her heart pounded madly. “I was so worried about you. You didn’t come back to the car and then I found that note.”

“You thought that note referred to me?”

She nodded.

“As you can see, I’m alive,” he said. “So who does it refer to?”

She gasped as that guilt flashed across her face again.

And he remembered the sign. “Michael?”

“Yes,” she miserably replied. “Some people blame me for his death.”

“Did you kill him?”

She gasped again in shock and outrage. “No. I would never…”

“It’s not a good feeling to have people thinking you’re a killer,” he remarked.

Her brow furrowed with confusion as he set her away from him. “Where have you been all this time?” she asked. As he turned and headed back down the steps, she followed him. “You’ve been down here?” Then as she realized exactly where he’d been, she ran ahead of him and tried blocking the doorway to her den.

Bookshelves lined knotty pine walls. But it wasn’t there he’d found what he’d spent the past four years looking for.

“You broke into my filing cabinet!” she said.

He could have lied and blamed it on whoever had thrown the brick through her window. But that person would have had no interest in what he’d discovered. So he just shrugged.

"You had no right!" she said, as she hurried over to where he'd spread the files across her desk.

"I think I have more right to those records than you do," he pointed out. "They're all about me."

She trembled as she shoved the papers back into folders. "But you shouldn't have seen them."

"That's what you were working on when we were together," he said, his gut aching as it had when he'd found the folders. If the drawer hadn't been locked, he probably wouldn't have bothered to jimmy it open. But he'd wanted to know all her secrets so that he might figure out who was trying to kill her. "You thought I killed my own father? That's the story you were after when you came after me."

She released a shuddery sigh. "That was a lifetime ago."

"But you're still a reporter."

She shook her head. "No."

"You teach journalism," he said, gesturing toward a framed award that sat among the books on the shelves of the den. She had given up so much of her old life, except for that. No matter where she was or what she was calling herself, she was still a journalist.

"I teach," she said, her tone rueful, "because I can't *do*."

"Because you can't give it up." Not for him. Not even for their son.

"I had to give up everything," she said. "My home. My family."

Family.

"Where's CJ?" he asked, glancing around the shadows. She'd been alone on the stairs. Where had she stashed their child this time?

"He's at his sitter's," she said. "He's safe."

"Are you sure?" He never should have let the boy out of his sight.

"I can trust the people here."

Skeptical, he snorted. "She wouldn't have thrown the brick?"

"Absolutely not," she said. "It must have been one of my other students. Or one of Michael's friends."

"What happened to Michael?"

Sadness dimmed her eyes and filled them with tears. "He was killed pursuing a story."

He touched his fingers to the scratch on his temple. It didn't sting anymore; it throbbed, the intensity of it increasing with his confusion and frustration. "How could you be responsible for that?"

Her eyes glistened with moisture. "It was a story I suggested that he cover." She blinked back the tears. "But that brick—that has nothing to do with what happened in Chicago. Nobody here knows who I really am. Nobody here would have tried to kill me."

"Just scare you," he said. But the brick and the note were nothing in comparison to gunfire and explosions. "You should be scared," he said. He reached out and jerked one of the folders from her hand. "This story could have gotten *you* killed."

She sucked in a quivering breath. "It almost did. It is why someone tried to kill me four years ago."

"Someone," he agreed. And now he knew who. "But not me."

She gestured toward those folders. "But you see why I suspected you. All the people I talked to named you as your father's killer."

People he should have been able to trust—men who'd worked with his father since they were kids selling drugs for Brendan's grandfather. And his stepmother. When his father had first married her, she had pretended to care about her husband's motherless son. But when Brendan had returned to claim the inheritance Margaret O'Hannigan thought should have been hers, she'd stopped pretending.

Josie continued, "In all the conversations I overheard while hanging out with you at O'Hannigan's, only one suspect was ever named in his murder."

"Me." Did she still suspect him?

"I was wrong," she admitted, but then defended herself. "But I didn't know you very well then. You were so secretive and you never answered my questions."

She didn't know him very well now, either. But it was obvious she couldn't stop being a journalist, so he couldn't trust her with the truth. He couldn't tell her who he really was, but he could tell her something about himself.

"We wanted the same thing, you know," he told her.

"We did?" she asked, the skepticism all hers now.

"I didn't want an award-winning exposé," he clarified. "But I wanted the truth."

She nodded. "That's why I never printed anything. I had no confirmation. No proof. I could have written an exposé. But I wanted the truth."

And that was the one thing that set her apart from the other reporters who'd done stories about him over the past four years. She wouldn't print the unsubstantiated rumors other journalists would. She'd wanted proof. She just hadn't recognized it when she'd found it.

"I want to know who killed him, too," he said. "I came back to that *life* because I wanted justice for my father." After years of trying to bring the man to justice, it was ironic that Brendan had spent the past four years trying to get justice for his father—for his cold-blooded murder.

"You spent a lot of time reading through everything," she said, staring down at the desk he'd messed up. "Did you find anything I missed?"

Because he didn't want to lie outright to her, he replied, "You weren't the only one who must have gone through those papers. If there'd been something in there, one of the marshals would have found it."

"Nobody else has ever seen this stuff," she admitted.

The pounding in his head increased. If anyone familiar with his father's murder case had looked at her records, they would have figured it out. They would have recognized that one of her sources knew too much about the murder scene, things that only the killer would have known. She never would have had to go into hiding, never would have had to keep his child from him. "Why the hell not?"

She lifted her chin with pride. "My dad taught me young to respect the code."

"What code?"

"The journalist code," she said. "A true journalist *never* reveals a source."

Ignoring the pain, he shook his head with disgust. "After the attempts on your life, I think Stanley Jessup would have understood."

She chuckled. "You don't know my dad."

"No," he said, "you never introduced me. I was your dirty little secret."

"He would have been mad," she admitted. "He wouldn't have wanted me anywhere near you, given your reputation."

"Good," Brendan said. He'd worried that the man had put her up to it, to getting close to him for a story.

"And if he cared that much for your safety, he would have understood you breaking the code."

She nodded. "Probably. But I didn't think so back then. Back then, I figured he would have been happier for me to die than reveal a source."

"Josie!" He reached for her, to offer assurance. He knew what it was like to feel like a disappointment to one's father. But when his arms closed around her, he wanted to offer more than sympathy. He wanted her… as he always did.

"But I realized that he wouldn't have cared about the code. He would have cared only about keeping me safe when I had CJ," she said. "CJ!"

She said his name with guilt and alarm, as if something bad had happened to their child.

"What? What about CJ?"

PULLING HIM OFF her, leaving him, had killed her earlier. She hated disappointing her child. So she'd kept her promise and had brought Brendan with her to pick up their son.

And for the entire day they had acted like a normal family. CJ had proudly showed Brendan all his toys and books, which the rumored mob boss had patiently played with and read to the three-year-old boy. Brendan had also looked through all the photos of their son, seeing in pictures every milestone that had been stolen from him.

Through no fault of his own. It was her fault for not trusting him. But she'd felt then that he had been keeping secrets from her. And she had imagined the worst.

As Brendan, with CJ sitting on his lap, continued to flip through the photo albums, she felt every emotion that flickered across his handsome face, the loss, the regret and the awe. He loved their son.

Could he ever love her?

Or had her lies and mistrust destroyed whatever he might have been able to feel for her? If only she'd known then what that damn story would wind up costing her…

The only man she would ever love.

He glanced up and caught her watching them, and his beautiful eyes darkened. With anger? Was he mad at her?

She couldn't blame him. She was mad at herself for all that she had denied him and her son. So today she'd tried making it up to them. She'd made all CJ's favorite foods, played all his favorite games, and she'd pretended that last night had never happened.

The gunfire. The explosion.

She was actually almost able to forget those. It was making love with Brendan that wouldn't leave her mind. She could almost feel his lips on hers, his hands on her body.

Feel him inside her…

She shivered.

"Why don't you take a shower," he said. "Warm up."

God, did she still look like hell?

"It's getting late," she said. "CJ should go to bed, too." The little boy had already had his bath. Brendan had helped give it to him. His rolled-up shirtsleeves were still damp from playing with the ducks and boats in the tub.

"I'll put him to bed," Brendan offered, as if he didn't want to waste a minute of the time he had with his son.

She had longed to clean up, so she agreed with a silent nod. But knowing that her little boy had to be tired, she leaned down to press a kiss to his forehead. "Good night, sweetheart."

Over the red curls of their son, she met Brendan's gaze. His eyes were dark, but not with anger. At least not anger she felt was directed at her. But he was intense, on edge.

As if he were biding his time...

To leave? Was his desire to tuck CJ in so that he could say goodbye?

THE HOUSE WAS small, but it had two bathrooms. So while she was soaking in the tub in the one off her bedroom, he'd used the small shower in the hall bathroom. But when he pushed open the steamed-up door, she was standing there—wrapped in a towel, waiting for him.

His pulse quickened, and his body hardened with desire. Her gaze flicked down him and then up again, her pupils wide with longing.

"Guess I should have locked the door," he remarked even as he reached for her. He slid his fingers between her breasts, pulling loose the ends of the towel she'd tucked in her cleavage, and then he dragged the towel off her damp body. He pulled the thick terry cloth across his own wet skin as she squeaked in protest.

"Hey!"

"Oh, I thought you'd meant to bring me a towel, like a good hostess." All day she'd played the perfect host, making sure that he and CJ had everything they'd needed. As if she'd felt guilty for keeping them apart.

Was that why she was here now? Out of guilt?

He wanted her, but not that way. God, he wanted her though. She was so damn beautiful, her silky skin flushed from her bath, her curves so full and soft.

He curled his hands into fists so that he wouldn't

reach for her. He had to know first. "Why are you here?"

"Why are you?" she asked. "I figured when I got out of my bath that I would find you gone."

He'd thought about it. But he'd had trouble getting CJ to keep his eyes closed. Every time he'd thought he could leave the little boy's bedside, CJ had dragged his lids up again and asked for Daddy.

Brendan's heart clutched with emotion: love like he'd never known. He'd felt a responsibility to his father to find his killer. But the responsibility he felt to CJ was far greater, because the kid needed and deserved him more. Brendan had to keep the little boy safe—even if he had to give up his own life.

"Why would you think that I would be gone?" he asked. Had becoming a mother given her new instincts? Psychic powers?

"I can feel it," she said. "Your anxiousness. Your edginess."

"You make me anxious," he said. "Edgy…"

She sucked in a shaky breath. And despite the warmth of the steamy shower, her nipples peaked, as if pouting for his touch. He wanted to oblige.

"You make me anxious," she said, "that you're going to sneak out."

"Why would I do that?"

"Because you learned something from going through my files earlier," she said, and her eyes narrowed with suspicion.

"Are you ever not suspicious of me?" he asked, even though this time he couldn't deny that she had reason to be. She'd nearly lost her life, several times, because of him. He wouldn't let her put herself in danger again.

She had so much more to lose now than she'd been forced to give up before.

"I wouldn't be," she replied, "if I ever felt like you were being completely honest with me. But there are always these secrets between us."

"You've kept secrets, too," he reminded her. "One of them is sleeping in the other room."

As if remembering that their son was close, she grabbed a towel from the rack behind her and wrapped it around her naked body.

He sighed his disappointment and hooked the towel he'd stolen from her around his waist. He'd wanted to make love with her again. He'd needed to make love with her again…before he left her.

But she opened the door first as if unable to bear the heat of the bathroom any longer. He followed her down the hall to her bedroom. Like the rest of the house, she'd decorated it warmly. The kitchen was sunny-yellow, the living room orange and her bedroom was a deep red. Like the passion that always burned between them.

"The difference between us," she said, "is that I don't have any more secrets."

He closed the door behind his back before crossing the room and grabbing her towel again. "No, no more secrets."

"You can't say the same," she accused him.

"I know how you feel," he said. "How you taste…"

And he leaned down to kiss her lips. Hers clung to his. And her fingers skimmed over his chest. She wanted him, too.

He slid his mouth across her cheek and down her neck to her shoulder. She shivered in reaction and moaned his name. "Your skin is so warm," he murmured. "So silky."

He skimmed his palms down her back, along the curve of her spine to the rounded swells of her butt. She'd been sexy before, but thin with sharp curves. Now she was more rounded. Soft and so damn sexy that just touching her tried his control.

He had to taste her, too. He gently pushed her down onto the bed. He kissed his way down her body, from her shoulder, over the curve of her breasts. He sucked a taut nipple between his lips and teased it with the tip of his tongue.

She squirmed beneath him, touching him everywhere she could reach. His back. His butt…

He swallowed a groan as the tension built inside him. Another part of him other than his head throbbed and ached, rubbing against her and begging for release.

But he denied his own pleasure to prolong hers. He moved from her breasts, over the soft curve of her stomach to that apex of curls. He teased with his tongue, sliding it in and out of her.

She clutched at his back and then his hair. She arched and wriggled and moaned. And then she came—shattering with ecstasy.

While she was still wet and pulsing, he thrust inside her. And her inner muscles clutched at him, pulling him deeper. She wrapped her legs and arms around him and met each of his thrusts.

Their mouths mated, their kisses frantic, lips clinging, tongue sliding over tongue. He didn't even need to touch her before she shattered again. He thrust once more and joined her in madness—unable to breathe, unable to think…

He could only feel. Pleasure. And love.

He loved her. That was why he had to make certain she would never be in danger again because of him. If he had to give up his life for hers and their son's, he would do it willingly.

Chapter Fourteen

Her body ached. Not from the explosion or even from running from gunmen. Her body ached from making love. Josie smiled and rolled over, reaching across the bed. The sheets were still warm, tangled and scented with their lovemaking. He'd made love to her again and again until she'd fallen into an exhausted slumber.

And she realized why when she jerked awake to an empty bed. An empty room. He'd left her. She didn't need to search her house to confirm that he was gone. But she pulled on a robe and checked CJ's room before she looked through the rest of the house.

Her son slept peacefully, the streetlamp casting light through his bedroom window. It made his red curls glow like fire, reminding her of the explosion.

And she hurried up her search, running through the house before reaching out over the basement stairwell to jerk down the pull chain on the dangling bulb. It swung out over the steps, the light dancing around her as she hurried down to her den. He wasn't there and neither were her folders.

He had found something in them. What?

What had she had?

Notes she'd taken from the conversations she'd overheard in the bar and from informal interviews she'd done with other members of the O'Hannigan family. News clippings from other reporters who'd covered the story. Sloppily. They hadn't dug nearly as deep as she had. A copy of the case file from his father's murder, which she'd bought off a cop on the force. Brendan wasn't wrong that many people had a price. They could be bought.

But not Charlotte.

Too bad the former U.S. marshal wasn't close enough to help her now. Maybe Josie wasn't close enough, either—to stop Brendan from doing what she was afraid he was about to do: either confront or kill his father's murderer.

"But who? Who is it?" she murmured to herself.

She'd gone through the folders so many times that she pretty much had the contents memorized. Brendan had figured it out; so could she. But she couldn't let him keep his head start on her. She had to catch up with him.

No doubt he had taken her SUV. But she had another car parked in the garage off the alley, a rattletrap Volkswagen convertible. It wasn't pretty, but mechanically it should be sound enough to get her back to Chicago. She had bought the car from a student desperate to sell it for money to buy textbooks.

She had never had to struggle for cash as her community college students did. Her father had given her everything she'd ever wanted.

Brendan's father had not done the same for him. In fact, if rumors could ever be believed, Dennis O'Hannigan had taken away the one thing—the one person—who had mattered most to Brendan: his mother.

Why would he want to avenge the man's death? Why would he care enough to get justice for him?

Was it a code? Like the one her father had taught her. She shrugged off her concerns for now. She had to wake CJ and take him over to Mrs. Mallory's.

The little boy murmured in protest as she lifted him from his bed. "C'mon, sweetheart," she said. "I need to take you to Mrs. M's."

He shook his head. "I don't wanna go. Gotta p'tect you like Daddy said."

She tensed. "Daddy told you to protect me?"

"Uh-huh," CJ murmured. "He's gonna get rid of a bad person and then he'll come home to us."

The words her sleepy son uttered had everything falling into place for Josie. Brendan may not have trusted her enough to tell her the truth. But he had inadvertently told their son.

BRENDAN WASN'T SURE who he could trust, especially now that he knew who'd killed his father. But he knew that Josie had at least one person she could trust—besides himself.

Charlotte Green's outraged gasp rattled the phone. "You thought I might have given up her location?"

He pressed his fingers to that scratch on his head. If the bullet hadn't just grazed him…

No, he wouldn't let himself think about what might have happened to Josie and his son. She'd had the gun though—she would have defended herself and their child.

He glanced around the inside of the surveillance van, which was filled with equipment and people—people he wasn't sure he should have trusted despite their federal clearances. If U.S. marshals could be bought, so could FBI agents. He lowered his voice. "After gunmen tracked us down at my safe house and tried to kill us…"

"I didn't even know where you were when you called me, and if I had," she said, her voice chilly with offended pride, "I sure as well wouldn't have sent gunmen after you and Josie and my godson."

He still wasn't so sure about that. But, he realized, she hadn't told anyone where she'd relocated Josie. Why keep that secret and reveal anything else?

"You must have been followed," she said.

He'd thought about that but rejected the notion. "No. Nobody followed us that night."

"Maybe another night then," she suggested. "Someone must have figured out where you would take her."

The only people who knew about the safe house were fellow FBI agents. He glanced around the van, wondering if one of them had betrayed him, if one of them had been bought like Charlotte's former partner had been bought and like he'd thought she might have been. "You didn't trace the call?"

"No."

He snorted in derision. "I thought you were being honest with me. That's why I trusted you."

More than he trusted the crew he'd handpicked. The other men messed with the equipment, setting up mikes and cameras, and he watched them—checking to see if anyone had pulled out a phone as he had. But then if they were tipping off someone, they could have made that call already, before they'd joined him.

"But you must have a GPS on that phone you gave her," he continued, calling her on her lie. "You must have some way to keep tabs on her."

She chuckled. "Okay, maybe I do."

That was why he'd left Josie the phone. "That's what I thought."

"Until recently she was easy to track," Charlotte said. "She was at home or the college."

"Teaching journalism," he remarked. "That's why you kept my secret from her. You realized that I had reason to be cautious with her. That no matter how much you changed her appearance or her identity, she was still a reporter."

"A teacher," Charlotte corrected him.

He snorted again. "Of journalism." And she'd still had the inclination to seek out dangerous stories. For her, there was no story more dangerous than this one. He had to make certain she was far away from him.

"Use your GPS," he ordered, "and tell me where she is now." Hopefully still at home, asleep in the bed he'd struggled to leave. He had wanted to hold her all night; he'd wanted to hold her forever.

Some strange noise emanated from the phone.

"Charlotte?"

"She's on the move."

"But I took her car." She must have borrowed a neighbor's or maybe Mrs. Mallory's. Hopefully, she'd left their son with his babysitter.

"The Volkswagen, too?"

"I didn't know she had another." As modestly as she'd been living in that small, outdated house, he hadn't considered she'd had the extra money for another car.

Charlotte sighed. "I'm surprised that clunker was up to the trip."

"Trip?"

"She's in Chicago."

"Damn it," he cursed at her. "I could have used you

here. I'm surprised you didn't come to help protect her. She thinks you're her friend."

"I am."

"You're also a princess. What is it? Couldn't spare the time from waving at adoring crowds?"

"I'm also pregnant," she said, and there was that sound again. "And currently in labor…since last night. Or I would have come. I would have sent someone I trusted, but they refused to leave me."

Brendan flinched at his insensitivity.

"So like you asked me to, I trusted you," she said. "I thought if anyone would keep Josie safe, it would be the man who loves her."

"I'm trying," he said. And the best way to do that was to remove the threat against her.

He glanced at the monitors flanking one side of the surveillance van. One of the cameras caught a vehicle careening down the street, right toward the estate they were watching on the outskirts of Chicago.

For all the rust holes, he couldn't tell what color the vehicle was. "Her second car," he said. "Is it an old convertible Cabriolet?" Even though the top was currently up, it looked so frayed that there were probably holes in it, too.

"Yes," Charlotte said.

"I have to go," he said, clicking off the cell. But it wasn't just the call he had to abort. He had to stop the whole operation.

"Block the driveway!" he yelled at one of the men wearing a headset. That agent could communicate with the agents outside the van. But he only stared blankly at Brendan, as if unable to comprehend what he was saying. "Stop the car," he explained. "Don't let her get to the house."

"From the way you're acting, I'm guessing that's the reporter you dated," another of the agents inside the van addressed Brendan. He must have been eavesdropping on his conversation with Charlotte. Or he'd tapped into it. "The one you just discovered was put into witness protection and that she had the evidence all this time?"

This agent was Brendan's superior in ranking, and even though he had worked with him for years—four years on this assignment alone—he didn't know him well enough to know about his character.

Could he be trusted?

Could any of them, inside the van or out?

His blood chilled in his veins, and he shook his head, disgusted with himself for giving away Josie's identity so easily. All of his fellow agents had been well aware of how he'd felt about Josie Jessup.

"It isn't?" the agent asked.

"No, it's her," he admitted. "And that's why we have to stop her." Before she confronted face-to-face the person who'd tried to kill her.

The supervising agent shook his head, stopping the man with the headset from making the call to stop her. So Brendan took it upon himself and reached for the handle of the van's sliding door. But strong hands caught him, holding him back and pinning his arms behind him.

Damn it.

He should have followed his instincts to trust no one. He should have done it alone. But he'd wanted to go through the right channels—had wanted true justice, not vigilante justice. But maybe with people as powerful as these, with people who could buy off police officers and federal agents, the only justice was vigilante.

He was going to kill her.

Josie had to stop him—had to stop Brendan from doing something he would live to regret. Taking justice into his own hands would take away the chance for him to have a real relationship with his son.

And her?

She didn't expect him to forgive her for thinking he was a killer. She didn't expect him to trust her, especially after she'd come here. But she had to stop him.

She hadn't seen her white SUV along the street or along the long driveway leading up to the house. But that didn't mean he hadn't exchanged it for one of those she had seen. The house, a brick Tudor, looked eerily similar to Brendan's, just on a smaller scale. Like a model of the original O'Hannigan home.

Brendan had to be here. Unless it was already done....

Was she was too late? Had he already taken his justice and left?

The gates stood open, making it easy for her to drive through and pull her Volkswagen up to the house. But she hadn't even put it in Park before someone was pulling open her door and dragging her from behind the steering wheel. She had no time to reach inside her bag and pull out the gun.

Strong hands held tightly to her arms, shoving her up the brick walk to the front door. It stood open, a woman standing in the doorway as if she'd been expecting her.

Yet she acted puzzled, her brow furrowed as if she was trying to place Josie. Of course, Josie didn't look the same as she had when she'd informally interviewed Margaret O'Hannigan four years ago. Back then the woman had believed Josie was just her stepson's girlfriend. And since they'd only met a few times, it was no wonder she wouldn't as easily see through Josie's disguise as Brendan had.

But Margaret must have realized she'd given herself up during one of their conversations. That was why Margaret had tried to kill Josie.

While Josie had changed much over the past few years, this woman hadn't changed at all. She was still beautiful—her face smooth of wrinkles and ageless. Her hair was rich and dark and devoid of any hint of gray despite the fact that she had to be well into her fifties. She was still trim and tiny. Her beauty and fragile build might have been what had fooled Josie into excluding her as a suspect in her husband's murder.

But now she detected a strength and viciousness about the woman as she stared at Josie, her dark eyes cold and emotionless. "Who the hell are you?" she demanded.

"Josie Jessup," she replied honestly. There was no point clinging to an identity that had already been blown.

"Josie Jessup? I thought you were dead," the woman remarked.

Josie had thought the same of her. That Brendan might have killed her by now.

"Are you responsible for this?" Margaret asked, gesturing toward the open gates and the dark house. An alarm sounded from within, an insistent beeping that must have driven her to the door. "Did you disable the security system, forcing open the gates and unlocking the doors?"

Brendan must have. He was here then. Somewhere. Josie wasn't too late.

"Search her car," Margaret ordered the man who'd held her arms.

Josie stumbled forward as he released her. But the woman didn't step back, didn't allow Josie inside her house.

"I wouldn't know how to disable a security system," Josie assured her. "I am no criminal mastermind."

"No, you're a reporter," Margaret said. "That was why you were always asking all those questions."

"And you were always eager to answer them," Josie reminded her. Too eager, since she hadn't realized she'd given herself away. But then neither had Josie. She still wasn't sure exactly what it was in those folders that had convinced Brendan of the woman's guilt. "You were eager to point the blame at your stepson."

"A man shouldn't benefit from a murder he committed," she said, stubbornly clinging to her lies.

"Brendan didn't kill his father," Josie said, defending the man she loved.

Margaret smiled, but her eyes remained cold. "You weren't so convinced back then. You suspected him just like everyone else."

"And just like everyone else, I was wrong," Josie admitted. "But you knew that."

The woman tensed and stepped out from the doorway. She held a gun in her hand.

For protection? Because of the security breach? Or because someone had tipped her off that either Brendan or Josie was coming to confront her?

"How would I know something that the authorities did not?" Margaret asked, but a small smile lifted her thin lips. "They all believed Brendan responsible, as well."

"But they could never find proof."

"Because he was clever."

"Because he was innocent."

The woman laughed. "You loved him."

It wasn't a question, so Josie didn't reply. Or deny what was probably pathetically obvious to everyone but Brendan.

"That's a pity," the woman commiserated. "It's not easy to love an O'Hannigan. At least you don't need to worry about that anymore."

"I don't?" Josie asked.

"Brendan is dead."

Pain clutched her heart, hurting her as much as if the woman had fired a bullet into her heart. He'd already been here. And gone.

"You didn't know?" Margaret asked. "Some journalist you are. How did you miss the reports?"

Had his death already made the news? The Volkswagen had no radio—just a hole in the dash where one had once been. The kid who'd sold her the auto had been willing to part with his car but not his sound system.

Margaret sighed regretfully. "And it was such a beautiful estate. I'd hoped to return there one day."

"The house?"

"It blew up…with Brendan inside." Margaret shook her head. "Such a loss." With a nasty smile, she clarified, "The house, not Brendan."

The explosion. She was talking about the explosion. Brendan wasn't dead. Relief eased the horrible tightness in Josie's chest, but the sigh she uttered was of disgust with the woman. "How can you be so…"

"Practical?" Margaret asked. "It's so much better than being a romantic fool."

Josie hadn't been a fool for being romantic; she'd been a fool for doubting Brendan. Then. And maybe now.

If he'd intended to kill his stepmother, wouldn't he have already been here? Where was he?

"You're better off," Margaret assured her. "You were stupid to fall for him."

"You didn't love your husband?" Josie asked. That would explain how she'd killed him in cold blood.

She chuckled. "My mama always told me that it was easier to love a rich man than a poor man. My mama had never met Dennis O'Hannigan." She shuddered but her grip stayed steady on the gun. "You were lucky to get away from his son."

"Brendan is—was—" she corrected herself. It was smarter to let the woman think the explosion she'd ordered had worked. "He was nothing like his father."

"You don't believe that or you wouldn't have gone into hiding," Margaret remarked. "You even changed your hair and your face. You must have really been afraid of him."

She had spent almost four years being afraid of the wrong person.

"Were you afraid of his father?" Josie asked.

Margaret shrugged her delicate shoulders. "A person would have been crazy to *not* be afraid of Dennis."

Dennis wasn't the only O'Hannigan capable of inspiring fear. Neither was Brendan.

Despite her small stature, Margaret O'Hannigan was an intimidating woman.

So Josie should have held her tongue. She should have stopped asking her questions. But maybe Brendan was right—maybe she wasn't capable of *not* being a journalist. Because she had to know…

Even if the question cost her everything, she had to ask, "Is that why you killed him?"

Chapter Fifteen

Brendan fought against the men holding him. He shoved back with his body and his head. He knocked the back of his skull against one man's nose, dropping him to the floor while the other stumbled into the equipment. Then he whipped a gun from his holster and whirled to confront his attackers.

Men he had hoped he could trust: fellow FBI agents.

"I should have known," he berated himself. "I should have known the leak was inside the Bureau. I should have known there was no one I could trust."

Special Agent Martinez, the man supervising the assignment, calmly stared down the barrel of Brendan's gun. "I've heard about this happening to agents like you, ones who've been undercover more than they've been out. Ones who get so paranoid of the lives they're living that they lose their grasp on reality. On sanity. You're losing it, O'Hannigan."

"No, we're losing *her,*" Brendan said, as one of the monitors showed Josie walking inside the house with a killer. Margaret O'Hannigan held a gun, too, pointed at the woman he loved.

"We've got the house wired," Martinez reminded him. "We're going to hear everything that they say."

"But the plan was for *me* to get her to talk," he said and lowered the gun to his side. He wasn't going to use it. Yet…

Martinez nodded in agreement. "But once she sees you're alive, you wouldn't get anything out of her."

"Neither will Josie," he argued.

"Josie Jessup is a reporter." Martinez was the one who'd confirmed Brendan's suspicions about it, who'd tracked her back to the stories written under the pseudonym of Jess Lcy. "A damn good one. She fooled you four years ago."

And allowing himself to be deceived and distracted had nearly gotten Brendan thrown off the case. But because he'd inherited his father's business, he had been the only one capable of getting inside the organization and taking it apart, as the FBI had been trying to do for years.

"She won't fool Margaret." Because Margaret had fooled them all for years. Even his father.

Martinez shook his head. "She's Stanley Jessup's daughter. She has a way of making people talk. She knows what buttons to push, what questions to ask."

That was what Brendan was afraid of—that she'd push the wrong buttons. "If Margaret admits anything to her, it's only because she intends to kill her."

"Then we'll go in," Martinez assured him. "The evidence you found got us the federal warrants for the surveillance. But there isn't enough for an arrest. We need a confession. You were the one who pointed that out."

And he'd intended to get the confession himself. He hadn't intended to use Josie—to put her in danger. Their son needed his mother; Brendan needed her, too.

On the surveillance monitors, one of Margaret's

bodyguards walked into the house, something swinging from the hand that wasn't holding a gun.

"We won't get there fast enough to save her," Brendan said, as foreboding and dread clutched his heart. The van was parked outside the gates. Even though they were open, thanks to the security system being dismantled, they were still too far down the driveway.

"There are guys closer," Martinez reminded him.

But were they guys he could trust? Could he really trust anyone?

SHE SHOULD HAVE trusted Brendan. Just because he'd discovered the identity of his father's killer didn't mean he was going to avenge the man's death.

But she'd thought the worst of him again. And she'd worried that CJ would lose his father before he ever got a chance to really know him. Now a gun was pointed at her, and the risk was greater that CJ would lose his mother. At least he had his godmother; Charlotte would take him. She would protect him as Josie had failed to do.

With the lights off and the draperies pulled, it was dark inside the house—nearly as dark as if night had fallen already. Except a little sliver of sunlight sneaked through a crack in the drapes and glinted off the metal of Margaret O'Hannigan's gun.

She looked much more comfortable holding a weapon than Josie was. Maybe she should reach for hers. Her purse was on the hardwood floor next to where Margaret had pushed her down onto the couch. Even the inside of the home was a replica of Dennis O'Hanningan's.

"Are you insinuating that I killed my husband? What

the hell are you talking about?" the older woman demanded to know.

"The truth." A concept that Josie suspected Margaret O'Hannigan was not all that familiar with. "And I'm not insinuating. I'm flat-out saying that you're the one. You killed Brendan's father."

"How dare you accuse me of killing my husband!" she exclaimed, clearly offended, probably not because Josie thought her capable of murder but because she hadn't gotten away with it.

Hell, she would still probably get away with it. Josie glanced down at her bag again. She needed to grab her gun, needed to defend herself. But then it was no longer just the two of them.

Heavy footsteps echoed on the hardwood flooring. "There was nothing in her car," the man who had dragged Josie from the Volkswagen informed his boss as he joined them inside the house. "But this."

Josie turned to see CJ's booster seat dangling from his hand.

"You have a child?" Margaret asked.

She could have lied, claimed she'd borrowed a friend's car. But she was curious. Would Margaret spare her because she was a mother? "Why does it matter that I have a son?"

"How old is he?" Margaret asked.

"Three." Too young to lose his mother, especially as she'd been the only parent he'd ever known until a day ago.

Margaret shook her head. "No. No. No..."

"It's okay," Josie said. "You can let me go. I don't really know anything. I have no proof that you killed Dennis O'Hannigan."

The man glanced from her to Margaret and back.

Had he not worked for her back then? Had he not realized his employer was a killer?

Maybe he would protect her from the madwoman.

"You have something far worse," Margaret said. "You have Brendan O'Hannigan's son."

"Wh-what?"

"The last time I saw you, I suspected you were pregnant," Margaret admitted. "You were—" her mouth twisted into a derisive smirk "—glowing."

Josie hadn't even known she was pregnant then. She hadn't known until after her big fight with Brendan, until after she'd had the car accident when her brakes had given out and she'd been taken to the hospital. That was when she'd learned she carried his child.

"You—you don't know that my son is Brendan's," Josie pointed out.

"All I'll have to do is see a picture," she said. She pointed toward Josie's purse and ordered her employee, "Go through that."

He upended the contents of the bag, the gun dropping with a thud to the floor.

"You should have used that while you had the chance," Margaret said. "I didn't waste my chance."

"Are you talking about now?" Josie wondered. "Or when you shot your husband in the alley behind O'Hannigan's?" She suspected this woman was cold-blooded enough to have done it personally.

The man handed over Josie's wallet to his boss. The picture portfolio hung out of it, the series of photos a six-month progression of CJ from infancy to his birthday a couple of months ago. Usually people smiled when they saw the curly-haired boy. But his step-grandmother glowered.

"Damn it," Margaret cursed. "Damn those O'Hannigan eyes."

Josie could not deny her son's paternity. "Why do you care that Brendan has—had—a son?"

"Because I am not about to have another damn O'Hannigan heir come out of the woodwork again and claim what is rightfully mine," she replied angrily. "I worked damn hard for it. I earned it."

"So you didn't kill your husband because you were afraid of him. You killed him because you wanted his fortune," Josie mused aloud.

The woman's eyes glittered with rage and her face—once so beautiful—contorted into an ugly mask. "He was going to divorce me," she said, outraged at even the memory. "After all those years of putting up with his abuse, he was going to leave me. Claimed he never loved me."

"You never loved him, either," Josie pointed out.

"That was why it felt so damn good to pull the trigger," she admitted gleefully. "To see that look of surprise on his face as I shot him right in the chest. He had no idea who he was married to—had no idea that I could be as ruthless as he was. And that I was that good a shot."

So she had fired the gun herself. And apparently she'd taken great pleasure from it. Josie had no hope of this callous killer sparing her life.

Margaret chuckled wryly. "The coroner said the bullet hit him right in the heart. I was surprised because I didn't figure he had one."

"Then why did you marry him?"

"For the same reason I killed him—for the money," she freely admitted.

She stepped closer and pointed the barrel right at

Josie's head. "So your kid is damn well not going to come forward and claim it from me now."

Margaret thought Brendan was dead—that CJ was the only threat to her inheriting now. But if Brendan had really died, the estate would go to his heirs, not his stepmother. Then Josie remembered that Dennis O'Hannigan had had a codicil in his will that only an O'Hannigan would hold deed to the estate. Before Brendan had accepted his inheritance, he'd had to sign a document promising to leave it only to an O'Hannigan. Margaret must have thought she was the only one left.

"He's only three years old," Josie reminded her. "He's not going to take anything away from you."

"I didn't think Brendan would, either. After he ran away I thought he was never coming back." She sighed. "I thought his dad had made sure he could never come back, the same way that he had made sure Brendan's mother could never come back."

"You thought Dennis had killed him?"

"He should have," Margaret said. The woman wasn't just greedy; she was pure evil. "Then I wouldn't have had that nasty surprise."

She was going to have another one when she learned that once again Brendan wasn't dead. But if he wasn't… where was he? Shouldn't he have been here before now?

Could someone else have hurt him? Or maybe the authorities had brought him in for questioning about the explosion and the shootings at the hospital.…

Maybe if she bided her time…

But Margaret pressed the gun to Josie's temple as if ready to squeeze the trigger. The burly guard flinched as if he could feel Josie's pain. "Now you are going to tell me where you've left your brat so we can make sure I don't get another nasty surprise."

"He doesn't need your money," Josie pointed out. "He's a Jessup. My father has more money than CJ will ever be able to spend."

"CJ?"

Josie bit her tongue, appalled that she'd given away her son's name. Not that his first name alone would lead the woman to him.

"So where is CJ?"

"Someplace where you can't get to him," Josie assured herself more than the boy's step-grandmother. He was safe now, and Brendan would make certain he stayed that way. No matter what happened to her.

"You'll tell me," Margaret said as she slid her finger onto the trigger.

Uncaring that the barrel was pressed to her temple, Josie shook her head. "You might as well shoot me now, because I will never let you get to my son."

The trigger cocked, and Josie closed her eyes, waiting for it. Would it hurt? Or would it be over so quickly she wouldn't even realize it?

The gun barrel jerked back so abruptly that Josie's head jerked forward, too. "Help me persuade her," Margaret ordered her guard.

And Josie's head snapped again as the man slapped her. Her cheek stung and her eyes watered as pain overwhelmed her.

"Where is he?" Margaret asked.

Josie shook her head.

And the man slapped her again.

A cry slipped from her mouth as her lip cracked from the blow. Blood trickled from the stinging wound.

"I'm never going to tell you where my son is," she vowed. "I don't care how many times you hit me."

"I care."

Josie looked up to see Brendan saunter into the living room as nonchalantly as if he were just joining them for drinks. But instead of bringing a bottle of wine, he'd brought a gun—which he pointed directly at Margaret. Probably because she had whirled toward him with her weapon.

But her guard had pulled his gun, and he pressed the barrel to Josie's head. Brendan may have intended to rescue her, but Josie had a horrible feeling that they were about to make their son an orphan.

She should have thought it out before she'd chased after Brendan. She had been concerned about CJ losing his father, but now he might lose both his parents.

"I THOUGHT YOU were dead," Margaret said, slinging her words at him like an accusation.

"You keep making that mistake," Brendan said. "Guess that's just been wishful thinking on your part."

"I thought the explosion killed you."

"You were behind that?"

"I wanted you dead," she admitted, without actually claiming responsibility.

But she'd already confessed to enough to go away for a long time. Martinez had been right about Josie making her talk. Now that Josie had gotten what they'd wanted, he needed to get her to safety.

"I've wanted you dead for a long time," Margaret continued. "This time I'll personally make sure you're gone. You've disrupted my plans for the last time." She cocked her gun at him now. "Then we'll retrieve your son."

She gestured at Josie as if they were co-conspirators. Had she not heard anything Josie had said to her? Josie would die before she would give up her son's location. That was what a mother should be like. CJ was one lucky boy. And Brendan would make sure they were reunited soon.

But Margaret was not done. She was confessing to crimes she had yet to commit. Crimes that Brendan would make damn certain she never got the chance to commit. "And when I get rid of that kid, I'll be making damn sure there will be no more O'Hannigans."

"You're the one who'll be going away forever," Brendan warned her as he cocked his gun. But if he shot her, would the guy holding Josie surrender or kill her?

Chapter Sixteen

"Don't kill her," Josie implored Brendan. Maybe she had been right to be concerned that he would take matters into his own hands. But why had he taken so long to show up here? Where had he been?

Brendan narrowed his eyes as if he were still thinking about pulling the trigger, about taking a life. He could even excuse it as he had the others—that he'd done it to save another.

"Josie, I have to," he said, as if he'd been given no choice.

She had been thrilled to see him, thrilled that he might protect her from this madwoman. But she didn't want him becoming her—becoming a killer.

"You told me you wanted justice," she reminded him. "Not vengeance."

"He's a killer," Margaret said, spit flying from her mouth with disgust. "All O'Hannigans are killers. That's why it's best to get rid of the boy, too. Or he'll grow up just like Brendan has."

"Brendan isn't a killer," Josie told her—and him. "He came back for justice. He figured out you killed his father."

"How?" the woman arrogantly scoffed. "No one else has figured it out in four years."

"She did," Brendan said. "And she has evidence."

"What evidence?" Josie asked. He had to be bluffing or at least exaggerating the evidentiary value of what he'd found. She'd gone through those folders so many times but hadn't figured out what he'd discerned so quickly.

Margaret snorted. "Evidence. It doesn't matter. It's never going to get to court. I will never be arrested."

That was Josie's concern, too. And then Brendan's name would never be cleared.

"I already brought the evidence to the district attorney," Brendan said, answering one of Josie's questions.

Now she knew where he'd been. He had gone through the right channels for justice.

"The arrest warrant should have been issued by now," Brendan continued. But he was looking at her henchman instead of Margaret, as if warning him. Or trying to use his bluff to scare him off. "Do you want to go to jail with her?"

"I had nothing to do with her killing your dad," the man said. "I didn't even work for her then."

"But you're working for her now," Brendan said. "You've assaulted a woman and threatened the life of a child. I think those charges will put you away for a while, too, especially if you're already on parole for other crimes."

The man's face flushed with color. He shook his head, but not in denial of his criminal record. Instead he pulled the gun away from Josie and murmured, "I'm sorry."

"Don't let him get to you," Margaret said. "He's bluffing. He's just bluffing."

The man shook his head again, obviously unwilling to risk it. It wasn't as if they were playing poker for money. They were playing for prison.

"Where are you going?" Margaret screamed after him as he headed for the door. "How dare you desert me!"

The man was lucky that she was having a standoff with Brendan or she probably would have fired a bullet into his back. She was that furious.

"You should just give it up," Josie told her. "You have no help now."

Margaret glared. "Neither does he."

"He has me," Josie said.

"Not for long," Margaret said. "He's going to lose you just like you're going to lose that brat of yours."

"You just shut the hell up," Josie warned the woman, her temper fraying from the threats and insults directed at CJ. "Don't ever talk about my son."

Margaret chuckled, so Josie struck her. She'd hoped to knock the gun from the petite woman's hand. But the older lady was surprisingly strong. She held on to her gun and swung it toward Josie, pressing it into her heart—which was exactly what her insults and threats had been hitting.

"You get involved with a killer, sooner or later you're going to wind up dead," the woman said. "Too bad for you it's going to be sooner."

Wasn't it already later—since Margaret had first tried to kill her four years ago? But Josie kept that question to herself.

"YOU'RE THE KILLER," Brendan corrected Margaret. So she would have no compunction pulling the trigger and killing Josie. It was what she'd intended to do from the moment she'd forced her inside the house. That was why she'd confessed to her—because she planned to make sure Josie could never testify against her.

"If you had really turned over proof to the district attorney, the police would be here already," Margaret said. "You have nothing."

"You confessed to Josie."

"Just now," she said. "And she'll never live to testify against me."

"No," he said, "you confessed to her four years ago."

Margaret laughed. "She doesn't even know what evidence you had. I think she damn well would have known had I confessed to her."

"You weren't confessing," Brendan admitted. "You were trying to convince her of my guilt. You told her that it must have been someone he trusted since my father had never pulled his gun."

Josie gasped. "And all the other reports—except for the official police report—claimed he'd been killed with his own gun."

Since Dennis O'Hannigan was legendary for turning a person's weapon on them, it had been the height of irony that he'd had his own gun turned on him.

Brendan shook his head. "But all his guns were in their holsters." He'd learned from his father to have more than one backup weapon. "Only the killer would know that he hadn't pulled any of them, that he'd trusted his killer."

Margaret snorted. "Trusted? Hell, no. Underestimated is what he'd done. He thought I was too weak and helpless to be a threat."

"And he would have considered me a threat," Brendan said, because his father had known what his son had become. What he really was.

So why had he left him the business?

"You underestimated me, too," she accused Brendan. "You never considered me a threat, either."

He hadn't realized just how dangerous she was—until she'd turned her gun on the woman he loved. "It's over, Margaret."

"On that flimsy evidence?" she asked, nearly as incredulous as the district attorney had been.

"No, on the confession that the FBI has recorded."

She glanced at Josie as if checking her for a wire.

"When your security system was hacked, the house was bugged. Every intercom in the place turned on like a mike."

She glanced around at the intercom by the door and another on the desk behind her.

"You're under arrest for the murder of Dennis O'Hannigan," he said, "and the attempted murders of Josie Jessup and—"

The woman raised her eyebrows and scoffed. "You're arresting me? On what authority?"

"FBI," he said. "I'm an FBI agent."

Josie's eyes widened with surprise. He'd hoped that she might have figured it out, that she would have realized he was not a bad man.

"You are not," Margaret said. "You're bluffing again, treating me like a fool just like your father did."

With his free hand he pulled out his credentials, which he hadn't been able to carry for the past four years, and flashed his shield at her. "No. Game over."

She stubbornly shook her head and threatened, "I am going to pull the trigger."

"Then so will I," he replied. And he was bluffing now.

"You won't risk her life." Margaret knowingly called

him on his lie. "I saw how you were when she disappeared four years ago. You were as devastated as you were when your mother disappeared."

He couldn't deny the truth—not anymore.

"So you're going to step back and let me leave with her," Margaret said.

"And what do you think you're going to do?" Brendan asked. "Talk her into taking you to our son?"

Margaret's gaze darted between him and Josie. That had been her plan—all part of her deranged plan.

"She'll never do that," Brendan said. "You won't be able to kill all the O'Hannigans. And even if you thought you did, you still wouldn't be the last one." He chuckled now at how incredibly flawed the woman's plan was. "You're actually not even a real O'Hannigan."

Anger tightened her lips into a thin line. "I married your father."

"But it wasn't legal," he informed her.

She glared at him. "I have the license to prove it, since you're all about evidence."

"It wasn't legal because he was still married," he explained.

"What?" she gasped.

"My mother isn't dead."

"Yes, she is," Margaret frantically insisted. "Your father killed her. Everyone knows that."

"He'd beaten her...." Which Brendan had witnessed; he'd been only eleven years old and helpless to protect her. "He sent her to the hospital, but she didn't die. She went into witness protection."

But still she wouldn't testify against him. Not because she had still loved the man but because she'd loved Brendan. And to protect him, she had struck a bargain with the devil.

Maybe he would have to do the same to protect Josie.

"You're lying," Margaret said. She was distracted now, more focused on him than Josie.

He shook his head, keeping her attention on him while he tried to ignore Special Agent Martinez speaking through his earpiece. Brendan was calling the shots now. And he wouldn't do that until Josie was out of the line of fire.

"Where do you think I ran away to when I was fifteen?" he asked. Thank God he hadn't wound up living on the streets, which he'd been desperate enough to do. He'd found a place to go. A home.

"I didn't think you really ran away," Margaret said. "I know you tried, that you stole one of your father's cars. But that car was returned that same night—without you. And you were never seen again."

As he relived that night, his heart flipped with the fear he'd felt when his father's men had driven him off the road and into the ditch. At fifteen he hadn't had enough experience behind the wheel to be able to outmaneuver them. And when they'd jerked him from behind the wheel and left him alone with his father, he'd thought he was dead, that he'd be going to see his mother in heaven.

His father had sent him to her with a bus ticket and a slip of paper with an address on it. His mother had been relocated to New York, where she had built a life fostering runaway kids. And somehow, either using money or threats, Dennis had found out exactly what had happened to his wife and where she was. Brendan had used that bus ticket to reunite with her and become one of those kids. And in exchange for getting her son back, his mother had agreed to never testify against Dennis O'Hannigan.

"My mom will actually be here soon," he said with a glance at Josie. "But the other agents will be here before her."

That was the cue, sent through his headset, to make all hell break loose.

Chapter Seventeen

Josie was reeling from all the answers she'd just received to questions she hadn't even known to ask. Was it true? Was any of it true?

Brendan had flashed the badge, but she hadn't had a chance to read it. Was it *his* name on it? Was he really an FBI agent? And what about his mother being alive all these years in witness protection?

It all seemed so unrealistic that it almost had to be real. And it explained so much.

She heard the footsteps then. And so did Margaret. Before the woman could react and pull the trigger, Josie shoved her back and then dropped to the floor as shots rang out.

The house exploded. There was no bomb, but the effects were the same. Glass shattered. Footsteps pounded. Voices shouted. And shots were fired.

She wasn't sure she would feel if any bullets struck her. She was numb with shock. She'd thought she had fooled and deceived Brendan four years ago. But she had been the fool. In her search for what she'd thought was the truth, she had fallen for the lies. This woman's lies. The other news reports about him.

He could have set her straight, but he had chosen instead to keep his secrets. And to let her go…

A hand clutched her hair, pulling her head up as a barrel pressed again to her temple. How many times could a gun be held to her head before it was fired? Either on purpose or accidentally?

Josie worried that her luck was about to run out.

"Let her go!" Brendan shouted the order. And cocked his gun.

Another shot rang out, along with a soft click, and Josie flinched, waiting for the pain to explode in her head. But then Margaret dropped to the floor beside her, blood spurting from her shoulder. Her eyes wide open with shock, she stared into Josie's face. Then she began to curse, calling Josie every vulgar name as agents jerked her to her feet.

Then there were hands on Josie's arms, hands that shook a little as they helped her up. Her legs wobbled and she pitched slightly forward, falling into a broad chest. Strong arms closed around her, holding her steady.

"Are you all right?" Brendan asked, his deep voice gruff with emotion.

She wasn't sure. "How—how did she not shoot me… when she got shot?"

"She'd already fired all her bullets," he replied.

She realized the soft click she'd heard had been from the empty cartridge. "Did you know?"

"I counted."

How? In the chaos of the raid, how had he kept track of it all? But then she remembered that he was a professional. She was the amateur, the one who hadn't belonged in his world four years ago and certainly didn't belong there now.

She belonged with her son. She should have never left him.

Exhausted, she laid her head on his chest. His heart beat as frantically as hers, both feeling the aftereffects of adrenaline and fear. At least Josie had been afraid.

She wasn't sure how Brendan felt about anything. She hadn't even known who he really was.

PARAMEDICS HAD PUT her in the back of an ambulance, but she had refused to lie down on the stretcher. She sat up on it, her legs dangling over the side. She wasn't a small woman, yet there was something childlike about her now, Brendan thought. She looked…lost.

"Is she okay?" he asked the paramedic who'd stepped out of the ambulance to talk quietly to him.

"Except for some bruises, she's physically all right," the paramedic assured him. "But she does appear to be in shock."

Was that because she'd been held and threatened by a crazy woman? Or because she had finally learned the truth about him?

"It looks like you were hit," the paramedic remarked, reaching up toward Brendan's head. He hadn't been hit, but not for lack of trying on his stepmother's part. As lousy a shot as she was, she must have been very close to his father to have killed him.

Too close for his father to have seen how dangerous the woman really was. His father had been so smart and careful when it came to business. Why had he'd been so sloppy and careless when it had come to pleasure?

Four years ago, when Brendan had found out his lover was really a reporter after a story, he'd thought he had been careless, too. And his carelessness had nearly gotten Josie killed.

"I'm fine," he told the paramedic. "That's not even recent." Two nights ago seemed like a lifetime ago. But then it had been a different life, one that Brendan didn't need to live anymore. He'd found the justice for which he'd started searching four years ago.

As he watched an agent load a bandaged and handcuffed Margaret into the back of a federal car, he knew he had justice. But he held up a hand to halt the car. Her wounded shoulder had already been treated, so she'd been medically cleared to be booked. But he didn't want them booking her yet, not before he knew all the charges against her.

"It's not scabbed over yet," the young woman persisted, as she continued to inspect the scratch on Brendan's head.

"I'm fine. But maybe you should double check the suspect," he suggested. After the paramedic left, he turned back toward the ambulance and found Josie staring at him.

She had lost that stunned look of shock. Her brow was furrowed, her eyes dark, and she looked mad. She had every right to be angry—furious, even. "I'm sorry," he said.

"Are you sorry that you saved my life?" she asked. "Or are you sorry that you lied to me?"

"I never lied."

She nodded her head sharply in agreement. "You didn't have to. You just let me make all my wrong assumptions and you never bothered to correct me. Is that why you're sorry?"

"I'm sorry," he said, "because I never should have gotten involved with you—not when I had just started the most dangerous assignment of my career." But he'd been sloppy and careless. He'd let his attraction to her overcome his common sense.

Special Agent Martinez had urged him to go for it, that having a girlfriend gave Brendan a better cover and made him look more like his dad. That it might have roused suspicions if he'd turned down such a beautiful woman. But Brendan couldn't blame Martinez. It hadn't been an order, more so a suggestion. Brendan hadn't had to listen to him.

It was all his fault—everything Josie had been through, everything she'd lost. She hadn't died, but she'd still lost her home, her family, her career. If only he'd stayed away from her…

If only he'd resisted his attraction to her…

But he'd never felt anything as powerful.

"You thought I was going to blow your cover," she said. "That's why you didn't tell me what was going on. You didn't trust that I wouldn't go public with the story."

"I know you, Josie. You can't stop being a reporter," he reminded her. "Even after they relocated you, you were ferreting out stories."

"But if you had asked me not to print anything, I would have held off," she said. "I wouldn't have put your life in danger."

No. He was the one who'd put her life in danger. And he understood that she would probably never be able to forgive him, especially if her father didn't make it.

"But you didn't trust me," she said.

"You didn't trust me, either," he said, "or you wouldn't have raced here to make sure I didn't kill Margaret for vigilante justice. You still suspected that I might be a killer."

"I didn't know who you really are," she said.

She hadn't known what he really did for a living, but she should have known what kind of person he was. Since she hadn't, there was no way that she could love him.

"How did you figure out where I had gone?" he asked. "You had all that information for years, but you never put it together. And then I took everything to present to the district attorney. So how did you realize it was Margaret?"

"CJ told me."

He laughed at her ridiculous claim. "CJ? How did he figure it out?"

"*You* told him," she said, "when you told him that you were going to get rid of the bad person so he'd be safe."

He hadn't even known if the little boy was truly awake when he'd told him goodbye. It was wanting to make sure that goodbye wasn't permanent that had had Brendan going through the proper channels for the arrest warrant.

"You said bad *person,*" she said, "not bad man, like we'd been telling him the shooters and the bomber was. Since Margaret was the only female I'd talked to about your father's murder, it had to be her."

He glanced to that car where his stepmother sat and waited for him. He needed to question her. But he dreaded leaving Josie after he had nearly lost her. He couldn't even blink without horrible images replaying in his mind—the burly man slapping her so hard her neck snapped and then the gun pressed to her temple…

Josie shivered as she followed his gaze. "I need to get home to CJ. I need to make sure he's safe."

"You don't need to go home," he said. "He should be here very soon."

Her brow furrowed. "How? Is Charlotte bringing him?"

"Charlotte couldn't come." He wondered if the former U.S. marshal had had her baby yet. "So I sent someone else to get him from Mrs. Mallory's."

She clutched his arm with a shaking hand. "You shouldn't have trusted anyone else, not with our son.

"I sent the only person I trust," he said.

She shivered again as if his words had chilled her. He didn't mean to hurt her feelings, but he hadn't been able to trust her—any more than she had been able to trust him.

The arrival of another vehicle, a minivan, drew their attention to the driveway. He smiled as an older woman jumped out of the driver's seat and pulled open the sliding door to the back. A redheaded little boy raised his arms and encircled the woman's neck as she lifted him from his booster seat.

"Looks like CJ likes his grandma," he murmured.

Josie gasped. "That's your mother? She really is alive?"

The dark, curly-haired woman was small, like Margaret, but she had so much energy and vibrancy. She would never be mistaken for fragile. She was the strongest woman he had ever known…until he'd witnessed Josie's fearlessness over and over again. She would have taken a bullet in the brain before she would have ever led Margaret to their son.

Almost too choked with emotion over seeing his mom and son together, Brendan only nodded. Then he cleared his throat and added, "My dangerous assignment is over now." And given what he now knew he had to lose, he didn't intend to ever go undercover again. "So I'd like to have a relationship with my son."

"Of course," she immediately agreed. "I'm glad he's met your mother. She sounds like an amazing woman. She gave up so much for you."

Just as Josie would have for their son. For him, Brendan's mother had given up justice for all the pain his father had put her through.

He nodded. "She is."

Josie smiled as the little boy giggled in his grandmother's arms as she tickled him. "I would like CJ to meet my father now—if you think it's safe."

"It's all over now," Brendan assured her. "Margaret knows that. Anyone who worked for her knows that now." The burly guard was sitting in the back of another car. Agents had apprehended him as he'd hightailed it out of the house. "It will be safe."

She bit her bottom lip and sighed. "For us. I'm not sure how safe it'll be for my father though. I don't want to risk giving him another heart attack. It's bad enough that he was attacked to draw me out of hiding."

And that was probably his fault, too—Margaret's wanting to make sure no other O'Hannigan heirs stood in the way of her greed. He needed to interview the crazy woman and find out who she'd been working with—who she'd bought.

"I'm sorry," he said again. He couldn't apologize enough for the danger in which he'd put Josie and their son.

BRENDAN WANTED A relationship with his son but not her. Would he never trust her? Would he never forgive her for deceiving him?

He had deceived her, too. Of course he'd had his reasons. And his orders. He couldn't tell her the truth and risk her blowing his cover.

Now she understood why he'd been so angry with her when he'd realized she had initially sought him out for an exposé. It hadn't been just a matter of pride. It had been a matter of life and death.

After all the times she'd been shot at and nearly blown up, she understood how dangerous his life was. That was why he'd kept apologizing to her.

He'd said he was sorry, but he'd never said what she'd wanted to hear. That he loved her.

She sighed.

"Everything all right, miss?" the driver asked.

She glanced into the back of the government Suburban where CJ's booster seat had been buckled. Her son was safe and happy. Of course he hadn't wanted to leave his daddy or his grandma, but he'd agreed when she'd explained he was going to meet his grandpa.

"Yes, I just hope that my dad is better." That he would be strong enough to handle the surprise of seeing her alive and well.

The older man nodded. She hadn't noticed him during all the turmoil earlier in Margaret's house. He didn't have a scratch on his bald head or a wrinkle in his dark suit. Maybe he hadn't been part of the rescue. Maybe he'd been in the van that they'd passed as they'd left the estate.

"Thank you for driving me to the hospital, Agent…"

"Marshal," he replied. "I'm a U.S. marshal."

"Did Charlotte send you?" she asked. Brendan had told her why her friend had been unable to come to her aid herself; she was having a baby. She hadn't even known Charlotte was pregnant. It had to be Aaron Timmer's baby. Josie had realized her friend was falling for her former bodyguard shortly after he'd been hired to work palace security, too. Had they married? She'd been so preoccupied with her own life lately that she hadn't gotten the specifics of what Charlotte and Princess Gabriella had endured.

"Charlotte?" the man repeated the name.

"Charlotte Green," Josie explained. "She was the marshal who relocated me in the program."

The man nodded. "Yes, she didn't tell anyone else where she'd placed you. Not even her partner."

Josie shuddered as she thought of the man who would have killed to learn her whereabouts. He must have been working for Margaret O'Hannigan. But then why had the woman thought she was dead?

"It's a shame that Trigger was killed."

"In self-defense." Josie defended her former bodyguard. Whit was the one who'd found the bomb in the safe house and called the marshals. Everything had moved so quickly after that—Josie had moved so quickly.

"He was a friend."

Josie shivered now and glanced back at CJ to make sure he was all right. "Trigger was a friend of yours?"

"Yes, a close friend. We used to work together," he said. "But then things happened in my life. I took a leave from work and lost Trigger as my partner with the Marshals. We also lost touch for a while…until recently. Then we reconnected."

"You had talked to him recently?" she asked.

"Right before he died…"

"Do you know who he was working for?" Josie asked. It might help the district attorney's case against Margaret to have a witness who could corroborate that she'd hired the hit on her.

"He wasn't working for anyone," the man replied. "He was doing a favor for a friend."

God, no...

She realized that this man was the friend for whom Trigger had been doing the favor. This man was the one who'd wanted her location, and from the nerves tightening her stomach into knots, she suspected he had not wanted her found in order to wish her well. She glanced down at her bag lying on the floor at her feet. Could she reach inside without his noticing? She didn't have the gun anymore. It had been left at the crime scene back at Margaret O'Hannigan's house. But if she could get to her phone…

She couldn't call Charlotte, but she could call Brendan. He would come; he would save her and their son as he had so many times over the past few days.

She should have trusted him four years ago. If she had showed him the information she'd compiled, they would have figured out together that it was Margaret who had killed his father. But apprehending Margaret earlier wouldn't have kept Josie safe.

"You were the friend?" she asked, as she leaned down and reached for her purse.

"If you're looking for this," he remarked as he lifted a cell phone from under his thigh, "don't bother." The driver's window lowered, and he tossed out the phone. "That way Charlotte Green's little GPS device won't be able to track you down."

He must have taken the phone from her purse while she'd been buckling CJ into his seat in the back. She was so tired that she hadn't even been aware of what the man was doing. She had barely been aware of him.

"Who are you?" she asked, her heart beating fast with panic and dread.

"You don't recognize me?"

She was afraid to look directly at him. A hostage

was never supposed to look at her kidnapper. If she couldn't identify him, he might let her live.

But as her blood chilled, she realized this wasn't a kidnapper. Unlike Margaret O'Hannigan, this person wasn't interested in money. He had an entirely different agenda.

"I—I don't know," she replied, but she was staring down at her purse, wondering what might have been left inside that she could use as a weapon. "I've been away for so many years."

"You're the one who looks different," he said. "But I know the doctor Charlotte Green sends witnesses to, so I got him to show me your files. I knew what you'd look like. I recognized you in the parking garage."

"That—that was you?" she asked.

He nodded his head. "And the other so-called orderly was at O'Hannigan's place, setting up the backup plan."

She glanced again at CJ and whispered, "The bomb?"

"But you were just so quick," he murmured regretfully. "Too quick."

"And Brendan's apartment?"

"I have a friend with the Bureau, one who knew that your little mob friend is really an agent, so he knew where his safe house is."

The guy had gotten to another marshal and an agent. Which agent? Were Brendan and his mother safe?

"Is—is this agent going to hurt Brendan?"

He chuckled. "He thinks O'Hannigan walks on water. He didn't realize why I was asking about the guy."

"He'll put it together now," she warned him. "Since the bomb and the shooting."

The man shook his head. “No. No one would ever consider me capable of what I’ve done and what I’m about to do.”

“Because you’re a U.S. marshal?”

“Because I’m a good marshal,” he said, “and I’ve always been a good man.”

Then maybe he would change his mind. Maybe he wouldn’t shoot her and her son....

“But you and your father changed all that,” he said. “That’s why you have to pay. You and your father took everything from me, everything that mattered. So now I’m going to do that to your father. I’m going to take away what matters most to him. Again.”

So even four years ago, this man had been the one—the one who’d cut her brakes and set up the bomb. All of it had been because of him.

“Mr. Peterson,” she murmured as recognition dawned. How had she not remembered that Donny Peterson’s father was a U.S. marshal? Her former college classmate had brought it up enough, using it as a threat against whoever challenged him. She hadn’t heeded that threat, though; she’d continued to pursue the story that had led to Donny’s destruction. So all of it had been because of *her.*

Neither of the bombs or the shootings at the hospital and the apartment complex had had anything to do with Brendan’s job, his family or his relationship with her.

It was all her fault and she was about to pay for that with her life. But Brendan, who’d had nothing to do with it, would pay, too—when he lost his son.

“Now you know who I am.”

If only she’d realized it earlier...

If only she and CJ hadn’t gotten inside the SUV with him.

"I understand why you're upset," she assured him, hoping to reason with him. "But you should be upset with me. Not with my son. Not with my father."

"You fed him the information, but he wrote the damn story." He snorted derisively. "Jess Ley."

"I'm Jess Ley," she corrected him. "I wrote the story."

He sucked in a breath as if she'd struck him. He hadn't known. "But if your father hadn't printed it and broadcast it everywhere…"

His son might still be alive.

"That was my fault," she said.

She alone had caused this man's pain—as she was about to cause Brendan's. Because this man must have originally planned to take her from her father in his quest for an eye for an eye. Now he would also take her son from her.

Chapter Eighteen

"I think you should have gone with them to the hospital," his mother chastised Brendan.

While other agents slapped him on the back to express their approval, his mother leaned against her minivan with her arms crossed. Her brown eyes, which were usually so warm and crinkled at the corners with a smile, were dark and narrowed with disapproval.

"I have to talk to Margaret," he said.

"Why?" she asked with a glance at the car in which her husband's killer sat. "She confessed, right?"

"To killing my father," Brendan said.

"Isn't that all you need?" she asked. "It's not like there's any mystery as to why."

He shook his head. "No, she explained that, too. Dad was going to divorce her and leave her with nothing. She wanted it all. That must be why she wanted to hurt Josie and my son, why she wanted to kill them, too—to make sure there were no more O'Hannigans."

"Your father's damn codicil," she remarked.

He grinned as his mother and stepmother glared at each other through the back window of the police car. "She didn't know about you."

His mother shrugged. "Doesn't matter. I'm not an O'Hannigan anymore."

No. She'd dropped her married name when the marshals had moved her. To the runaways she'd fostered, she'd been just Roma. Perhaps they'd all known the Jones surname was an alias.

"She thought you were dead," Brendan remarked as he opened the back door to the police car.

"What the hell is it with you people?" Margaret asked. "Is anyone really dead?" She turned her glare on Brendan. "First you come back from the dead and show up to claim what was mine. And then your nosy girlfriend comes back from the dead with a kid. And now her..." She curled her thin lips in disgust.

He'd been so scared that Josie had been alone with a suspected killer that he hadn't been paying much attention to the conversation coming through the mike. But now he remembered Margaret's surprise that Josie wasn't dead. He'd thought it was because she'd incorrectly assumed Josie had been killed with him from the bomb set at his house, but he realized now that she'd never admitted to planting it.

But why? When she had confessed to murder, why would she bother denying attempted murder?

"You didn't know Josie was alive?" he asked.

She shrugged. "I didn't care whether she was or not until she showed up here with pictures of your damn kid in her purse and all those damn questions of hers. How could you have not realized she was a reporter?"

Especially given who her father was. Brendan had been a fool to not realize it. But then he hadn't been thinking clearly. He never did around her.

He had just let Josie walk off with their son before

he'd confirmed that she was safe. Hell, he'd told her she was—that Margaret wouldn't be a threat anymore. But had Margaret ever been the threat to Josie?

"You didn't know Josie was in witness relocation?"

"I didn't know that anybody was in witness relocation," the woman replied. A calculating look came over her face. "But perhaps I should talk to the marshals, let them know what I know about your father's business and his associates."

Despite foreboding clutching his stomach muscles into tight knots, he managed a short chuckle. "I gave them everything there was to know." Along with the men who'd disappeared—either into prisons or the program.

"You have nothing to offer anyone anymore, Margaret," he said as he slammed the door. Then he pounded on the roof, giving the go-ahead for the driver to pull away and take her to jail. He couldn't hear her as the car drove off, but he could read her lips and realized she was cursing him.

But he was already cursing himself. "Where did Josie go?" he asked his mother.

"To see her father," she said, as if he were being stupid again. "You and I should have gone along. I could have talked to her father and prepared him for seeing his daughter again after he spent the past four years believing she was dead."

"Yeah, because you prepared *me* so well," he said. He nearly hadn't gone to the address his father had given him. But after he'd gotten off the bus, he'd been scared and hungry and cold. So he'd gone to the house and knocked on the door. And when she'd opened it, he'd passed out. Later he'd blamed the hunger and the cold, but it was probably because he'd thought he'd seen a ghost.

It had taken him years to live down the razzing from Roma's other runaways.

"You're right," he said. "I should have gone with her."

"Do you know which hospital?"

He nodded. He knew the hospital well. He just didn't know how she'd gotten there. "What vehicle did she take?"

Roma shook her head. "She got a ride in a black SUV."

"With whom?"

"A marshal, I think. The guy had his badge on a chain around his neck." That was how the men who'd taken her into the program had worn theirs, or so she'd told him when she'd explained how she had disappeared. "He offered to drive her and CJ to see her father."

How had the man known that her father was in the hospital? And why had a marshal walked into the middle of an FBI investigation? The two agencies worked together, but usually not willingly and not without withholding more information than they shared.

Brendan had become an FBI agent instead of a marshal because he'd resented the marshals for not letting his mother take him along—for making him mourn her for years, as he'd mourned Josie.

He had a bad feeling that he might be mourning her again. And CJ, too, if he didn't find her. Charlotte wouldn't have sent another marshal; she had trusted Brendan to keep Josie and their son safe.

And he had a horrible feeling, as his heart ached with the force of its frantic pounding, that he had failed.

"WHY—WHY DID you bring us here?" Josie asked as she rode up in the hospital elevator with her son and a madman.

Before Donald Peterson could reply, CJ answered, "We came to see Grampa." He'd even pushed the button to the sixth floor. "We shoulda brought Gramma."

No. Brendan was already going to lose one person he loved—if Josie didn't think of something to at least save their son. She didn't want him to lose his mother, too.

She looked up at their captor. "We should have left him with his grandmother," she said. "And his father. He isn't part of this."

"He's your son," Peterson said. "Your father's grandson. He's very much a part of this."

She shook her head. "He's a three-year-old child. He has nothing to do with any of this."

The elevator lurched to a halt on the sixth floor, nearly making her stomach lurch, too, with nerves and fear. With a gun shoved in the middle of her back, the U.S. marshal pushed her out the open doors. She held tight to CJ's hand.

He kept digging the gun deeper, pushing her down the hall toward her father's room. A man waited outside. He was dressed like an orderly, as he'd been dressed the night he'd held Brendan back from getting on the elevator with her and CJ. She'd been grateful for his intervention then.

He wasn't going to intervene tonight—just as his partners in crime had refused to be swayed from the U.S. marshal's nefarious plan. But still she had to try. "Please," she said, "you don't want to be part of this."

"He's already part of it," Peterson replied. "Even

before he set the bomb, he was already wanted for other crimes."

She understood now. "You tracked them down on their outstanding warrants but you worked out a deal for not bringing them in."

Peterson chuckled. "You can't stop asking questions, can't stop trying to ferret out all the information you can."

She shuddered, remembering that Brendan had accused her of the same thing. No wonder he hadn't been able to trust her.

"But you and your father won't be able to broadcast this story," he said.

"You're not going to get away," she warned him.

"I know. But it's better this way—better to see his face and yours than have someone else take the pleasure for me." He pushed the barrel deeper into her back and ordered, "Open the door."

"I—I think someone should warn him first," she said. "Let him know that I'm alive so that he doesn't have another heart attack."

"It was unfortunate that he had the first one," Peterson agreed. "He was only supposed to be hurt, not killed." He glanced at the orderly as he said that, as if the man had not followed orders. "But the doctors have put him on medication to regulate his heart. He's probably stronger now than he was when he thought you died four years ago. That didn't kill him."

His mouth tightened. "It would be easier to die," he said, "than to lose a child and have to live."

He wasn't worried about getting away anymore, because he had obviously decided to end his life, too.

"I'm sorry," she murmured.

"Not yet," he replied, "but you will be." He pushed her through the door to her father's room.

"Stop shoving my mommy!" CJ yelled at him. "You're a bad man!"

"What—what's going on?" asked the gray-haired man in the room. He was sitting up as if he'd been about to get out of bed. He was bruised, but he wasn't broken. "Who are you all? Are you in the right room?"

"Yes," CJ replied. "This is my grampa's room number. Are you my grampa?"

Stanley Jessup looked at his grandson through narrowed eyes. Then he lifted his gaze and looked at Josie. At first he didn't recognize her; his brow furrowed as if he tried to place her, though.

"You don't know your own daughter?" the U.S. marshal berated him. "I would know my son anywhere. No matter what he may have done to his face, I would recognize his soul. That's how I knew he couldn't have done the things that article and those news reports said." He raised the gun and pointed it at Josie's head. "The things—the lies—your friend told you, claiming that my Donny had tried to hurt her."

"Donald Peterson," her father murmured. He recognized her attempted killer but not his own daughter.

"Your son told me, too," Josie said. "He had once been my friend, too."

"Until you betrayed him."

"Until he tried to rape my roommate," she said. If not for her coming to her father with the article, he might have gotten away with it—just as he'd gotten away with his drug use—but the athletic director hadn't wanted to lose their star player from the football team. So they'd tried paying off the girl. When she'd refused money, they'd expelled her and labeled her crazy.

So just as she had done with Margaret O'Hannigan today, Josie had gotten Donny Peterson to confess.

"Josie…" Her father whispered her name, as if unable to believe it. Then he looked down at the little boy, who stared up at him in puzzlement.

Poor CJ had been through so much the past few days. He'd met so many people and had been in so much danger, he had to be thoroughly confused and exhausted. He whispered, too, to his grandfather, "He's a bad man, Grampa."

"Your mama and grandpa are the bad ones," Donald Peterson insisted. "My Donny was a star, and they couldn't handle it. They had to bring him down, had to destroy him."

After the confession and the subsequent charges, Donny Peterson had killed himself, shortly before the trial was to begin, shortly before Josie's brakes were cut. Why hadn't she considered that those attempts might have been because of Donny? Why had she automatically thought the worst of Brendan? Maybe because she'd already been feeling guilty and hadn't wanted to admit to how much to blame she'd been.

"And that is why I'm going to destroy them," Donald continued.

"You're a bad man," CJ said again, and he kicked the man in the shin.

Josie tried to grab her son before the man could strike back. But he was already swinging and his hand struck Josie's cheek, sending her stumbling back onto her father's bed. Stanley Jessup caught her shoulders and then pulled her and his grandson close, as if his arms alone could protect them.

CJ wriggled in their grasp as he tried to break free to fight some more. "My daddy told me to p'tect you," he reminded Josie. "I have to p'tect my mommy until my daddy gets here."

Donald Peterson shook his head. "Your daddy's not coming, son."

"My daddy's a hero," CJ said. "He'll be here. He always saves us."

"It is a daddy's job to protect his kids," Donald agreed, his voice cracking with emotion. "But your daddy's busy arresting some bad people."

"You're bad."

"And he's too far away to get here to help you."

Tears began to streak down CJ's face, and his shoulders shook as fear overcame him. He'd been so brave for her—so brave for his father. But now he was scared.

And Josie could offer him no words of comfort. As Donald Peterson had stated, there was no way that Brendan could reach them in time to save them.

They had to figure out a way to save themselves. Her father shifted on his bed and pressed something cold and metallic against Josie's hip. A gun. Had he had it under his pillow?

After the assault, she couldn't blame him for wanting to be prepared if his attacker tried again. But Donald's gun barrel was trained on CJ. And she knew—to make her father and her feel the loss he felt—he would shoot her son first. Could she grab the gun, aim and fire before he killed her little boy?

THE CAMERAS HAD still been running inside the van, and they'd caught the plate on the black SUV that had driven off with Brendan's son and the woman he loved. The vehicle had a GPS that had led them right to its location in the parking garage of the hospital.

When they'd arrived, Brendan hadn't gone down to

check it out. He already knew where they were. So he ducked under the whirling FBI helicopter blades and ran across the roof where just a few nights ago he'd nearly been shot. Once he was inside the elevator, he pushed the button for the sixth floor.

It seemed to take forever to get where he needed to be.

His mom was right. He should have taken Josie here. He never should have let her and CJ out of his sight. And if he wasn't already too late, he never would.

Finally the elevator stopped and the doors slowly opened. He had barely stepped from the car when a shot or two rang out. He fired back. And his aim was better.

The pseudo-orderly dropped to the floor, clutching his bleeding arm. His gun dropped, too. Brendan kicked it aside as he hurried past the man. The orderly wasn't the one who'd driven off with his family. He wasn't the one with the grudge against Josie.

That man was already inside and he had nothing to lose. Running the plate had tied it to the marshal to whom the vehicle had been assigned, and a simple Google search on the helicopter ride had revealed the rest of Donald Peterson's tragic story. There was no point in calling out, no point in trying to negotiate with him. The only thing he wanted was Josie dead—as dead as his son.

So Brendan kicked open the door, sending it flying back against the wall. He had his gun raised, ready to fire, but his finger froze on the trigger.

The man holding a gun was not the marshal but the patient. The marshal lay on the floor, blood pooling beneath his shoulder. His eyes were closed, tears trickling from their corners. But his pain wasn't physical.

It was a pain Brendan had nearly felt himself. Of loss and helplessness…

"See, I knew my daddy would make it," CJ said, his voice high with excitement and a trace of hysteria. "I knew he would save us."

Brendan glanced down at the floor again, checking for the man's weapon. But Josie held it. He looked back at his son. "Doesn't look like you needed saving at all. Your mommy and grandpa had it all under control."

Stanley Jessup shook his head. "If you hadn't distracted him with the shooting outside the door, I never would have been able to…" He shuddered. While the man was a damn good marksman, he wasn't comfortable with having shot a person.

"Are you okay, Daddy?" Josie asked.

He grabbed her, pulling her into his arms. "I am now. A couple of nights ago I heard a scream and then a female voice, and I recognized it. But I didn't dare hope. I thought it was the painkillers. I couldn't let myself believe. Couldn't let myself hope… You're alive…"

"I'm so sorry!" she exclaimed, her body shaking with sobs. "I'm so sorry."

It was a poignant moment, but one that was short-lived as police officers and hospital security burst into the room. It was nearly an hour later before the men had been arrested and the explanations made.

Finally Stanley Jessup could have a moment alone with his daughter and grandson, so Brendan stepped outside and pulled the door closed behind him. He walked over to his mother, who had insisted on coming along in the helicopter with him and the other agents.

"I'm going to get some coffee and food," Roma said. "I'm sure my grandson is hungry. He's had a long day." She rose on tiptoe and pressed a kiss to Brendan's cheek. "So has my son."

"It's not over yet," he said.

Her brow furrowed slightly. "Isn't it all over? All the bad people arrested?"

"There's still something I need to do," Brendan said. For him it wasn't all over. It was just beginning.

She nodded as if she understood. She probably did; his mother had always known what was in his heart.

Josie didn't, but he intended to tell her.

After patting his cheek with her palm, his mother headed down the hall and disappeared into the elevator, leaving him alone. He had spent so much of his life alone—those years before he'd joined his mother in witness protection. Then all the years he'd gone undercover—deep undercover—for the Bureau. He'd been young when he'd started working for the FBI, since his last name had given him an easy entrance to any criminal organization the Bureau had wanted to investigate. And take down.

He had taken down several of the most violent gangs and dangerous alliances. But none of them had realized he was the one responsible.

If the truth about him came out now, his family could be in danger of retaliation—revenge like that the marshal had wanted against the Jessups because of the loss of his son.

Pain clutched Brendan's heart as he thought of how close he had come to losing his son. CJ had told him how he'd tried to "p'tect" his mommy as he'd promised. The brave little three-year-old had kicked the man with the gun.

He shuddered at what could have happened had Josie

obviously not taken the blow meant for their boy. She'd had a fresh mark on her face.

As she stepped out of her father's room and joined him in the hall, he studied her face. The red mark was already darkening. He found himself reaching up and touching her cheek as he murmured, "I should have kicked him, too."

She flinched. "I used to worry that CJ was too timid," she said, "but now I worry that he might be too brave."

"Are you surprised?" he asked. "You've always been fearless."

"Careless," she corrected him. "I didn't care about the consequences. I didn't realize what could happen to me."

He'd thought that was because she'd been spoiled, that she'd been her father's princess and believed he would never let anything happen to her. Now Brendan realized that she'd cared more about others than herself.

"You're the brave one," she said. "You've put yourself in danger to protect others. To protect me. Thank you."

He shook his head. He didn't want her gratitude. He wanted her love.

"I thought you might have left with the others," she said, glancing around the empty hall. "With your mom..."

"She's still here," he said. "She's getting food and coming back up." The woman had made a life of feeding hungry kids—food and love.

"I'm glad she's coming back," she said. "CJ has been asking about her. He wants his grampa to meet his gramma. I think he thinks they should be married like other kids' grandparents are."

A millionaire and a mobster's widow? Brendan chuckled.

"I'm really glad that you're still here," she said.

His heart warmed, filling with hope. Did she have the same feelings he had?

"I owe you an apology," Josie said. "It was all my fault—all of it. And my mistakes cost you three years with your son." Her voice cracked. "And I am so sorry...."

He closed his arms around her and pulled her against his chest—against his heart. She trembled, probably with exhaustion and shock. She had been through so much. She clutched at his back and laid her head on his shoulder.

"My father knew who you were," she remarked. "What you were. From his sources within the FBI, he knew you were an agent. If I'd told him what story I was working on when the attempts started on my life, he would have told me to drop it—that there was no way you could be responsible. I should have known...."

"He knew?" Brendan had really underestimated the media mogul in resources and respect. He could be trusted with the truth, so Brendan should have trusted his daughter, too.

"He's a powerful man with a lot of connections," she said, "but still he didn't know that I wasn't dead. I hate that I did that to him. I hate what I did to you. I understand why you can't trust me."

"Josie..."

She leaned back and pressed her fingers over his lips. "It's okay," she said. "I understand now that sometimes it's better to leave secrets secret. There will be no stories about you or your mother in any Jessup publications or broadcasts. And there will never be another story by me."

"Never?"

Tears glistened in her smoky-green eyes, and she shook her head. "I should have never..."

"Revealed the truth?" he asked.

"Look what the consequences were," she reminded him with a shudder.

"Yes," he agreed, and finally he looked at the full picture, at what she'd really done. "You got justice for your friend—the girl that kid assaulted. If you hadn't written that article, it never would have happened. And I know from experience that it's damn hard to move on if you never get justice."

"That's why you went after all those crime organizations," she said, "to get justice for what your dad did to your mom."

"She gave up her justice for me," he said.

"So you got it for her and for so many others."

He shook his head. "No, Margaret got it for her. Go figure. But *you* helped your friend when no one else would. You can't blame yourself for what the boy did. And neither should his father."

"He needs someone to blame," she said.

Just as the people in her new town had blamed her for her student's death. Someone always needed someone else to blame.

"And so did I," she added. "I shouldn't have blamed you."

"You shouldn't have," he agreed. "Because I would have never hurt you, then or now." He dragged in a deep breath to say what he'd waited around to tell her, what he'd waited four years to tell her. "Because I love you, Josie."

"You love me?" She asked the question as if it had never occurred to her, as if she had never dared to hope. Until now. Her eyes widened with hope and revealed her own feelings.

"Yes," he said, "I love your passion and your intelligence and—"

She stretched up his body and pressed a kiss to his lips. "I didn't think you'd ever be able to trust me, much less love me."

"I don't just love you," he said. "I want to spend my life with you and CJ. No more undercover. I'll find a safer way to get justice for others, like maybe helping you with stories."

She smiled. "That might be more dangerous than your old job."

"We'll keep each other safe," he promised. "Will you become my wife?"

"It will thrill CJ if his parents are together, if every day is like that day at my house," she said.

That had been such a good day—a day Brendan had never wanted to end. His heart beat fast with hope. She was going to say yes....

"But as much as I love our son, I won't marry you for his sake," she said. "And you wouldn't want me to."

He wasn't so sure about that. But before he could argue with her, she was speaking again.

"I will marry you," she assured him, "because I love you with all my heart. Because even when I was stupid enough to think you were a bad man, I couldn't stop loving you. And I never will."

"Never," he agreed. And he covered her mouth with his, sealing their engagement with a kiss since he had yet to buy a ring. But it was no simple kiss. With them, it never was. Passion ignited and the kiss deepened.

If not for the dinging of the elevator, they might have forgotten where they were. His mother stepped through the open doors, her eyes glinting with amusement as if she'd caught him making out on the porch swing.

"We're getting married, Mom," he said.

"Of course," she said, as if there had never been any question in her mind. "Now, open the door for me." She juggled a tray of plates and coffee cups and a sippy cup.

He opened the door to his son, who threw his arms around Brendan's legs. "Daddy! Daddy, you're still here."

"I'm never leaving," he promised his son.

"Gramma!" the little boy exclaimed, and he pulled away from Brendan to follow her to his grandfather's bedside.

With a happy sigh, Josie warned him, "We're never going to have a moment alone."

"Our honeymoon," he said. "We'll spend our honeymoon alone."

Epilogue

"We're alone," Brendan said as he carried Josie over the threshold of their private suite.

Since his arms were full with her and her overflowing gown, she swung the door closed behind them. It shut with a click, locking them in together. "Yes, we're finally alone...."

And she didn't want to waste a minute of their wedding night, so she wriggled in his arms, the way their independent son did because he thought himself too big to be carried. As she slid down Brendan's body, he groaned as if in pain.

"Was I too heavy?" she asked.

He shook his head. "No, you're perfect—absolutely perfect." He lifted his fingers to her hair, which was piled in red ringlets atop her head. "You looked like a princess coming down the aisle of the ballroom."

"Well, technically..." She was. It had made her an anomaly growing up, so she'd often downplayed her mother's royal heritage. When she'd married Stanley Jessup, her mother had given up her title anyway. But here it was no big deal. Josie was only one of three princesses in the palace on St. Pierre Island. Four, actually, counting Charlotte Green-Timmer's new daughter.

Charlotte and Aaron had married shortly before their daughter's premature birth.

There was a prince, too—Gabriella and Whit Howell's baby boy. The princess had fallen in love with and married her father's other royal bodyguard. There were so many babies…

So much love. But she'd felt the most coming from her husband as he'd waited for her father to lead her down the aisle to him. In his tuxedo, the same midnight-black as his hair, he looked every bit the prince. Or a king.

And standing at his side, in a miniature replica of his father's tuxedo, had stood their son—both ring bearer, with the satin pillow in his hand, and best little man.

"It was the most perfect day," she said. A day she had thought would never come—not four years ago when she'd had to die, all those times she nearly had died, and during the three months it had taken to plan the wedding.

"As hard as you and my mom worked on it," he said, "it was guaranteed to be perfect."

She blinked back tears at the fun she'd had planning the wedding with Roma. "Your mother is amazing."

"She's your mother, too, now," he reminded her.

And the tears trickled out. "I feel that way." That she truly had a mother now. "And my dad loves you like a son." He couldn't have been prouder than to have his daughter marry a hero like FBI Agent Brendan O'Hannigan.

"I'm glad," Brendan said. "But right now I don't want to talk about your dad or my mom." He stepped closer to her, as if closing in on a suspect. "I don't want to talk at all."

Her tears quickly dried as she smiled in anticipation. "Oh, what would you rather do?"

"Get you the hell out of this dress," he said as he stared down at the yards of white lace and satin.

With its sweetheart neckline, long sleeves and flowing train, it was a gown fit for a princess—or so his mother had convinced her. Josie was glad, though, because she had wanted something special for this special day. A gown that she could one day pass down to a daughter.

"Your mom told the seamstress to put in a zipper," she told him. "She said her son was too impatient for buttons."

He grinned and reached for the tab. The zipper gave a metallic sigh as he released it, and the weight of the fabric pulled down the gown. She stood before her husband in nothing but a white lace bra and panties.

"You're the one wearing too many clothes now," she complained and reached for his bow tie.

He shrugged off his jacket, and for once he wore no holsters beneath it. He carried no guns. When their honeymoon was over, he would, but as a supervising agent, he wouldn't often have occasion to use them. He wasn't going undercover anymore—except with her.

She pulled back the blankets on the bed as he quickly discarded the rest of his clothes. "In a hurry?" she teased.

"I don't know how much time we'll have before CJ shows up," he admitted.

"His grandparents promised to keep him busy for the next couple of days," she reminded him. "And he's more fascinated with the royal babies right now than he is with us."

Brendan grinned and reached for her.

"He wants one, you know," Josie warned.

Brendan kissed her softly, tenderly, and admitted in a whisper, "So do I."

She regretted all that her unfounded suspicions had cost him—seeing her pregnant, feeling their son kick, seeing him born, holding him as a sweet-smelling infant…

But she would make it up to him with more babies—and with all her love. She tugged her naked husband down onto the bed with her. "Then we better get busy…"

Building their family and their lives together.

* * * * *

CLAIMING THE ROYAL INNOCENT

JENNIFER HAYWARD

This one is for my brother, Andrew, and his
unfailing belief in me in following my dream.
It's true – dreams aren't too expensive to keep! xx

CHAPTER ONE

"The Count and Countess of Agiero."

A soldier in ceremonial uniform announced the exquisitely dressed couple queued in front of Aleksandra Dimitriou in the foyer of the Akathinian royal palace ballroom, his booming voice with its perfect elocution sending her heart plunging to the marble floor. She had hoped arriving late for Princess Stella's twenty-fifth birthday party would mean the introductions would have been long concluded.

But then again, what did she know? She had never attended a high society party before, let alone an official royal function. The blue silk gown she wore was rented from one of those designer dress services that mailed the couture creation to you in exchange for an exorbitant amount of money, her shoes were those of her fashionable friend Kira, her jewelry unearthed in a knockoff boutique in the city. In fact, not even the invitation belonged to her. She had *stolen* it with the intent of slipping in unnoticed.

The furor in her head, gathering momentum by the minute, suggested her ploy was about to be revealed to the hundreds of people gathered to celebrate the princess's birthday. Not to mention the dozens of paparazzi who stood poised like a flock of vultures behind the stanchioned-off red carpet waiting for a money shot.

Her palms went sweaty. A shot of *her* in handcuffs, a *royal intruder* caught red-handed during a time of high security for the country, would be great fodder for them. She could just see the residents of her small, sleepy coastal village waking up to her face splashed across the front page of the daily newspaper. Picture them doing a double take, their bemusement quickly turning to horror…

Her heart pounded madly against her ribs. There was no way she was going to pull this off. She should turn around and go back to Stygos and forget she'd ever had this stupid, foolish need to know a piece of herself. To right a wrong that had long since been undoable.

But it was too late to back out now. The palace official was reaching for her blue and gold-embossed invitation, an expectant smile on his face. She handed it to him with frozen fingers. He checked his list. Frowned. Ran his finger over the names again, then looked up at her. "*Lypamai, despoinis*, but your name doesn't seem to be on the list."

Alex swallowed hard. Summoned composure from a place deep inside her she hadn't even known existed. "I originally had to decline the invitation," she said smoothly. "When I found out I would be in the country, I sent another note accepting."

He procured another list, scanned it, consulted someone by radio, then nodded. "*Kala.* It's fine. You're on the original list." He passed the invitation to the soldier with the booming voice and nodded for her to proceed. "Enjoy your evening."

She pinned a smile on her lips, picked up the hem of her gown and moved toward the entrance to the ballroom.

"Kara Nicholson," the soldier announced, his deep baritone seeming to hang on the air forever. Alex's step faltered, a thin layer of perspiration breaking out on her brow as she waited for someone to point out that she was *not* Kara Nicholson. That she was a *fraud.*

The din of the crowd remained unchanged. The soldier gave her a curious look. Exhaling the breath she'd been holding, she propelled herself forward on legs that shook so badly it was hard to put one foot in front of the other.

The powder room was her first priority. There, she restored her outward composure with her makeup compact. Inner composure, however, was somewhat more elusive.

That she and Kara, the American heiress who'd stayed in her family's tourist hotel a few weeks ago, were both slim with dark hair and blue eyes had just saved her from certain disaster. It was Kara's discarded invitation she'd picked out of the trash can to gain admittance to the party. Kara's identity she'd assumed. But resembling the beautiful socialite and being in any way prepared to do what she'd come here to do, to mingle with the exclusive crowd Kara frequented, were two entirely different things.

You just have to fake it long enough to get this done. Jaw set, shoulders back, she made her way into the elegantly clad crowd that filled the magnificent sweeping ballroom, champagne flutes in their hands. The upper echelons of Akathinian society were in attendance to celebrate the princess's birthday—assorted celebrities and a smattering of royalty from across Europe. The kind of people she checked into her hotel for a quiet, idyllic week where they wouldn't be bothered, the best view in all of Akathinia offered from their seaside window. Not those she socialized with.

She plucked a glass of champagne off a waiter's tray and moved deeper into the thick crowd, searching for a spot to locate her target. Taking a long sip of the delicious, clearly outrageously expensive bubbly, she swallowed, the champagne fizzling its way down to her stomach, where it spread a slow warmth through her. Exactly what she needed.

Securing a quiet corner from which she could survey the room, she tucked herself against a pillar and drank in her spectacular surroundings. Lit in the same blue and gold tones as the invitation, the richly appointed ballroom was a feast for the eye. The Akathinian royal crest was projected onto black marble floors, which looked as if they were threaded through with real gold vein. Massive antique chandeliers glittered from the ceiling, serving as a brilliant counterpoint for the dark accents in the room, while precious, larger-than-life paintings adorned walls that soared to impressive thirty-foot heights.

Her head spun at the opulence of it all. None of it seemed real. But then again, nothing *had* seemed real since her mother, a former lady-in-waiting to the elder Queen Amara, had broken a twenty-five-year silence with a bombshell that had blown her life apart.

Her father had not been an Akathinian businessman who had died before her birth. He was King Gregorios, the former monarch of this country, with whom her mother had carried out an extended affair before the queen discovered her betrayal and fired her.

Her hand trembled as she downed another swallow of champagne. That her mother, whom she'd considered above reproach, whose strength and courage symbolized everything that was good in the world, had indulged in a dangerous, illicit affair with the king, a married man, then manufactured a series of elaborate stories to paint a rosy view of her childhood, for whatever altruistic reasons she cared to offer, seemed inconceivable. *Unimaginable.*

And yet it was the truth. She had a father she'd never known. The siblings she'd longed for as a child, all of whom would have been lost to her if her mother hadn't broken down and told her the truth.

A bright burst of laughter drew her gaze. Princess Stella, *her half sister*, clad in a dazzling silver gown, held court in the center of the room, a handful of handsome men arranged around her, vying for her attention. She looked every inch the Grecian goddess with her slim figure and sleek blond hair caught up in an elaborate twist. Every inch a princess.

How different would her life have been had her mother told her the truth? Would she have become a princess, glittering alongside her sophisticated elder sister? Would she never have known her quiet, idyllic life in Stygos?

A fist tightened in her chest. How her half siblings would receive her was yet to be determined. Her priority, however, was her father's ill health, which had made tonight's subterfuge necessary. A heart attack had sent King Gregorios back to the hospital, his absence tonight marked. She needed to meet him before he died. It was the only thing that *had* been clear in the confusion of the past few months.

She scanned the room, locating the young, strikingly handsome King Nikandros mingling with a group of guests, his wife, Sofía, by his side. *Her brother.*

Nikandros had ascended to the throne after his father's initial heart attack during a difficult time for Akathinia, with its aggressive sister island Carnelia threatening to annex Akathinia back into the Catharian island group to which it had once belonged. Many feared the seventy-year-old Carnelian King Idas might finally have lost his mind, his recent mobilization of the Carnelian military suggesting a war might be on its way.

Thus the reason she had chosen tonight as her avenue to speak to the king. Securing an audience with him under any other circumstances would have been nearly impossible given the security that surrounded him and the demands on his time.

So tonight it was. She set her flute down on a waiter's tray with a determined *clink* of crystal. Took another. The expensive vintage was boosting her confidence by the minute, easing the tightness in her chest as it filled her with its insidious warmth. After this glass, she'd work up the courage to do what she needed to do. To rock the royal family with a scandal at a time when it needed it the least.

* * *

Aristos Nicolades leaned against a column in the packed ballroom, watching the stunning brunette in the sexy blue gown toss back her second glass of champagne with a speed that suggested she needed courage of some sort.

For what? he wondered idly, studying the play of shimmering light as it highlighted every dip and curve of her petite, shapely figure. Considering she'd lied about who she was to gain admittance to the party, he'd thought it best to keep an eye on her.

He'd been behind her in the lineup to the ballroom, his flight from the United States delayed, making him almost an hour late for the party. His every desire had been to skip the event, go home, take a long, hot shower and sleep after a grueling week abroad. But considering the king had finally granted him a license to build the jewel in his crown, a new casino on the sparkling, glitterati-strewn Mediterranean island of Akathinia, giving the occasion a miss had not been an option.

Bemused when the blue-gowned angel had swanned up to the doors of the ballroom and announced herself as Kara Nicholson, he thought he'd been hallucinating after almost thirty-six hours without sleep. The Kara Nicholson he'd divested of her clothes before he'd taken her in a long, hot encounter in Vegas six months ago, the Kara Nicholson known to travel in Stella's circles, was *not* the brunette standing in front of him.

With her near-angelic look—all big blue eyes and long, satiny dark hair—she hardly seemed the type to be one of Carnelia's spies or, God forbid, worse. But nothing could be discounted in this time of tension—spies had been pinpointed; separatist factions had emerged—and considering that a satellite company of his was in charge of security tonight, he wasn't taking any chances.

He studied the nerves the beautiful brunette was clearly

fighting despite her attempt at outward composure. She had come alone, hadn't attempted to talk to anyone, clearly knew no one here. The only person she had shown an interest in, other than the fleeting glances she'd been sending his way as an immediate attraction had sparked between them, had been the king. She had been inordinately interested in his whereabouts ever since she'd arrived.

It was possible she was simply one of those women who couldn't seem to accept that King Nikandros was happily married. There were enough of them around. Perhaps a jilted ex-lover? It would fit with the lost look she had at the moment…the inherent aura of vulnerability that surrounded her.

She sensed his perusal. Turned her chin to meet his gaze. The confusion, the anxiety in her beautiful blue eyes, stoked his curiosity higher. Confusion that quickly morphed into the unmistakable interest he'd seen there before. He held her gaze. Sustained the connection. Electricity arced between them, a rosy pink staining her cheeks.

Dipping her chin, she broke the contact first in one of those shy gestures that didn't seem to fit with the sexy image. A plus B plus C wasn't adding up.

His curiosity got the better of him. Downing his last swallow of scotch, he set the glass on a table and headed toward her. He'd played games he'd enjoyed far less than the one he was playing now. *This* could prove highly enjoyable.

Thee mou. He was headed over here.

Alex swallowed hard, wondering what on earth she was doing. She was here to talk to her father, to know him before he died, not flirt with the most strikingly good-looking male she'd ever seen, in a tuxedo or out of one. Yet *he* had been staring at her, making no effort to hide his interest. Difficult to ignore, particularly since every time she worked up the courage to speak to King Nikandros, he had moved on to another group.

Meanwhile, doubts were piling up about whether it had been an extremely bad idea to choose this party as the venue for her mission as the king glittered as an untouchable force. Would her father even want to see her? Would he even care she existed? Would he toss her out without acknowledging her?

Her ruminations were interrupted by the scent of expensive aftershave, followed by the man who wore it. He was tall, well over six feet, his height backed up by the lean, hard-packed muscle that covered every inch of him. With his dark-as-sin eyes and designer stubble, he made every other man in the room look effeminate in comparison.

Undeniably intimidating. Insanely attractive.

"I was standing over there wondering why a beautiful woman finds herself alone throwing back champagne like water." The rich, velvety undertone to his voice stoked every nerve ending to full attention. "Rather than allow my imagination to conjure up all sorts of creative possibilities, I thought I would simply come over and ask."

Her eyes slid to her empty glass. "It's only my second."

"In rapid succession." He swept his dark gaze over her in a perusal that scorched her skin. "To provide courage perhaps?"

She tossed her hair over her shoulders. "Why would I need courage?"

His eyes glittered with amusement. "You tell me. You are here alone. Perhaps that makes you feel uncomfortable?"

Very. She lifted a shoulder in what she hoped was a nonchalant gesture. "I have business to attend to. It's not so much a social occasion for me."

"Business at a birthday party? How distasteful."

"A personal matter."

He inclined his head. "Perhaps you could combine your

personal matter with a little…*pleasure*. I find myself at loose ends."

She suspected this man hadn't spent one second of his life at loose ends, but his sexy drawl had the intended effect, tangling her up inside.

"You look quite comfortable at loose ends."

"I prefer to find a…*diversion*. And you," he said, holding her gaze, "are the most beautiful woman in the room."

Her stomach flip-flopped, a wave of betraying heat rising from her chest to fill her cheeks. "Hardly true. The princess is hosting, after all."

"She has a layer of ice that surrounds her. You do not."

Alex swallowed past the sudden dryness in her throat, finding herself unable to pull her gaze away from his smoky, sexy one. "I'm afraid I'm not available as a diversion."

"Because you are here for someone else?"

"Because I really must see who I need to see, then go."

"One dance." He held out a lean-fingered, bronzed hand. "Then you can get on with your business."

He made it seem rude, *impolite* to refuse. Over his shoulder, she could see the king and queen still immersed in conversation. Perhaps it *would* be better to say yes to a dance rather than stand around at loose ends looking painfully out of place as she clearly had been.

"All right," she said, placing her palm in his much larger one. "I would love to."

He wrapped his fingers around hers. "Aristos," he drawled. "And you are…?"

Her brain froze, her clear thinking not aided by the two glasses of champagne she'd consumed. "Kara," she said after a pause. Better to continue the facade.

Not that it was easy to keep anything straight in her head with the energy that pulsed between them, moving from his fingers through her body until she was buzzing with the intensity of it.

His tall, impressive physique parted the crowds easily as he led her toward the dance floor, where a live band was playing a slow, sexy jazz number.

Aristos laced his fingers through hers, slid his arm around her waist and pulled her into a close hold that had her pulse racing. His smooth, skillful steps as he directed her around the packed space surprised her for such a solidly built male.

"So," he said, leveling his gaze on her face, "how do you know the princess?"

Her stomach seized. *A natural question*, she told herself. *Relax.*

"We're friends," she said, repeating what Kara had told her. "We're on a few of the same charitable boards."

He inclined his head. "And what do you do when you aren't tending to these…*charitable endeavors*?"

She blinked. Thought furiously. But a few scattered conversations with Kara hadn't provided that depth of information. "Mostly that," she murmured awkwardly. "My father has a large philanthropic portfolio. He needs the help."

"And where is home?"

"Texas," she said faintly, as if that would make up for her lack of a drawl.

"Funny, you don't *sound* like a Southerner."

Her mouth went even drier. *Diavole*, but this had been a bad idea. "I think I've lost my accent," she prevaricated. "I travel so much I've become somewhat…international."

His mouth twisted. "I get that one hundred percent. It's the same with me." His hand tightened around hers as he spun her in a smooth circle. "Texas is a big state. Which part?"

She had no idea. "Dallas," she said, guessing.

"The home of J.R. Ewing…"

She smiled a tight smile. "The very same. And you?"

she asked, attempting to regain control of the conversation. "How do you know Stella?"

"I'm a business partner of the king."

Oh, no. Not good. Swallowing her panic, she lifted her gaze to his. "What business would that be?"

"Hotels and casinos. A bit of this, a bit of that."

She thought that fit perfectly with his dark, edgy vibe. "That must be a very…*interesting* world."

His mouth quirked. "You don't sound so sure about that."

She lifted a shoulder. "I'm not a gambler. It seems to me you prey on the vulnerable. Take unsuspecting people's money."

"Those who walk into a casino do so of their own volition."

"Yes," she agreed, "but do they always know their limits?"

"They should. I find there is an epidemic of late of people who have no sense of personal responsibility. We are all responsible for our own actions."

Yes, she agreed silently, hysteria biting at the edges of her composure. That concept was top of mind at the moment.

"Perhaps true," she conceded. "Although I'm not sure it's a fair comparison. I'm an idealist. I think we all need to be looking out for the greater good."

"A dying breed," he said softly, his dark gaze resting on her face. "Idealists…"

He left it at that. She shut up before she said something she shouldn't. She should have protested when he tugged her closer so his tall, muscular body brushed against hers, his chin resting atop her head. But when there was no talking involved, there was no danger in exposing herself.

She couldn't resist allowing herself to melt into all that strength, just for a moment, of course, until the dance was over. It felt hedonistically good, frankly exciting to be in his arms, and when would she ever have another chance to meet a man like him? Stunning-looking members of the opposite sex were a precious commodity in Stygos. She'd known all of them since childhood.

The plaintive, haunting notes of the saxophone were beautiful. The champagne had kicked in full force now, leaving in its wake a heady buzzing feeling that instilled a confidence in her she hadn't had before. It made the dangerous attraction she felt toward the man holding her even more powerful. Made her even more aware of the strong column of his thighs as they pressed against her, driving home how powerfully built he was. How the spicy scent of his cologne mixed with the heady male musk of him was doing crazy things to her insides…

The warmth of his hand splayed at her waist burned her skin like a brand through the thin silk of her dress. It made her wonder what it would be like to be touched by him. *Truly* touched by him.

Her champagne-clouded brain was floating in a sea of pheromones when the song came to an end. She moved to extract her fingers from his, but he tightened his hold. "One more."

She should have ended it right there. But it was far too tempting to say yes. A glance over his shoulder revealed the king still deep in conversation. How harmful was one more dance?

He pulled her closer, their bodies perfectly aligning as they moved to the sultry notes of the song. It was an inappropriate hold, she knew, the heat of him moving through her like the most potent of caresses, his hand drifting lower to lie against the small of her back. But her sensible side seemed to have deserted her. He was the dark, mysterious hero of her favorite novels come to life, with a dangerous, presumptive twist that was impossible to resist.

A couple more minutes and she'd go.

She thought maybe a third song had come and gone when she finally pulled her head from where it was nestled under his chin and realized they had gradually worked their way from the couples dancing along the edge of the ballroom to the shadows of the small terrace that led off it.

She looked up into the mesmerizing heat of his black gaze, suddenly aware of exactly where this was going. "I told you I'm not interested in being a diversion," she reminded him a little too breathlessly.

"No?" he said derisively, bending his head toward her. "Your signals are saying the contrary." Sliding his fingers around her jaw, he captured her lips in a kiss unlike any she'd had before. Cajoling and demanding her acquiescence all at the same time, it was sensual, playful and masterful, enticing her to respond to his seductive expertise.

Her lips clung to his, helpless to resist his slow, intoxicating kisses. She swayed closer to him, her hand settling on his waist. He drew her into his warmth, the proximity of their bodies sending a shiver through her.

He lifted his lips from hers, their breath mingling. "Open your mouth, angel."

She hadn't been aware she was denying him anything. Obeying his command, she allowed his firm, beautiful mouth to part hers in a hot, languorous exploration she felt right down to her toes.

Her sigh split the air. He moved his hands down to her hips and shaped her buttocks, drawing her even closer to him until their bodies were molded together without a centimeter between them. She could feel the hard heat of him burning against the juncture of her thighs, as impressive as the rest of him. It made her knees weak.

"Aristos," she gasped, pulling her mouth from his. "Stop."

Satisfaction laced his gaze as she stared up at him, the supreme control she found there snapping her out of her haze. She put a palm against his chest to put some distance between them, but the hand he held at the small of her back kept her where she was. He slid it down over her buttock to wrap around her thigh.

"What *are* you doing?" she demanded, pushing harder against the rock-solid wall of his chest to no avail.

"Checking for weapons."

"Weapons?" Her brain struggled to compute. "Why would I be carrying weapons?"

He ran his palm over her other buttock and down the back of her thigh in a leisurely exploration that brought a heated wave to her cheeks. "Maybe you should tell me, *Kara*."

The edge to his voice made the hairs on the back of her neck stand up. *He knows. Had known all this time.*

She pushed a hand against his chest and this time he released her, setting her away from him. She bit down into her lip. *Hard.* "You know I'm not Kara."

He raked his gaze over her face. "Correct, angel. So maybe you'd care to tell me what you're doing here. And why you impersonated Kara Nicholson to get in."

A buzzing sound filled her ears. "How did you know?"

"Well, let's see… Your accent, for starters. Second, Kara is from *Houston*, not Dallas. And finally, I happen to know Kara. *Intimately.* And *you* are not her."

Thee mou. She closed her eyes, cheeks flaming. He and Kara Nicholson were lovers. How could she have ever thought she'd get away with this?

She opened her eyes. "You were behind me in line. Why didn't you call me out then?"

"I wanted to see what your intentions were."

"What did you *think* I was doing?"

"We have a country trying to draw us into a war, in case you hadn't noticed."

Disbelief sank through her. "You think I'm a spy? An *assassin*?"

"I think when anyone enters an official royal engagement under false pretenses, it needs to be investigated."

"So you thought you'd appoint yourself investigator? *Maul me* while you're at it? Make a game of it?"

"I wouldn't call it mauling. You were as into that as I was. And as for my *interest* in you, it's my security team the palace is using tonight. A side business of mine, angel, along with my *big, bad* casinos. I wasn't about to set you loose with the king in the room."

She clenched her hands at her sides, her gaze fixed on his. "You are going to regret this."

An amused glimmer filled his eyes. "Really? Do tell. My guess from the way you've been eyeing the king is that you're an ex-lover. A jilted one, perhaps… You don't seem—how should I put it?—*off your rocker*, so I'm assuming you've come with some misguided belief he'll take a lover. I hate to break it to you, but he's madly in love with his wife. It isn't going to happen."

A jilted lover? She gaped at him. "Are you out of your mind?"

He lifted a shoulder. "I've seen the women who throw themselves at the king. They crash parties to meet him. They go to ridiculous lengths to get his attention. So even though you," he said, stripping the clothes from her with a look that singed her skin, "are undoubtedly every man's type, *this* was a wasted escapade."

Fury swelled up inside her. "I came tonight because I need to speak to the king about a personal matter. Just like I said earlier."

"Why do it under false pretenses?"

"It's complicated."

"Complicated *how*?"

"That's my business."

"I'm afraid it's mine if you don't want me to have you handcuffed and hauled out of here right now."

"You wouldn't."

"Try me."

Her heart surged painfully against her chest. Pressing her hands to her face, she paced to the other side of the terrace. "I can't tell you why. I admit my methods for getting here were unconventional, but they were necessary given the security surrounding the king. I would never have gotten an audience."

"That security is in place for a good reason."

"Yes," she said, turning around. "It is." She took a deep breath. Fixed him with an imploring look. "I promise you it's imperative I speak to the king. In fact, if you would just take me to him right now, I would highly appreciate it."

"Not happening until you tell me who you are and what your business is."

"I can't."

"Kala." He spun on his heel and stalked toward the door.

"Aristos, stop."

He turned around. "No one knows this," she said. "You can't say anything to anyone."

"Spit it out," he growled.

She lifted her chin. "My name is Aleksandra Dimitriou. The king is my half brother."

CHAPTER TWO

ARISTOS'S MOUTH WENT SLACK. *Nikandros's half sister.* He couldn't have heard her correctly.

"Can you please," he said deliberately, "repeat that?"

Aleksandra, *if that was even her right name*, rubbed a hand against her temple. "My mother, Melaina, was Queen Amara's lady-in-waiting. She had an affair with King Gregorios during her tenure at the palace. The queen knew about her husband's indiscretions, but when she discovered the affair with my mother, it was one step too far. She fired her. No one knew my mother was pregnant. She went home to her village and raised me by herself."

He blinked. "Why keep it a secret? By Akathinian law, you would have been a royal."

"My mother knew I would be taken away from her if anyone found out. She didn't want that life for me. She told everyone, including me, that my father was an Akathinian businessman she'd met while she worked at the palace who was killed in a car accident before I was born. It wasn't until the king had his heart attack that I learned the truth."

Thee mou. His head spun. The queen's lady-in-waiting. *The ultimate betrayal.*

It was well-known that King Gregorios had indulged in countless affairs. But a child kept secret this long? Born to the queen's most trusted aide? If true, it was a scandal that would put all before it to shame.

He scrutinized the woman in front of him. Was she telling the truth? Her skin was pale beneath her olive-toned complexion, the vulnerability that emanated from her a quality he didn't think could be manufactured. Nor did he think she was a threat to anyone. She was not a practiced liar, that was clear. But he had learned long ago never to trust first impressions. Particularly when it came to a woman—the most deceptive creature on the face of the earth. One who wanted an audience with the king.

It hit him then, that same feeling of familiarity he'd experienced from the first moment he'd seen her. *Those eyes...* That particular shade of blue belonged to only one bloodline he knew. They were Constantinides blue. It was like looking at Nikandros and Stella.

His blood ran cold. She was telling the truth.

Aleksandra pressed her lips together. "I told you you were going to regret doing *that*."

He closed his eyes. For once in his life, he did. He and the king had just gotten their relationship on a solid footing after an adversarial start. *This* he didn't need.

"Just because you have the Constantinides eyes, as rare as they are, doesn't mean your story is true," he said roughly. "It will need to be verified, as I'm sure you will appreciate. You can understand my suspicions."

Her eyes flashed. "Your suspicions, yes, but not your tactics."

"Like I said, it took two to make *that* kiss."

That shut her up. He paced to the edge of the terrace, his brain working furiously. They were smack in the middle of a royal function with every paparazzo camera, gossip and royal watcher in the country in their midst. This could not get out before it was verified and the ramifications considered. But that was the king's job—not his.

He closed the distance between them. "What were your intentions coming here tonight? What do you want from the king?"

"I want to see my father. Talk to him. That's all."

He studied her for a long moment. Cursed under his breath and pulled his mobile phone from the inside pocket of his jacket. A phone call to the man in charge of security brought a detail in a dark suit out to the terrace.

"This is how this is going to go," he said to Aleksandra. "*You* are going to stay here with him. You do not move from here, you do not talk to anyone and if you do, he will restrain you. Understood?"

Her eyes widened, skin paling. "Yes."

She looked as if a good gust of wind might blow her over. Intensely vulnerable. His heart contracted despite his effort to stay distanced from the explosive situation unfolding in front of him. It had taken an immense amount of courage for her to come here and do what she'd done. He could only imagine how terrified she felt.

Closing the gap between them, he slid his fingers under her chin and brought her gaze up to his. "The king is a good man. You have nothing to fear."

He, on the other hand, did, if she spilled what had just happened to Nikandros.

Alex's heart thudded painfully beneath her ribs as her rather ominous-looking security detail nodded at her to precede him into the room. She stepped inside the palace library, its elegant chandeliers and wall sconces illuminating shelf upon shelf of precious volumes.

With her voracious passion for literature, the shelves might have stolen her attention had it not been fixed on the man who stood at the far end of the room looking out the windows, hands buried in his pockets.

She stood there, fingers biting into her tiny silk clutch as the king turned around and studied her, his expression intent. His eyes widened imperceptively, then that perfectly controlled countenance that made him vastly intimidating resumed its tenure.

He turned to Aristos. *"Efharisto."*

Aristos nodded and headed for the door. She fought the crazy urge to beg him to stay—he who had threatened to put her in handcuffs and have her tossed out—but after a long glance at her that seemed to say *keep your head up, you can do this*, he left, the door clicking quietly shut behind him.

The king nodded at the two leather chairs beside the window. "Please. Sit."

She obeyed, her weak knees only too happy to find a resting place. The king sat down opposite her. All at once, she was struck by how much they looked alike. The bright blue eyes, high cheekbones, dark ebony hair her brother wore short and cropped.

"You are Melaina's daughter."

"Yes." She cleared her throat as the response came out faint, raspy. "You knew her?"

"I was only eight when she left, but yes, I remember her. My mother and she were very close."

Until my mother had an affair with your father and was thrown out of the palace.

"Aristos has filled me in on your conversation. On your claim that my father is your father."

She lifted her chin. "It isn't a claim. He is."

"Forgive me," he said bluntly, "if I cannot accept that as fact. For over two decades your mother has kept you a secret, but now when my father is nearly in his grave, she's seen fit to speak out. *Why?*"

"She was afraid I would be taken from her. She didn't want my life marked by her mistake. She thought I would be better off with her, rather than carry the stain of my illegitimacy. But your father's heart attack hit her hard. I think she realized she had made a mistake in denying me my birthright."

He raked a hand through his hair. "So you came here tonight to..."

"Know my father. To know you and Stella. I—" Her gaze held his vivid blue one. "I don't have any siblings. I don't want anything else. I have a life in Stygos that I love."

He narrowed his gaze. "You can't be so naive as to think everything will stay the same if it's confirmed you are a Constantinides. You will be of royal blood. Third in line to the throne."

She shook her head. "I don't want any of that. I am not so *naive* as to think I would be welcomed into this family given the nature of my birth."

The king's eyes flickered. "There is a...*complexity* to the situation. But if you are telling the truth, the blood that runs through your veins cannot be denied. It must be dealt with. Acknowledged. But that is dependent upon us having the facts. A DNA test will need to be performed."

She nodded. Had assumed as much would be required. Knew she couldn't have expected more. So why did her insides sting so much?

The king stood up. "I must get back to my guests. You'll understand, given the need for security at the moment, if I have you escorted to a suite where you will remain for the evening. In the morning, we will address this."

"Of course." She got to her feet.

The beautifully appointed suite she was shown to at the back of the palace overlooked the formal gardens. It was done in gold and a soft moss green, the shimmery, wispy fabrics of the sweeping brocade curtains and the romantic overlay of the big canopy bed like something straight out of one of the fairy tales she'd devoured as a child.

When a maid showed up minutes later with a beautiful silk nightgown and inquired if she needed anything else, Alex fought back the hot tears that gathered in her eyes.

She'd accomplished what she'd come here to do. She *would* see her father. But what she wanted in this moment was for her brother to have believed her.

She assured the maid she had everything she needed. Unable to sleep, she wandered out onto the terrace. The band, whose lazy serenade had been drifting through the open windows of the ballroom, stopped playing. Then there was only the buzz of the cicadas as she contemplated row after row of perfectly tended, riotous blooms in the floodlit gardens.

A quiet knock reached her from inside the suite. Frowning, wondering who it could be at this late hour, she padded inside and inched the door open. Standing in the dimly lit corridor stood the princess, still clad in her silver gown.

"I had to come."

Alex stared at her sister. The princess's startling blue eyes were counterbalanced by a wide mouth and the high cheekbones that were a signature of her mother's aristocratic haughtiness. Arresting rather than classically beautiful, Stella stared back at her, all of her earlier poise stripped away, her carefully applied dramatic makeup standing out in stark contrast against the pallor of her skin.

Her quick intake of breath was audible. "*Thee mou*, but you two look alike."

"Who?"

"You and Nik."

Alex swallowed hard, a tightness gripping her chest. Her legs felt unsteady, consumed by the emotion of the day, as if one more blow would fell them. She forced herself to move past it, stepping back to allow her sister in.

Stella slipped inside and shut the door. "The party just finished. I hope I didn't wake you."

"I couldn't sleep."

"I expect not."

They regarded each other in silence, wariness and shock

filling the air between them. She searched her sister's gaze for the mistrust her brother had displayed, finding only bemusement and curiosity in return.

"The king told you I was here?"

"Of course not." The princess's lips curved in a wry smile. "At least not willingly. Nik is too protective for that. I overheard him and Aristos talking."

Her lashes lowered. "He is suspicious of me."

"My brother has to be cautious. He has a million grenades being lobbed at him every day with King Idas's descent into lunacy."

Alex bit her lip, chewing uncertainly on flesh she'd already made raw. "You don't doubt my story?"

"When you look more like Nik's sister than I do?" The princess shook her head. "My father's affair with your mother was common knowledge. I think we've all lived with the possibility that something like this might result from his indiscretions. Although for it to happen now is a bit...*startling*."

"I didn't know. I only found out a few weeks ago."

"Nik told me." The princess regarded her silently. "I hope you are not disappointed. My father is an imperfect man. A great king, but an imperfect man. Manage your expectations. Do not expect him to be warm and fuzzy."

"I thought my father was dead," Alex said quietly. "I'm not sure *what* I'm expecting."

The princess's golden-tipped lashes fanned her cheeks. "I can't imagine how you must feel. To find this out now."

Alex exhaled an unsteady breath. "Confused. Bewildered. I'm angry my mother lied to me. I feel...betrayed. And yet I know she did it for the right reasons. She wanted to protect me. How can I be angry about that?"

"Easily." Stella waved a hand around them. "She denied you this. Your birthright."

"Is it?" A vision of her beautiful, serene village filled her head. "I love my life in Stygos."

"You are a royal," Stella countered. "A Constantinides. You could have had the world at your fingertips. Instead she took that away from you."

Had she? Or had her mother given her the safe, loved existence she'd always known?

"Perhaps it's about destiny," Alex said. "Maybe mine was to live the life I have."

"Perhaps." A glimmer filled the princess's eyes. "The life of a royal has its challenges. I will be the first to admit that."

The reticence in her sister's voice stirred her curiosity. "But the benefits outweigh the challenges?"

"I'm not sure that's an analysis I can make." Stella's lips firmed. "Do I think it's my destiny to be where I am? Yes. Would I have chosen it if given the choice? That is the million-dollar question."

It certainly was. The cicadas buzzed their musical song as a silence stretched between them. Stella set a probing gaze on her. "I saw you dancing with Aristos."

Heat rose to stain her cheeks. She had been hoping *that* part of the evening would go unnoticed. Her inappropriate behavior had been uncharacteristic for her, foolish, particularly damning in light of her mother's scandalous reputation.

"It was a mistake," she said quietly. "I was nervous. I'd had a couple of glasses of champagne..."

"Aristos has that effect on women." The princess's mouth twisted. "A word of warning. He takes what he wants until you are too blind to see the danger. Before you know it, you're hooked. Then he turns you loose."

She was clearly speaking from experience. Alex set her jaw resolutely. "It's never happening again. After I talk to my father, I'm going home."

The princess regarded her silently. "I just met my sister," she said softly. "I find I quite like the idea of having one. It would be a shame to lose her so quickly."

A throb consumed her chest. It grew with every breath, threatening to bubble over into an emotion too big to contain. Stella seemed to sense it, the thread that was close to breaking inside her. She stepped toward the door. "It's late. We can talk in the morning. Better you get some sleep so you have a clear head as all of this unfolds."

And then she was gone, her exotic perfume wafting through the air. Alex's mouth trembled as she shut the door. She stood, leaning against it, every muscle, fiber, of her body shredded, spent.

As all of this unfolds. She was terribly afraid of the chain of events she had set into play tonight. A force she couldn't retrieve. That in needing to know her father, by taking a risk that was so totally outside of her nature, she had not only stepped outside her safe little world in Stygos, but entered one that could consume her. A world her mother had done everything she could to protect her from.

CHAPTER THREE

Two days passed, and with them Alex's premonition came true. As the blood test undertaken by the royal physician was rushed through the requisite channels, rumors of her presence spread through the palace in a flurry of gossip only a royal household could induce.

By the time the results of the test were delivered to the palace, confirming that Alex was indeed King Gregorios's daughter, the gossip had spilled to the press, who were demanding confirmation.

Nikandros made it clear they could not wait long in issuing a statement from the press office confirming her as a Constantinides. The longer they waited, the more time the press had to speculate on the story, something the family didn't need as the country fretted about a coming confrontation with its sister island.

It was with this daunting scenario in place that Alex met her father for the first time. Accompanied by Stella to his suite in the west wing of the palace where the king was convalescing, they were told Queen Amara was out for the day. Alex had the distinct impression she was avoiding her as the scandal she was.

Propped up against a pile of pillows, his leathery olive skin lined and craggy from almost four decades of rule, her father was pale beneath his swarthy complexion, his abundant shock of white hair looking out of place on a man who was clearly fighting what might be his last battle.

Stella left. Frozen with indecision, Alex stood in the

center of the room. The king opened his eyes, directing a brilliant beam of Constantinides blue at her. "Come. Sit."

She forced herself to move, perching on the chair drawn up beside the bed. Ruthless, arrogantly sure of his rule, beloved by his people, perhaps one of the last of an impenetrably powerful group of monarchs, her father was vastly intimidating.

He scoured her face. "You look like your mother."

She nodded. Cleared her constricted throat. "We are very much alike. In looks and disposition."

"How is she?"

"She is fine. We run a hotel, my family. It does well."

The king nodded. Contemplated her silently. "You are a Constantinides. As Nikandros will have told you, that gives you royal status. A place in this family."

"Yes." She drew a deep breath. "That's not why I'm here. I came to see you. To know my brother and sister. Not to cause upheaval."

His eyes darkened, a hint of emotion entering his gaze for the first time. "Upheaval there will be. Many mistakes have been made on all sides." He lifted a hand. "I am not long for this world, as you can see, so it will not be up to me to right my wrongs. My wife will come to terms with this. It is *you*, Aleksandra, who must step up and claim your rightful place in this family."

Her hands, clasped together in her lap, tightened their grip, nails digging into her flesh. No outpouring of warmth from this man. No declarations of love for his own flesh and blood. No regret he hadn't been there for her…

Stella had been right. She shouldn't have gotten her hopes up. And yet she had.

Knowing her father was alive had instilled a sense of longing in her. To have that illusion her mother had painted for her, that of a father who'd be excited at the thought of her. Perhaps not the one who would have taken her fishing, who would have taught her about boys, because that was not who this man was to her. Perhaps one with whom she could have forged a more mature bond. One who would have considered her a gift he'd never known he had.

It knocked the wind out of her, the hope. A dull, dead throb pushed its way through her.

"Did you love her?" she rasped, needing to know if her mother's feelings had ever been returned. Needing to salvage *something* from this.

The king fixed her with that steely blue gaze. "I cared about your mother, but no, I did not love her. A king's priority is to the state. There is no room for anything else."

She could have begged to differ, because clearly her brother was very much in love with his wife, but the frozen feeling invading her, siphoning off the emotion that threatened to corrode her insides, made it impossible to speak. Buffered her from more pain.

She had come for answers and she had gotten them. Perhaps not the ones she'd wanted, but answers nonetheless.

Alex spent the rest of the day attempting to wrap her head around the decision she had to make, the media circus going on outside the palace walls making her imminent decision a necessary one.

The decision should have been easy, because she'd never wanted to be a princess. Her visit with her father had been desperately disappointing. Her loyalty lay with the promise she'd made to her mother and the hotel they ran. No one could *force* her to become a royal, but the fact that she was third in line to the throne wasn't a minor detail she could ignore.

What played a larger role in her decision-making were her brother and sister. Now that she'd met her siblings, it was hard to think of walking away from them. But what did she know of being a royal? A princess? It was perhaps the most important question of all, one only Stella could answer.

She pulled her sister aside before dinner and picked her brain. Was life as a princess the endless round of royal engagements and charitable commitments that it looked from the outside, or was there more to it? Would she have any freedom to chart her course, or would it all be decided for her?

Stella answered honestly, which seemed to be her default setting. Yes, it was much as she'd described. But there was an opportunity to own the role, as she herself had proven.

Armed with the full scope of Stella's perspective, not that it cleared her confusion much, she and her sister joined her family for a predinner drink. Nik and Sofía were already enjoying a cocktail, minus two-month-old Theo, their infant son, who was with his nanny. Queen Amara walked into the salon just as the butler handed Alex a glass of wine. All eyes focused on the elder queen as she made her way toward Alex. Breath stalling in her throat, she dropped into a quick curtsy, entirely forgetting Stella's instruction that it wasn't necessary.

The elder queen waved it off with a flick of her hand. "You are a member of this family now."

Am I? I haven't made that decision yet. Her brain rifled through safe things to say. "It's an honor to meet you, Your Majesty."

The queen inclined her head. "Amara will be fine."

The cocktail hour seemed stilted and forced compared with the previous night. When they sat down to dinner, Alex was thrilled to have a knife and fork to devote her attention to.

"When will you be announced as princess?" Queen Amara directed her cool green gaze at Alex. "I would expect soon, given the throngs of media driving us all mad."

"I—" Alex put down her fork and knife. "I haven't actually decided yet what I'm going to do."

Queen Amara lifted a brow. "What do you mean, *decide*? You are third in line to the throne."

"I have a life." Alex lifted her chin. "My mother and I run a hotel together."

"You are a royal. There is no *decision* to be made. Duty says you take your place as an heir to this country."

Her mouth tightened. "My *duty*," she said, "is to my mother and the business we have built together."

Silence fell over the table. "This is all a great deal for Aleksandra to take in," Nik interjected smoothly. "Of course we hope she stays. She is family."

Her stomach tightened at the warmth in her brother's gaze. It was as if he'd been withholding emotion until it was safe to express it. It unraveled something inside her, an almost unbearably bittersweet swell consuming her chest. She picked up her water glass and drank, giving in to the impossibility of eating.

By the time the meal mercifully came to an end, she felt raw in her skin.

Nik headed off to a meeting in his palace office, Sofía upstairs to bathe Theo, Stella out for a drink with a friend. After a call home, an emotional conversation in which her infinitely wise mother told her she needed to do what was right for her, her voice breaking as she did, Alex curled up in the library to think. Process.

But when even that peaceful setting felt too stifling to think, she headed for the magnificent palace gardens instead. If she was going to find a clear head, it would be there.

Aristos emerged from his second visit to the palace in under a week with a strong sense of foreboding that Akathinia had yet to see its most trying times. The king had requested the unusual after-dinner meeting to inform him he'd called all his troops up for active duty after Carnelia had summoned its own reservists, signaling a possible imminent aggression by Akathinia's sister island.

Nikandros had requested he release the rest of the financial commitment he had made to the armed forces to enable the country to protect itself, to which he had agreed.

His head mired in what this would mean for his casino, a potentially devastating delay in breaking ground next month looming, he headed for the front doors of the palace. He was almost there when he saw an undeniably eye-catching female in a white dress headed across the foyer in the opposite direction. *Aleksandra.* He would have recognized that sweet derriere anywhere.

He couldn't deny he'd been wondering how she was. The apprehension in her eyes when he'd walked out of the library the night of the ball had been playing on his mind. Why that was, why he felt in any way protective toward her, was a mystery to him. Out of sight, out of mind wasn't a cliché in his world; it was how he lived his life.

If you didn't invest in people, it was impossible for them to disappoint you. For *you* to disappoint them.

His step faltered on the gleaming marble floor. *Don't do it, Aristos. You already crossed the line with her once. You have far too much on your plate already.* If the $2.5 billion Akathinian hotel and casino didn't get off the ground, his personal investment went down the drain with it, a loss that could threaten his company's existence.

Why he then found himself changing direction and heading toward the back of the palace was anyone's guess. Aleksandra had been headed toward the gardens. He chose the path toward the spectacular fountains and pool at the center of the sprawling botanical extravaganza and found her perched on the wide lip of the fountain, looking like something out of an Impressionist painting.

Wearing a simple white summer dress that left her tanned legs bare, her silky dark hair caught up in a high ponytail, her full mouth pursed as she contemplated what appeared to be a significant issue, she looked good enough to eat. Undeniably edible to his far-too-jaded palate. And yes, this, he decided, had been a big mistake.

Too late, however, as she looked up at him, blue eyes widening. "Aristos."

"Sit," he said as she scrambled to her feet, brushing off the back of her dress. Dumping his jacket on the edge of the fountain, he sat down beside her. Noted the distance she put between them as she returned to her perch with an amused pull of his mouth.

She slid him a wary look from beneath dark lashes. "Overseeing your security again?"

"Meeting with the king. I saw you on the way out. I thought I'd check to see how you're doing."

"You who hunted me down, seduced me to find out what I was up to, then threatened to put me in handcuffs?"

His amusement intensified. She was embarrassed about what had happened between them. About the undeniable chemistry they shared…

"Let's get one thing straight," he drawled. "I *kissed* you because you are one hundred percent my type, angel. Petite brunettes with insane curves do it for me. *Seducing* you would have required more privacy than we had. Although I am not against a bit of voyeurism to add some spice to a sexual encounter, a palace party would *not* have been the occasion I'd have chosen."

Her mouth went slack. "You would not have had the chance, regardless."

He raked his gaze over her pink cheeks, ramrod-straight spine, the faint dip of cleavage the neckline of her dress revealed. The flush staining her chest. The thin material did little to hide the peaks of her breasts thrusting against the material, hard delectable buttons he knew would be a rosy slice of heaven. All signs of a very obvious sexual attraction between them.

"No?" he challenged silkily. "When was the last time you let a man put his hands on you like that?"

She shut her mouth and kept it shut this time. He reached out and ran the pad of his thumb down her cheek, her silky soft skin hot to the touch. "Just for the record, I *am* disappointed, Princess. Your little bombshell that's rocking the country has put you on the endangered species list. Not to be touched under any circumstance. Unfortunate, when that kiss proved just how spectacular we would be together."

Alex hauled in a breath, her insides collapsing into a pool of molten heat. She knew she should be saying something smart back to this unholy man who appeared to say and do anything he deigned, but she was too busy imagining what it would be like to be seduced by him in the true sense of the word. *Hot, forbidden, unbearably exciting.*

He was insufferable, had done a job on her sister, who refused to admit it, and still, she couldn't deny she was disappointed, too.

She pulled her gaze away from the dark vortex it was sinking into. Lifted her chin. "Stella isn't petite and curvy."

His gaze narrowed. "Exchanging notes, you two?"

"She saw us."

"We were like oil and water." He lifted a shoulder. "It was a mutual decision."

She gave him a long look. "Is there a woman on earth you haven't taken to bed?"

"Dozens," he drawled. "Too bad you'll be one of them."

She blinked. "*Wow.* Just wow."

He threw her the most charming of smiles. "I *did* come out here to see how the meeting with your father went."

She considered him. He looked sincere. "It was…fine."

"Fine?"

"I wasn't expecting an outpouring of affection."

"So what did you get?"

She hesitated, unsure if she should be sharing this with him. He spread his hands wide. "The king trusts me with his military secrets..."

"He was aloof," she said. "Abrupt. He said he cared for my mother but never loved her. That there is no room for love when you are married to the state."

"It's a tough job," Aristos offered. "Your life can't be your own."

She was sure that was true. "My mother painted me a rosy picture," she said in response to his continued study. "She led me to believe she and my father were very much in love, to protect me I know, but I think I would have preferred the truth."

"Love is a concept we've all been trained to believe in. It gives us false expectations of our relationships, convinces us monogamy, a lifelong, eternal love, is the norm, when in fact it isn't. Human biology, the study of other animals, tells us that. And yet we continue to aspire to it because we think it's the right thing to do. The golden ideal."

She absorbed the depth of his cynicism. "So you don't believe love exists?"

"No, I don't. I think love is actually sexual attraction disguised as something deeper. When that fades, as it always does as evolutionary history has proven, people drift apart."

She didn't want to believe that was true. Didn't want to let go of her idealism so easily. For if the king of England was willing to abdicate for Wallis Simpson, didn't true love have to exist? If Scarlett and Rhett's passion could survive a civil war and two marriages, wasn't a once-in-a-lifetime bond possible? If it wasn't, if it was only the stuff of fiction, then all her daydreaming during her stolen moments with a book had been an exercise in foolish fantasy.

She wasn't letting *him* burst yet another bubble, she decided. Not at this particular moment when she needed some illusions to hang on to.

"So what happens now?" he prompted.

"I have to decide whether I want to be a princess."

"There's a decision there? I thought every woman wanted to be a princess."

"Not me. I love my life in Stygos."

"So you're going to spend the rest of your life living in a tiny coastal village when you could be exploring the world?'

"Lots of people would give their right hand to live in Stygos." She couldn't help the defensive note in her voice. "What's wrong with a quiet life?"

"Nothing if you're fifty. What do you *do* there?"

"I run my family's hotel with my mother."

"And when you're not working?"

"I see friends or I…read." Her chin rose at his mocking look. "The hotel business is a 24/7 occupation."

"I know that, Alex. I run several of them. I also know what hard work it is if you own a small property and have to do everything yourself. You could leave that behind. Hire someone to work with your mother."

She shook her head. "My mother and I made a pact when my uncle turned the hotel over to her to run. We promised we would always be a team, that we would do this together. To leave her seems like a betrayal."

"But these are extraordinary circumstances. Are there other family members who can help?"

"My cousin, yes. Much of my extended family is involved in the business."

"Then you shouldn't worry about it."

"But I *love* it. I love getting to know people. I love making them happy for a week or two out of their year. I love being busy. If a person has a calling, this is mine."

"Because you don't know any differently." He eyed her. "I think it's wonderful you and your mother are so close. But someday you're going to have to break free of that bond."

She bit her lip. "You think it's a crutch for me?"

"Your words… What I'm saying is that life is about living. Having the freedom to live. When was the last time you went out on a date?"

A long time.

"That long, huh?"

"A year. Since my boyfriend and I broke up."

"And he was?"

"Sebastien Soukis. He's the butcher from the next village."

An amused glint entered his eyes. "Don't tell me… He knows how to *handle* a woman."

Her mouth tightened. "It's a very respectable profession. Whereas yours is questionable."

"Right." He nodded. "I steal unsuspecting people's money."

"I didn't quite put it like that."

"Yes, you did. So what happened between you and Soukis?"

"I—" She waved a hand at him. "We decided to split."

"You were bored."

"He asked me to marry him."

"And you said no because?"

"It didn't seem right. I couldn't…envision it."

"Because it would have been too limited a life for you. You are young, Aleksandra. If you accept this opportunity, you'll have a life, experiences few people will ever have. A life most people would give their right arm for. What's the hesitation?"

"The fear of the unknown." The anxiety that had been

plaguing her all day tipped over into an honesty she couldn't contain. "I'm happy with my life. What if I do this and I'm terrible at it? What if I give up everything and find out it was a big mistake?"

"Then you go home," he said softly. "But don't shy away from this opportunity because you're scared. It's harder to run from your fears than face them. Trust me."

She took in his ultra-confident, ever-so-self-assured persona. "That's easy for you to say."

"Why? Because I'm a powerful man? It wasn't always that way. I've had my own conflicts. Two different roads I could have taken. It would have been easy for me to take the simpler one, the one I was drifting toward at the time, but it wouldn't have been the right one. Taking yourself out of your comfort zone is the most powerful thing you can do."

That intrigued her. "What were they? The two roads?"

"Ancient history." He tucked a wayward curl behind her ear. "My point is you should take the jump, Princess. Privilege is a powerful thing. Use it wisely and it'll be worth the reward."

His touch sent an electric impulse firing through her. She sank her teeth into her bottom lip as a shiver of reaction chased up her spine. If she'd been hoping her visceral response to him was a product of the champagne that night, she'd been sadly mistaken. She hadn't touched but two sips of her wine before dinner, and still she was so aware of him she wanted to jump out of her skin.

His dark, sinful gaze commanded hers. Dragging his thumb along her lower lip, he nudged the tender flesh free of the bruising grip her teeth had taken of it. "Stop fretting," he murmured, "and make the decision."

She got all tangled up in him. In the intimate claim he was staking on her mouth, the pad of his thumb stroking the vulnerable curve of her lower lip. Her stomach went into free fall as heat built between them, wrapped itself around her like an invisible force she was helpless to resist.

Her mouth went dry, anticipating, *willing* the kiss she knew would be worth the insanity of allowing it.

He brought his lips to her ear, his warm breath playing across her skin like an intimate caress. "That would be breaking the rules. I have a great deal of incentive not to do that, angel."

Rolling to his feet, he picked up his jacket. She hauled in a breath, attempting to corral her racing pulse.

He tossed his jacket over his shoulder, his gaze on her. "The woman who sashayed her way into the royal ball insisting on speaking to the king would see this for the opportunity it is. Guess you have to decide which one you are."

Turning on his heel, he sauntered off into the night. She watched him go, head spinning. Inhaling a long, steadying breath, she digested the encounter. Attempted to determine the veracity of what he'd said.

Had she been missing out on the world in Stygos? Would she regret it if she stayed there? It had been easy to work most of her waking hours, to devote herself to the family business in the pursuit of a better life for her and her mother. To satisfy her need to know the world by burying her nose in a book, lost to the adventures she'd found there. *Safe.*

She thought about everything that had happened since her mother revealed her shocking news. How it had seemed as if the world had shifted beneath her feet. How everything she'd thought she'd known seemed like an illusion, and everything she hadn't, her earth-shattering new reality.

She had a choice. To take back control of her life or have it control her. Because one thing was for sure; Nik had been right. Her life would never be the same no matter what she decided. She was a royal. A princess.

Perhaps it was not duty that would inform her decision, but a desire to truly know herself. To expose herself to the world and see what it reflected back at her. To stop living her life on the pages of a book and instead experience it for real.

Did she have the courage to take another huge leap? To leave everything she knew behind? If she did, what would she find when she got there?

CHAPTER FOUR

"How does it feel to be a princess, Aleksandra?"

Terrifying. Bewildering. Like I have no idea what I am doing.

Alex swallowed hard, her knees knocking together as she looked out at the sea of reporters crowding the palace gardens for the official announcement of her appointment as Her Royal Highness, Aleksandra, Princess of Akathinia. Packed into the center of the labyrinth of neatly trimmed hedges in the Versailles-style gardens, there were hundreds of them toting cameras of all varieties, the buzz in the air palpable as they waited to grill the new royal.

It was the largest showing of a press contingent since the king and queen's wedding the year before, a showing Alex had been well prepped for since making her decision to take her place as a Constantinides. And still her tongue was cleaved to the roof of her mouth, a rivulet of perspiration running down her back under the handpicked designer dress she wore.

Stella gave her an encouraging look from her position beside her, Nikandros flanking her other side. Taking a deep breath, Alex addressed the reporter in the front row.

"I'm still getting my feet wet. Perhaps you can ask me that again in a few months and I'll have a better idea."

"What is your role going to be?" the reporter followed up. "Do you have any causes you currently support?"

She was still trying to figure that out. It was her number

one point of anxiety, in fact, since getting the hotel in the black had been her "cause" to date.

"I'm working through that," she said. "More to come."

"Why hasn't the world known about you before now, Aleksandra?" another reporter called out. "Is it true your mother kept your birthright a secret?"

"That's a personal matter I won't comment on."

"What about your father's affairs? Is it possible there are more of you out there?"

"Again," she said, "I won't comment on my family's personal affairs."

"How do you anticipate handling the glare of the spotlight?"

"Day by day. Like any new job, I will have to learn my role. Luckily," she added, nodding at her siblings, "I have my brother and sister by my side."

A reporter directed a question at Stella about her new sister. Alex took the opportunity to breathe. A tall figure leaning against a tree behind the reporter claimed her attention. *Aristos.*

Clad in another of his bespoke suits, he sent her pulse scattering. *What was he doing here?*

"Aleksandra." The reporter turned her attention back to her. "Overnight you have become one of the country's most eligible women. Are you single or in a relationship?"

"I'm single."

"What are you looking for in a potential husband?"

"I'm not looking," she countered. "I have enough on my plate at the moment. But if I were, integrity, intelligence and kindness would be high on the list."

Aristos's mouth kicked up at the corners. Heat flamed her chest, rising to her face. *Diavole*, but why was he here?

"It's rumored the duke of Catharia is quite taken with you. Perhaps there's potential for a romance there?"

Her eyes widened. The duke had been seated beside

her at an official dinner two nights ago. He was charming and attentive, and she'd enjoyed his company, but since she'd been told to keep a low profile considering today's announcement, she hadn't given him any encouragement. Perhaps also because her head had kept going back to her encounter with Aristos in the gardens. Charming as he might be, proper like the duke, he was not.

"The duke is lovely," she said, lifting her chin. "But nothing to report there."

The press flung a dozen more questions at her, covering everything from her life in Stygos to her favorite color. When they had exhausted anything that could be considered remotely interesting, a reporter in the middle of the pack directed a question at Nikandros.

"What do you make of the fact that Carnelia has called its reservists up to active duty?"

Her heart jumped. *It had?* Nikandros moved to the mike. "I think we're doing everything we need to be doing to ensure Akathinia's safety, now and in the future.

"Are you anticipating an invasion by Carnelia?"

"We hope it won't come to that."

The media peppered the king with a series of questions on the Carnelian situation. Alex kept her gaze on the press corps rather than on the man making her feel utterly conspicuous. *Naive* and conspicuous.

The press conference thankfully came to an end. The PR liaison appeared to usher them back into the palace. Stella stopped to talk to a reporter she knew, while Alex continued on with her minder, anxious to get away from the frenzy.

Aristos appeared at her side, his long strides easily gaining him even with her as she walked toward the palace. "Well done," he murmured. "You took the leap."

His designer stubble was thicker than usual, giving him a wicked, pirate-like appearance. It kicked her insides into high gear despite her better sense. She gave him her best haughty princess look. "Surely you didn't come just to laugh at me?"

"You've been busy," he noted. "Taking my advice. A duke already… And no, angel, I didn't come to see your performance. I have a meeting with the king."

Oh. Her stomach dropped. And why was that? She needed to be staying away from him, not courting his attention.

"There is no duke. He was seated beside me at dinner. That's all."

"And you flashed those baby blues at him and he didn't stand a chance."

She turned to face him. "I was *not* flirting."

"You don't have to. You're a natural." He gave her a pained look. "But kindness, integrity and intelligence? Really, Alex? You might as well have posted a neon sign inviting all the Sebastiens of the world to come running. That was *not* what I meant when I said expand your horizons."

She narrowed her gaze. "That is just…*rude.* Any woman would be lucky to have Sebastien."

"Except you," he pointed out. "You're far too hot-blooded for that, Princess."

"Oof." She stuck her hands on her hips. "I tell you what. The next time I need dating advice I *won't* come to you and your heartless reputation. I'll figure it out myself."

"Ouch." He pressed a hand to his chest. "Heartless. That hurts."

"I'm sure you are withering away inside." Noting that Stella was directly behind them, she pressed her lips together and flung him a cool look. "Enjoy your meeting, Mr. Nicolades. Good afternoon."

She turned on her heel and swished her way through the palace doors. Stella caught up with her in the hall. "What was *that*?"

"Nothing." Absolutely *nothing.*

Alex headed to her meeting with her cultural adviser. A familiar anxiety worked its way through her as she sat through two hours of princess training. How was she ever going to get this all right? It all seemed unnecessarily complex and…*antiquated.*

She reminded herself why she was doing this. Stella and Nik were amazing. She hadn't been able to resist the chance to get to know them better. And perhaps because Aristos had been right. She had been playing her life safe with a whole world out there to explore.

Which didn't mean she had to pay attention to *him* and his condescending, provocative comments. If she was going to master this princess thing, she couldn't allow Aristos Nicolades to distract her at every turn.

Firming her mouth, she gave her adviser her undivided attention.

Aristos was still smiling over his confrontation with the feisty Aleksandra when he walked into the king's office. Nikandros's personal aide ushered him into the inner sanctum without delay.

"Thank you for coming," the king said, gesturing for him to take a seat in the sitting area by the windows. "I need a favor."

Aristos's always-opportunistic side perked up. The more goodwill he could bank with the king, the better. Construction on the casino on the shores of the Akathinian harbor would mean surprises—rude, *expensive* surprises a royal influence could help smooth out. Accelerate solutions for.

"Always," he said, crossing one long leg over the other and sitting back in the chair. "What can I do?"

Nik sat down opposite him. "My sources say Idas may make a move on this country as soon as his armed forces are at full strength. As such, we need to shift to a high alert."

His stomach plummeted. It was the worst-case scenario he'd hoped would not come to pass. What would his investors think of such an uncertain environment? A war that could destabilize the region? Would they jump ship? Let their nerves get the better of them?

A knot formed in his gut. He had doubled down on this one. Put the better part of his personal fortune up to back this casino. If it failed, *he* failed.

Your ambition will be the thing that fells you, Aristos, unless you learn to control it.

"Aristos?" Nik was frowning at him.

He shook his mentor's words out of his head. "Sorry, yes?"

"I want both princesses off the island. Stella has a good friend she can stay with in Athens. I need you to take Aleksandra to Larikos."

He blinked. The king wanted him to take his stunningly beautiful, unwittingly sexy, *very* innocent half sister to his private island in the Aegean Sea for safekeeping?

"Of course I'm happy to do whatever you require," he said carefully, "but of all people, Nik, you must know *I* am not a babysitter."

The king fixed his laser-sharp blue gaze on him. "I'm not asking you to babysit Aleksandra. I'm asking you to provide a safe place for an heir to the throne until this is settled. The security on Larikos is impenetrable."

Because he had a casino there where some of the richest men in the world came to play…in a few weeks, actually. "She would be better off with Stella," he suggested. "Wouldn't that be more reassuring for her?"

"Akathinian law says I can't have two heirs to the throne, however distant, together in a situation like this."

He firmed his mouth. "I'm not the man for the job, Nik.

I am scheduled to be all over the globe the next few weeks. I'll ask friends to host her."

Nik pinned his gaze on him. "That you are precisely *not* the man for the job is exactly why I want her with you. It's the last place anyone would think to look for her."

It was not a request. It was a command if he valued the casino license he'd spent the past five years chasing.

"All right. When?"

"Friday."

"Friday?"

"Friday," the king said firmly. "And, Aristos?" Nikandros shot him a deadly look. "I don't think I have to say that Aleksandra is off-limits."

Aristos absorbed the underlying message. The insinuation he wasn't good enough to fraternize with a royal. It had been this way, too, when rumors of his and Stella's brief liaison were circulating. He would have hoped with all the respect he and Nik had gained for each other over the past year working together, the king's opinion of him might have changed. Yet clearly, Nikandros still considered him beneath his family's blue blood.

His jaw hardened, his fingers tightening around the arms of the chair. He'd made an art of not caring what anyone thought of him. It had been a necessity in the life he'd led, in the business he operated in, with the checkered past he carried with him that was always in danger of resurfacing. The tightness in his chest suggested he hadn't quite perfected it.

"Consider it done," he said curtly, rolling to his feet. He had bigger fish to fry than a princess, including a flock of investors whose hands needed holding. A plan B to execute he'd hoped he'd never have to use.

His ambition wasn't the problem. It was the universe and how it was unfolding that was messing him up. Fortunately, he'd never met a calamity he couldn't conquer.

This casino *would* happen. His business would not fail. He was never going back to where he'd come from. *Ever.*

Alex and Stella were summoned to Nik's office after dinner, an unusual request given that the king had been burying himself there of late, forbidding interruptions. Alex rose from her chair, darting a look at Stella. "Do you know what this is about?"

Stella shook her head. "No idea. Could be Carnelia."

The worried look in her sister's eyes had *her* worrying. She followed Stella down the hall to Nik's office, where her brother waved them into chairs.

"You heard the speculation today about Carnelia calling up its reservists," he began, without preamble. "We have confirmed this is true. We have no idea whether Idas is bluffing or planning to make a move on Akathinia."

Her heart dropped.

"He wouldn't dare," Stella exclaimed. "He knows the world is against him."

"I'm not sure he is in his right mind. Regardless, I think it's prudent to remove both of you from the island for the next little while until we can determine the situation."

"And Sofía and Theo?" Stella asked.

"They stay. Sofía refuses to leave."

"Then I'm staying, too," Stella said. "I'm not leaving you."

Nik's gaze softened. "I appreciate the show of solidarity, but I can't have the three heirs to the throne here. Nor do I have the energy to fight with you. My wife is making it hard enough."

"He won't do it," Stella said. "He's bluffing. Why doesn't Kostas talk some sense into his father? What is *wrong* with him?"

"The crown prince remains noticeably absent. Do what

I ask. *Please.* We are well defended, Stella. It's just a precaution."

Stella clamped her jaw shut. Nodded. "We can stay with Cynthia, then."

"You can. Aleksandra will stay on Larikos with Aristos. It is written in our laws the heirs must be separated in a time of war."

"Aristos?" The sisters said the word in unison. Stella's jaw dropped. "Why?"

"Because his casino is impenetrable. She'll be better protected there than anywhere else."

"I'll go home," Alex interjected.

"I'm afraid that's impossible. You would be too vulnerable there."

She bit her lip. "What about my family? I can't leave them unprotected."

"I will make sure they are looked after."

Her head spun. This was *madness*. "I really don't think this is a good idea."

"Why?" Nik threw the question at her with the look of a man who'd just about reached his limit.

She exchanged a meaningful look with Stella. "I just… don't."

Nik's gaze moved between the two of them. "If you have something to say, spit it out."

I can't be marooned with Aristos on his private island for Lord knows how long when I am clearly, inadvisably attracted to him.

Unfortunately, the next day, she was packing to do exactly that.

CHAPTER FIVE

LARIKOS, ARISTOS NICOLADES'S private island in the heart of the Aegean Sea, sat to the east of Greece. Surrounded by sparkling cerulean-blue water, it comprised seventy acres of priceless real estate upon which Aristos's much-buzzed-about, invitation-only high-roller casino was situated, as well as his private estate and guest residences.

"The famous Great House." Aristos's pilot pointed at a massive, sprawling thatch-roofed structure that sat perched on a hill overlooking the sea. He listed off names of celebrities, politicians and royals who'd stayed in the €10,000-a-night suites. "The villas," the pilot said, "for those who wish for more privacy, are the structures scattered down the hill."

Alex absorbed the spectacular aerial view, then sat back in her seat, fingers clutching the armrests. Having never been on a plane before in her life, let alone a helicopter, she had been torn between terror and exhilaration as they'd made the trip from Akathinia to the place she would call her home for the foreseeable future.

She had, of course, not been about to tell Nik about her disreputable behavior with Aristos the night of Stella's party, thus the inevitable conclusion of her conversation with the king. There had been time only to call her mother to assure her she would be taken care of before she and Stella were whisked away from the palace for safekeeping.

Safekeeping. Her stomach dropped as the helicopter dipped and made its way toward the landing pad near the

Great House. She was worried about her family. Worried about what Idas would do. Sure she should be there by their sides and not *here* hidden away with the man she'd practically thrown herself at the other night.

Being uprooted again, separated from everything she knew under the most worrying of circumstances when she'd only just begun to settle into her new life, had been disconcerting. Unnerving. As if she were frozen midjump.

She wanted to know she'd done the right thing in abandoning the life she'd loved, to know everything would fall into place. Instead she'd been handed complete uncertainty.

Her fingernails sank deeper into the leather as the pilot set the helicopter down on the landing pad. A tall, dark male stood waiting, his shorts and T-shirt whipping in the wind. *Aristos.* Her stomach did a flip-flop of a whole other kind. She'd thought maybe he'd send one of his staff to greet her, hadn't even known if he would be here. Just because he was hiding her away didn't mean he had to play host.

Aristos pulled the door of the helicopter open and greeted the pilot. It gave her an opportunity to inspect him in casual clothes during the short exchange that followed.

The show began with the close-fitting T-shirt that stretched taut over his broad shoulders and cut abs, not an excess centimeter of flesh in sight, and ended with the most impressive set of powerfully built thighs and calves she'd ever seen. Pure masculine perfection that hinted at the fact that the rest of him she *couldn't* see was just as mouthwatering as what was on display.

He eyed her as he lifted her down to the ground. "You okay? You look a bit green."

"Fine," she managed past a churning stomach. "I've never flown before. It was an adventure."

He kept his hands on her waist. He smelled like earthy sexy male today, with a hint of sandalwood as opposed to his usual spicy urbane sophistication. Little pinpricks of heat flared beneath her skin as he studied her face, multiplying with unnerving speed until she was drowning in her awareness of him.

"You mean you haven't flown in a *helicopter* before," he corrected.

"No. I haven't flown, period."

His eyes widened. "Surely you've been outside of Akathinia?"

"Only to the Greek islands. Perfectly accessible by boat and automobile."

He looked at her as if she were a creature from Mars. She stepped back, pressing her palms to her flaming cheeks. "There's been no opportunity. You said it yourself. Running a small business means you have no personal time. Every time we hired someone we thought was reliable enough to take part of the workload on, we found we couldn't trust them."

"Staff will always be your biggest headache and asset. Has your cousin stepped in to help your mother?"

She nodded, a throb filling her chest. *Taken her place* was how she saw it.

"How did your mother take the news?"

"Not well." Her mother had been trying to mask her feelings, but she knew she was devastated by her decision, feeling the loss of their bond as much as Alex was.

His gaze softened. "No one said taking the untraveled road was easy."

Brutally hard was more like it. She was getting the sense this new life of hers was going to be a one-challenge-a-day kind of affair.

Aristos picked up her suitcase and headed toward the Great House. She trotted along behind him, half running to keep up.

"I'll show you to your room. Get you settled. Yolande,

my manager, is going to give you a tour of the island this afternoon. She'll be your point person for anything you need while you're here."

Because she was a pain in the neck to him. Because having her here was a huge inconvenience, likely the last thing he needed with a potential war delaying his casino.

"Thank you for opening your home to me," she said, drawing alongside him. "But please, don't feel like you have to play host. I'm sure you have a million things to do."

His dark gaze glittered in the sun. "Unfortunately, you and I are stuck together, angel. I am your official babysitter for however long it takes Carnelia to realize Akathinia can't be taken."

She blinked. *That could be weeks. Months.* "Surely you have to travel… You can't stop doing business because of me."

"I'm going to do it from here. I'll do day trips if I need to."

"That's ridiculous. Your business is all over the world. I don't need a babysitter. I can take care of myself."

He stopped and looked down at her. The warmth in his gaze had vanished, replaced by a cold black stare. "The king has entrusted you to my care. You are a potential target in these games Carnelia is playing should they elect to make a point out of you. You are therefore my responsibility and will do what I say while you are on this island. Understood?"

An icy feeling invaded her. She wasn't sure if it was this vastly intimidating version of Aristos that did it, or the fact that he'd just marked her a kidnapping target.

She swallowed past the lump in her throat. "You don't really think Idas would come after me or Stella, do you?"

"No. I think it would be highly unwise of him. But taking chances would be equally foolhardy."

Right. She shut her brain down before her imagination

ran wild and considered, instead, Aristos's distinctly cool demeanor as she followed him up the steps of the sprawling, airy structure with its incomparable views of the sea. Gone was the incorrigible, devilish version of him she'd come to expect, replaced by the Aristos she'd met the night of the ball.

Apparently Aristos ran hot and cold. Too bad the last time he'd run hot she'd practically begged him to kiss her.

"You can pretend I'm not even here," she suggested. "Better yet, put me to work. I've managed a hotel. I'm sure there are things I can do."

"There are no guests here right now. And what," he tossed over his shoulder, "would the king think of me putting you to work?"

"He'd be happy that you've kept me occupied?"

"I don't think so, Princess. Not going to happen."

She and Aristos were alone on this island. Well, them and a few dozen staff, likely. She digested that fact as she followed him up to the third level.

"When do the next guests come?"

"I'm not hosting any groups while you're here for security reasons. With the exception of an invitation-only poker game in three weeks. Everyone attending is a personal acquaintance of mine, each one thoroughly screened with background checks."

Oh. Her heart plummeted as she stepped onto the third-floor landing. His gaze speared hers. "What's the matter, Princess? Afraid to be alone with me?"

Not in your current chilly state, no. She lifted her chin. "Why would I be?"

Their gazes clashed, black battling with blue. "Oh, that's right," he said silkily. "You're looking for 'integrity, intelligence and kindness.' You'd best go find your duke."

She pressed her lips together. "I already told you, there is no duke."

He turned and strode down the hall. She followed, staring at his broad back. What had she done to annoy him? Or maybe he was simply irritated with the situation?

Her confusion fell to the wayside as she stepped into the ridiculously large, high-ceilinged bedroom Aristos had entered at the end of the hall. Her suite at the palace had been straight out of a fairy tale, but *this*, this was something else. Paradise, perhaps.

The three walls that enclosed the room were a cream-colored canvas for the bright, beautiful island art that covered it. The final wall that faced the sea comprised floor-to-ceiling glass with sliding doors that opened onto a terrace, offering a spectacular view of the endless blue horizon.

With that jaw-dropping perspective as a backdrop, the suite descended into sumptuous, hedonistic heaven. Gauzy cream-colored curtains were drawn to either side of the dark wood canopy bed. A decadent-looking daybed enjoyed a perfect view of the sea, promising hours of reading pleasure.

"Aristos," she breathed. "This is incredible."

"Nothing too good for the princess in residence."

She ignored the gibe, too caught up in the magic of the ethereal room. "I love it. It's perfect."

"Good. My bedroom is there," he said, pointing to the terrace beside hers. "So I can keep an eye on you. My office is in the casino. Yolande will show it to you this afternoon so you know where to find me." He turned and gestured toward the writing desk tucked away in the corner of the room. "There's a secure phone and internet line. You're not to use your usual devices. Turn them off and keep them off."

She bit her lip. "Okay."

"As for meals," he continued, "the chef on the main level is at your disposal. As are any of the water sports and activities. The staff are available to accompany you. The only thing you will *not* do is swim unaccompanied. The undertow can be strong with the *meltemia*."

"I'm Akathinian, Aristos. I was born on the water."

"The rule still applies." He leaned against the wall. "A few things. You will notice armed guards posted on the island. They carry *big* guns. There's no reason to be alarmed—they're for the protection of the guests we host, many of whom are VIPs whose safety is a top priority. To that end, there is no way on or off this island without my personal knowledge and approval. There's a three-mile blackout around us, meaning no aircraft or boat crosses it without my team's knowledge."

Armed guards with big guns and a no-fly zone? What had she walked into?

"Is that really necessary?"

"Yes. More than one of my guests have been kidnapped and held for ransom. It won't happen here."

That word again. *Kidnapped.* She wiped a palm over her brow.

"I thought we could have dinner. Sometime around eight?"

She met his cool gaze with one of her own. "I meant what I said. You don't need to babysit me or keep me company. I'll be fine."

"I have time tonight." He headed toward the door. "Enjoy your tour."

She tried to. Yolande was lovely, and Larikos *was* paradise. Whereas Stygos relied on its wild, natural beauty to attract visitors, its way of life virtually unchanged from a hundred years ago except for the most necessary of modernizations, Larikos was sleek and sophisticated.

From its sensational tropical gardens to the world-class clay tennis courts to the Romanesque-inspired casino, the island sparkled with an opulence that was reflected in every detail. But all that sophistication only made her pine for home. For beaches that were just as beautiful, views just as spellbinding. Her mother, who must be terrified as to what was to come…

She would have given anything in that moment for everything to be back to normal, where life had made sense. But nothing was normal anymore—perhaps never would be again. Her world as she knew it had vaporized, and she felt completely, utterly adrift.

Aristos spent the afternoon in his office, immersed in conference calls to make up for where he was supposed to be had he not been babysitting a princess. Almost all of them were to pacify nervous investors about the Akathinian situation, including one of his biggest, Russian oligarch Dimitri Smirnov, who had seemed even more wily and elusive than ever, marking the Akathinian political situation as "worrying" and refusing to give him a firm commitment that he would stick with him.

He'd therefore put plan B into motion: using his shrouded-in-secrecy, much-anticipated, invitation-only annual poker game on Larikos to keep everyone happy.

He never messed with the sanctity of the game. Any of the business contacts he mixed with the pros were players who could hold their own, but this year, he had invited all his key financial backers, including a wild card in Dimitri, so he could keep a finger on the pulse of them all. He only hoped it wouldn't destroy the game.

Frustration swirled through him, singeing his skin. *Too many calls. Too many uncertainties.*

He slammed a fist on his desk. If he'd been in Moscow as he was *supposed* to be, he could have talked Dimitri into a commitment. Instead he was here, protecting a princess he was supposed to have dinner with in a few minutes. Entertain. He could only hope the Russian would take the bait and attend the game he'd long coveted a place in. It wasn't looking promising.

Noting the espresso he'd spilled in his tirade, now eating up the pages of a report on his desk, he uttered another choice word, grabbed some napkins from his drawer and started mopping it up. He refused to consider the graveyard of men who'd conquered Vegas and Atlantic City, only to end up destitute, consumed by their own greed.

That would never be *him*. He wadded up the napkins and threw them in the trash. His risk had been big but calculated. Bold but not foolhardy. He couldn't imagine a day when he forgot what it was like to wonder where his next meal was coming from, where he was going to sleep that night. It was the kind of desperate clawing existence that was burned into your brain forever, no matter how far your star shot up in the sky—no matter how distant a memory it became.

It was something every human being knew if they were reasonably self-aware. Everything you had could and would go away in the flash of a neon Sin City sign if you didn't keep your eye on the prize.

Just as his own life had once vaporized in the space of a head-poundingly hot Athens night in which heated accusations had been delivered, ultimatums issued and decisions made that could never be taken back.

He pulled himself out of his ruminations with a scowl. It was the thinking of a man who hadn't slept enough, who had subsisted on a diet of far too much coffee and too little food today, his hesitation in heading toward sustenance with only one name: Alex.

She'd had another of those lost, disoriented, utterly out-of-her-element looks on her face when she'd arrived. And why wouldn't she? She'd been ripped away from her family once again with a war looming in Akathinia, clearly no happier to be here with him than he was to be stuck with her.

He had been cold with her, yes, stifling what seemed to be his natural desire to comfort her, because it was the only way to manage the attraction between them.

The women he dated were sophisticated creatures with the benefit of a world of experience. Who knew the score with him. Who didn't complain about his lack of commitment because they'd known from the start it was never coming, and for the time they were together, he provided them with everything money could offer.

It had been that way since his early days in Vegas. Since he'd discovered that having money meant an endless supply of women who cared more about his wealth than the man behind it. Which had suited him just fine. After his parents' disastrous marriage that had seen his mother kick his father out after years of vicious fighting and his infidelity, he had no desire to ever enter into the illusionary institution of marriage.

Carin, his PA, stuck her head in his office and prompted him about dinner. He rolled to his feet, threw his laptop into his briefcase and headed toward trouble. Trouble he was going to neutralize. If Aleksandra's innocence wasn't enough of a deterrent for him to keep his hands off her—which quite honestly, he suspected it might not have been under different circumstances—the fact that the king had warned him off her was.

Which meant keeping Alex at a distance by whatever means necessary.

Showered, changed, dressed in jeans and a T-shirt, and still not entirely free of his filthy mood, Aristos found the princess waiting for him on the terrace of the Great House. The fragile image she cut against the dusky pink-and-red sky, a tiny figure versus the big, scary universe she'd been thrown into, tugged at his heart. He was, after all, partially responsible for encouraging her to embrace this brave new world.

"I should have told you the dress is casual here unless we're having a formal night."

She turned around, a wry smile curving her mouth. "And here I was just getting used to the training that's been drilled into my head. *"Refined dress on all occasions, Aleksandra. Classy yet understated."*

He could have told her that on her, with her perfect curves, anything looked sexy. That the very proper turquoise wrap dress she had on only made a man want to unwrap her as a most fortunate present. That her hair, plaited down her back, elicited the same urge. But since his mind was supposed to be out of the gutter when it came to Alex, he declined to go there.

He crossed to the wine bucket sitting on a table and began uncorking the bottle of sparkling white. "You aren't supposed to let them turn you into a robot."

"I'm not." She frowned. "It's just…there are rules. So many rules. Standards to uphold. It's all a bit much."

"Stella knows her own mind." He filled two glasses, waiting for the fizz to die down to top them up. "Use her as an example."

She took the glass he handed her, a contemplative look on her face. She was curious, he knew, about his relationship with Stella, but there was nothing to tell. They had been two consenting adults scratching an itch, whereas Alex was vulnerable, *emotional*.

He surveyed the dark circles that lined her eyes, their red-rimmed appearance. Her emotions were not his concern; her safety was. But the tug on his heart at her obvious misery was too strong.

"So," he drawled, "what's eating you? You've been off since you arrived."

Her eyes widened. She opened her mouth to say something, then clamped it shut. "I'm worried about my mother," she said quietly. "I feel like I should be there by her side, not here, as lovely as it is."

A twinge of guilt assailed him. He should have been more reassuring earlier rather than scaring the hell out of her. "There's no need to be concerned about the political situation in Akathinia. The minute Idas makes a move, which I still have doubts will ever happen, the world will respond. Akathinia is too important a symbol for its former colonial interests to watch its democracy be compromised."

She gave a doubtful nod. "I suppose you're right."

"I am," he said firmly. He lifted his glass. "To your leap. May it lead you to many fantastic adventures."

She lifted her glass to his. Remained pensive as she drank.

He cocked a brow. "What?"

"I feel like I've been ripped away midjump. I was just getting settled, trying to figure out what I'm going to do, and then all *this* happened." She pursed her lips. "I need to find my 'thing.' My cause to support. All I've learned so far is how to smash a bottle of champagne against a ship without maiming myself and how to cut a ribbon without making it fray. It's making me crazy."

He leaned against the railing, balancing his glass on the top. "Rome wasn't built in a day. Have you been given any direction? Perhaps Stella has some ideas."

"She took me on a tour of the new youth center the charity she represents is building. It's very impressive."

"Youth Compass?"

She nodded.

"I'm on the board of directors. It's a good organization."

She crossed her arms over her chest and tucked her glass beneath her chin. "What got you involved with them?"

"A percentage of the profits from each of my casinos is diverted to the homeless and youth organizations in the cities we operate in."

Her blue gaze turned assessing. “So the big bad casino mogul has a heart.”

“Oh, I wouldn’t go that far, Princess. Corporate social responsibility is smart business.”

“And that explains the staff you’ve hired to work on Larikos who were living on the streets? Who had no particular skill when you hired them and now they’re the head groundskeeper and the engineer who maintains your solar project?”

He must remember to tell Yolande to cut down on the personal anecdotes. “It’s an issue society has to tackle.”

She pointed her glass at him. “I need something like that.”

“You need to be personally invested in it. What turns you on, Princess? Gets those creative juices of yours flowing?”

Her face went a rosy pink. He knew exactly where her head was, because it was where his was. Where it was every time they were within five feet of each other. *In bed, satisfying their intense sexual curiosity about each other...*

“Other than me, angel,” he drawled. “We’ve already established that as a nonstarter.”

Her eyes widened, a deep flush staining her chest to match the one in her cheeks. “You are insufferable sometimes, you know that? And just...*deluded*.”

His mouth curved. That was better. Feisty he could handle. The sad puppy-dog look, not so much.

“Insufferable, yes,” he agreed. “Deluded, I’d argue. You were craving a follow-up to that kiss that night in the gardens as much as I was.” He moved his gaze over her soft, pink, very consumable mouth. “You aren’t exactly subtle with your signals.”

Her mouth thinned. “Wanting something and acting on it are two different things. In actuality,” she said, pinning her gaze on his, “the duke *is* much more my type than you. There is a civility about him I enjoy.”

"Really?" The blatant lie, yet another slight from a Constantinides insinuating he was beneath their blue blood, evaporated his good humor. *His rules.*

"If I took that glass out of your hand right now," he said, holding her gaze, "picked you up and carried you upstairs to my bedroom to do exactly what we both want to do, you would *not* be complaining, Princess. You would be *begging* for me to finish it. And *that* is the truth."

She blinked. "That would never happen."

"You want to *try me*, angel?"

Color leached from her cheeks, leaving behind a pallor that told him he'd gone too far. And still the nerve she'd hit pulsed in his jaw, making it difficult to summon the self-control he knew he needed.

"Perhaps you're right," she acknowledged quietly. "But hormones don't have a lot to do with common sense, do they?"

She slayed him with that one simple line.

Alex almost turned on her heel and skipped dinner with Mr. Hot-and-Cold after that display. Her deeply ingrained good manners, however, wouldn't allow her to do it. Mr. Hot might be back, but she could manage him. Manage *this*. At least she thought she could.

What plagued her as Aristos seated her at the candlelit table for two on the edge of the large formal dining room, in the cooling breeze of the sea, was that she was afraid he was right. That if he'd done what he'd said, she might not have protested, might have been unbearably excited instead. And that was a head-scratcher, given what she knew of Aristos's reputation. Given the fact that Sebastien hadn't been able to persuade her into bed with him during their yearlong relationship, her boyfriend resorting to asking her to marry him in an attempt to get her there.

She wasn't sure what she'd been waiting for. Lizzie and Darcy's spark-strewn courtship? Gatsby's grand obsession with Daisy? Or perhaps the inescapable attraction she felt toward Aristos—as if a magnet kept pulling her toward him no matter how hard she tried to escape. Made worse by the fact that now she knew he had a heart. That the man behind the stunning good looks was one who cared enough to pluck two strangers off the street, one in Rio and one in Las Vegas, pay for their education and give them a job on Larikos, his most exclusive property. A second lease on life…

He liked to paint himself as the devil beyond redemption, but he was far more than that. It was dangerous to even let herself go there; she knew it as she lifted the glass Aristos had refilled and sipped her wine. But she couldn't seem to help herself.

"What about your reading?" he said, breaking the silence that had fallen between them with a return to their earlier discussion. "You said you love to read. Why not literacy as a cause? Youth illiteracy is a major issue. You could team up with Stella on activities…"

She thought about it. She had never thought of her reading that way, as a privilege, when in fact, it was. For her, a story that transported her to another world had always been a part of her life. Her mother had taught her English as a little girl, considering it an invaluable skill. The nook in her family's hotel where guests left their discarded books had become her gold mine. And yet not everyone had been granted that privilege, even for critical, life-sustaining purposes.

"I love that idea," she said quietly, recognizing it as the peace offering it was.

"Then use the time here to pick a short list of organizations you might like to work with."

She would. She attempted to focus on her salad as a

silence fell between them again. More peaceful this time. But she found her appetite had waned. Or was it just difficult to concentrate on anything with Aristos sitting across a candlelit table from her? When it looked as if he had been poured into the white T-shirt and dark blue jeans he had on, his current level of intensity only making him that much hotter.

"Enough about me," she said, offering a peace branch of her own. "What's been keeping *you* up at night?"

An amused expression crossed his face. He sat back in his chair, his wineglass cradled in his palm. "The list is too numerous to bore you with."

"You have to be worried about the casino."

"Yes, but much of that is out of my control. All I can do is try to convince my investors there is no need to worry."

"And is that working?"

"Most seem fine. One in particular, Dimitri Smirnov, a Russian oligarch, seems shaky. I've invited him to come to Larikos for the poker game, so I can firm him up."

Her stomach sank. "Which you could be doing now if you weren't babysitting me."

He shot her a reproving look. "We've had this conversation."

Yes, but she hated that she was standing in the way of something so important. "How does the game work?" she asked. "Who gets to come?"

"I thought you found my profession distasteful, Princess."

She sighed. "Hector Rigatos, my best friend's father, lost all his family's money gambling in Las Vegas. I know it's an extreme case, but that's why I have a problem with gambling. And could you *please* stop calling me Princess? You know very well I dislike it."

"There are some unfortunate cases like that," he acknowledged. "Most people, however, learn to enjoy responsibly.

As for calling you Princess," he drawled, "I like it. I find it reminds me *who* you are."

As if he'd forgotten for one second. She shook her head. "How long has the game been going on?"

"Five years. The players like it because it's private. They can let their hair down. What happens on Larikos stays on Larikos, so the saying goes. Social media, any type of reporting, is banned."

She could only imagine what happened when men, money, power and competition got together. "Do they get up to very naughty things?"

"Sometimes. Nothing that's fit for your ears."

"Please. How much is the opening ante?'

"One hundred thousand US dollars."

Thee mou. "And by the end of the game?"

"Last year it went as high as one point three million. We ended with twenty million worth of chips on the table. Which," he advised, "is not a public figure."

Her head spun. This was *beyond* fascinating. Unlike poor Hector Rigatos, these men knew what they were doing.

"You give a percentage to charity," she guessed.

"Yes."

"Do you play?"

"Sometimes."

She'd bet he'd be the most formidable of players…bet he looked smoking hot doing it.

She pursed her lips, regarding him thoughtfully. "So how do we get Dimitri Smirnov here?"

"You mean how do *I* get Dimitri here?"

"I can help. I can do some research… We've done some really great events at the hotel to draw in high-profile guests."

"I run a poker game, Princess, that's all. Dimitri's always wanted to play. We'll see if he bites."

She chewed on her lip. “Why the hesitation, then?”

“It’s his wife’s birthday that weekend. I already offered them an extended stay on Larikos to celebrate. If that doesn’t do it, I’m not sure what will.”

She couldn’t imagine what woman in her right mind would turn down a week on Larikos. When they weren’t in captivity, of course... But maybe, she thought, her brain percolating, there was more, something personal they could offer Dimitri Smirnov’s wife as a birthday present. An experience she couldn’t find anywhere else.

Her lips curved. Research was what was needed. Good thing Aristos had given her a laptop. If she just so happened to surf up some information on Mrs. Smirnov that might help, was that a crime?

Aristos eyed her. “No, Alex.”

“No, what?” she countered innocently, spearing a tomato with her fork.

The conversation remained on neutral, innocuous topics after that, topics Aristos seemed to handpick to keep their interaction in a safe zone. She played along with it because she knew it was the smart thing to do.

After dinner, he walked her upstairs, likely to ensure she was ensconced in his heavily guarded fortress for the night. Each step along the long hallway, toward a bedroom, *another* foreign existence that was now hers for weeks, perhaps months, brought with it a low-grade anxiety. She didn’t want to be alone. She didn’t want to be *here.* She wanted her life back. Which one she wasn’t sure.

“Can I get you anything?” Aristos asked as they reached her bedroom door.

It was the wrong question to ask. She bit her lip, hot tears burning the backs of her eyes. “No,” she said huskily, blinking them back. “I’m fine.”

He reached out and traced her cheek with the tip of his finger. “Alex—”

She flinched. Shut herself into her room with a murmured thanks and told herself to stay there before she did something really, really stupid.

Aristos stood outside Alex's room for a good minute, torn between the desire to go after her and comfort her and knowing exactly where it would be headed if he did. In the end, he turned and went to his own room, where he answered a few last emails from his overseas teams.

The storm rolled in about an hour later. One of those vicious assaults that came out of nowhere and packed the wrath of God. It brought with it a stunning display of thunder and lightning that seemed to shake the walls of the Great House, although in reality it was far too well-built for that.

He got up from his chair on the terrace, went inside and checked that the lightning strike detection system was activated. When he saw that it was, he poured himself a drink and went back outside to watch the show.

White and gold streaks of lightning arced across the inky black tropical sky, jagged, intricate fingers of pulsing light that dazzled the eye with their spectacular patterns. The thunder grew louder with every pass, its powerful roar shaking the floorboards beneath his feet. Faster and more frequent it came until there was virtually no pause between the cracks of thunder. It must be close. Almost directly overhead.

He wasn't sure what alerted him to Alex's presence on the terrace adjacent to his. The storm was too loud for him to have heard her. She stood, wrapped in the white silk robe the resort provided its guests, her arms wrapped around her. A bolt of lightning zigzagged through the sky, hitting the water not a hundred feet from them. It illuminated Alex's pinched white face. *She was terrified.*

Turning on her heel, she ran inside. He headed toward

her room, expecting the door to be locked. She must have forgotten to do it, because the handle turned and he walked into the room, colliding with a wall of frightened female.

"Whoa." He gathered her into his arms. "What's going on?"

"Th-that strike," she stuttered. "It was too close. It was—"

"We're fine." He ran a soothing hand down her back. "We get these storms all the time."

"So do we. I *h-hate* them."

"They sound worse than they are."

"What if it hits us?"

"We have sophisticated detection systems. We'd be on it in a minute."

A crack of thunder made her jump. She was shaking so hard her teeth were chattering. Uttering a curse, he set her away from him, walked to the bar and poured her a finger of cognac. Drawing her down on the sofa, he pulled her into his arms, her back nestled into his warmth.

"Drink," he said, pushing the tumbler into her hands.

He was staying for a few minutes until she calmed down. That was it.

She curled her fingers around the glass. Took a sip. "That's really strong."

"It'll calm your nerves."

She took another sip. He smoothed his palm over her hair, still bound in the tight plait. It made him hurt to look at it. "This *has* to be giving you a headache."

"My hair was a little wild. I'll take it out before I sleep."

He undid it for her, sliding the elastic from the bottom of the plait and methodically working the braid free with his fingers as the storm continued to roll over them. "Why are you so frightened? A bad experience with a storm?"

"My uncle Rasmus was hit by lightning when I was a little girl. He was a fisherman. He went out on his boat one morning, early, very early, when a storm like this rolled in. Luckily, one of his fellow fishermen saw it happen. They took him to the hospital, but his left side was paralyzed. He could never man a boat after that."

"That must have been frightening for a little girl."

She nodded. "I know the chances of it happening are one in a million, that it's an irrational fear, but you think if it can happen once, it can happen again."

He worked the last section of the braid free. Her hair fell around her shoulders, like warm silk under his hands. It was beautiful. She should never wear it up. If she were his, she never would.

The bizarre train of thought made him scowl. He never kept women around long enough for them to be "his." Where was *that* coming from?

The beats between thunderclaps lengthened, the bright bursts of lightning lessening in their intensity, becoming fewer and further in between. He moved his fingers to her scalp, his slow, easy massage meant to distract.

"Aristos…"

"Mmm?"

"Your two roads. What were they?"

His fingers paused in her hair. "Ancient history. Like I said."

She twisted around to look at him. "If it's ancient history, why won't you tell me?"

"Because it doesn't matter anymore."

"If it doesn't matter, why can't you tell me?"

Because it involved intimate details of his personal history. Because barely anyone knew the story. Because she *would know him if he did.*

And yet she'd had the courage to tell him her deepest fears. Had taken a massive leap few would ever have had the courage to take in leaving her life to become a princess.

Surely he could tell her a story that didn't matter anymore? That had nothing to do with the man he was now?

Or perhaps had everything to do with the man he was now…

He pulled her back against his chest, his hand returning to the satiny fall of her hair. "When I was sixteen, I was living on the streets in Athens. Running with a gang. I was distanced from my family for various reasons, bitter about the lot the world had handed me and headed down a very dark road. My mentor, David Tennyson, one of the men who revitalized Las Vegas, was visiting Athens. He was in front of a restaurant one night, smoking, when I attempted to relieve him of his wallet.

"He was too street savvy to let that happen. But instead of turning me in to the police, he wanted to know why I was on the street. I told him my story. He saw something in me, saw past the anger and the bitterness. He wanted to help me, he said, but only if I gave up my lawless ways. He handed me twenty one-hundred-dollar bills and a business card that night and told me if I wanted to learn the casino business to come to Las Vegas."

She twisted around to face him. "You went."

He nodded. "You only get a chance like that once in your life."

"Or never." She sank her teeth into her bottom lip, a habit he found himself once again wanting to correct. Only, he knew how he'd do it, and there wasn't anything innocent about the vision that filled his head. "That's quite a story."

"It wasn't a match made in heaven. Not in the beginning. I had a lot of baggage I had to work through…anger issues. David has a tough background himself. He wasn't about to put up with me breaking the rules. There were no easy shortcuts, I would come to realize. The path to success was a great deal of hard work."

"What's your relationship like with David now?"

He thought about it. "Like father and son, really."

"And your own family? Did you reconcile?"

"No."

"Why not?"

"Some paths you can never reconcile."

His tone was hard. Final. She opened her mouth, then closed it. "Does David come to your poker game?"

"Yes." He held her gaze. "That story is not for public consumption, Alex. David and I are the only ones who know the history, the only ones who ever will."

"I won't tell a soul," she said. "Thank you for telling me. I understand now about the choices you were speaking of. How difficult it must have been for you to choose. How we all have a choice."

He tucked a chunk of her hair behind her ear. "What were you upset about earlier?"

"I was homesick." She waved a hand at the sea. "It's so beautiful here. Your island is incredible. But it makes me think of Stygos. How much I miss it..."

"Did you call home?"

"Yes. It's just...I feel lost. I want to know I've made the right decision giving up my life. I *think* I have, then the doubts creep in."

"That's when you have to stay the course," he said firmly. "It gets harder before it gets easier, just as I said about my early days in Vegas. Once you've passed the point of no return, doubt is normal. It's what you do with that doubt, the strength of spirit you put behind it, that makes the difference."

Her lips curved in a heartbreakingly vulnerable smile. "You are wise, Aristos Nicolades."

"Along with being insufferable and rude?"

"Yes." Her smile grew. "Perhaps you are my David. Pushing me on the right course..."

He shook his head. "I identify with your struggle, that's

all. I know how hard it is to walk away from everything you know. To tell yourself you're doing the right thing even when it's terrifying. Even when you *know* it's right."

Her gaze darkened. Stayed on his. The moment hung, suspended between them. She was soft and warm against him, still within the circle of his arms, that brilliant blue gaze of hers eating him up.

"Alex," he growled, blood drumming in his ears. "We have rules."

"I know." She whispered the words even as she drifted closer. Her scent, a mix of jasmine and something he couldn't put a finger on, wound its way around him. To have all those curves within touching distance, that amazing mouth close enough to touch, *taste*, was playing havoc with his common sense. His rules.

She had drifted so close now, her lips were mere centimeters from his. He could have stopped the madness; he was still in possession of all his faculties, whereas Aleksandra was on the far side of vulnerable and clearly not. Perhaps because of that and not in spite of it, he didn't push her away. Didn't listen to the voice in his head asking him if he had a death wish.

She was seeking comfort. Surely he could keep it to a kiss? One kiss. Then he'd put her to bed, *alone*, and be on his way.

He could do that.

He let his breath mingle with hers. "What's the matter, angel? Don't have the guts to take it all the way?"

She brushed her mouth against his. He almost groaned out loud at the pillowy softness of it…how good she tasted.

The alpha in him couldn't leave it like that. Capturing her jaw in his fingers, he took control. Firmer, lusher, the kisses went until they had fully explored the texture and shape of each other. Then he slid his tongue into her mouth and rediscovered the intoxicating flavor of her. She tasted like peaches and pears from the wine she'd consumed, as heady as he remembered.

His blood heated, his body responding to the perfection of their connection. He should stop it now. Do what he'd said he'd do. But when he moved to disentangle them from each other, Alex protested and moved closer. "Soon," she murmured against his lips.

Soon? She was too tempting beneath his hands not to touch. Too tempting *to* touch. *A couple more minutes*, he told himself. Max.

Sinking his hands into her waist, he lifted her up so her knees came down on either side of his thighs. It gave him access to all of her. Perhaps not so smart.

Moving his lips to the smooth column of her throat, he satisfied a burning need to taste more of that silky smooth skin with lazy openmouthed kisses that revealed she tasted that good all over. *Christe mou.* Lust coiled low in his gut at the sweet, honeyed flavor of her. It made him wonder if she'd taste like that between her thighs…like some kind of forbidden ambrosia he'd never get to sample…but desperately wanted to.

He traced the pulse that raced at the base of her throat with his tongue, absorbing her indrawn breath.

"Aristos." His name on her lips sounded so sexy with the perfect roll of the *r*, all the blood in his body fled south.

"You are so perfect," he murmured, dipping lower to the hollow between her breasts. The plunging neckline of the robe gave him easy access to the beginning of those beautiful round curves. Succumbing to temptation, he slid his fingers beneath the silk, rasping his thumbs across the twin hard peaks. Alex gasped and arched into his touch, her breathy moan kicking him low in the gut.

He wanted to look at her, to wrap his mouth around her, to lavish his attention on her naked flesh. Instead he brought his lips back to hers in a kiss that flouted sanity, searched for it even as Alex buried her fingers in his hair, urging him on. Unable to resist those sexy moans, he rolled her nipples between his fingers, teased the aroused peaks even tauter, her answering groan heating his blood.

This is madness. Somewhere deep inside his brain the thought registered, finally clicked with unerring precision. Lifting his mouth from hers, he pulled the silk lapels of her robe together and set her away from him on the sofa. Alex stared at him, a stricken look on her face.

"*Soon* is over," he bit out. "*Soon* was a bad idea."

"Aristos—"

He got to his feet. Hardened his heart against the vulnerability that cloaked her like a second skin. "The storm has passed. Get some sleep."

Turning on his heel, he left before his common sense deserted him completely, his rules in tatters.

CHAPTER SIX

IT WAS NO USE.

Alex set her laptop on the table, swiped up her espresso and sat back in the plush lounge chair, drinking in the idyllic view of an endless blue horizon from her private terrace. Perhaps more caffeine might kick-start her brain into working order, because all it could focus on right now was *the kiss*. Well, not just the kiss. The way Aristos had taken intimate possession of her body *after* the kiss.

She closed her eyes as the memory singed her skin. How utterly and completely lost she'd been…how it had felt as if she were playing with fire but she hadn't cared… the knowledgeable rasp of his thumbs across the peaks of her breasts igniting a need she hadn't known existed…

Her blood pumped through her veins at the memory, warming her cheeks. In the cold light of day she recognized her actions as foolish, inspired by the loneliness enveloping her the night before, by the need to know if that kiss the night of the ball had really been *that* good, that that kind of passion existed off the pages of a book. And perhaps, most of all, because uncovering the Aristos who was so much more than the ruthless casino scion he was made out to be had proved undeniably fascinating. Lethally compelling.

She wondered at the strength of character he must have displayed to get where he was today. Wondered what could have happened in his family to drive him onto the streets. She wanted to feel special because he'd confided something to her he'd never confided to anyone else, but she knew that would be taking her foolishness to a whole other level.

She was sure the Aegean Sea was littered with the emotional corpses of countless women who had crashed and burned in their attempts to get to the bottom of Aristos. Who'd thought *they* would be the one. She would not be one of them. Not when he was the same kind of philanderer as the one who had broken her mother's heart. Stolen her dreams. Left her pining for a love that would never be hers.

That he was fast becoming an anchor for her, that Aristos Nicolades, notorious playboy and ruthless take-no-prisoners force of the business world, was serving as a fountain of wisdom on this new road she was traveling, seemed a rather bizarre development. But last night she'd seen he was far more than the image he presented to the world. She had a feeling it had been only the tip of the iceberg. So perhaps not so crazy after all...

Still, even if all that were true, even if she wanted to know that kind of passion for real in this new, more-daring version of herself, Aristos was the last man she should do it with. The way he'd dumped her on the sofa and left last night should be more than enough incentive to convince her of that. It had been vastly...*humiliating.*

She took another long draw on the espresso, attempting to drown her mortification in the dark eye-opening brew. She would be far better off doing what Aristos had suggested, working on her future, taking back control of her life in constructive ways, than fixating on a kiss.

She spent a couple of hours doing just that, looking at literacy organizations that not only appeared as if they were doing good work but also might benefit from her support as a spokeswoman. She jotted down the names of a couple of charities that looked interesting, then put her research aside for her more pressing task.

Typing in *Dimitri Smirnov* and *wife*, she searched

everything she could find on the oligarch's significant other, Galina Smirnov, a glamorous London-based socialite. The oligarch himself seemed to be of questionable reputation, some of his interests on the shadier side, it seemed. It made her wonder why Aristos did business with him, but that wasn't her mission here.

Working her way through the articles, she unearthed a profile from a glossy magazine. It was rife with information. Skimming her way through the stories of the Smirnovs' legendary soirees, weekend residences and politically notable connections, she found a paragraph about the hostess's not-to-be-missed London dinner parties.

> Galina Smirnov entertains with a glamour that harkens back to a golden age, when the jazz greats dominated and the making of a superior cocktail was an art. Cocktail hour at the Smirnovs' is sacrosanct, vodka-based, of course, Galina's collection of the jazz masters incomparable, enjoyed by the guests on an antique gramophone.

Jazz music. Her lips curved. This she could work with. Her mother just so happened to be old friends with the retired jazz legend Nina Karvelas, who had once come to Stygos to sing for their guests at the hotel's grand reopening.

Could she convince Nina to come out of retirement to sing on Larikos as a birthday present for Galina Smirnov? Perhaps the singer would do it if a donation were made to one of the charities she'd spent her retirement working with.

Exhilaration flooding through her, Alex threw on shorts and a T-shirt and went in search of Aristos at his office. His PA, Carin, told her he was booked solid until nine that evening with conference calls. Cooling her heels with difficulty, she headed to the beach, read a classic, took a surfing lesson from the water sports instructor, Diego, then ate dinner by herself. Still no Aristos.

She rose the next day only to be told by Carin that Aristos was in Athens for meetings. *Diavole.* Was he avoiding her because of that kiss? Was he going to avoid her forever?

Humiliation dogging her footsteps, she buried her head in another book to fill the day. By the time dinner rolled around, the thought of consuming another meal by herself didn't appeal. She wasn't even hungry. It felt as though all she'd done was sit around and eat.

She went for a hike up into the cliffs instead, the early-evening air still hot and humid. Sitting on a rock at the top, she took her time enjoying the view, then walked back along the beach toward the Great House.

Passing the tiny little cove off the main resort, a slice of heaven with its pristine white sand crescent bounded by the walls of the cliffs, she was irresistibly tempted. What she wouldn't do for a swim right now, her body grimy and sweaty from the hike. But Diego was off for the evening, Aristos nowhere in sight, the helicopter pad empty. She couldn't even *swim* by herself.

Frustration coursed through her, tightening her fists by her sides. She was a prisoner…a damn prisoner on this island. In this fortress Aristos called paradise. She was an excellent swimmer, there was no risk.

Heat pushed through her, egging her on. She glanced around the deserted little cove. There was no one to see her…

Mouth set, she stripped off her T-shirt and shorts to the bathing suit she had underneath, waded into the heavenly water and sighed. It was perfect.

Aristos landed on Larikos just before nine, the resort sparkling with light against a sky full of stars. Retrieving his briefcase, he thanked the pilot, jumped to the ground and propelled his weary body toward the Great House.

It had been quite the day. Still no word from Dimitri, and a score of meetings with suppliers in Athens persuading them to hang tight, that the ground-breaking for the casino would not be delayed long.

His thoughts turned to Alex as he climbed the stairs toward his suite. He had been ignoring her ever since that kiss, hoping the cloud of vulnerability that surrounded her would fade along with his instinct to comfort her and spill pieces of his past while he was at it.

Kissing her was one thing, a mistake he never should have made, but revealing so much of himself had been worse. If he pretended his past had never happened, refused to acknowledge it, it held no power over him; others couldn't use it as a weapon against his undeniable success. Telling the story to Alex, however, had established it as fact. Brought it into his present. And even though he trusted her and knew it would go no further, it still felt like a chink in his armor.

He climbed the final set of stairs, mouth flattening. The problem was, now he felt guilty. Alex must be lonely. Perhaps she hadn't eaten? Perhaps they could have dinner together? Dinner was safe.

He dropped his things off in his room and knocked on her door. When there was no response, he knocked again. No answer. Turning the knob, he pushed the door open and called her name. Nothing. *Strange.* The dining room had looked empty on his way up.

He went downstairs and found Yolande. "Do you know where Alex is?"

"I haven't seen her since this morning. I thought she might be having a rest."

"She's not in her room. Could she be using the spa?"

His manager made a call. Frowned as she hung up. “She’s not there.”

Then where the hell is she? An uneasy feeling slid across his skin. Alex had mentioned the cliffs the other night, how she’d thought the view would be amazing. He’d told her the rocks could be treacherous, unstable; it was a hundred-foot drop to the water below; better to do it together sometime.

His unease intensified. Had she gone and done it anyway? Even if she had, it was a short hike; it wouldn’t take hours.

“Go ask the staff,” he told his manager curtly. “Find out who saw her last.”

When Yolande reported back to say no one had seen Alex in hours, a web of apprehension snaked its way around him. His brain flipped to the Carnelians, a thought he immediately dismissed. The island’s perimeter was unbreachable. But it remained in the back of his mind, eating away at him, as he called his head of security and ordered a search of the island.

The cliffs worrying him the most, he jumped into a Jeep and headed toward them, his progress hampered by the darkness and the rutted track. Had she fallen? Hurt herself? There were venomous snakes up there…scorpions that could incapacitate a person in seconds.

His brain spun in a million directions. If anything had happened to her…she was his responsibility…under his care.

He hit the gas and the Jeep jumped ahead. This was why he hadn’t wanted her here. Why he never wanted to be responsible for anyone. Because every time he had been he’d failed, too caught up in himself to be there when the person he was responsible for needed him.

He had exhausted every possible scenario in his head, his insides in knots as he neared the cliffs, when his pilot called him. He had located Alex. Swimming. In the cove below the cliffs.

What he had strictly forbidden her to do.

He slammed on the brakes, a red mist descending over his vision. She would not have done that. She would *not.*

He sent his pilot home, pulled his security team in, turned the Jeep around and headed back along the track. By the time he reached the path to the cove he was beyond furious; he was apoplectic.

Pulling the vehicle to a screeching halt, he jumped out and headed down the path toward the beach. There, lying on her back, floating in the water, was Alex, illuminated by the light of the moon.

A choked sound alerted Alex to the fact that she was not alone. Flipping onto her front, she trod water, eyes widening when she saw Aristos in a designer suit standing on the shore. Her heart hammered in her chest as he headed toward the water. Surely he wasn't going to… *Thee mou.* Her hand flew to her mouth as he stalked into the sea, a lethally dangerous expression on his face.

She was in so much trouble.

Her tongue, cleaved to the roof of her mouth, could manage only a helpless "Aristos—"

He pushed through the water, sank his fingers into her waist, picked her up, slung her over his shoulder and headed for shore. She gasped, fingers grasping his jacket. "What are you *doing*? Put me down… You're ruining your suit."

He stalked up onto the shore and set her on her feet.

"While you were enjoying your swim, which I expressly forbade you to do, my search team, the entire island, has been looking for you."

"The entire island? Why?"

"You didn't show up for dinner. No one's seen you in

hours. You didn't deign to tell anyone where you were going."

Her heart sank. "I was on my way back. I was just going to be a few minutes more. It's—" she waved her arm around them "—it's so nice here. I told you I'm an excellent swimmer. Isn't this a bit of an overreaction?"

He stepped closer, his powerful body a wall of heat that bled into her skin, sending her heart racing in her chest. "You forget, you are a target, Princess. You are under *my* care. How do you think I'm going to react when you disappear? Do a whistling little stroll around the island calling your name like my dog's gone missing?" He raked his gaze over her face. "There are poisonous creatures on this island. A hundred-foot drop from that cliff. I was worried you'd fallen, were lying somewhere in need of help."

A tight band wrapped itself around her chest. She pressed her palms to her cheeks. "*Lypamai.* I'm sorry… I wasn't thinking right. I was so bored, I didn't—I didn't think to tell anyone."

"Bored?" His breath rasped across her cheek, the intimidating bulk of him pushing her heart rate from fast to furious. "I'll tell you who isn't bored. My pilot, who was finally settling down to dinner… My security team, who've already had a full day's work… Yolande, who is frantic about you."

Tears burned the backs of her eyes. "I said I was sorry. I'm just trying to explain."

"Why?" he demanded. "Why would you disobey my direct request not to swim?"

"I was…frustrated."

"About what?"

"About being here. I have nothing to do. You won't let me help."

His lip curled, wisps of pure fury coiling in his gaze. "You know what you need to do, Princess? *Grow up.* Stop whining about being here and thank your lucky stars people care enough about you to want you safe. Some don't have that luxury."

She flinched. Knew he was right, but the humiliation blanketing her lifted her chin. "What about you, Aristos? How grown-up are you being? We share one kiss and you go running for the hills."

"I was *working*, not running for the hills."

"And you couldn't spare five minutes to say hello?" She shook her head. "What are you afraid of? That I won't be able to keep my hands off you? That in my naive, vulnerable state of being, I can't resist you? Because I promise you, I know that kiss was a bad idea."

A smoky, sultry edge laced his furious expression. "Quite the opposite, Princess. I am afraid *I* won't have the discipline to walk away the next time you throw yourself at me. My next move after that kiss would have been to carry you to my bed, remove your clothes and explore every inch of your beautiful body with my hands and mouth to see if you tasted as sweet in all the places I'd fantasized about. And then where would we be?"

Thee mou. Heat uncoiled under her skin, a soft, sinuous unfurling of something molten that scalded her insides. Swallowing hard, she lifted her chin. Halted the insanity. "I know the kiss can't happen again. I would have told you that if you hadn't been avoiding me. As for tonight, I am truly, *truly* sorry for the mess I've caused. It was thoughtless of me."

"Hurricane Aleksandra," he murmured silkily, watching her with a hooded look. "Blows in and sweeps everything up with it."

Her lashes lowered. A shiver moved through her as the breeze swept over her wet skin. Aristos stripped off his jacket and draped it around her shoulders, the brush of his fingertips against her collarbones sending electric shocks of awareness through her. She clasped the lapels together, refusing to show how much he affected her.

"I did," she ventured carefully, "have something I wanted to discuss with you."

He lifted a brow.

"I did some research on Galina Smirnov."

The dark look reappeared on his face. "*No*, Alex."

"Hear me out. I read a profile piece on her. She's a big fan of jazz music."

"And this is relevant why?"

"My mother is old friends with Nina Karvelas."

"*The* Nina Karvelas?"

"Yes. She did a concert once for us at the hotel. She's retired now, but I was thinking she's heavily into her charitable causes. What if you threw a birthday bash for Galina? Nina sings, you donate a sum of money to her charity, everyone wins. It's an experience money can't buy. Exactly what might entice Galina to Larikos..."

His brows came together. "How do we even know Galina is that much of a fan of jazz? People say all sorts of things in profiles to look interesting."

"She has one of the most complete collections in the world. The interviewer was wowed by it."

He rubbed a palm against the stubble on his cheek. "We don't have parties, Alex. It's a poker game."

"So you have an opening night reception before you start playing. This is *Nina Karvelas*. If we could get her to say yes, it would be the coup to end all coups. How could Galina not come?"

"If her existing birthday plans can't be changed."

"So you find out. I could ask my mother to ask Nina in the meantime."

He pursed his lips. Stuck his hands into his pockets.

"Have you heard from Dimitri?"

"No." He gave her a long look. "I need to think about it. And you need to get some clothes on."

They walked back to the Jeep and drove back to the Great House. She changed when they got there, had dinner with Aristos, throughout which she kept her mouth shut, a low profile…until he walked her to her bedroom door that was, when she couldn't resist speaking up.

"What you told me the night before last," she said, looking up at him as he rested a palm against the frame of the door, "about your past…about that strength of character you needed to survive, *that's* what I took away from our conversation. Not the mistakes, not the dark parts, but the courage, the strength you must have had inside you to not only walk away from a life you knew was wrong, but to cross an ocean, to leave everything you knew behind to be something different." She shook her head. "*That* I think is amazing."

His gaze darkened. "So good at building fairy tales, Princess. You're a natural."

There he went again, deflecting praise, admiration. Anything that might be construed as good about him. Refusing to acknowledge who he was beneath the layers, because heaven forbid, someone might get close to him.

She was getting the impression Aristos didn't know how to be intimate in anything but the physical sense. He didn't believe in love, treated his relationships like transactions and preserved that protective shell around himself at all costs because he had been built that way, because whatever had happened in his early years to drive him onto the streets had scarred him badly. Impaired his emotional IQ.

"All right," he said, still striking that same indolent pose, palm against the door. "You win, because frankly, I need the carrot to dangle in front of Dimitri. Call your mother and see if Nina could make an appearance here. But don't make any promises."

A surge of satisfaction flooded through her. *Finally something to sink her teeth into.* Now she only hoped Nina would say yes.

Aristos's gaze narrowed. "This game is a well-oiled machine, Alex. It runs itself. You're making one phone call, that's all."

"Yes." She nodded her head vigorously.

"As for tonight," he said softly, straightening away from the door, "you've signed your warrant. You have now earned yourself a babysitter in the truest sense of the word."

A wary skitter went up her spine. "What does that mean?"

"It means you and I are going to be joined at the hip, angel. I intend on returning you to Nik in one piece."

She pressed her lips together. "That isn't necessary. I've learned my lesson. I won't take a step out of line."

"No, you won't, because I will be there to make sure you don't."

"Aristos…"

He sauntered off down the hall toward his room. "Start thinking of creative strategies to keep ourselves in line, Princess. I'm already off and running."

CHAPTER SEVEN

ALEX MADE THE call to her mother the following morning on a still, quiet Akathinian day in which the Carnelian military exercises continued on the waters bounding the two nations, the only sign anything was amiss. Having assured herself her mother was okay, she explained the situation Aristos faced and how Nina could help.

I owe Nina a call, her mother had said. *I'll see what I can do.*

Setting down the phone, Alex crossed everything. Her impulsive and admittedly recalcitrant behavior last night had had far-reaching consequences. If she could pull this off and Nina said yes, if the Smirnovs took the bait and came to Larikos, she could make amends for her thoughtlessness by planning this party for Aristos. Channel her frustration into something constructive.

True to his word, Aristos was on her like glue. He had lunch with her, dropped by her surfing lesson in the afternoon and joined her for dinner that evening. When he didn't have an eye on her, he had one of his dangerous-looking guards keep vigil. It was all getting a bit old by the next morning when her mother called to tell her Nina had said yes—the singer would consider doing the appearance on Larikos in exchange for the proposed donation to the charity of her choice.

She almost jumped out of her chair with glee, particularly when Nina's charity turned out to be a program that encouraged kids to learn to read through the power of song.

As the singer talked her through it in their follow-up call, Alex's excitement grew. It was exactly the type of work she wanted to get involved in with her love of reading, she'd told Nina. Something she could really make a difference with.

She practically flew over the beach to Aristos's office, one of his professional shadows hot on her heel.

"You've made your point," she said, stopping in front of his desk. "You can call the dogs off now."

"I don't think so," he drawled, sitting back in his chair, gaze lingering on the sweep of her legs in the shorts she wore. "I like having you on a leash, Princess. It gives me great peace of mind."

"Call them off," she said firmly, "or I will phone my mother back and tell her Nina's services aren't required. She said yes, by the way."

A slow smile curved his mouth. "Nicely done."

"I have been negotiating contracts for the hotel for years," she said crisply. "Do we have a deal?"

"Yes. But if you ever wander off like that again, there will be consequences, angel." He crossed his arms over his chest, that lethal gaze resting on her. "Don't let my imagination run wild."

Her lashes lowered, heat shimmering through her. She couldn't help but imagine what those consequences would be. She *should* be ignoring him. Instead she couldn't stop thinking about that fantasy he'd painted of her in his bed, kissing, *tasting* her all over…

"Still working on those creative strategies?" Aristos's taunting gibe brought her gaze up to his. "Looks like it's still a work in progress."

Diavole. She folded her arms. "How are yours coming? You seemed quite interested in my legs when I walked in."

He lifted a shoulder. "I'm a leg man, Alex. I'd have to be dead not to look at yours. Besides, I have strategies."

"Like what?"

"I drew up a list of dinner topics. Wait until you sit down—you won't believe how dry it's going to be. The weather, the spectacular meteor shower that's coming and the fascinating scientific phenomena behind it, what a charitable board member does in all its intricate, excruciating detail so you have your expectations set..." He waved a hand at her. "All guaranteed to have us dying for a good book."

All guaranteed to ensure they didn't have to engage in the intimate type of conversation he clearly preferred to avoid.

"How studious of you," she said. "*My* strategy is to get Galina to bite so I can plan this event and have something to do."

"*If* I let you plan the event."

"Oh, didn't I mention that?" She put her fingers to her mouth. "That's part of the deal."

He gave her a long look. Summoned her into a chair to go through the details. She sat, crossing her legs to give him maximum view, enjoying the power that surged through her when he took advantage of the opportunity to study the scenery with unabashed fascination.

"The exciting thing," she said, "is that Nina's new charity is about engaging youth in education through the power of song. She said we can talk when she comes, and if it seems like a good fit, we could work together."

He tore his gaze away from her legs. "A match made in heaven. That's good news. A happy princess might actually allow things to return to normal around here."

She made a face at him. "Do you want to hear the details? Nina has some requests."

"Go ahead." She went through the list of conditions the jazz singer had detailed. When Aristos approved them all, she left him to call Dimitri.

It was midafternoon, her surfing lesson about to begin, when he found her on the beach, a triumphant glitter in his eyes. “He said yes.”

Her heart swelled, a buzz of excitement zigzagging through her. “Will you let me plan the party?”

“Yes.” His gaze narrowed. “You own those two hours before the game. Work with Carin on the logistics. She’ll have my security team do background checks on Galina’s guests. But not another foot out of the box, Princess. You and this game are not mixing.”

She gave him a salute. “Aye, aye, captain.”

“Also, you are not supposed to be here. You will simply be Alex that weekend. Understood?”

She nodded.

He waved her off to join Diego. She turned and headed toward her instructor, a huge smile on her face.

“Alex?”

She swung around.

“Thank you.”

A warm feeling spread through her. “Don’t thank me yet. I still have a party to throw.”

Alex took her mandate and ran with it. With the party only two and a half weeks away, there was a great deal to do in a short period of time. She created a menu for the party, a special bohemian decor for the bonfire setting and liaised with Nina on her requirements for the performance and her travel and with Galina on her guests and special requests for the evening.

Luckily, event planning was a skill she’d mastered at the hotel. She created a critical path of things to do and checked them off as the days slid by, working furiously to ensure that every detail of Nina’s performance would be perfect, because impressing the Smirnovs was so critically important to Aristos.

Aristos continued to work day and night between his spot checks on her, his tension palpable as the poker game approached. He rose with the sun and worked late into the night, more driven than any human being she'd ever encountered.

Now she knew where that drive came from. He had known what it was like to have nothing, had built his business from the ground up, and that business was being threatened.

If the questions in her head grew ever more persistent—about the early experiences that had caused him to cut himself off emotionally from the world, what had happened to send him out onto the streets—she kept them to herself as they tiptoed around their perpetual awareness of each other.

She was finding her feet. It felt good to be contributing. Her mantra was to stay out of trouble, pull off a great party. Which meant keeping her attraction to Aristos buried deep.

CHAPTER EIGHT

HIS KEY INVESTORS locked down for the game, Aristos turned his attention to the rest of his business he'd been neglecting as he attempted to hold the Akathinian project together.

It was a daunting task. With thirty-three hotels in eleven countries, he relied on his property and country managers to handle issues in his absence and keep things afloat. Luckily, the team he'd handpicked was superior, and by the Thursday before his poker weekend, he'd caught up to a point where things were once again running like a well-oiled machine. His creative strategies for avoiding his attraction to his princess, however, could use some work.

With both of them on their best behavior and Alex immersed in the party planning, he would have thought the undercurrent between them would have faded. Instead it had grown stronger.

If he'd found her undeniably attractive before, Alex in her element, brimming with confidence, was even sexier. It was impossible not to respond to the vibrant, enthusiastic flip side to her vulnerability as she chatted about how the party was coming along at dinner and the ideas she had. It was like watching her potential surface, and it did something funny to his insides.

She was smart, creative and perceptive, her glass-half-full approach to life a fascinating, compelling foil for his jaded view of the world. Which subsequently rendered his list of strategies, his attempts at dry, safe dinner conversation, wholly ineffective. He, a creature who thrived on self-inflicted solitary confinement, looked *forward* to her company at dinner every night.

A buzz sounded from his desk. His gaze flicked to his mobile. *David.*

"Just checking to see if you're still alive," his mentor said drily. "You've gone deep underground."

Which in the past had not always been a good sign. When his darkness caught up with him… He got up to roam to the window, the moon a thin new slice in a dark sky. "Been busy pinning down investors for the game."

"Got everyone you need?"

"Now I have. Dimitri was being elusive."

There was a pause on the other end of the line. "You sure you trust him? I can try to line something else up here."

"I've got it," he said, his tone clipped. He wasn't about to let his mentor, a man who owned half of Las Vegas, rush to his rescue. Especially when David had made it clear he thought he'd pushed it too far this time.

"I appreciate the offer," he added in a more conciliatory tone. "But I'm good. I am looking forward to seeing you, though. Going to ditch those amateur bets you were making last year?"

"Going to get over the need to prove yourself? You've done it a hundred times over, Aristos."

And there it was, David's usual slice of advice delivered in a succinct left hook. He picked up the stress ball sitting on the windowsill and crushed it between his fingers. "Maybe when Akathinia's done."

Maybe when he felt he had the respect due to him that had never quite seemed to come. When his critics finally stopped finding reasons, trumped-up flaws in his visions, to leave him waiting in the wings while his competitors graced the covers of glossy magazines.

David bantered on for a few minutes, then signed off to go to bed. Aristos put the phone down, rested his palms on the sill and looked out at the perfection of a clear Larikos night.

The sense of accomplishment the rush of the week had provided faded in the silence of the darkened room, a bone weariness settling over him. *When are you going to get over trying to prove yourself?*

He was tired of fighting, he acknowledged. Exhausted from attempting to one-up the competition to get to the pinnacle—to be the name on everyone's lips in a fickle entertainment industry that changed on a dime. He thought maybe Akathinia had to be it. *The one.* Wasn't sure how much he had left in him.

He stared out at the clear, bright sky, littered with a sea of stars. What weighed on his mind, ate away at him when he allowed himself time to think, was what he would find when that day came—when he'd exorcised his demons, what he'd find underneath. He suspected it would be an empty shell—that he'd traded his soul for success.

It was why being in perpetual motion was the only way he knew how to operate. Pushing away from the window, he was about to return to his desk to finish up the report he'd been working on when a flash of white caught his eye, picked up by the floodlights on the beach. Alex, who'd stopped working hours ago with most of the details for the party wrapped, stopped under a palm tree, reached into her beach bag and pulled out a blanket. Shaking it out on the sand, she sat down, her eyes on the sky.

The meteor shower was tonight. He'd totally forgotten. In actual fact, despite his sarcasm, he found them fascinating and stunningly beautiful.

Like the woman who sat waiting for the show.

He should finish the report. Instead he found himself shutting off the lights and heading for the beach, his footsteps measured and purposeful. Just like that night in the palace gardens, it was clear to him he should be walking in the opposite direction from the one he was. But he was afraid he'd think too much in his own head, so he walked toward temptation instead.

He'd been resisting her for two weeks. Surely he had this down by now?

Alex looked up as he approached. "There are still front-row seats available."

"You remembered." His gaze touched her tanned, shapely thighs revealed by the modest hem of the shorts she wore, the kind of curves that stopped a man in the street. He didn't need to see more to know they were the perfect toned framework for the fantasies he'd had. Fantasies that involved him ordering her to wrap them around him as he demonstrated what steady-as-they-go Sebastien had clearly not had in his repertoire.

Hot, hard and memorable.

Color darkened her cheekbones. "Your scintillating, well-versed recap of the sight to be seen wouldn't allow me to stay away. I will, however, point out those types of looks are not within our rules."

"True," he agreed, settling himself down beside her on the blanket. "I, however, am in a bit of a mood. You want careful, Princess, you should send me on my way."

She stayed where she was, still as a statue. His excellent peripheral vision caught the big inhale that lifted her chest before she pulled her knees up to it and wrapped her arms around them.

"I thought you'd solved your biggest problem with Dimitri."

He settled himself back on his elbows. "I'm not getting a good vibe from him. I still have to convince him not to bolt."

"What happens if he does?"

"It leaves me one hundred million dollars short of financing. Not to mention the precedent that could set for other investors."

"That must be worrisome. But like you yourself said, you can only control what's within your power."

His mouth twisted. "A little difficult to tell yourself that when you have a half a billion dollars riding on a casino. But I'll give it my best shot, Princess."

She gave him a long look. Sat back on her elbows, mirroring his pose. "It should start soon. It said nine thirty on the web."

A silence fell between them. He studied the push and pull of the sea as it ate up the sand, inching its way forward in a steady, ancient rhythm. *Inescapable, unrelenting.*

Alex was right. He had shored up every weak link within his power. Dimitri was a wild card who played outside the usual rules—he'd known that from the start.

"It's so quiet here," she said after a while.

His gaze flicked to her. "Your village must be quiet. How many people live there?"

"A couple hundred, many of them my mother's family. And yes," she said, a wry note to her voice, "it's sleepy, caught in a past generation. Important announcements are still posted on the *platias* in the village, the fish truck still delivers the catch of the day and the farmers bring the milk to our door."

"How quaint."

"I like it. It's the best way to start my day. Sam, the farmer's son, and I always have the most interesting conversations."

He smiled. He'd bet it was the highlight of Sam's day, too.

"On Sundays we work a half day, let our weekend manager handle things. We have a big dinner with family, family being a loose term that usually encompasses everyone—neighbors, anyone who's around from the neighboring village. It's a big gossip fest, a chance to catch up. Someone handles the grill, someone's playing music, there are kids, dogs everywhere…all a little maniacal. When it's over, my head is usually buzzing so much I'll escape to my favorite little cove to read, center myself, before the week starts."

"It sounds wonderful." A hollow feeling invaded him. His cynical wasteland of an existence couldn't be more different from the reality Alex had lived, from the warmth and community she had been surrounded with. It would be like setting Alice in Wonderland down in the middle of Dante's Inferno…or perhaps Purgatory, he conceded, although he wasn't sure he'd rid himself of all his vices before he'd climbed out.

A throb unfurled low in his gut, wrapping itself around him and squeezing hard. It had never bothered him before, the emptiness of his existence, the connections he'd severed, the absence of affection he'd grown up with. But tonight it did.

A bitter regret assailed him, a sorrow that lingered just beyond the edges—for what he hadn't had, for the things he'd craved so deeply he'd had to let them go before they destroyed him. Guilt. Guilt for what he'd done. Guilt for what he *hadn't* done. Guilt for all of it.

He pinned his gaze on the sea. Fought against the emotion that seemed ever so close to the surface. Alex sat quietly beside him, giving him space in that intuitive way of hers she had. In that way she had of *knowing* him.

If he was pretty sure he'd forgotten how to connect with people—if he'd ever understood the concept—he'd never had that problem with this woman. Their connection had been real from that first night at the ball. Powerful. It had prompted him to reveal parts of himself he'd sworn he never would. If that wasn't enough to make him run, he wasn't sure what would.

Alex absorbed the turbulence of the man sitting beside her. He was clearly working through something in this dark mood he'd announced upon sitting down, as if he wanted to be here and didn't all at the same time.

"You were right," she said quietly, when she'd decided his brooding had gone on long enough. "What you said in the gardens at the palace. I told myself it was enough, my life in Stygos, and it *was* wonderful, I am blessed to have had it. But it was too safe. I needed to leave to find out who I am. I needed to step outside my comfort zone."

His mouth curved. "You've done that, all right. Still feel like it's the right decision?"

"Yes." She pressed her palms to her cheeks, marveling at everything that had happened since that night. "Identifying where I want to put my energy, planning this party, I feel like myself again, only better. Because I know I have all these amazing experiences out there waiting for me."

He blinked, his dark lashes shading his cheeks. "You will be a force to be reckoned with. I have no doubt about it, Princess."

Something unfolded inside her, a warmth, a yearning that was shocking in its intensity. Pressing her lips together, she lowered her gaze, attempting to wrestle her feelings under control. Her eyes slid over the dark purple tattoo half hidden by the sleeve of his T-shirt. Reaching up, she traced it with her fingertips. "What's this? I've seen some of the guards with it."

He pushed his T-shirt higher. "It's a man-of-war. It's the marking my gang members and I carried."

"You brought some of them with you here to Larikos?"

He nodded. "I knew I needed the best in protection for the clientele we would host. Knew I could trust them. Their allegiance is unquestionable, as is their ability to keep a man alive."

A shiver went through her. She traced the intricate detailing of the beautiful design. Done in varying shades of purple and black, it perfectly represented the dangerous creature that had inhabited the seas she'd grown up in, an animal she'd been warned away from as a child. Fascinating, but to be avoided if you knew what was good for you. Like Aristos himself.

She absorbed the corded, impressive muscle beneath her fingertips. It was intoxicating to touch him, to give herself permission to explore his beautiful body for a purely innocent reason. Except she wasn't sure it was so innocent, touching him, not when she lifted her gaze to his and found a banked heat there that made her insides simmer.

She let her fingers fall away from his skin. "What is the significance of the man-of-war?'

"They are deceptively beautiful. Deadly in numbers."

Her lashes arced over her cheeks. "Were you? Deadly?"

He eyed her. "What are you asking me, Princess? If I've ever killed a man?"

"Yes."

"No. My organization, the Men of War as we were known, thought of ourselves as revolutionaries. We were soldiers, taking from the haves to give to the have-nots, reclaiming what society had taken from us. There was a sense of justice to it. It was mostly petty thievery, some armed robberies. There were a few instances where things got out of hand, yes, people got hurt, but those were the hard-core personalities, not the majority."

She stared at him, fascinated. "What was the background of the members? What led them into it?"

"Poverty, violence at home, single-parent families in which the mother was left to cope. The gang provided the bonds we didn't have at home, leadership figures, brother figures..."

"And you?" she asked quietly, her heart in her throat. "What kind of a home did you come from?"

"A broken one. A poor one. My father was a mechanic,

an alcoholic, chronically unfaithful to my mother, often out of work. They fought constantly."

"Was that what drove you out of the house?"

"Partially. I got older, stronger. My father and I would go head-to-head. It was either that or let my rage get the better of me."

"How did they react, your parents, about you joining a gang?"

"My father was furious. He gave me an ultimatum—quit, get back in school or stay away."

"So you chose to stay away?"

"Yes."

"How old were you?"

"Fourteen."

Her chest tightened. *So young. Cast out of his home for reasons that should never have been in the first place.*

"What about your mother? Your brothers and sisters? It must have been difficult to leave them behind."

A silence followed, so long, so pronounced, it made her fear she'd crossed the line, gone too far in her need to know. His reply when it came was low, tight. "My anger was tearing me up. I was afraid of what would happen if I stayed, afraid of what would happen if I left."

The band around her chest tightened. "An impossible decision," she said softly.

"Yes."

"Do you know how they're doing, your family?"

"My mother kicked my father out the year after I joined the gang. She'd had enough. When I sold my first hotel, I went home and bought her a house, made sure she never had to work again. Beyond that, we've had very little contact with each other."

And therein lay the key to so much about this man. Alienated from the family he'd loved, damned if he did, damned if he didn't, he'd cut himself off from feeling, from *allowing* himself to feel because, she suspected, it hurt too much.

She bit the inside of her mouth. "Family is everything, Aristos. Family is the thing you have when everything else is gone. I know you said those ties have been severed, but surely nothing is irreparable?"

"This is."

"But—"

"Angel." The warning in his voice was clear, the glitter in his dark eyes sending a shiver down her spine. "I know you love where you come from. I know you like to idealize that paradise on earth you think it is, but not everyone gets to have that. Sometimes you get hell on earth instead. Sometimes wishing for things you'll never have is too expensive a proposition to keep."

She digested that stunning proclamation, her heart thudding painfully in her chest. She knew the feeling well. She'd spent her life wishing for a father who loved her, only to be served up with reality instead. But Aristos was talking about his *life*. About the love and care he'd never had, not until David Tennyson had picked him up off the street at sixteen, perhaps too late to ever heal the wounds inside him.

If she'd been living her life on the pages of a book, Aristos had been living his in a bitter existence no one should ever have to experience. Making choices no one should ever have to make.

Her head was still spinning when Aristos pointed at the sky. "There's one."

She looked up, watching a bright ball shoot horizontally across the inky black sky, a trail of light flaring behind it. Not far behind was another, then another, until the heavens were a stunning display of bursts, streams and flutters of light.

Spellbound, she drank it in. On and on it went in a symphony of color. When a particularly jaw-dropping explosion scorched the sky, she reached for Aristos's arm to point it out to him, but her hand landed on his thigh instead.

Tight, hard muscle coiled beneath her palm; his heat bleeding into her. An electrical current vibrated from where she touched him up through her arm to encompass her entire body. It tore her gaze from the sky and planted it solidly on that of the man beside her. If her heart hadn't been firmly secured in her chest, it would surely have jumped right out of it at the look on his face.

Jaw set, expression predatory, the fire in his eyes made the blood pound in her veins.

The world could have exploded around her in that moment and it wouldn't have stopped her from drifting toward him, toward the imminent collision she knew would be as explosive as the ones happening in the sky above. Eyes darkening with an emotion she couldn't read, Aristos pressed a palm to her chest, stopping her before she got there.

"*No*, angel."

Her brain didn't immediately compute. She stared at him, confused. He dropped his hands to her waist and rose, lifting her along with him and setting her down on her feet in the sand. Retrieving the blanket, he shook it out, threw it over his arm and propelled her toward the Great House, a hand at the small of her back.

Up the stairs they went, the silence surrounding them deafening. Humiliation heated her cheeks, dragged her every step. When they reached the door to her bedroom, she turned to look at him, leaning back against the frame. "Aristos—"

"Alex." He cut her off with a clipped voice. "That would not have been wise, and you know it."

She brought her back teeth together, corralling her emotions. "You're right," she bit out. "There I go again, throwing myself at you. My deepest apologies…"

Turning, she reached for the door handle. Aristos's fingers clamped around her biceps and spun her to face him. "Alex—"

"Forget it," she snapped furiously. "Let me go."

He backed her up against the wall instead, his palms flattening on either side of her. "Princess," he murmured huskily, pressing his forehead against hers, "I am not rejecting you, I am choosing *sanity*."

Wasn't it the same thing? She sucked in air, attempting to find some of that particular attribute because he was right. Perfectly right. This shouldn't be happening. Except wrong, because she didn't give a flip about sanity. She wanted *this*.

A second passed, two, three maybe, their heat spilling into each other. His mouth was a fraction from hers, so close she was breathing his air. His hard thighs, pressed against hers, broadcasted his arousal.

The oath he uttered then as he levered himself back to stare at her made her stomach clench. "I don't know what I'm doing with you anymore," he rasped, his gaze raking hers. "And tonight is not the night to figure it out. Trust me."

Cool air drifted over her as he stepped back, turned and walked down the hall to his room. Pulse racing, blood pounding in her ears, she watched him go, waiting for her knees to assure her they would function before she pivoted, reached for the doorknob and let herself in the room.

Would her mistakes with that man never end?

CHAPTER NINE

A PICTURE-PERFECT LARIKOS night had presented itself for Galina Smirnov's birthday party, at which the jazz legend Nina Karvelas would sing in public for the first time in over five years.

A blood-orange sky streaked with fingers of yellow marked the occasion, drawing a dressed and ready-to-go Alex out onto the terrace to drink it in as the day sank slowly into night as only a Mediterranean evening could, with its intoxicating blend of vivid colors that stoked the senses.

A flock of butterflies traced a looping path through her stomach. She'd double-, triple-checked that every detail was in place, and still she felt nervous. She wanted it to be perfect for Aristos. Perfect for Nina, with whom she'd met earlier in the day to discuss her charity, another reason for the overabundance of adrenaline running through her veins. It seemed a perfect fit. If Nik approved the choice, she would be off and running.

The butterflies in her stomach intensified. Now if only the tension between her and Aristos could be resolved. He hadn't spoken to her since he'd left her at her door two days before with that cryptic line.

I don't know what I'm doing with you anymore.

What did that even mean? He was conflicted, to be sure. About her, about his feelings for her. He was charged with protecting her, yes, but she suspected his walking away had more to do with how much he'd revealed to her…

the intimate conversation they'd shared…the connection between them neither could seem to control.

What he'd shared with her on the beach that night had been heartbreaking, had followed her around ever since. Had changed *everything*. She could no longer label him a heartless philanderer. Instead she had discovered a complex, wounded man behind those walls he liked to build, a man who'd never been given the tools to connect or love.

She felt empathy for him, yes, but also something far more dangerous: the belief that whatever was happening between them was real, different. That *she* was different to him.

What she'd felt that night when he'd stood there outside her door fighting his emotions hadn't changed. She wanted to be with him, to know that kind of passion. Of all the jumps she'd taken, this might be the biggest, most dangerous, because it involved her heart. Because if they explored what they had, Aristos might break it.

But wasn't that what her new life was all about? Taking the risks she'd always avoided?

Her watch told her it was time to make her way down to the beach. Stepping her feet into crystal-studded flip-flops, a prerequisite for the sandy white beach, she joined the staff as the first guests began to arrive.

The hiss and crackle of the roaring bonfire that licked almost six feet into the air was the star attraction, surrounded by the sultry sounds of Nina's jazz band. Sleek-looking serving staff handed out vibrantly hued cosmopolitans, Galina's favorite cocktail, to inspire a celebratory mood.

She stood surveying the scene as the beach filled up, a satisfied smile curving her lips. Not only were the Smirnovs and their guests here, but every single one of Aristos's poker players was, too, clearly anticipating the show. As long as nothing went wrong with the acoustics, which weren't a given with the tricky winds of late, the evening would be a smash success.

Her gaze shifted to Aristos, who stood speaking to the guests of honor, Dimitri Smirnov and his wife, Galina. Galina was as lovely as her superior hostess reputation had suggested; her husband, on the other hand, was another story. His reputation preceded him; first impressions hadn't improved it. He struck her as cocky, not entirely transparent and full of himself.

Aristos, meanwhile, had a very different impact on her. Elegant in a silver-gray shirt and black pants, his short-cropped dark hair pushed back from his face in a ruffled, spiky look, he oozed intensity. He reminded her of the fire dancing and crackling behind him: beautiful, imminently combustible, undeniably dangerous, a dozen layers deep, each one a darker, more complex version than the last.

Her stomach dipped, a wave of heat shimmering through her. What would it be like to have that single-minded intensity focused on you and you alone? She'd had a taste of it. It had been enough to convince her it would be worth every heart-stopping second.

He looked at her then, before she had a chance to wipe the evidence from her face. Moved that intense gaze over the sophisticated French twist she'd engineered, down over her face, where ebony eyes tangled with blue for a long, suspended moment, then over the sleek black dress that skimmed her curves, cataloging every inch, every centimeter as he went.

She sucked in a breath, heat bleeding into her skin as if he'd physically touched her. It shook her in her shoes, vibrating every inch of her skin, as if for a moment, he'd forgotten to marshal his defenses, that impressive control of his, and all she could see was the truth. The hunger.

He didn't want to want her, but he did.

He moved his gaze back to her face. Tension thickened

the air between them. Held her frozen. Then rationality, in precious little quantity of late, thankfully kicked in. She wasn't letting Mr. Hot-and-Cold take her on an emotional roller-coaster ride tonight. Not when so much was riding on the success of this party, for her and for him.

Turning her back on his stare, she made her way into the crowd.

Aristos absorbed the princess's turned back with a blink and then another, noting, of course, her amazing behind in the formfitting black dress, because she had the best one he'd ever seen.

Was that just a kiss-off look? He thought it might have been… He'd never actually had one to compare it to.

It stirred an animalistic desire to wipe it off her face even though he knew exactly why she'd directed it at him. That he deserved it. This time he *had* been running for the hills. Sharing your life story with a woman you were clearly developing feelings for did that to a man. Well, that, and he'd been completely focused on the game, on clearing the decks so he could devote his attention to his investors tonight.

It ate away at him, that look. Festered as he found himself watching Alex rather than Nina's performance, as spectacular as it was, wondering what he was doing with her. He'd walked away from her the other night because Nik had told him in no uncertain terms that she wasn't to be his—that hadn't changed. Yet every time he came within a foot of her, those good intentions flew out the window, clouded by a complex set of emotions and lust he couldn't seem to make head nor tail of.

The lust he could handle, decipher. The other feelings Alex aroused in him, not so much. That he had cared for her from the start was clear if you shone a light on his behavior. What he felt for her now was more complex.

She was getting under his skin, making him feel things, question things, *want* things he couldn't have. He couldn't turn her off like a switch as he did with his other women.

That was the heart of the issue. The source of his problem. But he thought maybe he could have handled it better.

He pulled her aside after the performance as the guests mingled. Alex gave him another of those cool looks.

"Everything okay?" he asked deliberately.

"Kala." She lifted her chin. "Everything's going perfectly. Don't you think it's perfect?"

"Perfect," he agreed. "I came over to say thank you."

"It's the least I can do." The words rolled off her tongue in swift, robotic fashion, stirring the antagonism roiling his insides. "Galina would like to watch the game," she said. "Can I watch it with her?"

"Women are distracting."

"Then why do you have the two beautiful waitresses? I saw them earlier."

"Because they're meant to distract, entertain the men. You are not."

Her mouth firmed. "I will stay in the background. Firmly in the background. Let me come."

His better judgment told him no, but this was Alex and her big blue eyes he was up against—an unfair battle.

"In the background," he underscored. "You blend in with the paint."

The high rollers' room glittered with opulence: Brazilian-wood floors shone underfoot, the marble showpiece of a bar was lined with hundreds of colorfully hued bottles and the arched, elegant glass doors that lined the wall to the terrace were magnificent, cut crystal shimmering in the muted lighting.

The air was tense, thick, the players bent in concentration over their cards. Aristos, Dimitri, the sultan she'd met earlier, a senator from New York and six other men sat around the table in the center of the room. Whiskey glasses littered the surface of the table, ties lay discarded on the backs of chairs and the aroma of cigars lingered alongside the overpowering scent of competition.

One of the beautiful blonde waitresses clad in a black dress far sexier than Alex's ushered her and Galina around the edge of the room to the bar.

"Is it always this quiet?" Alex whispered, sliding onto a stool.

"No. Tense game."

"Who's winning?"

"Kako, then the sultan, then Aristos."

Kako, the pro who had won last year… "How much is on the table?"

"Eight million."

Thee mou. She almost swallowed her tongue.

Ensuring Galina had a drink in her hand, she procured a glass of champagne from the bartender. Off duty now and able to relax, a victorious rush moved through her. Nina's performance had gone perfectly, Galina was ecstatic and Aristos had spent much of the party with the Smirnovs.

For the first time in weeks, she didn't feel helpless. Didn't feel carried along by forces far greater than herself. She had proven she could execute a charity event for VIPs and make it a success. It gave her the confidence that when she resumed her real life as a princess and her upcoming work with Nina, she could do good things in the world, that she could own the role.

It sank into her bones, that heady feeling, as she watched the game. Aristos, sleeves rolled up to his elbows, corded, muscular forearms exposed, took the round, pulling the pile of chips toward the stacks he had in front of him. Triumph glittered in his ebony eyes as he leaned back and drained his scotch.

The dealer set out the next hand. The senator stretched while he did, noticing her and Galina sitting at the bar and smiling a greeting. She returned the smile, keeping it brief. Blending with the paint, that's what she was doing.

But the sultan, who already had two wives although he'd been flirting outrageously with Alex at the party, noticed her, too. His overt stare caused a ripple effect around the table as the rest of the men turned to look.

Aristos narrowed his gaze on her. Turning on her stool, she devoted her attention to her glass of champagne and Galina.

The next round began. The sultan took it, Kako the one after that, then Aristos in a nail-biting hand that stretched the tension in the room to a breaking point.

The sultan looked most displeased. Kako gave a shake of his head, requested a break and headed out of the room. The tension broke then, the table dissolving into good-natured ribbing, one of the professional players flirting heavily with the blond-haired waitress as she served him a drink. The sultan remained silent, pouty, if a man could be described as that, sitting back in his chair, arms crossed over his chest.

"Maybe," he announced, setting his gaze on Alex, "we should up the ante for the next round."

Galina sucked in a breath. Alex sat up straight. Aristos followed the sultan's gaze to her, eyes narrowing. "What are you proposing?"

"Her," said the sultan, nodding at Alex. "Winner of the next round."

Her stomach fell to the floor. A silence filled the room. Aristos sat back in his chair, the expression on his face unchanged. "We don't play by those rules here. You know that."

They did somewhere else?

"Maybe we need to shake things up a bit."

"Not happening," Aristos drawled.

"Why?" The sultan gave him a belligerent look. "Is she yours?"

One of the pro players made a choked sound. The senator's eyes went round. The icy expression that passed across Aristos's face sent a chill down her spine. "Yes, as a matter of fact," he drawled, "she is."

The sultan held up his hands, a rueful twist to his lips. "Fair enough. You have to admit, Nicolades, you weren't making it very obvious."

Because she wasn't his. Because this was insane.

Aristos pushed his chair back, stood and walked over to where she sat at the bar. His spicy cologne infiltrated her senses as he barked a request to the bartender for a scotch, his eyes never leaving hers. He waited until the drink was poured, wrapped his fingers around the tumbler, clamped a hand around her upper arm and pulled her off the stool.

Her breath caught in her throat. Too intimidated to protest, she allowed him to guide her out onto the terrace while the whole table watched.

She waited until they were out of sight and earshot of the others before she pulled her arm out of his grip. "Enough of your caveman tactics, thank you."

He leaned against the railing and knocked back a gulp of scotch. Fixed his gaze on her. "I told you this was a bad idea. These men are a different breed, Alex."

As was he. It thrilled and intimidated her all at the same time.

"Did he mean it?"

"Undoubtedly."

"Did *you*?"

His eyes flashed. "Alex," he growled. "There are millions of dollars on that table. We are not doing this now."

"I know," she said, moving closer to him. "But I'd like to know the answer to the question."

"You can't be mine," he rasped, his gaze tracking her. "You want my list again? You are off-limits. I don't do relationships. My affairs are short-lived, transactional entities where everyone knows the score."

"What if I did, want that, I mean? To explore what's between us."

His gaze narrowed. "You are a princess. Third in line to the throne in case you'd forgotten…whom I'm supposed to be protecting."

"There's no threat here," she derided. "The only thing you're protecting me from is you."

"Exactly."

Her pulse gave a tremendous flutter, then took off at a full gallop. "And if I weren't…off-limits to you?"

"There's no point in discussing it, because you are."

She fixed her gaze on his. "I saw your face tonight. That night on the beach…"

"*Christos*, Alex." He raked a hand through his hair. "You've just walked right out of *Alice in Wonderland.* I am not the man for you. I don't do flowers and chocolate."

"I'm not asking for that…for a relationship. I want to explore what's between us. What that kind of passion feels like. That's all."

"That's all?" He stared at her. Set his glass down on the railing with a deliberate movement. "Are you trying to wreck my head?"

She shook hers. "I'm merely suggesting, as you yourself said, that we do what we both want."

"No."

She eyed him, frustration coursing through her. "You know what I think? I think you're all talk, Aristos. I think you throw these challenges at me, these scenarios of what it would be like between us, because you know I won't act on them. It's *safe*. And when I do, you run." She lifted her chin. "I think you're scared. I think you have no idea what will happen between us if we actually face up to this attraction."

"Oh, I know," he rasped, eyes flashing. "We would be incendiary together, angel. We would blow the doors off my bedroom, and this would turn into an even bigger mess than it already is."

"Or it would solve our problem… We could address it and put it behind us. No one would have to know."

A long moment passed. "Just so we're clear," he ventured in a silky voice, "you're suggesting we have an affair? Confined to this island?"

"Yes."

"No."

"Why?" She tugged her bottom lip between her teeth. "You said I was bored with Sebastien and you were right. You told me to define my life, to go after what I want. Here I am, going after what I want."

He uttered one of the filthiest curse words in the Greek language. She winced, absorbing his fury. Taking her by the hand, he marched her back into the room, issued an "all non-players out" command directed at Galina, then propelled her out of the room past a sea of amused faces, a palm at her back.

Across the beach they went, up the stairs to the Great House and down the hall to her room. Her heart was pounding like a freight train by the time he opened her door and pushed her inside.

"*You*," he said, "will stay here. You will not come anywhere near the game. I will deal with you when it's done." He pinned his gaze on her face. "Understood?"

"Yes." She tucked a stray chunk of hair behind her ear. "But you could tell me—"

Thud. The door slammed behind him.

* * *

Aristos stopped drinking after that. It had only been his second scotch; he'd been pacing himself, as had all the men, except the sultan, of course, who didn't drink. But any amount of alcohol in his brain after what Alex had just done to him was too much.

He set his second-to-last hand down, a good one. Sat back in his chair as Kako grimaced.

No one would have to know. It would just be between the two of them... Theos. A synapse in his brain snapped. *You told me to define my life, to go after what I want. Here I am, going after what I want.*

He wiped a hand across his brow. He had created this monster. This was his mess to deal with. The question was, what was he going to do about it?

He allocated half his attention to the sultan's hand, the rest of it sitting firmly back in that room at the Great House with the woman he now conceded he wanted more than he'd ever wanted one in his life. The same one who had just offered herself up to him for a no-holds-barred, private affair.

She was right, he acknowledged as the sultan set down a full house, a better hand than his. What he'd been offering were excuses, excuses that had been protecting him from her. From the lust he felt for her. From whatever else he felt for her that he refused to examine. Except for the king and his casino contract, of course. That was a very real deterrent to taking what she was offering.

But if he and the princess kept this between them, no one would have to know.

Kako set down a brilliant hand. Aristos scowled and took a sip of water. Examined the last point to be considered. He was afraid he would hurt Alex. Afraid he had no idea how to play this game when his feelings were involved. When it wasn't just sex. He knew he couldn't give her what she needed in the long run, but she'd said she wasn't looking for a relationship.

Could she handle an affair, however, that ended when his interest waned? Which it would once he'd solved her mysteries. It was always that way with him: the allure of a woman fading when she was no longer an enigma to him. The thrill of the chase in its most classic format.

If he agreed to what Alex was proposing, she had to be clear on the rules. The boundaries. Truthfully, he was starting to think a controlled experiment, like allowing a fire to burn under carefully monitored circumstances, was the only way forward for them. To burn this attraction out completely.

She was affecting his head. Impeding his ability to focus at the most critical time in his career. He couldn't have it.

An image of himself on his knees, his hands on Alex's delectable body, tightened his fingers around the tumbler. Those sexy moans she made when she couldn't help herself…

An impatient sigh broke through his fantasy. "I know she's hot," said Kako. "Hell, I'd be long gone by now, but could you please," he said, waving his hand at him, "take a card or pass so we can find a winner?"

Ignoring the pro's gibe, Aristos lifted his hand and requested two more cards. It wasn't enough.

The final result: Kako first, Aristos second, the sultan third.

He offered Kako his congratulations, his own mood rather surly now as he watched his millions piled in front of the pro. He intended to exact retribution for the result, in only the most pleasurable way, of course.

CHAPTER TEN

ALEX STOOD, FOREARMS resting on the terrace railing, contemplating the floodlit beach as the clock ticked past 2:00 a.m. The lap of the waves against the shore and the persistent song of the cicadas were the only sounds that filled the air, not enough to drown out the pounding in her ears.

She'd seen some of the players disperse along the beach toward their private villas, which meant Aristos would be done soon. Adrenaline coursed through her, tightening her skin, quickening her heart. Had Aristos meant tonight when the game was over they would settle this between them? Or perhaps when all the players had gone home? Since that wouldn't be until tomorrow afternoon, she thought it might actually kill her. She'd stayed dressed just in case.

A knock on her door ten minutes later had her jumping out of her skin. Waiting for it, anticipating it, she froze, all of a sudden utterly unsure of what she was doing.

It came again. Pulling herself out of her suspended state, she walked inside, crossed to the door and released the bolt. Aristos, tie slung over his shoulder, a bottle of champagne in his hand, stood leaning against the wall.

Apparently the intensity he'd been wearing hadn't ended with the game. The look he sliced over her was pure predator. It held her feet rooted to the ground, eyes fixed on his.

"You going to let me in, Princess?" His low drawl raked over her sensitized skin. "A discreet affair might not entail me standing in the hallway with a bottle of champagne in my hand."

Her heart skipped a beat. Is that what they were having?

She stepped back before it appeared she'd lost all her brain cells. Aristos straightened away from the doorway and moved inside, leaving behind a waft of that delicious spicy scent he wore.

She closed the door.

"Lock it." His evenly delivered command told her exactly how this was going to go. Made her stomach cave to the floor. She twisted the bolt shut with hands that weren't quite steady. Turned around to find him uncorking the bottle.

"Who won?"

"Kako."

"Oh." She pushed a chunk of hair out of her face. "I'm sorry about that."

"You should be." A *pop* as he worked the cork free made her jump. "I was in it up until those last couple of hands. You destroyed my concentration."

She searched his face for some sign he was joking, but there was none. Just that same intensity, clawing its way across her nerves.

"I really am sorry. I had no idea the sultan would be so…outrageous."

"I told you that game is no place for a woman."

"Do they actually bet *women* in these games? Isn't that against some sort of law?"

"There are no rules for some of these men. The sultan, Dimitri, they live in a whole other universe. It would never happen in one of my games, though, and they know it."

She shivered. "I didn't like him—Dimitri. Doesn't his background bother you? His unethical business practices? The rumors of far worse?"

"They are rumors, *paidi mou*. Exactly that. Show me a rich man who doesn't have shadows."

The casual endearment stirred the anticipation churning her insides. Her stomach lurched as he moved closer, the bottle of champagne in his hand. Close enough she could feel the heat of his big body. It moved through her, stung her with its all-enveloping warmth.

He raked his gaze over her face. "So here's the thing. I think you're right we need to tackle this problem of ours. Face up to this attraction we share. An affair would do that. But I need to know you can handle this, Alex. That you're not jumping in with this newfound confidence of yours only to realize it's been a big mistake."

She shook her head, heart battering her ribs so hard she thought it might break free. "I won't. I know what I want."

He lifted a hand and brushed the back of his knuckles over her heated cheek. "This starts and ends here. Nobody gets hurt…"

She nodded. He was protecting her with his caveats, but he was also protecting himself.

Aristos's eyes darkened, the only outward sign he had acknowledged the decision they'd just made. He took a long swig of the champagne straight from the bottle, then passed it to her. She closed her fingers around the ice-cold glass. "Not very princess-like."

"Nothing about tonight is going to be very princess-like," he murmured, snaking an arm around her waist and pulling her into all that solid heat. "Except me granting your every wish… I might be persuaded to do that as long as I have leeway to make some demands of my own."

She didn't dare even wonder what those demands would be. Had enough on her plate at the moment, quite frankly. She lifted the bottle to her mouth and took a sip of the dry, fruity vintage. It tasted intoxicating, heady. When Aristos cupped the back of her head and took her mouth in a kiss that wasted no time in getting to the point, her head spun.

His tongue dipped inside her mouth, sliding against hers in a leisurely exploration. His throaty murmur of approval skated across her cheek. "I love champagne on you. You taste so sweet, *moro mou*."

Bringing the bottle to her mouth, he fed her another swallow. Dipped his head to consume it with her. She had never experienced anything so erotic, so intimate. He fed her a few more sips in between those sweet, hot kisses until she had melted against him, completely under his spell.

He captured her bottom lip in his and bit lightly, the sharp reprimand catching her off guard. "This mouth," he growled, "does something to me… Every time I tell myself I have to stay away, I can't. You are wrecking my head, Princess."

Her stomach folded in on itself. She leaned back, drinking him in. "I love kissing you. It's almost…spiritual."

His gaze darkened. Setting the bottle down, he took the weight of her hips in his palms, dragging her closer. "Do it again," he instructed, covering her mouth with his. She did, kissing him back, exploring his beautiful mouth with teasing nibbles of her own. He tightened his hands around her hips and pulled her into him, settling her against the erection that strained his trousers. She gasped at the size of him.

"That's right, angel…your kisses do that to me."

That they did blew her mind. A light-headed feeling descended over her as Aristos buried his mouth in her throat, seeking out her pleasure points while his palms held her hips in place for the sensual, intoxicating slide of his thick length against her core.

When Sebastien had kissed her, it'd been pleasant. *These* kisses were turning her insides to molten heat. Making her forget she'd ever had nerves.

A low moan escaped her throat.

"You want more?"

"Yes."

He slid his hands down the back of her thighs and pushed her dress up. Easing his knee between her legs, his hard muscle found her throbbing core. The friction, his purposeful movements, the heat of his gaze as he watched her, sent bolts of pleasure rippling through her. The aching flesh between her thighs grew wet, supple, his to command.

"Aristos."

"You like that, angel?"

"Yes."

The helpless, raspy note to her voice sounded foreign to her. She didn't know what she wanted. Needed. She knew only that she wanted more.

He dropped to his knees. Her spinning head attempted to determine what he was doing. Closing his hands around her thighs, he nudged them apart, a look of such wicked intent on his face, her breath stopped in her throat.

"Aristos—"

He looked up at her. Read the hesitation in her face. "You've never had a man do this for you?"

"No." She hadn't had a man do anything to her beyond kissing her. But she thought the timing was all off to tell him that now.

"Consider it another of your firsts," he said huskily. "I'm pretty sure it was the thought of you, spread out for me like this, that lost me the game."

Theos. "It's too—"

"Angel," he said firmly, "trust me."

She did. Had trusted him from the beginning. She relaxed her thighs, giving way to the firm pressure of his palms. His hands pushed her dress up to her waist. The look on his face when he discovered the wispy black thong she wore made her stomach dissolve. "You kill me," he murmured. "You are so beautiful, Princess. I want to *know* you. Every part of you."

Any further qualms she might have had dissolved with those words. His thumbs slid under the sides of the thong to ease it off her hips. She stepped out of it for him, blood pounding in her ears. She closed her eyes after that as he parted her thighs wider. One hand on her hip, he slid a finger down the length of her most intimate flesh. She jerked against his touch, but he held her in place. "So aroused," he murmured, repeating the caress with a more insistent movement. "As hot for me as I am for you."

When he parted her with gentle fingers, she thought her heart might jump through her chest. His breath was a warm, heady caress against her skin, announcing his intention to touch her just before his tongue made a leisurely foray where his fingers had been. She bucked into his hold. He held her firmly, sliding his tongue over her again, finding the tight bundle of nerves at the heart of her this time. A white-hot pleasure exploded through her.

She buried her fingers in his hair as he nudged her nub with his tongue. Over her, against her, he moved, increasing his rhythm until the almost-impossible sensitivity dissolved on a hot rush of sensation.

"This is how I wanted you," he rasped, lifting his mouth from her flesh. "Completely at my mercy. Begging for the pleasure you know I can give you."

She was too far gone to respond. Her eyes flew open as Aristos slid one of his long, elegant fingers inside her.

"Easy, angel," he murmured. "I've got you. I promise."

Her hands clenched his hair as he moved his finger in and out of her in an exquisite torture that stoked the fire inside her higher. When he added another, filling her completely, she started sliding down a starry path of no return.

She moaned his name, the desperate edge to her voice shocking her. Keeping up that delicious rhythm with his fingers, he brought his tongue back to the tight nub at the heart of her. "That's it," he murmured against her flesh. "Let go, angel."

She arched her hips against his mouth. He took her apart with a deliberate flick of his tongue that pushed the white-hot pleasure to its peak. Her orgasm racked her, blinding her, her legs giving way beneath her.

He held her up as, spent, shaken, she recovered, waves of aftershocks shivering through her. When the earth had righted itself, he slid an arm under her knees and picked her up, carrying her to the bed.

Setting her down beside it, he reached for the buttons of his shirt. Rapidly, his gaze on her the whole time, he undid it and dragged it off, then reached for the button of his pants. Her heart jumped into her throat as he pushed them off his hips and stepped out of them. He was all solid, powerful muscle. Vastly intimidating. Not to mention the part of him that was fully aroused beneath his black boxers. It made her mouth go dry. Excessively dry.

She headed straight for the champagne bottle, picked it up and took a healthy swallow.

He sat down on the bed. "Nerves, angel?"

He had no idea. He really didn't.

She took another sip of the champagne.

"Bring it over," he suggested.

"No," she said, taking another drink, "I'm good."

Aristos had no problem waiting her out. He might be way past gone where Alex was concerned, but he intended to take his time with her. Play to her inexperience this time around. Later was another story…

When she eventually set the bottle down and walked back over to him, he took her in from head to toe, watching a flush work its way across her beautiful olive skin as he did. "Take the dress off, Princess."

She blinked. Chewed on her bottom lip. “I need help with the zipper.”

He set his hands on her hips and turned her around. Reaching for the zipper, he slid it down to where it ended at the beginning of her delectable bottom. Snagging an arm around her waist, he pulled her against him, pressing his mouth to the delicate column of her spine. A shiver went through her. He moved his hands up to cup her breasts. She arched against him, seeking his touch.

Her responsiveness made the blood fire in his veins. “Take it off,” he ordered throatily.

She lifted her hands and pushed the dress off her shoulders. It fell to her hips and caught on the curve of her bottom. Bending, she slid it past her hips to the floor, stepped out of it and kicked it to the side. When she turned around, he knew he’d never seen anything so perfect. She was petite with a Venus-like voluptuousness that was all woman.

He wondered if that was why he needed to possess her so badly. The dominant side of him. The need to protect, to claim what was his. And yet, he reminded himself, frowning past that errant thinking, she would never be his. This was a fling to put their explosive chemistry to rest.

He caught her hand in his and pulled her onto his lap. A tinge of apprehension still lingered in her blue eyes. He covered her mouth with his and kissed her until she was soft beneath his hands, played with the erect points of her nipples with his thumbs until she let out a low moan.

Depositing her on the bed, she landed in a cloud of cream-colored silk. Riffling through his pants, he found the condoms he’d stashed there. Fishing one out, he threw it on the bedside table, slid his fingers under the waistband of his boxers and pushed them off.

Alex’s eyes were riveted to the proud thrust of his manhood. Ripping open the package, he slid the condom on, happy to give her a show. When he’d sheathed himself, he joined her on the bed. "This is where you get to tell me how you like it, Princess. Your choice."

Her eyes widened. "It—it doesn't matter. Just…slow, you know."

She was damn lucky he had some self-control left. *Barely.* "Maybe you don't know? Soukis was that tame?"

Her delicate throat convulsed. "I *don't* know. How I like it, I mean…"

Something twisted inside him. "No worries," he murmured, moving over her and caging her with his thighs. "I know how I want you. Underneath me. Wrapped around me, angel, so I can watch your face while I give you everything I have."

Her eyes were huge, sparkling sapphires. Bending his head, he took one of her perfect breasts in his mouth. Applied enough pressure to make her writhe beneath him. She thrust her fingers in his hair and hung on. Devoting the same attention to her other nipple, he slid his hand over her flat stomach, dipped into her warmth and found her wet and ready for him.

His control on shaky ground, he nudged her thighs apart. Guiding one of her legs around his waist, he lifted her bottom with his palm and slid his throbbing flesh against her slick opening. Alex closed her eyes, her fingers catching hold of the silk beneath her. Slowly, deliberately, he caressed her. Waited for the signal she was ready.

"Aristos." His name left her lips on a sigh. Sinking his fingers into the soft flesh of her bottom, he eased himself into her tight, hot body. She was small, petite here, too. He gritted his teeth and took it slowly, allowing her body to soften around his before he continued. The leg Alex had wrapped around his waist tightened, urged him closer. He sank deeper inside her, her snug body heaven and torture all at the same time.

"Okay, angel?"

She nodded, the hazy pleasure in her eyes inflaming his senses. Gripping her buttocks, he surged forward, filling her with all of him. Flinched at the resistance he encountered. His brain struggled to compute. Had it been physical? Mental? The shock spreading across her face, the different tightening of her body around his, the sudden easing now that she'd accommodated him, made it seem as if—

He froze. Surveyed the tension on her face.

"Alex," he said in a dangerously quiet voice, making those blue eyes flutter open. "Tell me you aren't what I think you are."

She bit her lip. He cursed.

Her fingers closed around his forearm. "I wanted it to be you. I made this choice, Aristos."

"And you didn't think to tell me?"

"I should have." She tightened her leg around him, holding him to her. "It's done now. *Parakalo*—I want this. I want *you*."

She was right. The damage was done. It was all his stunned brain could process.

"Please," she said again. "This is what I want."

It was the vulnerability, the hot desire in her gaze that did him in. The knowledge that if he was going to hell, which he surely was now, he was going to enjoy himself while he was doing it. He was going to make her first time the best experience it could be.

Palming her buttock, he began stroking inside her. Her natural eroticism, her passionate response as she lifted her hips to meet his thrusts, stoked the flame inside him back to life. Deepening his strokes, he brought his mouth down on hers and drank from her sweetness. Swallowed her low moans of pleasure.

"You like me inside you? How does it feel to have all of me?"

"Good. *So good.*" She dug her fingernails into his back. "Don't stop. Please don't stop."

There was no way he could now. There was no resistance left in him as he drove himself into her soft, willing body. *Spiritual*, she'd called it. He thought it particularly apt as he buried his mouth in her throat and tasted her racing pulse. Kissing Alex had been one thing. Possessing her another thing entirely. He had the feeling nothing else would satisfy him after this. That she would be imprinted on his brain, ruining him for anything less than what she was.

The tension in his body built to unsustainable levels. Lifting his mouth from hers, he filled his palms with her hips, angling her so he could find that pleasure point deep inside her that could give her an even more intense release than before. He saw it in her eyes, the way the blue turned deep indigo, that she felt it, too.

"Right there," he murmured huskily, stroking that spot again and again with deep, hard thrusts. "Feel me right there."

She started to tremble beneath him. He closed his mouth over hers as she came apart, her moan of pleasure raking through him, completing him in a way he'd never experienced before. It spurred his own violent release. Uttering a hoarse cry, he drove into her sweetness, slaking the lust that had been consuming him for weeks.

A thick silence filled the room as they lay spent, catching their breath. Shifting his weight off Alex, he went into the bathroom and cleaned himself up. When he returned, she was sitting up on the bed, her dark hair in wild disarray, blue eyes wary. "Are you angry?"

"Yes." He raked a hand through his hair. "You should have told me. *Diavole*, Alex, I just took your virginity."

"So?"

"So how does that happen in this day and age? You are twenty-five."

She lifted a shoulder. "I told you. There wasn't much of a chance to meet anyone in Stygos. Sebastien was my only serious boyfriend."

"And he never got you into bed?"

"That's why he asked me to marry him. Because I wouldn't."

She might have been worth it. He shook off that rather insane thought. "So you blithely decided to toss it all away tonight? Just for the hell of it?"

"You know it wasn't like that."

He didn't know anything anymore. Not one damn thing.

"Aristos," she said quietly. "This changes nothing. I'm an adult. I made a decision."

"A decision you didn't consult me about. A decision that has repercussions."

She frowned. "What repercussions?"

He didn't know that, either. Biting out a curse, he gathered his clothes from the floor and threw them on. Alex watched him from the bed, a frozen look on her face. But this time, *this* time, he wasn't going there. He needed to go find his common sense instead.

"Get some sleep. I have guests to see off tomorrow."

"Aristos—"

He left without looking at her. Before temptation led him astray yet again.

CHAPTER ELEVEN

ALEX WOKE WITH a pounding headache, sunshine from another glorious Larikos day streaming in through blinds she'd forgotten to draw. But it wasn't just her head that hurt. She was sore in places that made her cheeks heat.

Burrowing her aching head in the pillow, images from the evening before came at her fast and hard. Her night with Aristos had been hot, tender and passionate, had surpassed any expectations she'd had. Reading about that type of passion on a page and experiencing such heart-stopping intimacy were two entirely different things.

She felt different, changed, more of a woman in every way, as if the universe had opened up yet another facet of itself for her to explore. She didn't regret for one second giving her virginity to Aristos, but apparently he did.

Her head gave another vicious throb. Cradling it in her palm, she closed her eyes. The way he'd vacated her room with the speed of a hotel guest short of funds took the edge off her glow. Killed it dead. Spoiled what should have been perfect.

So she'd been a virgin. What was the big deal? It hadn't seemed to throw off what had surely been an extremely sensual encounter. Or maybe it had? Maybe it had turned Aristos off completely. Maybe she'd disappointed him with her inexperience. Maybe he'd just done a good job of hiding it.

Perhaps it hadn't been as spiritual as she'd felt it to be at all.

Ugh. Opening her eyes, she maneuvered herself into a sitting position. She wasn't going to be *that* girl. Not when she'd promised herself no regrets.

Untangling herself from the silk sheets, she padded to the bathroom, rooted through her toiletry bag and unearthed some aspirin. Downing them with a swig of water, she told herself Aristos's running had more to do with him being Aristos. Because he was a commitment-phobe and she had been a virgin. A deadly creature.

She dressed and went for breakfast on the main terrace, thinking perhaps it would help her head, but when the man in question strode into the dining room with Dimitri Smirnov, offered her a curt nod, then ignored her completely, her stomach shriveled up into a ball unsuitable for the consumption of food.

She gave up and left. Her head finally cleared in the cool breeze of the beach and a swim in the heavenly water. She would not backslide. She had vowed to approach her life with less fear. Taking risks sometimes meant making the wrong call. Getting hurt. And Aristos had always been a wild card.

Aristos's last guest left on a Cessna just after three. Only David remained beside him, waiting for his helicopter to take him to Athens, then Las Vegas.

"So how was Dimitri?"

"Hedging. He still wouldn't give me a straight answer at breakfast. Says he needs to look at his portfolio."

"The offer's still open. I can work my channels..."

Aristos shook his head. "He'll come around."

David raked a hand through his thick graying hair. "You'll pull this one out of the fire, Aristos. I've no doubt about it."

A faint smile touched his mouth. "It will be my biggest

magic act to date. Maintaining funding for an illusionary casino that may never be built."

"It will." David sank his hands into his pockets. "I like her, Aristos."

"Who?"

"You know who I'm talking about." His mentor shook his head. "I worry sometimes you think you don't deserve happiness. That you consider it unattainable to you."

"Maybe it is."

"And maybe you're just afraid to reach for it."

Maybe it wasn't worth it. He'd watched his family fall apart under the weight of the burdens it carried—financially, emotionally—his mother turning into a shadow of her former self when life had worn away at the very edges of her. Had watched the rosy glow slip from his life as a so-called revolutionary when it became clear the term was only used to perpetuate the violence, the control, those in charge had sought to exercise over them all as foot soldiers.

Happiness, those myths the storytellers liked to weave, they had always turned out to be lies for him. *How could you want what you didn't even believe existed?*

Returning to his office after David left, their conversation continued to dominate his head. *Content* was a state of being he could get on board with. Money went a long way toward providing that. Except he didn't seem to even have that state of mind in his possession anymore. Being around Alex reflected back at him the image of a man he wasn't sure he wanted to be any longer, a problem when you thought maybe that was all you had in you.

He'd thrown most, but not all, of his dark past at her and she hadn't blinked. Didn't seem to think any less of him for it. He wondered what she'd think if she knew the truth. How he'd walked away from the people who'd needed him most, not once, but twice. How being the man who always put himself first made him a selfish creature who wasn't about to change his spots.

He put his feet up on his desk and closed his eyes as he waited for Carin to put his call through. Allowed himself to consider the implications of last night after spending all day avoiding them. Alex had claimed her virginity changed nothing between them, that it had been her decision to make and she'd wanted her first time to be with him.

He could convince himself she had been right, it was that simple, that the damage was done and the only way was forward. The question was what *was* the way forward? Either he shut this down, likely the path he should take, or he made the conscious choice to do exactly what Alex had proposed—see where this thing between them went in a time-limited, short-term affair.

Expelling a breath, he hit the intercom and asked for an espresso to go with his call. His brain didn't seem to be in working order, because the only thing that did seem to be computing about this whole mess he'd predicted so accurately was that, in his lust, he'd recklessly claimed something that hadn't been his to own—the innocence of a royal. There would be consequences; he just didn't know what they were yet.

Alex was debating whether to go down to dinner alone or have it in her room when Aristos showed up at her door. Propped up against the jamb, all earthly male in khaki shorts and another of those T-shirts that showed off his muscles, it was all she could do to look completely unaffected.

"Everyone gone?"

He nodded. "Up for dinner?"

She eyed him. "Are you still angry with me?"

His mouth curved. "My feelings toward you are a whole lot of things, but anger isn't one of them."

"You walked out last night..."

"Because I needed to think."

Right. Where was that anger that had fueled her all day? The aloofness she so desperately needed? She looked down at the sundress she wore. "I'm not dressed for dinner."

His gaze slid over her. "You could wear a garbage bag and still look utterly edible, Princess. Grab your shoes. Sneakers, actually. We're going sailing."

"Sailing?"

"Thought you might like to see the sunset from the water. Chef made us dinner."

Her disobedient pulse fluttered. A sunset cruise would be intimate... But perhaps exactly what they needed at the moment to resolve last night. Slipping on sneakers and sunglasses, she walked with him to the beach. His gaze rested on her as they walked along the sand toward the dinghy waiting for them. "You look pale."

"Headache. It's going now."

"The champagne?"

"I didn't drink enough for that." Fire filled her cheeks. He'd consumed *her* before that had gone very far.

For once he made no smart comeback. Guided her instead to the motorized dinghy that took them out to the forty-five-foot sailboat waiting for them.

Once they were on the water, she found herself immersed in the rush of the wind. While anything but an accomplished sailor, she knew which sail was which and made a decent team member for Aristos, who *was* an extremely competent sailor, athletic and commanding as he guided them in a loop of the surrounding islands.

When they finally dropped anchor in a perfect little cove, the sun beginning to sink into the horizon in yet another of those spectacular blood-orange sunsets, another set of muscles she hadn't used in a while was making itself known. Wincing, she sank to the deck.

"Sore?" Aristos asked.

"Yes. And thirsty."

He unearthed a cooler from below deck, handed her a bottle and took a beer for himself. She eyed the vodka-based cranberry drink with amusement. "A girl drink for me?"

He moved his gaze over her in one of those totally inappropriate looks that made her breath catch in her throat. "Yes," he drawled, "definitely a girl."

Pinpricks of heat unfurled beneath her skin. She took a sip of the surprisingly tasty drink to cover her fluster. When Aristos stripped off his T-shirt to enjoy the dying rays of the sun, she followed suit. As far as bikinis went, hers was modest, far from attention-seeking. Aristos, on the other hand, sprawled out beside her, beer in hand, was the definition of the term in dark blue swim trunks, his long, bronzed limbs all tight, corded muscle. A couple of days' worth of stubble lining his cheeks and jaw added to his dangerous appeal.

"We should talk about last night."

She pulled in a breath. "Yes."

"First of all," he said, training that deadly dark gaze on her, "I wanted to say that you were amazing last night. Last night was amazing."

Her stomach clenched. "I thought what happened might have ruined it for you."

"It caught me off guard. I did not expect it."

"I was going to tell you but it didn't seem like the right time once we—"

"—consumed each other," he offered drily.

"Yes."

"Are you worried you disappointed me?"

She nodded.

"No chance of that, angel. It was off the charts."

A warmth engulfed her, radiating through her chest. "So why walk out?"

A long moment passed. "I'm insanely attracted to you," he said finally. "I care about you, Alex. I think that's clear. But anything beyond that, I can't offer. My longest relationship was three months—shorter than many of my contract negotiations."

Her jaw tightened. "To use your words, we've been through this. I've already told you I'm not looking for a relationship. I have a whole new life ahead of me I need to focus on. And second, as I said last night, me being a virgin doesn't change anything about our agreement. I was waiting for the right time. The right experience."

"Yes, but it creates…expectations."

"What expectations?"

"You gave me something special, Alex."

"Frightening, you mean."

"That's not what I said."

"It's what you meant. If you'd left my room any faster, you would have been running."

He sighed. "I'm not frightened. I'm concerned I'm going to hurt you. Relationships are messy, complicated entanglements I prefer to avoid."

"And now that we've reinforced the fact that I'm *not* looking for a relationship, where does that leave us?"

His dark gaze glittered. "I think that's up to you, Princess. As long as you're clear on who and what I am."

The antagonism that had been simmering just below the surface roared back to life. "I think that would be a difficult thing for me to swear allegiance to when you hide yourself behind your walls, Aristos. When you run at the first sign of intimacy. I wonder if *you* know who you are."

The glitter in his eyes intensified. "Oh, I know who I am, angel. An unashamedly, unapologetically solitary man.

Overtly ambitious and perhaps a bit spiritually corrupt. There is no redemption for me."

She blinked. Took a sip of her drink. "Actually," she said, "I think you forgot an inspirational success story for those who've walked your path, a person who gives back to others in need, a man who has a big heart he refuses to acknowledge."

A cynical twist curved his mouth. "I should make you my PR person. You'd have me on the most admired CEO list in no time, something even my own PR team can't seem to do."

She shook her head as he deflected again. "Nice try, Aristos. But I have your number now."

"Do you?" He downed a long swallow of beer, swiped his palm across his mouth, set the bottle aside and leaned back on his elbows. "Give it to me. I'm fascinated to hear what you think."

She took a deep breath. "I think David Tennyson might have picked you up off that street in Athens and helped build you a new life, an immensely successful life, but somewhere along the way, likely far before that, you closed yourself off from the broken relationships and promises that defined your life. You told yourself that love and relationships weren't to be trusted, were messy, complicated entanglements. To you they only meant hurt.

"You deflect people with sarcasm," she continued, "when they try to get close. You carry on your 'transactional' relationships because they are of no threat to you. You are a lone wolf, and you like to keep it that way."

She held his gaze. Found it full of an emotion she couldn't read. "How am I doing?"

Deadly accurate. Aristos waved a hand at her. "Keep going. I'll give my analysis at the end."

"Last night you ran because of the connection we share

as much as from taking my virginity. Because you've let me in and you don't like it. Because it breaks all your rules."

She sat back on her elbows and took a sip of her drink, apparently finished with her excellent summation of him. Her rosy cheeks, the nervous half glance she threw him, suggested she worried she might have gone too far. He thought that if it had been any other person on the planet, it might have been. But not her.

"Very perceptive," he drawled. "I like the lone-wolf analogy. But don't be fooled by our connection, Princess. It will only take you so far."

"I don't doubt it. But since we are only having an affair, if you've decided that's still going to happen between us, it's irrelevant, isn't it?"

He eyed her. Took another swig of his beer. "I feel like I've created a monster."

She gave him a self-satisfied smile. "Take the plunge, Aristos. Make the call."

Every muscle in his body coiled at the challenge. He was not unaware that indulging in what was in front of him meant taking his fledgling ability to be intimate with another person to the next level, but he couldn't have stopped himself if he'd tried.

"Get over here," he murmured.

Her lashes lowered. "I don't take orders from you."

"Yes, you do. Now get over here."

A flare of excitement lit those beautiful blue eyes. Setting her drink down, she pressed her palms to the deck and shimmied toward him. He snagged an arm around her waist and lifted her atop him so her legs were wrapped around him. His gaze rested on her quivering full lower lip, lust tightening his insides.

"I'm feeling a bit spiritually bankrupt," he drawled, lifting his gaze to hers. "You'd better send in the reinforcements."

Her mouth curved. “I thought you were a lone wolf.”

“Don’t you ever hear them howl at night?”

Her breathtakingly beautiful smile blinded him as he bent his head and took her mouth in a hot, searing kiss. Her hands clasped his jaw, anchored herself as he devoured her with a hunger he’d kept in check last night. She was with him all the way, arching into his hands when he stripped off her bikini top, moaning when he rolled her nipples between his fingers.

Then it wasn’t enough, not nearly enough, because he needed to own her as much as she owned him in that moment as he pushed himself into uncharted territory.

Sliding his palm down her flat, quivering stomach, he moved his fingers beneath the waistband of her bikini bottoms and cupped the warmth at the heart of her.

Her breathing fractured, those long, silky dark lashes lifting to reveal a brilliant blue. “Aristos,” she whispered, “we can’t— We’re—”

“—in the middle of the Aegean.”

“Yes, but—”

He squeezed her soft flesh. Stroked her silky skin. A stifled gasp filled his ear.

“Like that, angel?”

“Y-yes.”

His thumb found her core, rocking against her in a gentle rhythm that had her moving against his hand. Eyes closed, mouth parted, cheeks flushed, she was the hottest thing he’d ever seen, turning him hard as a stone.

She must have known he was watching her. Her lashes fluttered open, gaze meeting the heat in his. He increased the pressure of his thumb, moving in tight, deliberate circles now, his eyes seducing her as surely as his fingers.

A frown of concentration crossed her brow, her nails digging into his biceps as her orgasm built. Slipping his fingers inside her, he stroked her to the edge. *“Ei sai poly omora,"* he whispered, cupping her nape and bringing his mouth down on hers as he increased the rhythm of his fingers. *You're beautiful.*

A fractured moan left her lips, her hips pushing against his hand. Sinking his fingers deeper inside her, he whispered, "Come for me, angel."

Closing her eyes, she melted into him. Rocked harder until she came apart on a low cry he swallowed with a conqueror's satisfaction.

Fumbling in his pocket, he found a condom. He set her away from him long enough to roll it on, then lifted her with one arm and brought her down on him, his fingers pushing aside the thin strip of her bikini bottoms and guiding his shaft to her slick, hot flesh.

Her eyes widened, nails biting into his flesh as he penetrated her snug channel.

"Aristos. You're so big… I—"

"Slow," he muttered thickly. "We take it slow, *glykeia mou.*"

She closed her eyes. Trusted him with her body. Gradually, her body accepted his, melted around him until he was buried deep inside her. She opened her eyes then, an expression of wonder in those blue orbs that rocked him to his core.

Slowly, gently, he gripped her hips, moving her up and down on him, claiming her with every gasp-inducing thrust of his body. His eyes on hers, he reached between them and rubbed his thumb over the pleasure point at the center of her. Stroked her into another release.

When she came in a shudder, he claimed his own pleasure. A few quick thrusts was all it took, her pulsing, tight flesh shaking his body in a violent release that stole his breath.

She is mine. This time there was no going back.

CHAPTER TWELVE

ARISTOS TRACED THE perfect sloping line of Alex's voluptuous hip with a light touch designed to deify rather than wake. He'd had her in his bed for three days and still he couldn't get enough of her. It was like going to the well to drink and discovering you had a never-ending thirst that was impossible to slake. Like discovering something that might finally make you feel whole if you consumed enough of it.

In spite of that thought, or perhaps because of it, he eased himself away from her and slid his legs over the side of the bed. He was going to pin Dimitri Smirnov down to a meeting today. Spinning his wheels, wondering if the Russian was going to pull out on him, was killing his head, destroying his productivity. It needed to be settled. Cast in stone.

Showering and dressing, he left temptation alone, grabbed a croissant from the kitchen and made his way to his office. Carin greeted him, handed him a stack of messages and got up to get his espresso. Wandering into his office, he made for his PC.

Carin backtracked and came to the door. "Were you just whistling?"

"Whistling?" He frowned. "I don't whistle."

"That's what I thought." She gave him a look. "You *were* whistling."

"First time for everything. Anything urgent in this?" He waved the stack of messages at her.

"June. She said she sent you an urgent email."

Since his PR person bothered him only when something was truly important, he went right to his email, immediately thinking there'd been a crisis at one of his hotels. The last one had been a couple of rare birds who'd taken up residence in the facing of his London property. Threatened with eviction, the entire bird-loving population of London had revolted, placard-carrying activists and all. The birds had stayed.

He clicked open June's email, bracing himself for a political nightmare. It was a nightmare, all right, but not a political one. The photo June had sent made his head buzz. It was of him and Alex from that night on the boat, an intimate photo of them, Alex half naked, her legs wrapped around him.

His heart sank further as he read the caption from the European entertainment website it had been posted to.

> Princess Aleksandra busy canoodling with billionaire Aristos Nicolades in the Aegean while Akathinia sits in wait.

Canoodling? Who used that word?

Thee mou. The enormity of the disaster sank through him as he sat back in his chair and wiped a palm across his brow. How had this happened? Paparazzi couldn't access the island. It was impossible. It had to have been a staff member.

His vision went red. "Carin."

She came in with his espresso. Took in his expression. "I take it the whistling is over?"

"Get Yolande in here *now.* And Rolf." His head of security.

His PA departed. He took a deep, fortifying sip of the coffee to kick-start his brain. The damage was done, but he could inflict pain on whoever had done this. And he *would* find them.

He was picking up the phone to call June in New York when his cell phone buzzed. Glancing at the screen, he replaced the receiver. *Nikandros.* He contemplated the buzzing phone, a tight feeling in his chest. He could ignore it, gather a game plan, then talk to the king. Or he could pick it up and get it over with.

He picked it up. "Nik."

"You have sixty seconds to explain why I shouldn't fly there right now and kill you."

"I care about her, Nik."

"*Try again, Nicolades.* You've never cared about a woman in your life."

"I care about her."

Silence.

He rubbed a hand to his temple. "You were the one who insisted she come here. *I* didn't want her here."

"And it was too much of a stretch to keep your hands off her? Off *one woman*, Aristos."

"Why?" Aristos wanted to hear Nik say it. That he wasn't good enough for Aleksandra. That he was below her.

"You know why. You are the most notorious womanizer on the face of the planet."

He digested that. Wondered for the first time if that was the core of Nik's issue with him, rather than his bloodline.

He closed his eyes. "It's done, Nik. But I intend to make it right."

"How?"

"We'll marry, of course."

Another long silence. *Had he just said that?* The *M*-word?

"I haven't given you my permission."

Ah, there it was. He raked a hand through his hair. "You know it's the right answer."

Another silence. "Get your PR team in contact with

mine. Put a lid on this. Meanwhile, Alex stays on Larikos. The press can't get to her there, and I need to focus on Idas. The rumor is he's had a stroke."

His heart lifted for the first time since he'd seen that damning photo. "Substantiated?"

"We're working on it."

He prayed it was true. Crown Prince Kostas of Carnelia was a known proponent of peace and democracy. It would be a godsend for the country and for his $2.5 billion investment. "Nik—"

"I need to think." The line went dead.

He pulled the phone away from his ear, a knot growing in his stomach at what he'd just done. Getting bigger by the minute. He should have ignored the call. Should have gotten his thoughts together, made a plan. Instead he'd just announced he was marrying Alex. He, who had once called marriage hell on earth, had just committed himself to that very institution.

Rising from his chair, he paced to the window, espresso in hand. Looked out at the glorious, picture-perfect vista he so often took for granted. Was too busy to even enjoy. He'd spent three of those sun-soaked, unparalleled Larikos days with Alex, working, yes, because he needed to keep things moving, but also using the opportunity to take a step back. To allow himself a breather from the obsession with business that had consumed his life.

He'd found himself more even-keeled, without his usual restless vibe, a perspective settling over him, a contentment. Perhaps those obsessions that had fueled him all these years had blinded him to other things…to the things he'd told himself he couldn't have.

He rubbed a palm over his jaw. Could he have them with Alex? Was this the solution to a problem he'd already known he'd had?

He watched the sun reflect off an impossibly blue sea.

Surprisingly, the idea of marrying Alex didn't fill him with horror. His interest in meaningless assignations had waned months before. Having a beautiful, intelligent wife by his side to fill the empty life he'd been leading held appeal, a woman for whom his desire was showing no signs of abating, who seemed to be chipping away at his cynicism with every moment he spent with her, making him feel almost human again.

And yet, he wondered, how far could he take it? Was he deluding himself he could ever be *that* man? The one who deposited his briefcase on the kitchen floor, received a kiss from his wife, went back to work the next day and did it over and over again? The man who stuck? Nik certainly seemed to be questioning it. He hadn't even given him his permission to marry Alex.

Memories, too close to the surface in recent days, bubbled their way to the surface. His last epic battle with his father before he'd left home for good…

This family is better off without you, Aristos. You have no substance, no honor. Go waste your life away with those infidels. You are one of them now.

And he had been. He would have been anything to get away from the toxic atmosphere at home. Even if it meant leaving everything he knew behind, including the brothers and sisters he'd loved. Even if it meant cutting those ties for their own safety, keeping them away from the lawless men he associated with.

But there had been more. He'd been angry, so angry at his mother for choosing his no-good father over him, for allowing him to turn him out. Bitter to the core. That was when the murkiness of the street had climbed inside and claimed his soul.

A text from June buzzed his mobile. Pulled him out of the past, the bitter taste of regret staining his mouth. He swung away from the window to answer it. Whether he deserved Alex, whether he was husband of the year material, was irrelevant. What mattered was repairing this situation before it spiraled out of control.

He'd been gone only hours and already she missed him.

Lifting her gaze from the text blurring in front of her, Alex acknowledged that disconcerting thought. She'd started a business plan for Nina as they'd begun to define their partnership, the need to plan her future a necessary distraction from her present, a grounding force she desperately needed given her current reality that involved long, hot, heady nights with Aristos and the very real fact that she was half in love with him. Possibly more.

Her risk-taking had taken her down a road she knew it wasn't wise to go, but it really wasn't the sort of road you just turned back from. Not when you thought the man in question might finally be letting his barriers down, slowly but surely. When you saw a potential there that was too bright and seductive to ignore.

With every day that passed, her decision to leave Stygos seemed more right. She still got homesick, still missed so much about its peaceful allure, but she realized now how much living she had to do. How her aversion to risk-taking had limited her experiences. And Aristos was a big part of that.

It was disconcerting how much she wanted to be the one to do the same for him. To be the one to open *his* world up—to show him what he was missing by cutting himself off from his emotions. To make him believe some people could be trusted, that *she* could be trusted.

Dangerous thinking indeed, but not enough to prevent her from putting on her shoes and making her way over to his office with the excuse that she needed a break. Peeking inside, she found him on the phone. He beckoned to her with a crooked finger. She walked in, perched herself on the windowsill and waited for him to finish barking out instructions on how to enter the airspace at Larikos.

"Who's coming?" she asked when he hung up.

"A jeweler."

"A jeweler?" She frowned. "Why?"

Aristos sat back in his chair and patted the corner of his desk. She eyed the open door. His mouth curled. "As appealing as that idea is," he drawled, "we have a situation we need to deal with."

It was then that she noticed the edge to him. The ruffled hair, the tight set of his mouth, the rapid-fire intensity to him.

She slid onto the edge of the desk, a feeling of unease whispering across her skin. "What is it?"

"The night we were on the yacht, someone took a photo of us."

She froze, graphic images of what they'd done that night filling her head. "You said no one could get anywhere near the island."

"They can't. A staff member must have taken it."

A staff member? Her stomach sank, a sick feeling engulfing her. "What kind of a photo?"

"The incriminating kind." He sat forward and clicked a button. Her brain went into lockdown. The photo on his computer screen had been taken with a long-range lens, her in Aristos's arms, legs wrapped around him, stark naked except for her bikini bottoms, head tossed back as she looked up at him. *Thee mou.* Her mouth went dry. The angle of the photo had been artfully done so nothing indecent was showing, but it was the look on her face that sent heat rushing to her cheeks. She looked…love struck.

"Where?" she whispered. "Where did you get this?"

"A European gossip site. But according to my PR person the rights have been sold to a handful of other daily newspapers."

"Can you stop it?"

"We're trying, but injunctions take time."

"What are we going to do?" Her voice had risen now. "I am *naked* in that photo, Aristos. I am a *princess*. You need to do something."

"I *am* doing something." His dangerously low tone warned her to pull it back a notch. "I've done about fifteen things in the last two hours."

She pressed her knuckles to her cheek. "I'm sorry. This is a shock."

"Nikandros," he said evenly, "called first thing this morning."

The blood drained from her face. "What did he say?"

"That I had sixty seconds to give him a reason not to kill me."

Theos. She stared at him. "And how did you…explain it?"

He calmly took a sip of his coffee. "The funny thing about a photo like that. It explains itself… So I didn't so much explain it as offer a solution."

She didn't like the hard glint in his eyes. "Which was?"

"We marry."

Her mouth dropped open. "You— I— *No.* That's not a solution."

"By all means," he said, his voice dripping with sarcasm, "come up with an alternative. I'm all ears."

She swallowed hard. "We simply explain to Nik things got a little…out of hand and I'm sure he will understand."

"And do we tell that to the rest of the world, too? A short little concise press release? *After lusting after each other for weeks, Aristos and Alex took matters into their own hands and—*"

"Aristos."

"You need a better plan than that, angel. Akathinia is still under the threat of war. It does not look good."

She shook her head. "Nik will calm down. It will be fine."

"Did I mention he threatened to kill me?"

She bit her lip. "He didn't mean that. He was angry."

"Yes, Princess, very angry, which is why we are going to defuse the situation. Now. This afternoon, in fact."

"I am not marrying you. This is insanity."

"Insane but unavoidable."

She stared at his determined expression. *Diavole*, but he was serious! The phone call she had walked in on flashed through her head. "Why is the jeweler coming?"

"So you can pick the largest, most outrageously beautiful engagement ring you want."

"Oh, no," she said, rising. "We are not getting engaged."

He snared an arm around her waist and pulled her down onto his lap. "Nothing is going to defuse this situation but an engagement. Nothing is going to defuse *Nik* but an engagement. So wrap your head around it."

She stared at him, attempting to process the unreality unfolding around her. And suddenly, she understood what he wasn't saying. He did business with Nik. Nik had granted him his casino license. Nik could also take it away.

"Let me talk to him," she said. "I'm sure he will see reason."

"Alex," he said softly. "It's not just Nik. It's your reputation you have to consider now. You are not a normal citizen anymore. You are a princess. The rules aren't the same. You know it and I know it. We're both to blame for this. We need to own the consequences."

There it was—those consequences he'd been talking about. *And, oh, how right he'd been.*

"You don't want to get married. You swore you'd never do it." She poked a finger against his chest. "You'll be miserable. Why would I want to commit myself to that?"

"I've had a couple more hours to wrap my head around

this than you have," he said grimly. "I'm about ten steps ahead. Besides," he said, shifting her so her bottom fit more securely within the span of his hips, "there could be worse things than having you in my bed…*every* night."

Her chest tightened. "This is not funny."

"Believe me, I'm feeling a lot of things right now, Princess, but humor isn't one of them."

She took a deep breath. "Aristos—this is crazy. We can't do this. You don't want this."

"It doesn't matter what I want." He tucked a stray curl behind her ear. "We are good together. We knew we had a problem—now we have a solution."

She shook her head. "You're mad. It's not enough for marriage."

"Why not? I find myself…bored with my current lifestyle. It can't go on forever. We could do good things together."

Her back stiffened. "So you want me to marry you to *amuse* you?"

"Yes," he said silkily, "that and many more things."

"No." She scrambled off his lap. "There has to be another way. I need to think."

Unfortunately, thinking didn't provide solutions. Particularly after Nik's phone call that afternoon in which he was short and to the point. The family didn't need any more scandals; an engagement would be ideal. They would take an engagement photo after she'd chosen her ring today and send it out along with a press release tomorrow morning announcing her and Aristos's engagement. The strategy was to replace the scandalous coverage with the happy news of a pending royal match.

Alex didn't even think about refusing. She was too busy staring at the wall wondering how she'd gotten herself into this situation. Cringing at the disappointment that had stained her brother's tone. Another Dimitriou royal scandal—a PR nightmare for the palace.

Her stomach twisted, tying itself into a tight knot. How could she possibly have been so careless? So unthinking of her position when her mother's lesson should have served as the biggest one of them all?

Three hours later, she found herself trying on rings from one of London's most exclusive jewelers. Numbly she chose a square-cut sapphire surrounded by diamonds, requested by her soon-to-be fiancé because it reminded him of her spectacular eyes.

Aristos put it on her finger, the cold slide of metal against her overheated skin sending a shiver down her spine. It fit perfectly because, of course, Aristos always got the details right. Which meant it stayed there. Which meant they were engaged.

If it wasn't the romantic proposal she'd always dreamed of, with her suitor down on one knee, she was too dazed to much acknowledge it.

When the photographer left, she and Aristos sat down to a late dinner and a bottle of champagne that tasted flat to her frozen senses. She told herself this wasn't set in stone, that once the furor died down, an engagement could always be broken. Couldn't it? But she knew in her heart that part of her decision had stemmed from her feelings for Aristos. Because she was in love with him, and maybe they *could* make this work.

"What?" Aristos arched a brow at her when she was unusually silent during the meal.

"Nothing. Did you get Dimitri tied down?"

"Yes. He and Galina are going to come stay this weekend with us."

"*This* weekend?"

"Yes."

It was the last thing she needed, to host the Russians

when she was grappling with all of this, but she forced a smile to her lips. "That's a good sign, then."

"Who knows with him."

She told herself not to interfere, but the research she'd done on the Smirnovs had been too revealing: rumors of drug-taking in his clubs abounded, that he perhaps participated in that drug trade highly debated.

She shot him a look. "He's a bad man, Aristos. Why do you do business with him?"

"Our dealings are purely financial."

"Yes, but him being an investor reflects on you. On your business."

His jaw hardened. "Do you know how many squeaky-clean sources of money there are in the world? Very few."

"So you choose to look the other way?"

His lip curled. "Are you picking a fight, Princess? And here I thought we were celebrating."

Being railroaded into an engagement was putting her in a funny mood. She pointed her glass at him. "Why is this casino so important to you? Why, with all the other properties you have, is Akathinia such an obsession?"

His gaze narrowed. "Because it is the jewel of the Mediterranean…because the world's elite vacation there…because no one's been able to crack it before now. When it's done it will put any other hotel and casino on the planet to shame."

"And," she pointed out, "it's your roots. It will prove to those who gave up on you how far you've come. That they were wrong about you."

He smiled, but it didn't reach his eyes. "Putting words in my mouth, Alex? Maybe it's not so insightful as that. Every developer in the world would kill to build on Akathinia."

She conceded the point with a dip of her head. Pushed the piece of fish she hadn't the appetite for around her plate, her engagement ring sparkling in the muted lighting.

"You done with that?" His low drawl brought her head

up. "Because if you are, I thought we could continue the celebration in private."

The look of intent in his sinful eyes vibrated through her. She lifted her chin. "I have a headache."

His gaze sharpened. "Is that so?"

She lifted a shoulder. "A tension one from today."

He threw his napkin on the table. "Good thing, then, that I am an expert at working the knots out."

She eyed him. He held out a hand and pulled her to her feet. They stood toe to toe, taking each other's measure. "It's been a long day," he murmured. "You get a massage. Anything more than that, you can let me know. You won't ever get anything you don't want from me, Alex."

Her heart went into free fall. Feelings she couldn't suppress bubbled to the surface, enveloping her in a warmth, a hot headiness, that threw her mixed feelings into a tempest. "That would be perfect," she said softly. "My shoulders are a mess."

Aristos's suite was bathed in a muted glow when they arrived, dozens of candles burning from tapered silver holders scattered around the room's sleek, luxurious surfaces. Roses of dark pink and red tumbled from vases, filling the air with an intoxicating aroma.

Her gaze moved to Aristos's. "You did this?"

"I asked Yolande to." He nodded to the bathroom, where a rose-scented bath had been drawn. "Go take a bath first. It'll help with the knots."

She stripped off her dress and underwear and stepped into the heavenly water. It did wonders for her stiff muscles and disposition. When she climbed out and wrapped herself in the silk robe hanging on the door, Aristos was typing out a message on his phone. He nodded toward the bed. "Be right there."

She perched on the edge. He tapped out the rest of the

message and tossed the phone onto the dresser, his gaze eating her up as he closed the distance between them.

"You know what I was thinking that first night we were here," he said huskily, his fingers toying with the lapels on her robe, "when you had that blue wrap dress on…"

She shook her head, eyes glued to his.

"That I wanted to unwrap you like a present. That you are so beautiful, any man lucky enough to get his hands on you should savor the opportunity. Recognize his good luck."

A shiver went through her. He captured her left hand, blazing with his sapphire on it, and brought her fingers to his mouth. "That makes me an exceedingly lucky man tonight, angel."

The maelstrom of emotions swirling through her intensified, until she felt as if she were in the eye of the storm. "Always?" she asked quietly. "Are you always going to feel that way? Or will it fade as 'evolutionary history dictates'?"

His mouth twisted. "I'd say we're both in uncharted territory here. The truth is, we fit. I know when to give you the push you need and you—" her heart sat suspended as he searched for words "—you show me what's possible. You show me the things I want to have."

Her insides dissolved. She saw it then in his dark-as-night eyes, the infinite possibilities for them. The spectacular and never-ending kind, if she was patient enough to wait for them. Brave enough.

He reached for the sash of her robe. Tugged it open. Her breath caught in her throat as he took her in, his gaze tracing a line down to her breasts, to the vee at the apex of her thighs, down over the curve of her legs to her coral-tipped toes. It turned her insides to liquid.

"I think," she said breathlessly, "the bath worked out those knots."

His mouth curved. "The head?"

"Better."

She waited, nipples hardening, body anticipating his caresses. Still he didn't touch her.

"What do you want?" he asked quietly, eyes on hers.

She stepped closer. "You."

It was like sealing her fate, the kiss that followed. Gentle, passionate, never ending—it was all of those things. His hands moved to her shoulders, slipped the robe from her. Her fingers dispensed with the button on his shorts. When she reached inside his boxers and closed her fingers over the hard, thick length of him, he was velvet over steel.

Tentative, then gaining confidence, she explored him. Stroked him. He closed his fingers over hers, tightened her grip, showed her how he liked it. It was so erotic, heated her blood to a slow simmer to do this with him. To share this with him.

His hand at the small of her back, he pushed her toward the dresser, setting her hands on its polished surface. Her gaze met his in the mirror. "Stay there," he murmured.

The ripping sound of a condom wrapper pierced her sensual haze. It stoked her blood even hotter. He came back to her, ran his palms down her spine to cup her buttocks. His foot nudged her feet apart. She allowed herself to be put where he wanted her, the blood roaring in her ears as she watched him behind her. He sank his teeth into her shoulder in a wicked caress.

His palm cupped her between her thighs. She was ready for him, more than ready. His low rasp of approval as he parted her silky flesh sent another shiver through her.

"*Thee mou*, but you do something to me." He sank his fingers inside her. She moved into his touch, reaching for him. He pushed her hands back onto the dresser. "Leave them there."

She did. If his intent was to make her vulnerable, to

leave her wide-open to him, to demonstrate how completely he owned her, he had succeeded. Her breath left her in a gasp as he placed one hand on her buttock and brought himself to rest against her moist, willing flesh.

"Arch your back," he commanded, eyes burning into hers. She did. He slid into her with a slow penetration that set every nerve ending in her body screaming for more.

"Aristos."

"Look at me, angel. I've got you."

She anchored herself in his gaze. His hands cupped her buttocks as he stroked his way inside her. Harder, deeper, until she could feel him everywhere, touching the very heart of her. He was so big and powerful, the places he hit inside her so intensely pleasurable, she started to shake under his hands.

He leaned forward, capturing her earlobe in his teeth. Scoring it lightly. "Relax, angel."

Relax? She was ready to beg for him to touch her, to push her over the edge, but it was his body that did it instead. The power of him that made her tighten with a desperate clench, the throb of her orgasm radiating out from her center as a scream left her throat.

He gripped her hips tighter and thrust inside her, pleasure exploding in his eyes. Just when she thought it couldn't get any better—it always did.

He carried her to the bed when they'd recovered their breath. The weight of her engagement ring felt foreign as she curled up against him, her hand tucked against her cheek. Made her feel fidgety, restless.

Aristos pulled her tighter against him. "You're mine now," he said roughly. "Forget about the rest."

How could she? The shock in her mother's voice when she'd called to give her the news replayed itself in her head. Her pointed question as to whether she knew what she was doing with Aristos.

She was taking the longest of long shots. Risking it all for a man who didn't commit. Who'd sworn he wouldn't. And yet with the slide of Aristos's hand against her back, sleep consumed her.

CHAPTER THIRTEEN

"THE SASSICAIA OR the Excelsus?" Aristos's French chef lifted a brow. "Or both…?"

Alex surveyed the two bottles of wine. You really couldn't go wrong with either with the meal they were serving Dimitri and Galina Smirnov, but she was being a perfectionist because it was so important to Aristos, and he had put her in charge.

"I think both," she said, "but let me check with Aristos."

She made her way to the casino, the afternoon shower having given way to sunshine in anticipation of their guests' arrival. She had been happy to help with the dinner given the insanity of the past few days…the field day the press was having with both the nude and official engagement photos, although that sport seemed to play second fiddle to the fun they were having predicting how long the playboy billionaire's marriage would last.

They had been making bets. Taking polls. It was enough to make her think she *had* lost her wits in agreeing to marry him.

Carin's chair was empty, her fiancé on the phone when she walked into Aristos's office, his New York lawyer's voice coming through the speakerphone.

She sat on the corner of Carin's desk and waited, not wanting to hurry him as he and the lawyer went through a contract. Aristos, efficient as always, plowed through the terms in minutes. When they were done, his lawyer asked him if he needed anything else.

"Start working on a prenup for me."

Her shoulders stiffened.

"Sure. You got a ballpark figure in mind?"

Aristos named an outrageous number that made her mouth drop open.

"That's very...generous."

"I don't intend to give it away. I'm a lucky man. Not to mention Alex will bring considerable assets to the table herself. It's an advantageous union from all angles. A politically advantageous union for Nicolades Inc."

"No doubt," agreed the lawyer.

Her stomach tightened. *A politically advantageous union?* She told herself to focus on the "lucky man" part. But did that have more to do with what she brought to the table personally or her lineage as a Constantinides?

Aristos ended the call. She stayed where she was for a good couple of minutes so it wouldn't be clear she'd overheard the conversation, then slid off the desk and made her way into his office. She didn't mention what she'd heard. Wasn't sure why not. Maybe because she thought she was being oversensitive, that just because Aristos needed Nik's casino license for his current obsession it didn't mean that's all *they* were.

But it festered as she dressed for dinner that evening in a silver-beaded cocktail dress. Aristos came up behind her in the mirror as she stood choosing her jewelry.

"I haven't seen this one yet." He rested his hands on her hips. "I like it."

The smoky, intimate tone he'd undoubtedly used on every one of the women the papers had mentioned as notable exes inspired the usual flock of butterflies in her stomach, but she held herself stiff beneath his hands. "Stella chose it."

He gave her a long look in the mirror. "Anything wrong? More outrageous press coverage?"

Too much to count. She shook her head. "You should get ready. We need to go."

He surveyed the carefully schooled expression on her face. Pulled her back into him and set his lips to her jaw. "You playing hard to get, angel? I could like that game."

She pushed against him and stepped out of his arms. "No. I still need to do my hair."

The look he scorched her with could have stripped paint from a car, but he stepped back, made his way to the wardrobe and acquired a shirt. A fine pair they were going to make, she thought, grimacing, as she gathered her hair on top of her head. Aristos the powder keg in advance of the Russian's visit, her distinctly *off*.

The Smirnovs were waiting for them on the main terrace. Dimitri, a tall, thin, elegant figure with a sharp face and eyes that missed nothing, pressed a kiss to both her cheeks.

"Congratulations on your engagement. And here I had no idea you were a princess."

"We weren't broadcasting the fact given the political situation."

"Understandable."

Alex greeted Galina more warmly while her fiancé shook his nemesis's hand. They sat down to drinks, then dinner. Galina asked about her and Aristos's wedding plans. She tried to focus on the innocuous conversation, but her attention was captured by the cat-and-mouse game going on between the two men.

Aristos was direct and to the point. Dimitri was noncommittal and evasive, a game player. One who flouted the law and who could someday become a liability to her fiancé, but he wouldn't acknowledge it. Not that she was anything but polite to the Russian, if coolly so, but as the dinner wore on, her patience wore thin.

"I'm opening a new club in Moscow in October." Dimitri

directed the comment at Alex as dessert was served. "You should come."

"I'm afraid I'm not much into clubbing," she returned evenly.

Dimitri lifted a dark brow. "Oh, but this one is like no other. Lions in cages. Waitstaff suspended from the ceiling. It's something to see."

"I'm quite sure you're right."

Dimitri gave her a long look. Aristos gave her knee a squeeze.

She could have stood up and given a cheer when the meal was over. But it wasn't to end there, unfortunately. Dimitri declared himself in favor of a nightcap. The staff relieved for the night, Aristos went off to procure a bottle of brandy. When Galina got up to use the ladies' room, Alex rose to follow her. Dimitri put a hand on her arm. "Stay and keep me company."

What could she do? She suggested they move to the comfortable lounge area that overlooked the sea. That used up some time. When she sat down on the sofa, Dimitri sat beside her.

"I get the feeling you don't like me, Princess."

She widened her eyes. "Why would you think that?"

"I've asked you to call me Dimitri twice. You refuse to."

She'd never been a liar, nor was she about to start now. Crossing her legs, she lifted a shoulder. "Your business is with my fiancé."

He sat back, a hard glitter in his eyes. "I've offended you."

"Not at all."

"My reputation offends you."

"Perhaps we should choose another subject of conversation."

"I'd rather finish this one."

Oh, but he was a piece of work. There was no escaping

this. She set her gaze on his. "I don't like your business practices, Mr. Smirnov. But what I have to say is irrelevant to my fiancé's business."

He took a sip of his wine. "You think my association with Aristos will tarnish your family's reputation."

"I didn't say that."

He pressed the rim of his glass to his chin, his eyes on her. "The press like to print a lot of garbage about me, Aleksandra. Don't believe everything you read."

His smug they'll-never-catch-me look was too much for her. "Where there is smoke," she said softly, "there is usually fire, Mr. Smirnov."

Aristos returned from the cellar to find that Alex and Dimitri had moved to the lounge. Alex's stiff body language immediately had his antennae up. She excused herself not long after that, Galina at her side, happy to leave the business to the men.

Intent on solving his impasse with the Russian tonight, Aristos poured a liberal amount of brandy into their glasses. He wasted no time in getting to the point. "I need a firm commitment you're in, Dimitri."

The Russian lifted a shoulder. "I'm finding I need a faster return on investment these days. Your casino could be delayed for months. Years."

Aristos's blood pressure rose. "It won't be. Reports say Idas is ill. His son will come to the throne any day and it will be over."

"And if it isn't?"

His gaze narrowed. "Either you're in or you're out."

Dimitri sat back in the sofa, taking his tumbler with him. "I don't think your fiancée likes me."

"I'm sure you're mistaken."

"She doesn't like my business practices. She thinks

I'll be a detriment to your reputation. The royal family's reputation."

His back stiffened. "Did she say that?"

"That she doesn't like my business practices? Yes."

Alex had not said that. She would know better than to say that. Aristos's fingers tightened around the glass. "What the royal family thinks or feels is of no bearing to my business."

Dimitri inclined his head. "Still," he drawled, "I think the gestation time on this investment is going to be too long, I'm afraid. I'm out."

With those two words, the Russian put his casino on borrowed time. "I think you shoulder reconsider," he said tightly. "The prestige of this project will be like no other."

"Funny thing about that, Nicolades. It always seems that way until the next best thing comes along."

Aristos sat on the terrace by himself, putting away another glass of the brandy as he worked to control his fury… contemplated his future. He thought he had his temper under control by the time he let himself into the room where Alex was up, reading, but just looking at her made his vision go red.

She put the book down. "What happened?"

He threw his phone on the table. "He backed out."

"Why?"

"He said the gestation time of his investment was too long given the political situation in Akathinia."

"But that might change soon."

"He doesn't care."

"He won't change his mind?"

"No." He pinned his gaze on her. "Did you say you didn't like his business practices?"

A flush stained her cheeks. "He backed me into a corner, Aristos. You saw the games he was playing tonight."

"Which is why you should have said nothing." His voice rose. "Did you also tell him his business dealings with me reflected badly on the royal family?"

"No. He intimated that. I told him your business dealings were your affair."

"After you told him you didn't approve of his business practices!" He was yelling now and he didn't care. "How could you be so stupid?"

Her face lost all its color. She sat there for a moment, silent, then pushed the sheets aside, got out of bed and walked over to him. "You need to calm down. They'll hear you. I didn't say that. He did."

"After you said it at dinner the other night. Don't tell me it wasn't in your head."

"Yes, because I care about you. Because I don't think he's the type of man you should be doing business with. Because I worry about him being your downfall, not because it has anything to do with my family."

"If you cared about me, you would have said nothing." He threw his hands up. "All I asked you to do was entertain him, Alex, but you spent the night being the ice queen."

Her eyes widened. "Is that what I'm supposed to do? Keep my mouth shut? Perhaps I was not enough of a *political asset* to you tonight, then?"

He blinked. "What?"

"A political asset. Like you said to your lawyer on the phone today."

"You were eavesdropping on my conversation?"

"I came to ask about the wine."

"It was a throwaway comment." He turned and paced to the other side of the room, his head too full, too hazy with the alcohol he'd consumed to think clearly.

Alex watched him quietly. "I understand you are upset. I understand how important this night was for you. But this has been coming with Dimitri. You knew he was iffy.

So perhaps it was meant to be. You are meant to find a better fit."

Blood swirled in his head, making him feel as if it would blow off. He swung to face her, giving her a scathing look. "Oh, that's right. I'll just go round up another hundred-million-dollar investor. Give me a sec."

She bit her lip. "Do you know he employs underage girls in his clubs? Lord knows what they do beyond serving customers."

"Now you're letting your imagination go wild."

"And you're not seeing what's right in front of you. Or do you just not *want* to see it?"

"Alex," he growled. "I've never pretended to be a Boy Scout. I told you my world is full of gray areas."

"But *you* aren't." She shook her head. "You forget I know you now. You are a good man, Aristos, an honorable one. But if you don't watch it, this obsession with proving yourself *is* going to make you spiritually bankrupt."

His mouth twisted. "That happened a long time ago."

"No," she said. "It didn't. You did what you had to do to survive in the world. But now you have choices. Power. You need to decide which road to take."

Silence reigned between them. Lifting a shoulder, he went to the sideboard and poured himself a glass of water. When he turned around Alex was gathering up her things.

"What are you doing?"

"Going to my room. I think we could both do with some space."

"Running away, Princess?"

"No," she said, lifting her chin. "Walking away is your specialty. I'm calling a time-out."

CHAPTER FOURTEEN

ALEX'S TIME-OUT WITH Aristos lasted for two days. She was too angry with him for insinuating she was responsible for Dimitri's desertion to offer an olive branch, Aristos too busy working day and night to replace the Russian's investment to do so, either, apparently. Which had left them in a standoff that couldn't go on.

He had shut her out completely, rebuffed any attempt to talk as he made phone call after phone call to his contacts around the world. If she didn't break the impasse, she was worried he would build his walls back up completely before they worked this out, and she was far too invested in him for that.

She ate dinner alone for a second day, then decided enough was enough. Picking up the sandwich she'd asked the chef to make, she headed for Aristos's office. She found him standing at the window, hands braced on the sill, gaze trained on the remnants of the spectacular sunset.

She stood there for a moment, struck by what a solitary figure he cut. It clung to him like a second skin, as though he'd been wearing it so long it was his permanent finish. *The lone wolf.*

Her heart throbbed in her chest. For a while she thought she'd stripped it away, but now it was back.

She cleared her throat. "Any luck today?"

He turned to face her, his dark, fathomless gaze taking her in. "No. A couple of potential leads, but nothing substantial."

She put the sandwich on the desk. “You need to eat if you’re going to function.”

He didn’t even glance at it. She leaned against the desk. “Are there other solutions to the loss of Dimitri? Can you scale the project back?”

An emotion she couldn’t read flickered in his gaze. “I would have to withdraw the plans, make major adjustments, something I don’t want to do when I’ve been so public about my vision for it.”

His reputation would suffer. He would lose face. His big gamble to prove he had conquered the casino world a failure… “You would still be first,” she pointed out. “The first to build a casino on Akathinia. Isn’t that enough?”

His lashes lowered, framing the dark circles that rimmed his eyes. It would never be enough. He would constantly be chasing after the next big thing until he destroyed himself. The realization sent a chill through her.

“The industry is about vision,” he said finally. “About convincing the entertainment world you have the biggest and the brightest offering. You lose that cachet and you’re done.”

“Or you lose everything because you need to save face. You don’t need to prove yourself anymore, Aristos. You have achieved a success beyond most men’s wildest imaginations. Perhaps part of a dream is better than none.”

“I will find another investor,” he rasped.

“Or you will destroy yourself trying.”

He lifted his chin, his gaze a smoky, dark cauldron of antagonism. “Is your lecture almost done?”

“Not quite.” She folded her arms across her chest. “You’re still angry with me about Dimitri.”

He shook his head. “You were right. He was already lost.”

And he hadn’t bothered to convey that to her? To apologize? A wave of antipathy washed through her. “You can be a real *jerk*, you know that?”

He lifted a shoulder. "I come as advertised."

Wow. She shook her head. "You're shutting me out."

"I'm working, not shutting you out."

"Funny, it feels as if you are. If you weren't, you would have apologized. We'd be talking, working through this together like a normal couple. Maybe I can't solve it for you, but I can be here for you."

"I told you I don't do this well."

"Oh, that's right, your convenient no-promises excuse, yours to pull out of the bag whenever you don't feel like communicating. You'd rather tune me out than be in a real relationship."

His gaze narrowed. "My company is on the brink. Cut me some slack."

"You did it before the poker game, too. This is your routine, Aristos. Your MO." She shook her head. "I want to be that person you can trust. I want to be the other half of *us*. But if you can't let me in, this is never going to work."

A dark glitter entered his eyes. "Maybe it isn't. I've been clear about who I am, Alex, and you refuse to see it. You keep pushing your sanitized Hollywood version of me."

Her chin lifted. "It's not a Hollywood version. It's you."

"It's not." He clenched his hands by his sides. "You want to know who I am? Who I really am? I'm the man who can't stick. Ever. I'm the man who walked out on his family not once, but twice, because he couldn't stick. The one whose father told him his family was better off without him. And guess what? He was right."

"No." She shook her head, heart clenching. "No, he wasn't."

"Yes." His olive skin was ashen, drained of color. "When my mother kicked my father out, my older brother, Vasili, came to me and asked me to come home, *pleaded* with me to help because he couldn't handle all the responsibility he'd been given, and what did I do? I said no. I told him my mother had already made her decision. That I was done with them."

Her heart fractured, a million tiny shards scattering in every direction, piercing her with their jagged edges. "You were hurt. You expected your parents to put you first."

"I was a piece of dirt, that's what I was. A street kid who didn't care, and I haven't much changed." He wiped a hand across his mouth. "So do yourself a favor and walk in the opposite direction."

"Aristos—" She put out a hand to touch him, but he shrugged it off.

"I have a call coming."

In other words, leave.

"Kala." She held his gaze, its bleakness chilling her. "But you're wrong. You are wrong about who you are. You're trying to give yourself adult decision-making skills when you were a child. You were acting on emotion, hurt, and the people who loved you should have known better. Done better."

Turning on her heel, she left before he broke her heart.

Aristos did the conference call with California, with little hope that lead would go anywhere. Everything he could accomplish done, every avenue exhausted, he sat back in his chair and closed his eyes. He'd slept maybe six hours over the past forty-eight, his body felt as if it had lead weights attached to it, yet still he sat there, racking his brain for alternate possibilities.

There were none. If his Los Angeles–based investor didn't bite, he was done. He would need to scale the casino back or pull the project entirely. Either way, his reputation would be in tatters, everything he'd built subject to the whims of an industry that would call you old news before the year was out.

He wanted to believe everything Alex had said, to absolve himself of the responsibilities he'd had toward his family, but the guilt went too deep. At sixteen, he'd been old enough to know what he was doing when Vasili had come to him, and still he'd made the wrong choice, a choice he knew would haunt him forever.

He rubbed his burning eyes, attempted to think past the haze consuming his brain. He knew he should go apologize to Alex, but he was afraid of what he'd say in this state of mind…afraid of saying things he'd regret.

Being around her made it impossible not to look at himself, at what he'd become, because she was the good, the lightness in this world. She made him feel better than he'd ever felt in his life, so close to that magical happiness quotient he thought it might actually be attainable. But the more he allowed his need for her to rule, the more vulnerable he became; the more out of control he felt.

She had the power to hurt him. To twist his brain into so many directions he didn't know what he wanted anymore. Who he was. And that terrified him, took him back to a place and time where that was all he'd felt, to a chaos he never wanted to experience again. Had sworn he never would.

He stumbled to bed at midnight, his head no clearer. Sure he would pass out, he lay staring at the wall instead. When he could resist no longer, he got up, went to Alex's room, scooped her into his arms and carried her back to his suite.

She looked disoriented, confused, her big blue eyes searching for his as he tucked her into his bed. He couldn't have her there without touching her. Sliding his hands over her curves, he rediscovered her, memorized her. With a low moan, Alex sank into his touch.

Exhausted and sated, he fell asleep with her in his arms.

Alex woke by herself after a night wrapped in Aristos's arms, a night in which everything had felt right again and she'd thought she might have gotten through to him.

When dinner passed and he was still holed up in his office, she told herself she couldn't expect massive change overnight. She slept in his suite that night, hoping he would come to her when he was done. She was asleep before he came in, and he was gone before she woke the next morning. The pattern went on for two days before the ache in her stomach began to make her feel physically ill.

A phone call from Nik interrupted her ruminations. Kostas had taken over in Carnelia and declared peace with the region. It was over. They were free to come home.

She was deluged with a mix of feelings—happiness she could finally return home, anxiety about what this would mean for her and Aristos.

When he deigned to make an appearance at dinner that night, she told him of her conversation with Nik.

He nodded. "He called me earlier this afternoon. I've asked the pilot to be ready to take us at noon tomorrow."

Just like that. Her fingers tightened around her wine-glass. "What are we going to do?"

He gave her a quizzical look. "We fly home. Resume our lives."

Her heart, breaking piece by piece this week, fell apart a little further. "No," she said deliberately, "I mean what are we going to do about us?"

He frowned. "I need to get the financing for the casino sorted out."

"I think you need to get *us* sorted out while you're at it." She pushed her glass away. "You have to decide whether you're going to give me a meaningful place in your life or let me go, Aristos. It's as simple as that."

"It's not as simple as that," he growled.

"It is. I don't want to be a convenient wife, nor do I want to be a politically advantageous one. I want to be your partner. I want to be the one you come to when you're happy or sad. The one who licks your wounds for you."

The silence that followed was deafening. Hot tears pooled at the backs of her eyes. "Do you know the tabloids are making bets about how long we last? How long you can stay married?"

His eyes flashed. "They are garbage."

"Yes, but the funny thing about them is there's always a vein of truth there. It's how they survive."

She threw her napkin on the table and rose. "Tonight it's me who doesn't seem to have an appetite. If you'll excuse me."

Alex stepped into the helicopter behind Aristos the next morning with nothing between them resolved. She steadfastly refused to look down as they took off, bound for Akathinia. At all the memories the island held for her…the terrace where Aristos had held her through that wicked storm…the beach where he'd finally opened up and broken her heart…the beautiful, magical suite where she'd given him all of her, sure they were different.

She had no idea if they'd ever be back here together. If they'd even make it.

The journey was painfully silent, Aristos with his face in his laptop, her staring out the window. When the white Maltese stone Akathinian palace came into view, she knew what she had to do. She didn't want to live with a husband who cared about her the way her father had her mother, only commanding a piece of his heart; she wanted, needed, all of him.

The helicopter touched down. Aristos planned to continue on to his home on the outskirts of the city, then to his office, so the pilot kept the helicopter idling as her fiancé helped her out and onto the cement landing pad.

Stella and Nik appeared on the steps. Desperate to keep her emotions in check, she turned to Aristos. His expression was hidden by dark sunglasses, but what did it matter? He'd been emotionally unavailable all week.

He lifted a hand to run a finger down her cheek. "I'll call you later."

"Don't."

His head snapped back. She bit her lip, summoning a composure she wasn't sure she had. "We need some space, Aristos. Time to figure out how we feel about this. *Us.*"

"Alex—"

She put a finger to his lips. "I know how I feel about you. You know I love you. Now you have to figure out how you feel."

She kissed him. A brief touch of her lips to his. When he would have pulled her closer, she stepped out of his arms, turned and walked away, fighting back the tears that blinded her path.

He had taught her to grab hold of her future. Now she had. She wondered where it would take them.

Aristos stepped onto the helicopter after Alex threw those three loaded words at him and flew home. He spent the next week working the same insane hours, rattling around his too-big estate on the cliffs of Akathinia when he finally came home, its soaring ceilings and twenty-five rooms empty and without soul. They always had been, but it struck him now how utterly barren the place was.

He knew the difference was Alex, the effervescent presence she was, the spirit in her that reached out and surrounded him, refused to allow him to retreat into himself. But she had just walked out of his life.

It had been on the tip of his tongue to call her back, to rectify the mistake he knew he was making. But he'd known he wasn't ready. He had ghosts to exorcise, a future to shape. Wanting something, even as badly as he wanted Alex, wasn't proving you could stick. And that he had to do.

When word came that his final hope for an investor to replace Dimitri had fallen through, it was like being handed a life sentence he'd known was coming. All you could do was slide your hands into the shackles and admit your mistakes. Your failings.

Alex had been right. He would destroy himself trying to prove something that didn't matter anymore. He needed to stop. He needed to find a peace he could live with.

A lightbulb went off a few nights later, pulling him out of bed and to a sketch pad, where he drew until morning. He sent the amateurish result to his genius of an architect, asking him what he could do to modify the current casino design with that direction to save costs but still retain his vision. Then he waited. And waited. When Barry Schindler flew in two days later, arriving on Aristos's doorstep to find him unshaven and ready to pounce, he gave his client a wry look.

"Losing some sleep?"

"Just a bit."

"I might be able to help."

Two strong espressos sitting on the table beside them, the architect took Aristos through the redesigned plans. His design was inspired, based on lighter, more versatile materials and brilliant, indiscernible modifications that would provide no less of an impact.

"How much?" Aristos asked, chest tight.

"I've saved you fifty million."

Which left him fifty million short. Perhaps he could get his other investors to kick in the remainder… It was worth a shot.

He made his first phone call to his biggest investor at a US bank. He said yes. He made more calls. A funny thing happened then. As word spread that Dimitri was out, his investors started calling *him* to offer to make up the gap. They'd never liked the Russian's involvement.

By the end of the week he had his fifty million and a go-ahead from the Akathinian government to break ground. A front-page story ran in the business section of the newspaper with the new schematic included. It was garnering universal acclaim.

The story also included a feature on the program he had committed his company to—what he called the Hector Rigatos Gambling Addiction Fund. He wouldn't call it that, of course, but he would forever think of it as that. For what Alex had taught him.

An intense feeling of satisfaction, of rightness, settling through him, he set the newspaper down, walked out onto the balcony and took in the hauntingly beautiful view of the mountains. In the shadow of that quiet, majestic presence he knew it was time for him to take *his* leap. He couldn't right the wrongs he'd made with his family—they would forever be with him—but he *could* change the future. If he wanted to be with Alex, to deserve her, he needed to face his demons. He needed to go home. He needed to learn how to stick.

CHAPTER FIFTEEN

SMILING AND WAVING at crowds during Akathinia's annual Independence Day celebration, even one as joyous as it was this year with the prospect of war lifted from the national conscience, was no fun for a princess who'd rather be on an Aegean island with the man she loved.

Alex was navigating her new role with care, loving her work with Nina, settling back into palace life with its intricacies and formalities. If only she didn't feel so miserable. If only she could put last week's newspaper feature out of her head.

Aristos had secured his investment, the casino was a go, the ground-breaking to happen in two weeks' time. But what had made her put the paper down and leave the breakfast room in tears was the gambling addiction fund he'd created to help those who fell through the cracks.

She was so happy for him. And still he hadn't come.

Her heart throbbed painfully in her chest as they navigated the final length of the parade route on the float upon which she and her family stood. Perhaps she'd been wrong. Perhaps it was just too difficult for Aristos to let down his walls after decades of shoring them up.

Somehow, she managed to hold her smile as they reached the end of the parade route, bade the crowds goodbye and were ushered into the waiting limo. Only her father was missing, his recovery at home an unexpected development as his archnemesis, Idas, lay on his deathbed.

Her father hadn't seemed to warm up much to her, but

her budding relationships with her siblings gave her such joy. Stella, who was becoming the best friend she'd always wanted in a sister. Nik, whose quiet, wise philosophy held so much she could learn from.

Stella pounced as the limo came to a halt in front of the palace and Alex slid out, heading for the stairs.

"You have to stop moping around."

Alex swept up the stairs and through the doors. "Aristos isn't coming tonight He's playing poker on Vardis Melonakos's yacht."

"You told him you needed space."

"That was a cue for him to give his head a shake."

"Maybe you should give yours one, too."

She pulled to a halt. *"Really?"*

"Yes, really. He's crazy about you, Alex. I saw it on his face when you walked away from him at the helicopter… when he pursued you at the press conference."

Her mouth pursed. "I'm not sure he's emotionally capable of acting on it."

Stella followed her up the stairs and into her bedroom. "Perhaps not, but moping around on the biggest day of the year isn't going to help. Are we going to have fun tonight or are you going to act like a limp dishrag?"

She straightened her shoulders. Gave her head the shake she knew it needed. "Yes," she said firmly, "we are going to have fun."

She channeled her favorite literary heroine for inspiration. *What would Scarlett do?*

She would *not* sit around pining for Aristos while he played poker on Vardis Melonakos's yacht with beautiful women serving him drinks. She would show him what he was missing.

"I think we should go shopping."

"Shopping?" Stella looked at her as if she were mad.

"My legs are about to fall off. The ball starts in four hours."

"Do you want to help me or not?"

The two princesses entered the Akathinian royal ballroom arm in arm after a firestorm of paparazzi flashes documented their arrival.

"A prior engagement," Alex had said tersely when asked where her fiancé was.

Stella shoved a glass of champagne into her hand. "Drink."

She did. Her sister scanned the room, her gaze settling on Crown Prince Kostas of Carnelia, standing beside Nik in a group near them.

"Look at him walking around the place as if he owns it. I *hate* him. I don't care what Nik says, what they said in their little *chat* together, there is nothing on this planet that could make me like him."

Alex smiled. Prince Kostas's unexpected appearance at the Independence Day ball had been a shock to everyone. Nik had invited the prince as a symbol of the healing that needed to happen between the two countries. Stella, still brokenhearted over her eldest brother's death at what she called "Kostas's hands," had not taken it well.

"Perhaps you should listen to what Nik has to say," Alex suggested. "He seems to be at peace with it all."

Stella scowled. "Kostas is a coward. He spent the last year relegating our two countries to turmoil, afraid to stand up to his father. I have no respect for him."

As if the extraordinarily handsome crown prince's ears were burning, he turned his head toward them. Elegant in a black tuxedo, he wore his dark hair short and cropped above a face that could be described as nothing short of spectacular: high, aristocratic cheekbones; piercing, narrow eyes beneath thick dark brows; and a straight, prominent nose.

"He's awfully stunning, Stella."

"If arrogant brutes are your idea of attractive, yes."

"I thought you used to like him. They say he is progressive, pro-democracy, nothing like his father. Apparently very witty and intelligent."

"*Used to* being the operative words."

Alex's eyes widened as Kostas broke away from the group and headed toward them.

"Don't look now, but here he comes."

Hot color stained her sister's cheeks. "Here? Why is he coming over here?"

"We're about to find out."

The crown prince stopped in front of them and inclined his head in a greeting. Alex smiled politely, but Kostas's gaze had moved to Stella and stayed there. "Perhaps you would do me the honor of a dance?"

A loaded silence followed. The flush in her sister's face deepened, her lips pursing as if to refuse. But then her manners seemed to kick in, as if she knew they were being watched, and with a stiff nod, she accepted.

Which left Alex alone. Alone in the very sexy dress she'd purchased, the plunging neckline of the champagne-colored sequined gown skirting the limits of what a princess might get away with. Worn perhaps to show the world she didn't care her fiancé wasn't here—or perhaps the man himself.

She stood, back against a pillar, watching Stella and the prince dance. It was better than TV. Two men asked her to dance, the duke Aristos had liked to make fun of and a friend of Stella's, but she turned them both down, pleading sore feet, a poor excuse, but she didn't care. She was tired of pretending.

"I was standing over there wondering why the most

beautiful woman in the room keeps turning down dances," a deep male voice purred in her ear. "Instead of allowing my imagination to run wild, I thought I'd come over and find out for myself."

Aristos.

Her heart jumped into her mouth as she turned to face him. He was not in a tuxedo like the other men, but in a dark suit that made him look so handsome her heart stayed lodged right where it was, deep in her throat, making speech nigh impossible.

The tears she'd been fighting swamped the backs of her eyes, threatening a full release.

"Oh, no." Aristos's gaze darkened. "No tears, Princess, not when we've come this far."

She swallowed hard, fighting them back. *What did that mean?*

"Aren't you supposed to be playing poker?"

"I was. I found my attention was elsewhere, so I left."

She scowled at him. "I am not available as a *diversion*."

"Funny," he drawled, his gaze sliding over her. "That dress screams it with a capital *D*. It's not fit for public consumption."

"Absentee fiancés don't get a say in the matter."

Fire lit his gaze. "Ah, but we know they do. Especially since I am not absentee any longer."

He curled his fingers around her forearm and directed her out of the ballroom to the terrace. Bypassing the crowd there, he led her down into the gardens. They walked until they came to the fountain, the little square at the center of the maze where he'd challenged her to take her big jump.

She sat down on the lip of the fountain, the sounds of the party muted now, the square deserted.

Aristos sat down beside her, splaying his long legs in front of him. The scent of his spicy aftershave made her want to crawl into his arms. She wrapped hers around herself.

"You asked me for space," he said, setting his dark, inscrutable gaze on her. "And you were right—I needed it. Needed to figure myself out, determine my priorities, whether I could be the man you needed."

Her heart squeezed. He always had been.

"What I discovered is that my life as I've been leading it is not the life I want to live. You made me see that, angel, made me see the possibilities…what I want, and I want more. I want to wake up every morning with you beside me. I want to share my life with you. I want you to be there to lick my wounds when I stumble, and yes," he added a devilish glitter in his eyes, "other parts of me, too."

Her heart turned over, leaping with a joy that sent it tumbling nearly out of her chest. "Aristos—"

He held up a hand. "I have a lot of baggage, Alex. Maybe more than I can ever fully overcome. There's never going to be a day where I'm not cognizant of the fragility of life—of how everything can be taken away from you in the blink of an eye. It will always make me a fighter. It will always push my survivor instincts to the forefront, making my first inclination to push people away. It's a reflexive thing I'm going to have to work on."

A tear slid down her cheek. "All of us have those things…those crutches we rely on. For me it was retreating. Not taking the chances I should. You showed me that."

"For me it was burying the past. Trying to pretend it never existed, that it couldn't hurt me, but it was always there in the background, chasing me. I knew after you walked away from me I would regret it if I let you go. But I had to face my ghosts first. Find out who I am now. Who I *was*. So I went home."

Her heart leaped. "You did? How was it?"

"Painful. Awkward. Amazing."

She could so identify. And yet hadn't it all been worth it?

"I'm so glad you went," she said softly. "Were they glad to see you?"

"Yes." The rasp in his voice made her cover his hand with hers. "I think there is…potential there. My mother—she was very emotional. Vasili—he—he will be the hardest. I broke his trust. I need to get it back."

She crawled onto his lap then, because she couldn't resist. Her hands framed his face. "You've made the overture. Give it time."

He nodded, his eyes so full of emotion her tears became a steady flow, sliding down her cheeks and soaking his shirt. She kissed him, a long, sweet kiss full of salty tears and the future she knew they had in front of them.

He pulled back, his hands grasping hers and dragging them to her sides. His gaze was so serious, so full of intent, it made her stomach grow tight. "You saved my soul, angel. I was very nearly spiritually bankrupt. I need you with me to make sure that never happens again, that my demons don't take over."

She gave him a tremulous smile. "I think I already made that commitment."

He lifted her ring-clad finger to his mouth and brushed his lips over her knuckles. "I think I missed something when I gave this to you."

"What?"

"I love you, *agapi mou*. I think it was love at first sight, if the truth be known. I did everything but say no to Nik when he asked me to take you to Larikos."

He loved her. Her brain latched on to those three words and held them tight. "I told him it wasn't a good idea," she breathed. "I knew you were trouble, Aristos Nicolades."

"I am," he murmured and proceeded to demonstrate with a kiss that had no sweetness to it, only hunger, an insatiable hunger that seemed to have no end. She moved closer as he slid a hand to her bottom and brought her to him, his sexy, fiery kisses leaving her short of breath.

"Your bedroom," he murmured as they came up for air, "where is it?"

Procuring a bottle of champagne along the way, they climbed the stairs to the royal suites. She was in his arms kissing him before they made it halfway up, then again outside her bedroom door before he pushed it open and shoved her inside.

She pouted as he lost his jacket. "I thought it was spiritual for us."

"Yes, angel, it is." He started working on the buttons of his shirt. "Now I'd like to take it to another realm."

She took a drink from the bottle. Eyed him. "I love you, Aristos."

His gaze darkened as he looked up at her. "I love you, too, Princess. Now put down the bottle and get over here."

She did. Because sometimes dreams *were* too expensive to keep. And sometimes they were all that mattered.

* * * * *